DREAM PACK

JANE HANDLER

Dream Pack

Book Three: Into the Parallel Omegaverse

Jane Handler

Happily ever afters come in all shapes and forms. May you find yours.

About This Story

Welcome back to the parallel omegaverse! *Dream Pack* is a why choose, non-shifting omegaverse, fated mate, portal romance and is book *three* in the *Into the Parallel Omegaverse trilogy*. If you haven't read *Dream Girl* and *Dream Mates,* you're going to want to read those first, so that you know what's going on. This is a 'why choose' romance, so Grace gets her HEA with multiple people, and her story is m/m/m/m/f/m.

Grace is from our world and falls into another. Wes lives in a *parallel universe* that is like ours, and while some things are the same, there are *many* differences, given things have evolved a little differently. This has affected everything from physical places to laws and technology.

The biggest difference of all is that alphas, betas, omegas, and many other designations exist. Each designation has specific characteristics. Alphas are larger, faster, with better senses and are often leaders. Betas make up most of the population and are your average, ordinary people. Omegas are nurturers, and often physically smaller. They are the most physically compatible with alphas and are sought after as mates. Mate bonds between an alpha and omega are as legally binding as marriage.

Many people live in packs, and they have all the legal rights of families, no matter what designations comprise them. There are also plenty of couples and throuples. Same-sex and polyamorous relationships are legal and accepted in this world.

While this story and world aren't particularly dark, some characters have darker pasts. As a teen, Grace suffered physical and mental abuse at the hands of her religious mother and church. Brennan, too, had some significant mental health struggles. Other characters have also had their own mental health struggles, and/or have suffered the loss of family members or partners. There's some family drama, gun violence, and an attempted kidnapping. Some characters are hospitalized, there are also brief references to past genocide, gun violence, and child trafficking. While there's a whole lot of jokes about Grace having their babies, she doesn't get pregnant, though there are some pregnant side characters. There's also no third act breakup and the women causing drama aren't out to steal Grace's guys.

This book is meant for adult readers. There are graphic spice scenes, some of which include multiple partners. This book contains bonding, knotting, praise, group scenes, heat scenes, dvp, tvp, power dynamics, soft daddy doms, and other spicy things.

Enjoy your return to the Parallel Omegaverse. Because dreams aren't real—until they are.

Chapter One

Evan

"Evan, you can go to the waiting room now. Thank you," the police officer stated.

"Okay. Thanks. Where's my sister?" I asked, glancing around. As soon as our pack arrived at the hospital, we'd been split up and questioned by both the police and the Bureau of Investigation. There were also people who I suspected were from the Office of Designation Management, because they were asking about Rosalind, the woman Grace had thought was her mom.

"I'm sure she's either in the waiting room or still being questioned." She turned to talk to someone from the Bureau of Investigation.

Hopefully she wasn't alone. They hadn't let me stay with her. While I'd asked for one of my alphas, or at least someone from the Center, to be there with me during questioning, I'd just gotten tired looks and been told that I wasn't in trouble and things would go so much faster if I just cooperated.

It was clear that I wasn't a suspect, that they were just trying to figure out what the fuck was going on. Also, I couldn't wait to find out who Cassidy Silvers was and why the professor's alpha was arrested for trafficking her, not Grace.

Looking around, I didn't see anyone from my pack. Where did I even go? There were several waiting rooms here. Spencer and Grace had also been taken to different parts of the hospital–him for emergency surgery and her because she had another seizure.

I sent a message to the group chat, since I'd like to find my sister.

Me

Where are you all? Where's Riley?

Jett

Bren and Wes are still being questioned. I'm waiting for Riley. Ask about Spencer and Grace?

Me

Will do.

Wes was livid--I could feel it through the bond. Brennan, too, was close to breaking. Once again, someone attacked our pack, and the alphas hadn't been able to stop it.

"Hey, can you tell me where my mate is?" I asked the woman at the information desk.

"ID?" She snapped her gum, looked at my ID, and went to her computer. "Wait in the family waiting room for intensive care on the second floor. I'll note that you're there."

"Thanks. Wait, Grace isn't in the Omega Ward?" I scanned the directory on the nearby pole. Omega Ward was on the third floor.

She shook her head. "There's no Grace listed in your pack. This is for your alpha, Spencer."

"Oh, okay." That was my next question, anyway. "Could you please tell me where Grace Ellington is? She's Spencer's mate and was brought in at the same time. They just mated, so the paperwork for her to be part of the pack isn't finished." I turned on the charm.

Giving me a look that said she was immune to omega wiles, she typed on her computer.

"Sorry. You're not her emergency contact. But one of your pack-mates who's mated to her can ask about her." With a wave of her hand, she went to help someone behind me.

Not her emergency contact? Yeah, I was going to have to fix that.

I went up to the second floor and added what I found to the group chat.

Me

> **Unless you want me to wait with you, I'm heading up to the second floor where Spencer is. They won't tell me anything about Grace. Wes has to ask.**

Jett

> **Go find Spencer. We'll meet you there.**

At the desk on the second floor, I tried again to get information on Grace. She said she'd do what she could, and I should wait. The family waiting room was stuffy and smelled of sadness and fear.

I played on my phone trying to distract myself. Where was my sister? Should I go look for her or continue to wait here for her and Jett?

Was Grace okay? Maybe they'd take her to Spencer after he got out of surgery. That was pretty normal when mates were both hospitalized.

A nurse in blue scrubs came in. "Hi, are you Evan? I'm here to take you to your mate."

She was? I shot up out of my chair. I still couldn't feel anything from Grace, which was part of my agitation.

"Thank you." I followed her past the nurse's station and down a hall. The door stood open. Monitors beeped, and tubes were attached to the person on the bed.

But it wasn't Grace.

It was Spencer. They must have assumed that the omega waiting for Spencer was *his*. Still, I was so fucking glad to see him, even if he was unconscious or asleep, or something.

"He'll be okay, right?" A bit of fear shot through me. I'm not sure I'd ever seen him so still.

Spencer had to be okay. He just had to. The idea that he might not be, made my chest tighten. He was the frosting that kept our pack together.

"You can lie down with him, just make sure you're on his left side, not right. Purring for him will help. The surgery went really well. He's asleep because he's sedated. Alpha patients can be a bit... troublesome, so we usually keep them sedated a little longer when their mates are also injured so they don't hurt themselves trying to get to them," she assured.

I got a glimpse of a bond mark on her wrist as she checked his monitors.

"That makes sense. Thank you. Hey, could you get me any information about his mate, Grace Ellington? She was brought in at the same time. She's bonded to Spencer, but she isn't actually pack yet, so no one will tell me anything about her. I'm bonded to her, too, but you know, that doesn't count." I rolled my eyes, hoping she'd be sympathetic.

She snorted. "I hear you on that. They didn't want to let me in when my omega was having her baby because I'm a beta, so I'm not really her mate. I ended up having to say that I was the doula to get in. Well, I'm also her doula, but really, I think the laws need to get with the times. I'll see what I can do."

"Thanks. I just want to make sure that she's okay." I rubbed the center of my chest, getting a burst of anger from Wes.

The nurse left, and I went over to Spencer. The pack-sized room had a couch that probably pulled out into a bed, a couple of chairs, and a small table. It looked like there was enough room for Grace to be brought in with him. As she should be.

"Wake up soon, old friend. We need you. I need you. Grace needs you. The pack needs you." I squeezed his hand.

The group chat was quiet, but everyone's locations showed that they were here in the hospital. I texted them the room number. With the day weighing on me, I curled up with Spencer and purred for him for a few moments, like the nurse told me to.

Still, I needed to know Grace was okay. I sent her a shot of love. Nothing.

Wes sent me some back.

I wasn't sure how long I'd been there when there was a knock on the open door. Where was my sister?

"Hi there. I'm Liz and I'm with the Omega Center. The nurse on duty thought you might want to talk." A petite woman with a messy bun, a hot pink polo, and a large duffle bag stood there, Center credentials hanging around her neck.

"Sure, come in." The hot pink polo said *Crisis Response Team* underneath the Center logo. Ooh, there were probably snacks in that bag.

She looked over at Spencer. "We can speak somewhere else if you'd like."

"It's fine." I sat up on the bed.

"Are you sure? The cafeteria has ice cream." Liz pulled a chair over. "It's okay to leave him for a little bit."

"Ice cream is tempting. But I'm fine. Spencer and I have been friends since we were tiny. I have nothing to hide–or fear–from him. Full disclosure, I work for the Center. So, if you don't have time for me, or need to see other omegas, it's fine. I hope they didn't call you in just for me." Pulling up my Center card on my phone, she scanned it with her tablet.

"I'm assigned here and on duty, so it's fine." Liz looked at her tablet. "You're an advocate?"

"Yes, back in Rockland. I'd love to talk to you about being part of the Blanket Brigade. I'm supposed to start training in the fall."

"That's amazing. I'm happy to tell you whatever you want to know. First, can I ask you a few questions?" Again, her eyes flickered to Spencer.

I nodded, and she asked me the usual questions we always asked omegas, making sure they were safe and cared for.

"If you're hungry, I have snacks." She took a couple of packages out of her duffle. Each one had a drink and a variety of semi-healthy snacks and was tied with a bow.

"Thank you." I took the one that had my favorite color of vitamin water in it.

She put the others back and pulled out more cute packages. "Would you like a comfort kit? It sounds like you might be here for a few days."

"These are adorable; did you make these?" They contained things like slippers, eye masks, toiletries, vitamins, and tea.

"My mate and I put them together. So, your mates were attacked on the beach. That seems scary." She put the rest of them back after I selected one.

"It was–and not how I expected our beach day to end. But the past few days have been a shit show." I sighed.

"Oh no. I'm so sorry to hear that. Would it help to tell me about it?" Liz offered.

I shook my head. "Not really."

It was fucking weird—and that was without us learning that Grace was born *here* then somehow made it to another world with her biological mother's evil twin, who was also an illegal designation.

"Can you get me information about Grace Ellington? She's in the hospital, too, and no one will tell me anything. She's probably in the Omega Ward." I made a face.

"I knew there was an ulterior motive to my mate sending me here. She had her sneaky face on." Liz laughed. "I'll pay Grace a visit and report back."

"Thank you." Any news would be a relief.

"I'll return." She grabbed her bag and left.

I munched on my snacks and checked my phone. No Wes. But Jett and Riley were on their way.

"There you are." Jett came in, looking tired.

"Spence." Riley started crying.

"Hey, come here. Spence is going to be okay. His surgery went well." I stood and wrapped my arms around her. Riley was still in her black vintage bathing costume and holding a stuffed bear.

Someone at the hospital found me a shirt and shorts because I came in wearing only swim briefs. It looked like someone had found a shirt for Jett.

"That fucking bitch. I'm going to destroy her," Riley sobbed.

"We'll make sure that Adriana pays for stabbing Spencer, and whatever the fuck she did to baby Grace," Jett assured, rubbing her shoulder.

"Good," Riley mumbled.

"I feel bad for those kids though, seeing their mom dragged off like that," Jett added.

I'd tried my best to make sure that the little one didn't see everything. But I'm sure she was still traumatized because she not only had a big sister she never knew about, but one of her mothers was the reason. Not to mention the older ones knew what was going on.

Shit, I hoped those kids got therapy.

"Do you know anything about Grace? Is she okay? They wouldn't tell me anything." Jett asked.

"No. But I think she's awake. And pissed." I rubbed my chest. "Someone from the Blanket Brigade is here, and she's going to see what she can find out about Grace."

Brennan came in. He'd already been wearing a shirt with his swim trunks when we'd left the beach. "Good. Grace should be next to Spencer, not in some other part of the hospital. They wouldn't tell me anything about Grace, but I know that Spencer should be fine."

"Good." I sighed with relief.

"You okay, Love? They wouldn't let me be with you, I'm sorry." Brennan hugged me, squishing Riley between us.

"I'm right here, Fucker," Riley grumbled, though she made no attempt to struggle out of his grasp.

"It was fine. I still don't know what's happening." I relished in my alpha's touch.

"If I had my laptop, I could figure it out." Riley still didn't scoot out of Brennan's arms.

"Are you okay, Dear? Thanks for waiting for Riley," Brennan said to Jett.

"I'm fine, Honey," Jett replied. "But I also want to know what's going on."

Brennan sighed, his pine scent anxious. "I got some information. In my understanding, Grace *is* Cassidy. It was a separate record created so that Rosalind could pass Grace off as her biological child. Which could be why Grace was tagged as a *misfiled child* because it was suspected they were duplicate records but couldn't prove anything because they couldn't find Grace. Everything else was sort of lost in the bureaucratic shuffle because no one was looking too hard for the lost baby of someone with an illegal designation. Adriana was arrested for Cassidy, not Grace, because that's where the money trail leads. Though I think they've managed to confirm that Grace *is* Cassidy which is something they'll have to do to actually prosecute Adriana."

"Got it." I suspected as much.

"I'm sure the professor's alphas also kept Nate from looking too hard," Jett added.

Riley wiggled out of our arms, eyes focusing on the snack bag on the bedtable. "Can I have the rest of the snacks?"

"Sure. Maybe when she comes back, she'll give you some, too," I suggested.

Jett nodded. "Baby records don't have much on them either, so they're pretty easy to fake. The police were looking for a single woman, not a young mother. Smart."

"Yeah. I guess Rosalind's plan was to move somewhere else, have new identities made, and start over with the money Adriana gave her to take baby Grace and never be heard from again," I added.

This was why advocates and integration teams existed, so alphas didn't get rid of their omega's kids or omegas didn't ghost their pregnant girlfriends because they found their scent match.

"Right, only somehow Grace ended up in another world. We may never know how they got there." Brennan glanced over at Spencer.

Riley sat on the couch eating snacks and texting.

Jett plopped down next to Riley and made a play for the food.

"Mine." Riley hissed at him and held them to her chest. She rolled her eyes and handed him a fruit bar.

"Thank you." Jett unwrapped it.

Brennan eyed them. "The hospital has a cafeteria."

"You can go if you want. But I'd like to wait for an update on Grace," I replied, still clinging to my alpha, as I got annoyance from Wes and anger from Grace through the bond. No, not really interested in food right now.

"Do we know what crime Rosalind committed?" Jett asked.

"Rosalind and her brother helped rob a federal vault. They never found all the money, and they never apprehended everyone," Brennan explained.

Jett whistled. "Fucking shit. That's crazy."

"If she robbed a bank, why did she take money for Grace?" I frowned.

"Amateur." Riley rolled her eyes. "She might have needed funds to hide until it was safe to use the money. She might have had to go get her share or whatever. Someone could have taken her share. Also, Brennan said *vault*. They might not have stolen money."

"True. I don't know what's in the vault." Brennan shook his head. "Riley's right. It could have been anything. I was lucky they told me what they had."

"Damn alpha privilege. They asked me very different things. Also, they gave me a stuffed animal, juice, and cookies. They had a social worker there with me." Riley stuffed crackers in her mouth.

"Did they? I didn't notice that. But yeah, I didn't get cookies and juice." Jett laughed.

"I got tea. No social worker," I replied. "What did they ask you?"

"Mostly if I was okay being with you fuckers. They also asked me about Grace, and I had to recount watching that bitch stab Spencer. But it's fine." She brushed crumbs away.

Sure. I'd check in with her later.

"Where's Wes?" I glanced at my phone, worried.

"Still being questioned, I guess." Brennan shrugged.

After a while, there was a knock on the door.

"Hey, it's me. Oh, your pack is here." Liz waved.

"Well, everyone but Wes and Grace. What did you find out?" I asked her.

"Grace is in the Omega Ward. But there's an officer there in front of her door. She wouldn't let me in because people were talking to Grace. She was mean." Liz made a face. "Really, they should let someone in with Grace."

"I'm sorry that they were mean. She's awake, that's good." But I still was worried. Grace had blacked out, probably from Spencer's pain, then had a seizure.

"Maybe the other alpha mated to her can ask to have her brought here when the police are done," Liz told us.

"Thank you," Brennan replied.

Liz looked over at the couch and waved at Riley. "Hi, want some snacks?"

"Do you have good snacks? Though I'll take any snacks." Riley held out her hands.

"You know what? I have these that I keep for kids. How's this?" She rummaged in her duffle and tossed something colorful at Riley, who caught it.

"Ooh, I'll take it. There's even a coloring book. Thanks." Riley tore it open and took out a candy bar.

"I'll be here for a little longer if you need me. I'll also be here tomorrow so I can answer all your questions about my job." Liz waved and left.

"That's what you want to be, right?" Riley stuffed the rest of the candy bar in her mouth.

"Yep." I frowned and rubbed my chest. "Now, where the fuck is Wes?"

Chapter Two

Wes

"What do you mean I can't see her? That's my fucking mate in there," I growled at the woman at the desk in the Omega Ward as I tried to find out Grace's room number.

"She's being questioned by the police. No one can see her until they clear her," she replied.

I hit the counter with my hand. "She shouldn't be alone."

Why were they keeping Grace from me? First, I was questioned for so long, by so many people, and not told anything about her. Finally, they told me that Grace was awake and here but wouldn't let me in to see her.

"Sir, don't make me call security. Also, why are you shirtless?" She scowled at me and picked up a phone.

"Because we were at the beach. Look, she's scared and pissed, and I should be in there with her. Ugh. This is stupid." I strode past her, the need to be with Grace clawing at my chest.

"Hey, you can't go back there. I'm calling security," she yelled.

I jogged down the hall. Sure, I didn't know what room she was in, but I'd just look for the police.

An alpha female officer stood in front of a closed door. The windows looking into the room from the hallway were closed.

"Hi, I'm Grace's alpha, Wes. I'd like to be there with her, please. She's probably so scared." I tried to ramp up the charm a little.

Her arms crossed over her chest. "Someone will get you when you can be with her. Right now, all interviews have to be done individually."

"I told you, she's *dead,* okay," Grace shrieked. "I was told that she was dead. No, I didn't go and make sure. Why? Don't you know what she did to me?" Her anger shot through the bond.

"Grace." I reached for the door.

"I don't think so," the officer snapped, getting me in some sort of hold before I could blink.

"She's my mate. Let me in there." I clawed at her.

There were footsteps. "That's him," a voice said.

"Get him out of here." The officer scowled at me. "She's *fine.* The doctor said that it was okay to talk to her. You should be glad that I won't have you thrown out of the hospital for this."

"Please, just let me in there. That's my *mate.*" I struggled as security dragged me down the hall.

They pushed me through the doors. "He doesn't get in," one guard said to the other guard at the Omega Ward's entrance.

The doors slammed in my face.

"Don't make me have you thrown out of the hospital." The guard glared at me.

"But... that's my mate." Defeat ripped through me.

Fuck. My shoulders slumped, and I sent her all my love. *I'm sorry, Grace. I tried.* Checking the group chat, I saw that everyone was in Spencer's room on the second floor.

Okay, if I couldn't be with Grace, at least I could hold Evan and make sure Spencer was okay.

I also had a text from my sister.

Lexi

Are you okay? I saw that very dramatic stabbing on the news.

Oh fuck. But Spencer Thanukos being stabbed *was* newsworthy.

Me

I'm fucking pissed that the police are questioning Grace alone. But I'm fine. I think Spencer will be okay.

Lexi

Does this have to do with whatever was going on yesterday that Jett was working on?

Me

Yeah. Spencer was stabbed by the alpha of Grace's bio-dad. I'll fill you in later.

Lexi

Okay. Let me know what you need.

I checked in at the desk and found Spencer's room. Spencer lay there in the bed, eyes closed, face bruised where Adriana had punched him on Friday. Evan was curled into him.

Jett and Brennan talked softly on the couch. Riley sat in a chair at the table texting.

"Finally." Relief coated Brennan's face.

"He's going to be okay, right?" I looked over at Spencer.

Brennan nodded. "You just missed the doctor. He'll be okay."

"Good. Hey, Babe." I went over and ran my hand down Evan's arm.

"Hey, Babe. Where's Grace? She's pissed and scared." Evan rolled over to look at me.

I sighed. "They won't let me into her room and threw me out of the Omega Ward. I think it was the Office of Designation Management questioning her because she was yelling about Rosalind being dead."

Brennan nodded. "I'll go and check on her soon. I've been trying to see if we can get the pack paperwork expedited."

"Really?" While that was a good idea, I was surprised that he'd do that.

"It seems like so many problems could have been circumvented by her being in a pack." He exhaled sharply.

"It's okay to be cautious, Honey. We had no idea that all of this would happen." Jett gave Brennan a squeeze.

I saw some snack wrappers on the table. "Is there a cafeteria here? Should we get something to eat?"

If I just sat here, I might try to break into the Omega Ward again. I couldn't help Grace if I ended up in a holding cell.

"I ordered pizza. It's coming." Riley looked up at me.

"How do you order pizza to a hospital?" I blinked.

"Wouldn't you like to know?" Riley smirked.

Not knowing what else to do, I sat on the bed with Evan and Spencer, sending love to Evan. Of course, this would devastate him. While they weren't mated, he and Spencer were best friends.

"Hi. Please tell me that this is Grace's room?" A *tall* woman, with dark hair, and blue-green eyes, in heels and a lab coat, stood in the doorway, holding a plant.

"Um, no, Doctor?" I blinked at her.

She laughed. "Okay, it's Spencer's then? The desk person was being weird with me."

"I'm sorry, you are?" Brennan stood, frowning.

"Hi, I'm Verity. I'm not Dr. Thorne yet, but I will be in a couple of years. Though I'm a plant geneticist, not a medical doctor. I'm Grace's little sister. I haven't met any of you yet," she explained.

Little? She was like six-feet tall and in her early-to-mid-twenties. Unlike the other siblings I'd met, she bore no resemblance to Grace. Though that didn't mean anything, other than someone else in the pack was her bio-dad.

Riley looked up from her phone. "Hi."

"Hi. Are you Riley?" She smiled.

"The one and only." Riley nodded.

"Mercy was texting me all about you. I brought Grace an omega lily. It's from my latest batch." Verity put the potted flower on the table.

"You make omega lilies?" I asked. Omega lilies were a traditional mating gift for omegas. Evan forgot his in a box, and it died.

She laughed. "I do. You know the stories about omega lilies making happy homes? Well, omega lilies actually contain chemicals in them that make people happy. I'm genetically engineering them to be even happier."

"You make happy flowers? Nice." Evan sat up.

"I'm Brennan. This is Jett. That's Wes. Evan's on the bed with Spencer. Um, what are you doing here?" Brennan asked.

"I wanted to make sure that she was okay. What happened was awful." She bit her pink lower lip. "I can't believe Mom did that to her. To him. Also, I needed to get out of the house." Her look went pained.

Yeah. The past couple of days' events might cause some household disharmony that flowers couldn't fix.

"Mercy also said that she'd meet me here and wanted a ride home." Verity looked around.

Riley moved the plant from the table to the bedstand. "It's a pretty plant. I love the container."

"One of my classmates makes them," Verity replied.

"I think I'd like to take ceramics next year." Riley nodded.

"Pizza delivery." Mercy, one of Grace's other little sisters, walked in with several pizzas.

"Thank fuck. You're a legend," Riley said.

The teenager, who looked like she hadn't changed since the beach, put the pizzas on the table.

"Hey, Ver, thanks for the ride. Hale took Tru home. Tru pouted, but we didn't know if Grace was okay or if the hospital even allowed small children." Mercy looked a lot like a sharper-featured, tall and muscular, brunette Grace. She took a piece of pizza out of the box and started eating.

Yeah. Didn't have to ask me twice. I took two pieces.

"Yeah, thanks." I took a large bite.

Brennan got pieces for him and Jett.

"Dinner delivery, got it. Did you have trouble getting through the press? I'm glad I had my lab coat in the car," Verity said.

"Evan, there's pasta for you. Verity, have a piece and sit. You're making me nervous." Riley ate another slice.

"I walked in with a stack of pizzas, I was fine. Take that chair, I'll get another one." Mercy left.

"There's press? Fuck." Jett finished his piece.

"Yeah. Spencer Thanukos was *stabbed* on a beach holiday. Of course, the press is here." Brennan sighed.

Verity sat down at the table with Riley and took a piece. Mercy came back in with another chair.

Evan went over to the table. "Pasta? Thank you."

"My brother doesn't like pizza." Riley handed him a round container and a fork.

"You are a very large omega," Verity breathed. "Sorry, I didn't know omegas came in extra-large before Grace showed me your picture."

"Yeah, there aren't too many of us. I've only met a few. Though there's a hockey player that a lot of the teens at the Omega Center like, and an actor in a popular show." Evan brought the pasta back to the bed.

The giant omega actor was in Evan's favorite show. Omegas played *hockey?* My dad loved to watch the Rockland Daredevils on TV.

Mercy and Riley were having a very in-depth conversation about skate smash. The rest of us made small talk with Verity and ate our food.

"Is there any pizza left for Grace?" I asked.

"I saved her two slices," Riley assured me.

Verity glanced at her pink phone and sighed. "I'm being summoned. Mercy, I'm sorry, but we need to go."

"O-kay. I wanted to see Grace, though." Mercy gave Riley a hug.

"Me, too." Verity grabbed her pastel purse. "I hope everyone makes a full recovery."

"The Rockland Raiders have a skate smash camp for high schoolers. I'm going. There's still time for you to apply, though you'll have to do it tomorrow," Riley told Mercy.

Mercy grinned. "That sounds fun. I aged out of the one the Carolina Furies have. I'll check and see if the dates work."

The two of them left.

"You and Grace's sister are besties now?" Brennan looked at her.

Riley shrugged. "My therapist says making friends is a good thing."

"Verity seems like a nice person," I nodded. "A really smart person."

"Well, yeah. It makes sense that Grace would be from a family of fucking geniuses, or did you not meet her five-year-old sister who wants to solve an unsolvable equation?" Riley gathered up the pizza boxes.

"I should go find Grace." I stood. The anger had stopped; now she just felt sad.

"If you were kicked out of the ward, maybe I'd have more luck?" Evan threw away his empty pasta dish.

Brennan stood. "I'll go. If anyone wants to head back to the hotel, that's fine. We don't all have to be here. Also, they might not let everyone stay. I don't know what the rules are."

Riley's head tilted. "I like actual beds. But let's see how Grace is, first."

That sounded like a good idea.

Evan pulled me back down with him. "Stay with me, Wes."

How could I deny that? "Of course, I'll stay."

Maybe Brennan would have better luck.

Chapter Three

Grace

"Are you sure she's actually dead? You know that helping a fugitive is a criminal offense?" The officer from the Office of Designation Management scowled at me.

"My brother said that she was dead. There was no reason to not believe him." I scowled back. I was cold, tired, and hungry. My heart ached for Spencer. I wanted Wes and Evan.

Instead, I was alone, in a hospital room, hooked up to monitors, being questioned by someone from the Office of Designation Management. I'd already talked to the police and what was probably this world's FBI. The agent from the Bureau of Investigation was still with us.

"Look, Grace," she snapped. "We need to find Rosalind. Why don't you just stop covering for her?"

"Covering for her?" What? The audacity. Anger exploded inside me. "I told you, she's *dead*, okay," I shrieked. "I was told that she was dead. No, I didn't go and make sure. Why? Don't you know what she did to me?"

I turned so she could see the scars lacing my back. "She had them beat me until I forgot my soulmate. I'd *never* cover for her. She's the literal reason I'm a gamma. She knew the professor was my biological father and that my being an omega was likely. No, I was never tested. Probably because it was obvious that I'd be an omega. I was making nests in the laundry when I was three. Three! You know who smells like laundry? My soulmate, who I started dreaming of when I was ten. A mate I'd really like right now. Not to mention I have another mate who might still be in surgery."

Or dead. No. I think I'd know if he was dead.

I wanted my mates. Taking a deep breath, I tried to calm myself. *3.14159265359*

"What did Rosalind steal?" I looked up at the agent through blurry, tear-filled eyes.

She sighed. "You don't need to know that."

"Fine." I turned to the officer. "How did Thora die? Why did Thora die?"

"Being a sigma is illegal. It didn't hurt her. I promise," the officer assured.

"That doesn't make me feel better. I never even got to know her." Yeah, I absolutely was going to help Spencer figure out how to make Elaris' project to protect the illegal designations a reality.

"Now, can you just tell us the information I need?" the officer pressed.

"So, Thora was brought into the police because they thought she was her twin, or because they wanted to question her because of her twin and her brother. She gave me to Adriana, who turned me over to the baby shelter, who then gave me to Thora's mom." Who I supposed was my grandmother?

I frowned. "Thora's released, then picked up again, and somehow it's thought she was a sigma. You murdered Thora–and Thora's dad and brother. At some point, Rosalind sneaks in, reaches out to Adriana Thorne, takes a payoff, makes me a fake record, and we disappear. Thora's mom explains my disappearance by saying that she can't take care of me, and I was put into care. Do I have the timeline right? Because I'm confused. Until a couple of days ago I thought Rosalind was my mom, not Thora, and I didn't know who the professor was." I might as well get all the information they'd tell me.

Especially if it could help me figure out how we got to my world.

"Not quite. First, it's not *murder*. Also, your uncle and grandfather were found and tested later, when the whole family, minus you, Rosalind, and Thora, were brought in. If you were in the house, you would have been tested, and there would be mention of it under one of your records. They should have looked for you in care, but we don't always have the resources to search hard for someone," the officer told me.

"You test *babies?*" Horror coated me. But then my siblings were tiny, and they were tested.

Also, not murder? Really?

"You've had the test, it doesn't hurt. Small children will need to be tested again as teenagers."

"How can you be so calm about it?" My hands fisted as the tears started again.

"Can you just answer the questions?" Anger and frustration rolled off of the officer.

Ugh. It's not like I could tell them the truth.

Or could I?

"Fine. But I want my mates. Somehow, Rosalind accessed a smuggling network that helped people with illegal designations start over. We were sent elsewhere. No, I don't know who these people are. I'm making deductions here," I told them.

"Okay, now we're getting somewhere. Give me your address where you grew up." She tapped on her tablet.

I gave it to her.

"A *real* address, Grace. This city doesn't exist." Her eyes narrowed.

"Not here. Somehow, we were smuggled to another world. One like ours, but not quite. One where she wasn't illegal. The smuggling ring isn't around anymore, and I wish I knew how they did it. I mean, I know the basics of the math behind it, but not how you'd actually implement it," I elaborated.

She blinked. "You expect me to believe that you went to another world? How did you get back?"

"That's a whole different story," I replied. "But that's why you can't find Rosalind Ellington or her address."

Anger filled the room as the officer huffed. "I can't even."

"Grace, your genetics are fine. You said so yourself, she hurt you. Just tell us what we need to know, instead of making up stories about other worlds," the agent scolded.

"I did! A concussion gave me memory loss. It's in my file. She's dead, okay. So, you can rest easily that there's one less sigma out there, and you'll just have to recover her treasure later. That's what this is about, right? Not prosecuting her, but finding whatever it was she stole? Can I have my mates now?" I snapped, tired of all this.

"I'm done here." The officer stormed out, slamming the door behind her.

The agent shook her head and left.

Ugh. I wanted my mates. While I got love from Wes and Evan, I wanted *them*. But I had no idea where my phone was. Also, I was only in my swimsuit.

I used the bathroom, bringing the monitor with me. Maybe I'd go find them. I tried the door to the hall. Locked.

"Can I have some food? My mates? Anyone?" I banged on the door.

Nothing.

"Hey, I thought I didn't do anything wrong?" I opened the shades and tapped on the window that looked out onto the hallway.

Still nothing. Trudging back to the bed, I pressed the call button. Maybe a nurse could bring me some food?

The room was a little smaller than the one I'd been in back in Rockland. It had a couch and a small table. But it felt uncomfortable. Probably because I didn't have my hot man mattress.

Two people walked by, and I perked as the door opened.

"Hi, Grace. I came to check on you," the doctor I'd seen earlier said.

A male nurse in pink scrubs was with her, pushing a small machine.

She looked at the monitors and made notes on a tablet.

"I feel fine." Though I know I had a seizure.

"That's good. You have had a lot of seizures, and that's concerning. Though you blacking out because your mate was in pain isn't abnormal." She glanced at her tablet and nodded.

"Could I have my mate now? Also, some food?" My belly rumbled.

"One of your mates has been banned from the ward, the other is unconscious, so I think the answer is *no*," the nurse snapped as he attached me to a small device that, if I remembered correctly, read my brain.

"Spencer's unconscious? Did the surgery go okay?" I asked. Wes had been banned? I thought I'd heard shouting earlier.

"Well, he did get stabbed because of you," the nurse muttered.

The doctor shot him a look. "I believe the surgery went well, and he's now in recovery."

"Okay, can I see him? Could I get my phone? Maybe a T-shirt? Can I have my omega? One of my packmates? I'll take any of them?" Actually, Riley would be a good companion right now.

"Let me check. Usually it would be *yes*, but this is… extenuating." The doctor frowned.

My shoulders slumped. "Okay."

"I'll be back later. We're going to need to run some more tests. The nurse will finish up and bring you some food." The doctor left.

Muttering under his breath, he finished up the readings and unhooked me from the device.

"Thank you. I understand if I can't see my mates, but maybe the person from the Omega Center that they sent away can come back?" I asked. "Could I get a blanket? Please?"

"No," he huffed as he punched some buttons on the monitor I was attached to. "You don't even belong here. Ugh. I don't know why they're keeping you here and not at one of their facilities. Dirty fucking variants don't deserve medical care."

"What? I'm not an illegal designation. It's about someone I once knew. I didn't do anything." Why was everyone so mean here?

His eyes narrowed. "That's what they all say."

Pushing the machine out, he slammed the door, muttering, "Yeah, not bringing a variant food or a blanket, especially one that almost got her mate killed."

Well, someone needed to work on their bedside manner.

Still, what he said weighed on me. *You don't even belong here.*

But it *was* my fault. Spencer's injury was because of me. He put himself between me and the knife. I was the one that Adriana meant to stab. He could have died. He could still die. If we lost him because of me…

Spencer never would have been on that beach if it hadn't been for me. Actually, so many bad things happened to the pack because of me.

Not to mention, were they really okay with my bio-mom having illegal genes? It seemed like some people weren't. Like that nurse.

Maybe they'd just leave me here. For all I know, they were gone. I mean, she said Spencer was recovering, but she didn't say that he was here. Maybe he'd been sent to another hospital.

None of the guys signed up for a gamma with a mom with an illegal designation, a bio-dad with homicidal mates, and an aunt that somehow ran away to another world.

I was toxic. Dangerous. The entire pack could be in danger because of me.

Love and reassurance came through the bond from Evan and Wes. I tried to tamp down the bonds and shut it off the best I could.

I didn't deserve it. Them.

Yeah. They would have been better off if Agent Weigmier had never brought me here.

All I did was ruin everything. Curling up in a ball, I started to cry.

Chapter Four

Brennan

My phone buzzed as I walked back toward the Omega Ward.

Something's wrong. You need to get her.

Trying.

I checked my email again. There it was. I'd started trying to obtain the court order the moment they separated us from Grace at the hospital. It would cost me because this was the judge who helped me yesterday. But, I felt like she'd be sympathetic since she already knew some of Grace's story. A vacation at one of my resorts for her pack was well worth Grace's safety.

Guilt ate at me. Maybe we should have made Grace part of the pack sooner. No, Jett was right. Being cautious about bringing someone into the pack was normal. Also, the legal process of adding someone took time, especially with her falling under omega law.

How were we to know all this would happen?

The court order would work for now. Who knew what the universe would throw at us next?

No. I shouldn't tempt fate like that. With Grace, the literal universe could throw actual things at us.

The delta at the double doors leading to the locked Omega Ward glared at me. "I told you, I can only let in someone who's pack or an emergency contact, and not that guy who I was told not to let in."

I showed him my phone. "This is a court order placing Grace Ellington in my pack's care. I'll give you any documentation you need. But please, let me in. She's all alone and scared."

He studied it. I showed him my ID.

"I'll let you in, but they might not allow you to go to her room." He opened the door.

"Thank you." I went into the ward, which looked just as comfortable as the one in Rockland, with pastel walls, paintings, and soft music.

A woman in pink scrubs looked up at me from behind a desk. "Can I help you?"

"I'm here to see Grace Ellington." I smiled at her.

Her eyes narrowed. "I won't hesitate to throw you out like the other one."

Once again, I showed her everything. She printed out a sticker with Grace's name and room number on it.

"The officers left a bit ago, so I think you can go in? If there's still an officer at the door and they don't let you in, please don't tackle them?" She gave me a pleading look.

Is that what Wes did? Not that I blamed him. If someone was keeping Evan or Jett away from me, I'd do the same.

"Of course, thank you." I put the sticker on my shirt and went down the hall.

Two guys in pink scrubs were gossiping at one of the nursing stations.

"You brought the patient in 317 dinner, right, and called her pack? They said she could have her pack now," a doctor asked as she walked by.

"Yes, I brought her dinner along with a blanket," one of them nodded. "Her pack is unresponsive, I'm guessing that they abandoned her."

The doctor frowned. "They're probably busy with the pack member who is on the second floor. Maybe bring in Liz?"

"She's gone for the day, but I'll call for a social worker." He waved her off, and the doctor hurried down the hall.

What? 317 was Grace's room. I texted the group chat.

Me

> **Did anyone from the Omega Ward reach out to you? They're saying they did, and we were unresponsive.**

Wes

> **They didn't text me. Also, I have her phone.**

Evan

> **Not me. Not Spencer's phone either.**

Jett

> **Nope.**

Oh? I looked over at the nurses. The gossips paid me no attention.

"Did you really?" one asked, looking scandalized. "I wouldn't."

The other laughed. "Of course not. She shouldn't even be here."

I turned down the hall, and my belly twisted. Everything felt off. Evan's words came back to me. *Something's wrong.*

While all the other doors had placards with the patient's name and designation, Grace's had none. There was no officer at the door. The window blinds were open, and it looked like she was sleeping, in her bikini, no blanket.

A sour-sweet smell, like rotten fruit, made my nose twitch. I put my hand on the door. Locked.

Why the fuck was her door locked?

This wasn't right.

I kicked the door; then I kicked it again.

An alpha came out of the room next to hers. "What are you doing?"

"They fucking locked her in there." Anger bubbled inside me. How dare they treat anyone like that, let alone Grace?

"Isn't she a criminal? I saw the police here." The alpha gave me a wary look.

Another door opened, and someone stared at me.

"A criminal? Why would you even think of that? My mate is a police officer; they question people at hospitals all the time. Her mate was *stabbed,* and she had a seizure." I looked at him like he was an idiot.

I kicked the door again, and it flew open. The smell of rotten peaches rolled over me—a scent reminiscent of the night that she spiraled.

"Fuck." I ran into the room and pressed the call button, which didn't work. Why didn't it work?

Shouldn't an alarm have sounded when she started spiraling? A glance at the monitor that she was attached to showed that it was off. Shit. I started undoing her from everything so that I could get her out of here.

Grace's tiny form was crumpled into a ball. Her skin felt clammy. Tears stained her face.

What the fuck happened?

I scooped her up and kissed her forehead, which tasted of sweat, fear, and sadness. "Come on, Grace. Let's get you out of here. You'll feel better with your mates."

Hopefully. But I wasn't about to leave her here. How dare they?

"What are you doing? Are you supposed to be in here?" The doctor from before stood in the doorway.

"I'm her head alpha, and I'm taking her out of here. You locked her in a room, turned off her monitors, and disabled the call button. You're making her sick," I shouted, clutching Grace's clammy body to my chest, as I threw a sheet over her.

The doctor looked confused. "Locked? We unlocked it when the police left. It took a moment to make sure she was cleared, but her mates *were* notified that they could see her."

"I literally had to kick her door in—and no one notified any of us." I brushed past the doctor.

"You probably just missed the text. You can't just take her," the doctor said.

"Watch me. How can you even call yourselves medical professionals? No one should be treated like this, especially someone whose mate was stabbed. She should have been moved in with him as soon as he was out of surgery, not locked in a room and denied us." I carried her toward the exit. "It's going to be okay, Little Butterfly. I've got you."

"Security, security," shouted the guy in pink scrubs who said he'd called us.

"It's a good thing my arms are full, or I'd punch you. You didn't call us. Are you the one who locked her in? Did you turn off the monitors? Certainly, you didn't bring her a blanket or dinner. I'll have your license. If anything happens to her, so help me," I growled.

"She's a fucking variant. She shouldn't even be here," he snapped back.

Moving Grace to my right arm, my left fist hit him in the face.

"Variant? What the fuck are you talking about? She's a gamma and mated to Spencer fucking Thanukos. Do you have any idea what you've done?" I snarled. "Even if she was, how dare you treat *anyone* like that? Don't you all swear oaths?"

The scent of her spiral was strong, and everyone in this unit probably knew what it meant.

"Let's take her back into her room. We'll get her some medicine and blankets. You can stay with her. Spirals can be dangerous," the doctor said.

Security ran over. "Is there a problem?"

"Yes. We're wasting time. I need to get her to her mates since not only did this spiral happen on your watch, you caused it," I snapped, wishing I had time to punch that nurse again, but continuing to stride down the hallway instead.

"I think you should bring her back to her room." A security guard blocked me.

My growl filled the hallway–a primal noise that made some of the staff shake.

"And let you hurt her more? You'll be hearing from our lawyers." Holding Grace tight, I broke into a run, taking her down the hallway and going past the desk. No one messed with our pack–or treated us like this.

The woman at the desk shot me a startled look. "Wait, should you–"

Ignoring her, I burst through the doors, the guard looking surprised.

"Don't fucking try me, they could have killed her," I called, as I kept moving. I'd already wasted too much time.

"Hold on, Grace." I headed straight for the stairs. "We're going to get you tucked in next to Spencer. Evan can snuggle with you. Wes and Jett are there, too. Riley even saved you some pizza."

Exiting on the second floor, I ran straight past the desk and the nurses' station.

"Wait, sir?" Someone called after me.

"She's spiraling, I need to get her to her mates," I yelled, still not stopping.

I ran into the room, and everyone looked at me. Evan sat on the couch between Jett and Wes. Riley was on her phone.

"Here you go, Little Butterfly. You cuddle right there," I whispered, tucking her into Spencer's good side.

"I smell that. What the fuck happened?" Wes stood up.

"Evan, can you squish in here so that she's in between you two? Your snuggles fixed her last time. Can someone get another blanket? She's only in her bathing suit." I covered her with the one on the bed.

"I will." Riley ran out.

"Fuck." Evan squashed into the bed, sandwiching her between him and Spencer. "I've got you, Peaches. You're safe here between Spencer and me. Wes is with us."

Evan's purr filled the room. Wes got in as close as he could, stroking her hair as his purr joined Evan's.

The nurse who had been checking on him ran in. "You said that she's spiraling?"

"Yeah. But I don't want anyone from the Omega Ward anywhere near her, especially the person I punched in the face. I might get banned for that." But Grace was worth it.

"I'll get a doctor in here." The nurse left.

"What happened?" Jett put a hand on my shoulder.

Riley came back in with an armful of blankets and started heaping them over Grace and Evan.

Quickly, I told them what I'd found, what I'd overheard, and what happened.

Wes looked stricken. "They did what? Fuck. Maybe I shouldn't have tried to get to her."

I shook my head. "I think it had to do with the Office of Designation Management questioning her. The nurse called her a *variant*."

"Can they even do that?" Wes asked.

"I don't think so." I shook my head.

Wes pulled a chair over to the bed and stroked her hair, murmuring to Grace. Evan kept purring.

I sat down on the couch, Jett next to me, and emailed our lawyer everything.

A security guard came into the room. He stared at me. "You." He looked at Wes and sighed. "And you."

"Ban me if you'd like. But keeping her locked in a room and disabling her monitors while she spiraled is malpractice." I should probably email people at the hospital, too.

Hmmm. Did I know anyone on the hospital's board?

"Excuse me." A female doctor brushed past the guard, with the nurse behind her.

"This is my mate, it's okay. Liz already went home, or I'd have her come, too," the nurse assured us.

"What happened?" The doctor started checking her the best she could with Grace wedged between Spencer and Evan.

I repeated what I'd found.

"Is she on any medications?" the doctor asked.

"No." Wes shook his head.

The nurse hooked her up to a small, portable monitor.

"This is the right place for her to be, but I'm going to give her a shot to help things along." The doctor held a syringe.

The security guard stood there. He sighed and looked at me. "You punched a nurse."

I looked at Jett. "Should I call the police? What that nurse did has to be some sort of assault."

"I feel like the police not letting Evan and Grace have someone in there with them when they were being questioned is illegal?" Wes added.

Jett shook his head. "They just wanted information, so it's technically not illegal, just not general protocol. At least in Rockland, it could be different here."

"Do you need me to leave?" I eyed the security guard.

"Doc says not to kick you out, but you're banned from the Omega Ward. It's protocol." The security guard looked like it had been a long day.

"Okay. It looks as if they can treat her here just fine." I went back to my emails.

He sighed again and left.

The doctor and nurse finished up with Grace. The doctor who'd been tending to Spencer came in and talked to them.

"Grace should stabilize soon, just snuggle her. Purr for her if she needs it. We'll check on her again soon." That doctor left, but the nurse stayed.

Spencer's doctor checked him over.

"He's doing okay, though his heart rate is up. He's probably feeling her distress. We'll monitor him. Try reassuring him that she's okay. Once she's stabilized, we'll probably take him off sedation. Then he'll wake up after a few hours," the doctor told us.

I thanked him, and then he left. Wes and Evan talked to Spencer and Grace.

"Want me to take you back to the hotel, Ri?" Jett asked.

"Not yet." Riley shook her head. "But I'd like to go to the cafeteria. I need something sweet."

Evan nodded. "They have ice cream."

"Let's go see what they have," I told them. And maybe track down a hospital administrator.

Someone would answer for what had happened to Grace.

The hospital room was dark, though light crept in through the blinds leading to the hospital hall. Evan and Grace slept next to Spencer. The doctor hadn't roused Spencer yet, though Grace seemed to be doing better and sleeping normally.

Jett, Wes, and Riley had gone back to the hotel. Wes was going to return with things for Grace and Spencer. I'd take Evan back in the morning for a bit.

Well, if he'd leave them.

The couch turned into a small bed, and it wasn't uncomfortable. There were extra blankets and pillows, too. I just couldn't sleep. Normally I'd either work, workout, or fuck one of my mates.

None of those were options right now.

"No, no. Please, don't leave me," Grace screamed as her monitor beeped.

"It's okay, Grace. It's okay," Evan mumbled, draping an arm around her.

"I'm sorry, I'm so sorry. I didn't mean to put everyone in danger," she cried.

Evan sat up and shook her gently. "Peaches, wake up, you're having a bad dream."

"I didn't mean for anyone to get hurt. I... I'm sorry. Please don't make me go." Grace thrashed against Evan.

Spencer's monitor went off. Shit.

I hopped off the couch and strode over to the bed. "Hey, Little Butterfly, come here. Evan, comfort Spencer?"

Bundling her into my arms, I pulled her out of the bed and brought her over to the couch.

Evan draped himself on Spencer's good side. "She's okay, Bren's got her. It's just a nightmare."

A sleepy purr filled the room.

"I've got you." I lay on the couch bed, with her on my bare chest. Evan had on my shirt–she had on Evan's.

"Don't leave me, Bren. I didn't know my mom was illegal," she sobbed.

"What? No. Never." Pulling the blankets over her, I held her tight, kissing the top of her head, and stroking the back of her neck. Her peach scent was a little panicked but not rotten anymore.

Was this why she'd spiraled back in the Omega Ward? She thought that we didn't want her? Or perhaps they made her think that?

"He got hurt because of me. Bad things happened because of me," she wailed.

Spencer's monitor went off again.

"She'll be okay. She's a little upset, but she'll be okay." Evan gave him a pat.

"It's not your fault, Grace. Not the stabbing, not anything else. None of this is your fault," I assured her, giving her another kiss on the top of her head as I tried to put out calming pheromones to help settle her before she or Spencer got too distressed.

"Everything I knew is a lie." It came out as a sob.

"We still love you. Promise." Evan reached out to her.

I took one of her hands and extended it to his. "See, we love you. It'll all be okay. I'm going after the license of that fucker who was mean to you. I might even sue the hospital. Think of all the ice cream you could get."

Not only was our lawyer livid, but I'd told Katie what had happened in order to get some advice. Her pregnancy hormones were raging, and my twin was ready to inflict some wrath.

"Okay. Just don't leave me," Grace murmured, settling into my arms.

"We won't." I stroked her hair.

The door opened, and a nurse came in and ran over to the monitor. This was a different one, given the shift had changed.

"She had a nightmare." Evan patted Spencer again. "It's okay, Spence, she's okay."

"That's working," the nurse assured. "He's feeling her, but he's also responding to your reassurance." He came over to Grace and me and checked her monitor. "She looks okay."

"I've got her." I gave Grace a squeeze and made sure we had enough blankets.

"Let me know if you need anything." The nurse left.

The group chat went off.

Wes

Is Grace okay?

Me

She had a nightmare. I've got her.

I took a photo of us and sent it to him.

Wes

You look cozy.

Me

Jealous?

Wes

I'll share her with you. Oh wait, already have.

Wes liked to think he was funny.

Wes

No, seriously, take care of her however she needs. I'll be back soon. Still trying to sort things out with the hotel so we can stay longer.

Me

Thanks for doing that. Bring me a shirt? Evan took mine.

Wes

Sure.

We were supposed to check out of the hotel in the morning. But I didn't think we would be leaving here anytime soon. At some point, I should let Terrance know what was going on.

Grace mumbled and snuggled into me. Okay, it was more like she ground into my dick and nuzzled against my chest. While part of me felt like I should stop it, I was the one who'd brought her onto the couch for cuddles.

I also liked it *a lot*.

She's not yours.

But she could be. Maybe not now, but at some point. Jett was right; somewhere along the way I'd started to give a fuck about her.

Okay, I gave many fucks about her.

It's okay to care about the people who live in your house.

I suppose I could enjoy those snuggles. Sometime down the line, I might start something with her. But I'd let it happen naturally.

Jett was in love with her. Evan kept telling me about that fantasy of his involving the three of us having her while she was in the swing. Which was a pretty nice one–and much more attainable than the ones Jett and I had about her.

My dick grew hard as she ground into me again.

Wes was right. I'd give her just about everything–including my dick. At some point, I should make sure Spencer was okay with that.

Spencer. Fuck. If Grace ever went into heat, what was *that* going to look like? I had a feeling Little Miss Needy Butterfly would want *everyone* there. I'd never even seen that man naked, let alone shared someone with him.

If she wanted us all there, we'd figure it out.

She'd want me there, right?

I wasn't sure why the idea of her not wanting me there bothered me. After all, she wasn't mine.

But she was *ours.* She'd been through so much. We'd all been through a lot recently.

"Love, are you doing okay?" I reached out to squeeze Evan's hand. He was worried about Spencer, I could feel it through the bond.

His hand brushed mine. "When we go back to the hotel, I want dick."

"My dick is yours." I smiled at him through the darkness. Yeah, I'd give him all the comfort he wanted.

"Okay." Grace mumbled, her hand sliding down my pants.

I froze.

"I've had a shitty day. Be a good boy and let me nap on that." Her hand wrapped around my cock.

"Little Butterfly, I'm not your good boy. It's Bren whose lap you're on—not Wes, Spencer, or Evan," I said softly. She was half asleep, and while I didn't mind if she wanted my cock, I needed her to know that it was me.

Also, I wasn't anyone's good boy. Okay, sometimes I was Jett's good boy. But that was different.

Evan was now wide awake and watching us curiously.

"You are so my good boy. Mmmm, I like the texture. It's the best fidget toy." She toyed with my piercings.

"It feels good, doesn't it?" Evan chuckled.

"Get in there." Moving her bikini bottoms aside, she just impaled herself on it.

I stilled, waiting for her to move—or realize that I wasn't the alpha she wanted. Was I really going to do this? Yes. I cared about her, and it would calm her down. Evan's cock wouldn't hit the same pressure points as an alpha's.

Grace just hummed and laid her head back on my chest.

"That's what you needed?" I asked, this feeling far too comfortable.

"Much better." She patted me on my head, sleepily. "Now, hold me. Such a good boy."

"You're going to nap on his cock?" Evan laughed.

"Shhh. I'm sleeping." Grace made a contented noise.

I wrapped my arms around her. "I've got you. Go back to sleep, Grace."

"Good boy." Evan grinned.

I shot him a look. "That stays between us. She's probably high on whatever drugs they gave her. So, I just lay here, and she naps with my dick inside her?"

"Full body cuddles make her feel better. She cares about you, too, Bren. You know that, right?" Evan said softly.

"Yes." I planted a kiss on her head. "I care about her as well."

Hopefully, she wouldn't regret this in the morning.

Chapter Five

Spencer

Pain rippled through me. I moved and felt another jolt. "Ow."

"Spence?" a sleepy female voice croaked.

Opening my eyes, my surroundings came into focus. A hospital room? Oh. Memories of Adriana trying to stab Grace, and me stepping in front of her came back to me.

I looked over at Grace, who was curled into my side. She smelled of Brennan and Evan. Wes slept on the couch. No one else was here. I had no idea what time it was.

"Spence, you're awake." Grace's blue-grey eyes gazed at me.

"Hi, Darling." My hand reached out and stroked her hair. "I feel a little shitty."

"That bitch stabbed you. But you'll be okay. Alpha healing and all that. I'm sorry." She sniffed. "I'm so sorry you were hurt and had to have surgery because of me."

The angst in our bond hurt my soul.

"It's not your fault, Baby Girl. Don't think it is for one minute." I wanted to lean over and kiss her, but that took too much effort. So, I stroked her hair again and sent her reassurance through our bond.

"Okay. Bren, Wes, and Evan said that, too, but I needed to make sure," she whispered.

"I love you." I tried my best to pull her to me.

She snuggled into me more. "I love you, too. It's morning. They sedated you after the surgery and gave you the drugs to bring you out of it an hour or so ago. Bren dragged Evan off to the hotel. Jett and Riley are there too. They'll be back. Wes is here with us."

"Are *you* okay?" I had vague memories of her not being okay.

"I wasn't injured. But I had a seizure and a spiral and some nightmares. However, I'm okay. I don't really want to move right now, but I'll be all right." She headbutted me.

"You can stay next to me as long as you need." It was probably scary for her. It was frightening for me.

"Um, I texted your mom and your publicist." Grace looked up at me. "It hit the news. They were calling you. I told them what I knew. Also, I said that I didn't think they needed to come here. I also talked to Mrs. K. She was worried. Other people called and texted, but I didn't reply. Evan or Wes might have, though."

Oh. But then if Grace and I walking on the beach was news, my being stabbed absolutely was.

"Thank you. I'll call them later." Right now, I really didn't feel like moving.

A doctor came in, though she stayed near the doorway.

"I'm fine." Grace scowled at her.

"I know. I've been checking with the doctors on this floor. I'm sorry for how you were treated. I assure you, that nurse will be disciplined." She looked anxious.

"Disciplined? It's malpractice. He needs to never work in healthcare again." Wes sat up, scent going spicy with anger.

What happened?

"It's not indicative of how we treat our patients. Usually, our staff are professionals and don't let their personal beliefs cloud their professional judgement," the doctor said.

"Okay." Grace's lower lip quivered.

"We've got our lawyers on it. This is a clusterfuck, and you know it," Wes snapped.

"I know. I just wanted to say that I'm sorry." The doctor gave her a concerned look, then she left.

I turned to Grace and Wes. "What happened?"

"People are stupid." Grace buried her face in my shoulder.

Wes filled me in on all the questions the pack had from various agencies–and how Grace was treated in the Omega Ward.

"No, that won't do. I'm glad Brennan's on it." Horror coated me. They did what? She could have died if Brennan hadn't broken down the door. My poor baby girl. No wonder all she wanted to do was snuggle.

"Oh, he's on it, and is after that guy's license. The hospital's going to pay for letting that happen. Someone from the hospital administration already came with flowers. That's not going to fix the fact they could have killed her," Wes muttered.

"They're pretty flowers. I'm okay, Wes. It was scary, but I don't like the idea of someone losing their job–and you don't need to sue anyone and hurt the hospital's ability to care for others." She sniffed.

Wes pulled a chair over to the bed, not that the couch was far. "Grace, getting him fired means he won't do that to anyone else. Same with going after the hospital. Also, the hospital has insurance for this specific reason."

She gave him a skeptical look.

"He's right, Grace. Taking legal action means protecting others." I continued to play with her hair.

"Okay. I really don't want anyone to go through what I did. I don't want money from this, though." She frowned at Wes.

Wes took her hand. "If you get any money from it, you can put it away and have a little extra money of your own. Or you can save it for Wyatt, Hannah, Daisy, and Grayson."

Children. She, Wes, and Evan had named our pack's future children. Awww. I knew Evan wanted a daughter named Daisy. His mom *loved* daisies.

"Yeah, you and Evan do *not* get two kids each." Grace shook her head. "Honestly, I'd prefer those fraternal twins with different daddies, so I have your and Evan's babies in one pregnancy."

"I'm not sure it works that way." Wes laughed.

"Fraternal twins run on the professor's side and identical twins run on Thora's side. So, it's a possibility." Grace squirmed. "I don't have a twin, right? Like we'd know?" Anxiety shot through the bond.

"If you had an identical twin, we'd know," I reassured her. "You could have twins? Hmmm, identical twin girls that looked like a cross between you and Evan? They'd get away with *everything*."

"Right?" Grace chuckled.

"How many kids do you want, Grace? Two?" I asked.

She thought for a moment. "Maybe three, one for each of you? I want to wait a couple of years to get my career started, get our life going."

My heart exploded. I hadn't expected that. I'd always wanted children but knew it was a strong possibility that I'd never have any. Elaris couldn't have children.

"That makes so much sense, Darling. I'd love that, but only if you would, too." I could feel that something about children made her anxious. Was it work? Compass BioTek had very generous parental leave, flexible schedules, and on-site day care, but Grace also struck me as someone who didn't want to pause her research for long. It wasn't uncommon. We'd figure it out.

Wes grinned, revealing a dimple. "I think the world needs your and Spence's identical triplets. They'd be running their own company by middle school."

I laughed too, trying not to wince in pain. "Yes, they would."

"Wes. *Identical triplets?*" Grace laughed. "I do worry about being a good mom."

"You'll be a great mom," I reassured. "You'll have all of us to help you, and you absolutely won't need to give up your career or slow down if you don't want to. But if you do, you have so many options."

Wes kissed her hand. "You'll be the best mom."

"Also, I'm a little unsure about pushing out all of your giant babies," she chuckled.

"You're my soulmate, you're made for our giant babies." Wes gave her a kiss.

"Oh my god, Wes." She play-smacked him, still laughing.

The idea of her pregnant with our children turned me on. I'd cook her everything and anything she wanted and rub her back every night. Of course, I'd do that now. I was also so relieved that Adriana hadn't harmed her. Grace's safety was worth my discomfort.

"But all this with Thora's genetics? It's scary." Grace's scent turned anxious.

"Of course it is. But you're not a carrier, so it'll be okay," I reassured. "Also, don't feel like you *have* to allow the professor and his family into your life."

"I think I'd like to get to know my siblings more. Creed and I sort of clicked. Riley and Mercy get along amazingly well. I wasn't there, but apparently Verity came to visit and even brought us an omega lily," she told me.

"Oh, she did? How lovely." I spied an omega lily in a beautiful pot next to a giant bouquet of flowers.

"Hale's a lot. But Tru? How could I not love a five-year-old obsessed with math? I look forward to getting to know them. I'll give the professor a chance, but I don't know about the other parents." Grace frowned.

"That's just fine," I assured her.

"You don't even have to give him a chance if you don't want to," Wes added.

"I know." She sighed. "It would be nice to have siblings here—especially sisters."

"This pack needs all the sisters." Wes chuckled. "But hey, don't worry about everything with the hospital, okay. We'll let Bren and the lawyers handle it."

Grace made a noncommittal noise. "I guess. Bren said we could buy ice cream with the money. Can I just give it to the foundation so our scholarship kids can buy ice cream? They need ice cream money."

"I love that idea. Being able to give our students allowances would be helpful. For right now, at least, we've got all of Evan's omegas situated. We'll get everything else worked out eventually. We should probably create an application process," I said.

While I'd reached out to Rock Tech and Hadley Hall about the science scholarships for betas, I still needed to talk to Sonja, Evan's sister, about establishing one at Darthmore, which was the private academy primarily for gifted betas that she was dean of students for.

Grace nodded. "I think we should call the science ones *Starbright Scholars*. Because they're going to make the world brighter with all the good their science will put into the world."

"Ooh, I like that," Wes replied.

I did, as well.

"We should call the omega scholars *Starlight Scholars*. You know, like *Starlight, Starbright, first star I see tonight*." She beamed.

"Oh, we used to play that and make wishes," Wes breathed.

While I didn't know that game, it sounded just like her. "Perfect."

She frowned. "While I understand wanting to have applications for the omega scholarships moving forward instead of just Evan randomly awarding them, aren't most of his given out of urgency? Maybe we should still have the option to award emergency scholarships based on referrals?"

"I like that idea. It doesn't always have to be full scholarships either. It could be anything that gives them safety—such as a plane ticket or a deposit for an apartment. I know that the Omega Center has some of that, but the money gets allocated quickly. They also can't help non-omega siblings, but we could," I told them.

"*Stardust Scholars*—and the *Stardust Fund*." Grace snapped her fingers. "Because sometimes you just need a sprinkle of stardust to make some magic."

"Absolutely. You're right, there's a need for both. I love the names you came up with." I threaded my fingers through hers and squeezed.

While the talk of children made me happy, all these ideas for our family foundation made me equally pleased.

"Oh, you're awake, great." A doctor ducked in and checked my monitors. "How are you feeling?"

"Glad to be awake," I admitted honestly.

She looked over Grace, who just had a wrist monitor like before.

"You're looking great, Grace. How about if you and your alpha go get some tea? Getting up and moving around will make you feel better. We won't be long," she told them.

Grace whined a little. *I know.*

"Get me some coffee?" Giving her a task might help.

"Okay." With a sigh, Grace rolled out of bed and put on the shorts Wes handed her, which barely peaked out from her t-shirt. She put on some flip-flops and kissed me.

The two of them left, hand-in-hand, but not before Grace blew me a kiss.

"Is the news bad?" I looked at the doctor.

"Not at all. You should be fine. I just wanted to give you some privacy," she said.

"She's fine?" I frowned.

"She had scans and bloodwork first thing this morning, and everything looks okay," the doctor assured. "Now let's get you checked out before the rest of your pack returns."

"Oh, hey, where is everyone?" Brennan walked into my hospital room, holding a bag.

"Grace and Wes went down to the cafeteria, they'll be back," I told him. The doctor had just left. I'd called my mother, publicist, and Mrs. K, assuring everyone that I was fine.

"I brought some things for you. Evan's coming with more." Brennan set the bag down. "Wow, that's a gigantic bouquet."

"Apparently the hospital sent them for Grace." I used the controls on the bed to move me into a sitting position.

Brennan grunted. "They're scared that we're going to sue them."

"Grace wants to use the money to give all our scholars allowances." I chuckled.

"That's so Grace. Um..." His scent went a little anxious. "You don't have a problem if Grace starts something with Jett... or me... do you?"

"No, not at all, as long as it's something everyone wants." While Brennan might be a lot for Grace, I also trusted him to be attuned to her needs.

Relief flooded his face. "Oh good. I don't know if anything will ever really happen, but well, sometimes..."

Oh.

"If she needs to be taken care of, please take care of her. That's what packs are for," I assured.

"More like she had a nightmare and decided it was *my* cock she wanted a nap on last night. Then at some point she got up and crawled back in bed with you and Evan." He neatly folded the blankets that Wes had left strewn on the couch.

So that was why she smelled like them.

"Thank you for comforting her. I don't have any issues with it. Do you?" I knew that he'd really struggled with everything with his ex—and the feelings Grace's appearance had brought up. Personally, I hadn't liked Caroline much. I'd only tolerated her because she'd meant something to Brennan.

Brennan exhaled sharply as he pushed the bed back into a couch. "I don't know. She's so fragile, and I'm not sure I can meet her needs."

"I think really she just wants your acceptance and love. Maybe some ice cream after you play piano duets," I suggested.

"Maybe that's what I grapple with most. I'm used to people needing and wanting more from me. She is a good listener, though." Brennan rolled his eyes as he stacked the folded blankets on top of the pillows.

"She is. Maybe that's also what you need from her."

He turned and stared at me. "Must you be so profound right after surgery?"

"I'll try to be less insightful," I joked.

"We were worried. There was a lot of blood," he whispered.

"I'll have to go easy on the golf and tennis for a bit, but I'll be okay. Wes and I have a symposium soon, and I should still be able to make it." I'd forgotten about it. Mrs. K had asked if she needed to cancel everything.

Brennan sat down. "*Wes* is going to a conference?"

"There's a cybersecurity forum that he's quite excited about. He's less excited about the panel he's on. I'm on a couple of panels. I was considering bringing Grace, but you have on the calendar that you're taking her to a piano concert. If she wants to stay, will you, Jett, and Evan look after her? It's a short symposium, and it's not far, so we can come home quickly if she needs us. I'll also cancel if she wants us to." I hadn't expected to bond with her so soon.

"If she wants to stay, we'll watch over her. If she wants to go, I'll take someone else to the piano concert." His look went wistful.

"She's looking forward to it," I reassured him. "I'm so happy that you have a love of music to share with her."

"It makes things easier when you share an interest. I suppose I should order some sheet music for some Theodosia pieces considering that's her middle name." He got on his phone.

"*Danser Dans La Neige* is my favorite of Theodosia's works." I hummed it under my breath.

"Oh, that's a nice one. I was thinking of *Les Cloches de Mai* since it's a common competition piece in the upper levels." He looked up at me.

"Or both," I agreed. I didn't play the piano, but my mother did. I played the bouzouki a little, but it was back in Greece at my mother's. Perhaps I should ask her to send it to me.

He nodded. "Good idea."

"What's a good idea?" Wes came back in with Grace. Both carried coffee cups. Grace had a little sack.

"I got you coffee and a croissant. They only had plain, not chocolate." Pulling the bed table over, she set the coffee and bag next to me.

"Thank you, my good doctor." I gave her a fond smile.

"Hi, Bren. We didn't bring you anything. I'm sorry." Grace sat on the bed and leaned into me. I kissed her forehead.

"That's okay, Grace. Evan, Jett, and Riley are getting food for everyone," Brennan told us.

"Um. Hi. I... I wanted to make sure that everyone was okay." Nate Thorne stood awkwardly in the open doorway, holding something.

"Um, we're okay, Professor." Grace's scent went anxious.

"Fortunately, both of them will be fine. But they could have easily not have been," Wes snapped.

Nate bowed his head. "I'm sorry. We didn't expect Adriana to come after you. I'm so sorry for what she did."

"Thank you, Professor. Do you remember Spencer? Also, this is my mate Wes, and this is Brennan, he's head alpha. Everyone, this is Professor Nate Thorne," Grace introduced.

"Um, hi." Wes frowned and moved close to Grace.

"Hi. So, who called the police? They came after Adriana *quickly*, arresting her for baby trafficking." Bren looked pensive.

I had the same thought. Sure, I'd planned on turning everything over to the police, but I hadn't done so yet.

"I did." Nate's voice went quiet. "The others are angry with me for involving the law. They're worried about what it will do to the pack. But I... I... I can't believe that she just sat back and let me look for you all those years knowing that she sent you to live with someone else. She even came with me to meet some of the girls that I thought might be you." Nate sniffed.

Grace put a hand to her mouth. "I can't believe she did that."

How monstrous.

"How did you look for her?" Brennan asked.

"Mostly online. I'd reverse image search baby pictures of Creed, and my sister, hoping I'd get a hit. We got a few, but they were never you, though we found one of my brother Barrett's kids that way. At one point Barrett hired a PI for me. We traced Rosalind all the way to Europe, and then she just... disappeared." His look went wistful.

"Professor, you can sit down," Grace said softly.

Oh. Obviously, they would have had to come to Greece if my father and Dr. K helped them. Where was the equipment? I explored the university thoroughly and found nothing odd and didn't recall anything being off-limits. Maybe I should ask Mrs. K about it.

Nate sat down in a chair by the small table, moving the flowers and the omega lily so he could see it. "Did Verity visit? That looks like one of the flower pots she buys from her friend."

"Yes, she came by last night," Brennan said. "Rosalind got to Europe?"

"We're not sure how. By then she was wanted. Even if she had a fake record made, she'd probably want to minimize contact with authorities. She might have been smuggled by boat," he told us.

How did she know that they'd help her? Who got her there?

"You knew I was with her?" Grace asked.

He shook his head. "Not for certain. A woman fitting her description was seen with a baby at some points, though not at others. That's why I wondered if she trafficked you. She smuggled you to Europe, sold you, then took the money and disappeared.

But..." Nate frowned. "You weren't raised abroad. Somehow she came back here and raised you off the grid? Or maybe there she got really good fake records made? None of it makes sense."

No, not to him.

"We might never know what happened." I gave Grace a squeeze.

Yes, I needed to talk to Mrs. K.

Nate sighed. "I know. And I'm sorry Rosalind was the one who raised you and hurt you. I... I haven't told anyone other than the pack that I've found you. Is it okay if I tell my family?"

Grace thought for a moment. "I guess?"

"Thank you. They won't reach out, but if you'd like to meet them sometime, they'd love it, I'm sure. Also, I won't tell Thora's mother. I don't know if she's even still alive. But if at some point you ever want to talk to her, I'll help you make contact," Nate offered.

"Thank you." She leaned back into me. Wes squeezed her hand.

"Is Adriana still in jail? I worry that she'll come after Grace." Brennan asked.

"She's in jail waiting for the judge. I cooperated fully. Not taking you in was one thing. *Paying* Rosalind to whisk you away so that I'd never find you, then allowing me to look for you, is something else entirely. I... I've forgiven her for so much over the years. But I'm not sure I can forgive that." Nate sighed again.

I felt a little sorry for the children in the pack. If Adriana went to jail, it would massively affect their family. At the same time, what she did was terrible and wrong. How could she simply sit back and let her mate hurt like that?

Grace eyed the doorway. "I understand. It's a pretty horrible thing. Not to mention she *stabbed* my mate. Are you here alone?"

"Pip's here. But they wouldn't let her past the nurses' station. They let me in because I'm on your record as being your father. I hope it's not an overstep. I was worried when I heard what happened." He clutched something to him. "I'm sorry she stabbed you."

"It's okay," I assured. Okay, I'd be pressing charges, but it wasn't his fault.

"Are Tru, Hale, and Mercy all right?" Grace added.

"Tru was pretty scared. But she'll be okay. So will Hale and Mercy. Um, so, at one point, I thought I'd found you. I was so excited, and I got you this. Only it wasn't you. I kept it for when I found you. You don't have to take it, but I brought it in case you wanted it." He held it out, and I realized that it was a doll.

"Oh. Thank you, Professor." She got up from the bed. "Was the girl Barrett's? I remember you asking me if I was looking for him."

"Yes. Barrett has a few. Deep down I knew that she wasn't you. But one could always hope." The look on his face was mournful. "The others in the pack thought hiring a PI was a waste of money. Barrett hired the PI that traced Rosalind to Europe for me because he knew how disappointed I was that the girl I'd found was his, not you."

A waste of money? More like Adriana didn't want Grace found.

Grace sucked in a breath and took the doll. "Thank you. The doll is adorable."

She leaned in and gave him a little hug.

"I also brought you this." He handed her a card. "You don't have to open it, but I found a few pictures of Thora and printed them out so that you'd have them."

"Thank you." She returned to me, and I hugged her as so many conflicted emotions came through the bond.

Nate looked at me. "Hale and Mercy said that Adriana mentioned people murdering your other mate?"

I nodded. "While it was deemed a car accident, I always wondered if it was purposeful in retaliation for her beliefs. Adriana's statements about not knowing they were going to kill her, that she just thought they'd scare her, only cemented my suspicions. They being the organization she belongs to that's against the work my mate and previous company did."

Later, I'd have to see if my sources found any more information. Perhaps Jett would help.

Nate's look turned to one of horror. "Oh no. While I always found them to be a little... overzealous, I didn't think they'd go that far."

"They literally throw paint at people going into their workplaces." Brennan gave him a look.

"Adriana thought that I brought Grace into your life as revenge," I said softly. "It wasn't. It was all a coincidence that Grace met someone who knew Creed."

"I know Inara quite well and I can see the situation unfold in my head. Accident or not, I'm really glad that we finally found you." Nate looked a little anxious.

"Fuck of the morning, Bitches, we have brunch. Spence, you're awake, thank fuck." Riley burst in with brown handled bags, Jett and Evan following with another bag and drinks in a carrier.

Evan beamed. "Spence, it's so nice to see you awake."

Riley stopped short and stared at the professor. "Sweet baby cheeses."

"Um, hi. I'm Nate. Are you Riley? Mercy and Tru were telling me about you." Nate gave a little wave.

"Yeppers. Mercy and I want to go to skate smash camp together this summer." Riley put the bags on the couch next to Brennan.

Nate smiled and nodded. "That sounds fun."

"I'm Jett." Jett put the carrier of drinks on the table, then moved the flowers.

"And I'm Evan." Evan had a duffle bag.

"Well, I'll leave you to eat your meal. I just wanted to make sure that you were okay. Grace, Spencer, I wish you speedy recoveries.

Again, I'm so sorry." Nate gave us one last look and went toward the door.

"Professor?" Grace asked.

Nate turned, looking hopeful. "Yes?"

"We'll still have that lunch when you come to Rockland?" She sounded unsure and anxious.

He beamed. "I'd like that very much."

Nate left, and Riley handed out beverages.

"Are you okay?" I asked Grace, kissing her temple.

"Yeah."

Riley frowned as she handed something to Grace. "Who got Grace a fucking Everydoll?"

"The professor," I replied. They were a lot more expensive than the average doll but *very* popular. There was an entire store of them at one of the malls in Rockland.

"Oh. That's kinda weird?" Riley's head cocked.

"He got it when he thought he found me and saved it for when he actually did." Grace bit her lower lip. "I thought it was sweet."

"Oh, that is sweet. You have one of the older ones? Nice. I think her hair could use a trip to the doll salon," Riley replied as she gave Wes his drink.

"Would you like me to take the two of you to the Everydoll boutique like I did when you were younger? We could have tea, then you could have their hair done, and get new outfits for them? We haven't done that in a while." It was something Riley and I did every year for her birthday up until a couple of years ago.

Riley flinched. "I don't have one anymore."

"You don't?" Evan frowned as he put out the containers. "You loved them. They always had wild adventures. You used to send me videos."

Going to the Everydoll store was one of our first outings together and not long after her parents died. Her grandparents needed me to get her out of the house. She was very young. I didn't know what to do with her, so I'd brought her there and we'd had a lovely afternoon of tea and dolls followed by a movie and a trip to the pizza arcade.

"What happened to them? I won't be mad if you traded them for a dirt bike," I reassured her. From her look, I was pretty sure that wasn't the case.

Riley mumbled something as she set something for me on the tray.

"Um, Sasha did what to your dolls?" Evan turned and looked at her, stricken.

"She was mad at me, so she gave my dolls and all my doll things to the neighbor. Sasha said I was too old for them, anyway. Sonja and Grandma told her off but didn't make her get them back and wouldn't let me ask for them. They also told me not to tell either of you. Grandpa promised to get me a new one. And he did, but it wasn't an actual Everydoll, it was just from Swoop." Riley wrapped her arms around herself.

While it was nice of him, I could see a discount store doll not quite being the same. While she'd just had a couple of dolls, she had quite the collection of accessories and clothes.

"Shit, I'm sorry. Sasha can be mean sometimes." Evan wrapped his arms around her.

"I mean, I'm not a kid anymore. But that doesn't mean I didn't still like them. Lots of people collect them." She buried her face in her brother's shoulder.

"Ugh, it's not like she doesn't still have hers." Evan made a face. "I know because she left them at Grandma's when she moved."

Riley looked up. "You don't think I haven't thought of kidnapping them?"

"When was this?" I asked. My heart broke. Sasha was sometimes resentful of Riley, but that was pretty awful.

"The summer between seventh and eighth grade, around when you were talking about me moving to Rockland for high school," she mumbled. "It was one of the reasons I agreed. I knew you all wouldn't touch my shit."

That timing correlated with her saying that she wanted to do something else with me for her birthday.

"My mom did that, too–got rid of my toys and gave them to other kids," Grace whispered. "My dad saved one, but it still was awful."

"It won't replace what you lost, but you could choose a new one? Then we can have tea, and go to the doll spa, and you and Grace can select new outfits for them?" I offered.

"I suppose. But only because they just launched a line of official skate smash outfits for Everydolls, and I want a Rockland Raiders outfit for mine," she said.

Grace was on her phone. "Tiny skates and helmets? Count me in. Ooh, there are so many dolls to choose from."

"They're always putting out limited edition ones, too. Some of them are *really* fancy. I think it's fun to have one or two, but it's creepy when you have an army of them." Riley looked at Grace.

"We had something like this in my world. I always wanted one of those dolls, but I never got one," Grace said wistfully.

"Oh, they had a limited edition Theodosia one. You can still get her on some resale sites. She comes with a tiny working piano," Brennan said, looking at his phone.

Riley started laughing. "Fucking shit, Bren, really?"

He had it bad for her. Hmmm. That was going to be a courting gift, wasn't it?

"Fuck, Grace is going to amass a doll army, aren't you? We're going to have a creepy doll room." Riley rolled her eyes.

"I could buy lots of these, couldn't I? I want a room of dolls and stuffies and a permanent blanket fort." Grace's eyes went alight as she continued to scroll on her phone.

"I mean, there are worse hobbies. My sister had an army of them," Brennan said.

Wes shuddered. "I remember. My sister had *one*. It was always watching me."

"Watching, always watching." Grace laughed.

Riley let her brother go. "Thanks, Spence."

"Anytime, Riley," I told her. "Really. You can both amass creepy doll armies."

"Hard pass on the doll army. I will take a chicken army." Riley grabbed a container and plopped down.

"I'm not sure that's allowed in our neighborhood," Brennan said.

Grace snorted. "That's silly. I had a chicken army growing up. Maybe we'll get a duck, too. To the hardware store!"

"Right, because that's where your chickens come from." Brennan rolled his eyes.

Jett handed me a container. "Why don't we eat before it gets cold. Also, I vote for a bunny army."

"Hedgehogs. I had one when I was small." I nodded as I opened my container.

Evan handed one to Grace. "Oh, I remember Sir Pemberly."

"I want all the pets," Grace declared. "Let's get a kitten and a puppy, too."

"I like the way you think," Riley agreed. "Though I'd like a mini tiger."

"What?" Grace blinked.

"Oh, someone decided to genetically engineer a few animals to be tiny and sell them as pets, such as mini tigers," I explained, realizing she might not have them.

Jett shook his head. "Mini tigers don't actually make good pets. They might be the size of dogs, but they're still tigers. Also, they might eat the chickens and bunnies."

Riley rolled her eyes. "Fine."

I'm sure they'd find another pet for us. Yes, we were going to have an army of dolls, pets, and children, weren't we? I wouldn't want it any other way.

Chapter Six

Jett

"Jett, should we order lunch?" Brennan propped himself up on one elbow as we lay on the bed in the massive villa at the fancy beachside hotel.

"Yes, please. I need to look through some things as well. I'm going to be owing favors to Cam and Lexi forever. Not to mention all the time off I'm using. At least everyone at the station understands." My boss was pretty lenient with us needing off for pack emergencies as long as we could cover our shifts.

I reached over and smoothed Brennan's dark hair. With how much had been going on over the past couple of days, it was nice to have this time alone.

"Well, hopefully we can bring Spencer home to Rockland tomorrow. If not, I'll send you back along with Riley, and whoever else needs to go home," Brennan said.

"Sounds good. Though I'm enjoying this right now. What do you want to eat? We should order something for Grace, too."

I glanced at the clock. Everyone else was at the hospital with Spencer. Grace was asleep in one of the rooms downstairs.

"Yeah." His brow furrowed, and conflict flowed through the bond.

"Now what? Regretting how much you ended up paying for that Theodosia doll?" I teased, gazing up into his blue eyes. Never did I expect to see Brennan Morris get into an online bidding war for a doll.

He shook his head. "Her doll needs a working piano. Um…"

I propped myself up on my elbow, leaning in so we were nose to nose. "What?"

"When she took that nap on my cock she, um… she called me a *good boy,* and I liked it." Brennan frowned.

Oh? He hadn't mentioned that when he told me about it.

"You are a good boy." I leaned in and gave him a kiss.

"But *her* good boy?" His brows furrowed. More conflict poured through the bond.

Oh, Bren. It was quite amusing watching him fall for her.

I kissed his wrinkled brows. "Is it any different from her–or Evan–telling you that you're a good alpha? I'd love for her to call me a *good boy* as I fuck her against the wall with my hand around her throat like in one of her novels."

Grinning, I remembered having her on the chaise lounge in the cabana.

"I still don't know if she remembered doing it, or not. She never said anything. But, if you put it that way." He rolled over, taking me down to the bed with him, his nose touching mine, blue eyes alight with mischief and desire.

"Yeah?" I waggled my eyebrows, getting his need and want, both in his scent and through our bond.

"Always." Brennan's mouth crushed mine.

Brennan's phone rang. It was Terrance's ring.

"Leave it." My arms wrapped around him, pulling him closer as if I could unite our souls even more than they were already.

From the moment I pulled him out of the wrecked car, I knew that he was my alpha. Even when he annoyed or infuriated me, he was still my other half; what kept my heart beating. I put all that into my kiss.

"I'll call him later." Brennan straddled me, lips still locked.

Feeling playful, I rocked my body, flipping us over. "Pinned you."

"Oh, that's how it's going to be?" He laughed.

That's how it always was. I laughed as he flipped us over again, getting close to the edge of the comfortable, alpha-sized hotel bed.

The phone rang again.

"Ugh." Brennan shot it a look.

Using the distraction, I rolled us back to the center of the bed and pinned his arms over his head.

"You can call him later." I rested my forehead on his.

"I thought that we were going to order lunch?" He grinned boyishly, his desire filling the room.

I grinned back. "You started it."

Once again, his phone rang.

"I should get that." He groaned. "I'll make it up to you."

"You always do. Go." I unpinned him.

He rolled over and grabbed his phone. "Terrance, what's wrong?"

Pulling on some shorts, I grabbed my laptop and went downstairs. Using the console in the kitchen, I ordered lunch for me, him, and Grace. The door to the room she was in stayed closed.

She'd been through a lot. Not to mention, Evan and Wes had given her quite the workout earlier. Then again, I'm sure she needed it.

Actually, she probably needed Spencer, and I'm surprised she hadn't just helped herself to his cock. She'd be careful of his injuries.

Hmmm, maybe I could orchestrate some alone time for her later. Part of the issue could be that Wes was pretty much always with her. Sure, I understood that, but she probably wanted some privacy.

Grabbing a beer from the fridge, I opened my laptop and went back to analyzing everything that we'd found on Adriana and her science terrorists. While Adriana had admitted to knowing that the extremists were targeting Elaris at the conference where she'd died, she was adamant that she didn't know they'd kill her. She also wouldn't name names.

Spencer had amassed some information on them. I'd also gotten some of my own. We weren't sure if the police would pursue a closed case that had been ruled a vehicular accident. However, Spencer getting justice for Elaris was important, so maybe we'd find something that would get the case re-opened.

And this organization shut down. They were a menace and were probably impeding scientific progress with their protests and fear-mongering.

I continued working until the scent of annoyed pine permeated the kitchen. Brennan, in only some shorts, took the open bottle of bourbon, poured himself a glass and sat down with me.

"What happened? More issues with the estate? Did another team quit?" I closed my laptop so that I could give him my full attention.

"My mother has discovered that I now own the building she needs. I have her blocked, so when I wouldn't answer her, she stormed my offices and pitched a bitch fit, demanding that I give it to her." Brennan had a drink.

"Even I know it's not how business works. You're going to propose a trade, right?" I took a sip of my beer.

He nodded. "The papers are already drawn up. Our lawyer is sending it to her now. My father texted me saying that I should call and talk to her, but I'm just going to go through the lawyers."

"Good. Also, does she not know that Spencer's in the hospital?" I frowned. It had been international news.

"Oh, she does. She tried to get Ian Murphy's case for trying to keep my inheritance away from me dismissed, thinking that I'd be so preoccupied I'd miss her sneaky bullshit. She also tried to get my permits cancelled. Again. Thank fuck for Terrance. Oh, my brother has informed me that I'm officially off the Morris Family Foundation board." His scent went salty with sadness.

Reaching over, I squeezed his bare shoulder. "I know how much it meant to you. But we have our own foundation now. Since you no longer have to go to parties, you could use that time to do things for it."

"I was thinking that Evan and I would probably be the more involved members of the family. Grace and Spencer have a lot of ideas, and we're going to need more than an admin to take care of things. I didn't realize Spencer was already moving forward with the science scholarships. But that makes sense. Just like Grace wanting them to have allowances. The names she came up with for the scholarships are a little pretentious, but why not." Brennan swirled the amber liquid in the glass.

"I thought they were cute. Also, we're the Thanukos Family Foundation. We already sound pretentious." I took another sip of beer. I liked the names. "We're going through with our name changes, right? As much as I enjoy being Officer Morris, being Officer Thanukos is going to be fun."

"Yes. I'm looking forward to no longer being a Morris," Brennan agreed. "Did you order food?"

"I did. It should be here soon. Should we wake Grace?" I looked at the clock.

"I'm awake. Why did you let me sleep so long?" Grace stood there, in only one of Evan's shirts, pouting, arms crossed over her chest.

"You needed to sleep, Little Butterfly. You've barely left Spencer's side." Brennan opened his arms, and she crawled onto his lap. He started playing with the back of her neck the way she liked.

"That's what a good mate does." Her scent went salty.

"You're a wonderful mate, Peaches," I praised, scooting closer, so she was on both of our laps. "We ordered lunch, so we'll eat, shower, dress, and go back."

"Okay. Bren?" She hiccupped.

"Yes, Grace?"

"I'm sorry if I pushed your boundaries or took advantage of you. Evan told me what happened that first night. I'm so embarrassed that I don't remember." She kept her face buried, scent filled with regret.

"If I didn't want to comfort you, I would have said *no* and had Evan take over. I'm glad that you feel safe with me. It means everything. Also, you were probably high from whatever they gave you," he soothed.

High? Yeah, on hormones. They'd shot her up so good I was surprised she hadn't gone into heat.

They might call her a gamma, but there was something very omega-like in her. That part of her knew exactly what she was doing crawling on Brennan's cock and calling him a good boy. I liked that Peaches very much.

Also, I was happy that their relationship was growing. Between his trauma and their rocky start, I hadn't been sure.

"Okay." She sighed as he continued to stroke the back of her neck.

There was a knock on the door. I stood. "There's lunch."

I went over to the front door. Signing for our food, I pushed the cart into the kitchen and put out the food as Brennan just sat there, holding her.

That was too fucking cute.

While some of our fantasies would probably always remain just that, I think we both needed Grace in our lives. Her gentleness evened us out a little. Also, now I really wanted to hear her call Brennan a good boy–he needed reminding of that now and then.

"I just got us all burgers, since sadly the hotel's spicy noodles are not up to expectations." I uncovered the plates. Burger with fries for me–onion rings for those two.

"Thank you." Grace didn't move from Brennan's lap.

Like most alphas, he seemed to have the ability to fully function with someone on his lap–even someone the size of Evan.

"If you have work to do, I can wait a little bit before we go back. I have a bunch of things to synthesize from the conference and send to my co-worker." Grace shoved an onion ring in her mouth.

"I just need a little bit of time to deal with some things with the lawyers. It won't take too long," Brennan assured her.

"Okay."

I wasn't sure if they were Queen Mum things, work things, estate things, or Grace things. The nurse that locked her in the room had been fired and was going to the Nursing Review Board. Katie was having a great time going after the hospital.

"Peaches, later, if you'd like, I'll get everyone out of the hospital–even Wes–so that you can spend some time with Spencer." I bit into my burger.

"Really?" Her eyes lit up.

Yep. I knew it.

"Really," I assured. "Bren, should we take everyone out for a nice dinner or something?"

"Spencer took me on a sunset dinner cruise. What about that–or maybe sunset whale watching? Are there whales here?" Grace took a drink of beer.

"Sunset whale watching followed by dinner sounds like an excellent idea. There are humpbacks here," Brennan said. "We'll bring food back for you."

"That sounds good. I'll book something after we finish eating," I told them.

Yeah, I'd absolutely go whale watching so that Grace could have some hospital sex with Spencer. After all, that's what packs were for.

And I was glad that she was part of this one.

Chapter Seven

Grace

"Have fun." I waved at everyone as they left the hospital room, as I lay on Spencer.

"Are you sure you don't want to come with us?" Wes frowned at me.

I shook my head. "I'm exhausted. Bring me dinner?"

"Of course. Spence, we'll bring you food, too." Wes kissed me. "If you need me, call me."

"I'll be okay," I reassured him. They were going on a sunset whale watching tour, followed by dinner at a waterfront restaurant that Brennan wanted to try.

"We'll be fine." Spencer wrapped an arm around me.

He looked so much better now and had even asked me to bring his laptop so that he could get caught up on a few things. I knew he'd been answering emails on his phone and making phone calls...

...and that Mrs. K had been scolding him for it.

Supposedly, he'd be discharged from the hospital tomorrow, but we wouldn't know for sure until morning. If he was, we'd probably fly back to Rockland. Everyone needed to get back to school and work–including me. Though Deb, my supervisor, had been very understanding. Which was nice. My old bosses wouldn't have been.

I'd already been discharged, but the doctors were making me wear the small monitor again.

"Be good." Evan kissed me and winked, making me wonder if Jett had told him the real reason he and Brennan had a sudden urge to take everyone whale watching.

Brennan had closed the blinds on the windows looking out into the hall. Jett smirked as he took something off the back of the doorknob and closed the door.

It turned out that hospitals in this world were so used to packs getting busy that they had little door hangers to alert the staff. However, Jett warned me that they *would* just walk in if they had any reason–like loud noises, monitors going off, or simply taking too long.

"You're not feeling well, or did you just not want to go, Darling?" Spencer gave me a concerned look as he toyed with my hair.

"This was a ruse so that we could have some time together," I admitted. "Everyone is always around."

"Oh, that was sweet." Spencer kissed me. "Since it's just the two of us, is there anything we need to talk about? You know that I don't blame you in the slightest, don't you?"

"I know. Thank you for taking a knife for me. You literally put yourself in harm's way for me." I sniffed a little because it could have gone so wrong.

He stroked my face. "That's what mates do for each other."

"All of this is just so surreal. Um, is it weird to keep the doll?" I'd been wondering about that. Though I'd finally opened the card.

It was just a sweet little belated birthday card. But inside were a couple of letters that he'd written to me over the years, which made me cry, some pictures of my birth mother, and a couple of them together.

Growing up, no one had ever done anything like that for me. Even if I just left the doll on a shelf somewhere, I wanted to keep her.

"No. If anything, it shows that he was sincere about looking for you," he replied.

"From the moment that I saw the look on his face when he noticed me in the coffee shop at Briar University, I knew he had been." There'd never been any doubt of that.

The professor had been back to visit us and had brought Tru and Mercy. Verity had been by as well. Creed was busy with finals and graduation but had been texting me.

Tru kept taking Verity's phone and sending me messages, which was *adorable.*

"Hopefully, they'll discharge me tomorrow. I'm ready to get out of here. I have so much to do," he told me.

"Me, too. Though, they'll want you to go easy for a bit," I replied, gazing up at him.

He smiled. "I'll go easy on the golf and tennis until I'm healed."

"Good. What about... other things..." My hand slid under the blankets. He was only wearing a shirt because of the incision.

Sure, Spencer had tended to the mark he'd left on me–and I'd done the same–and we'd cuddled, but it wasn't the same.

Wes and Evan had made sure I was well cared for, but I wanted Spencer.

Now.

His cock went hard the moment my fingers brushed it as I let all my lust tumble through the bond.

"Mmmm, that sounds delightful," he murmured, lust, love, and devotion shooting through the bond as his oiled leather scent went sweet with desire.

I wrapped my hand around his cock and squeezed it. "Can you? Or do we need to wait a month or two? I mean, you did just have surgery."

"I'm an alpha. And yes, I should wait a couple of weeks. But the doctor also knows we're recently bonded. If you're willing to be gentle with me, mindful of the incision, and do most of the work, I believe we can do it?" Spencer leaned in and kissed me, long and deep.

"I could do that." I stripped off my shorts and panties but left my shirt on–just in case someone came in to check on us.

Straddling his hips, but not putting any weight on his upper body, I leaned in and kissed him. "I love you, Spencer Thanukos. Wait, do you have a middle name?"

"Sofoklis. My mother, who is Greek by heritage, but grew up in New York, picked my first name. My father chose my middle name." He pulled me down and kissed me again.

I tried to carefully balance myself so I wasn't putting weight on any place that would hurt him. I peppered his stubbly jaw with kisses.

Hmmm, Spencer with a beard? That could be so sexy.

"Does it hurt when I do this?" Once again, my hand wrapped around his cock. His knot was inflating.

"No, that feels nice. You could try to ride me, though we might end up on our sides." Spencer's hand tangled in my hair, desire from the bond and his scent making me wet and needy.

"I don't care, I just need you inside me. I don't even need your knot if it'll hurt you, I just need *you.*" It came out in breathy pants.

The incision was closer to his ribs than his hips, so if I was very careful...

"If it hurts, tell me to stop." My eyes met his as I lowered myself slowly down his cock. I leaned forward, hands on the pillows so I'd be less likely to put too much weight near his injuries.

"Grace," he gasped, eyes closing. "Yes. Take me, Darling. I'll let you know if it hurts. I promise that I'm feeling *very* good right now."

Feeling his pleasure, not pain, through the bond, I gently rode him, moving up and down. One of his hands tangled in my hair, the other moved under my shirt, caressing my back.

"Yes, yes, this is exactly what I need," he breathed.

"Me, too, Dearest," I told him. "Can I call you that, since you've stopped using that for me and mostly call me *Darling*?" I continued moving my hips, relishing in the sensation of us being united like this once again.

"You can call me anything you like, Baby Girl." His forehead touched mine. "This feels so good; you feel so good." The hand caressing my back moved to my clit. "Come for me. I think you can take my knot, but we'll have to roll to our sides."

"I'm just fine with that." Kissing him, pleasure grew inside me. I gasped as an orgasm took me. Sitting down fully on him, my greedy pussy enveloped his swollen knot.

"Oh, yes." Spencer moved us to our sides–his good side, arms wrapping around us as his hot cum shot inside me.

"Mmmm, so good." I sent him all my love, love from him coming back.

Content, I made sure we were covered by the blanket, and snuggled into him, us still joined.

"Do you feel better? I know I do." Spencer kissed my temple.

"That wasn't selfish, was it?" Biting my lower lip, I looked into his eyes.

"No. You were very gentle. It was perfect and exactly what I needed." He kissed me again.

"How did your parents meet? Your mom went to college with Evan's mom, right?" I asked.

"She and Evan's mom met at university in Rockland, Rock State, where Brennan went. She went to Rock Springs with Evan's mom a lot. Auntie Kim, Evan's mom, moved back to Rock Springs after graduation. That's part of why my mom and I moved to Rock Springs, and not back to New York, after my father passed. They both studied art. Evan's mother majored in art history, my mother majored in ceramics. The two of them went on a study abroad trip to the university in Greece that my father was getting his PhD at," he said.

"Awww, I love it. Love at first sight?" I asked.

He chuckled. "For him. She made him work for it. My mother was afraid that he was just on the hunt, thinking she would be an easy conquer because she was a beta studying abroad. But his intentions were genuine. They were long distance for a while, then after she graduated she moved to Greece. He researched and taught, eventually teaming up with Dr. Katsopolis, while my mother created pottery. My father made her a studio in our back yard. Eventually, they had me."

"I wish I had gotten to meet him. He sounds brilliant." My eyes closed.

"He is. I'm looking forward to you meeting my mother."

"Yes, we'll invite her to our party, and anyone else you want. If you wish for an extravagant party in a far off locale, we can have one, but given everything that's happened, I'd be just as happy renting out a nice restaurant in Rockland and having a meal with a little dancing and music. My mother, at least, will make the trip." He continued playing with my hair.

"I think your idea of having a party in Rockland is perfect. We can always have another when we see your family on our vacation."

"That's an excellent idea. Perhaps we can look and see if we can find any more of my father's research when we visit my mother," he added.

I nodded. "Yes, I'm so curious now about how Rosalind and I got to the world I grew up in. It's all so wild—and coincidental."

"The universe is like that sometimes. I'll talk to Mrs. K and see what else she knows."

"That sounds good. You... you can tell her about me, if you need to. She's trustworthy, right?" I liked Mrs. K.

"I'd trust her with my life."

There was a knock on the door. "I'm going to need to check on you in about five minutes," someone called.

"Shit." Spencer laughed. "I'm knotted inside you pretty good."

"You're just going to need to think unsexy thoughts," I chuckled, not wanting them to come in while we were still knotted together.

He kissed me again. "That is a very difficult prospect when I'm inside you."

Spencer and I snuggled together in the bed, fully dressed, watching a documentary. The nurse checked him over and brought some food.

Riley sent me tons of pictures. Whale watching looked fun, but I was glad to spend time with him.

The door stood open, and the nice nurse, whose mate worked for the Center, appeared.

"Hi, Grace. She says she belongs to you?" The nurse pointed to the small child next to her.

"Yes, that's my little sister. Um, hi Tru. I didn't know that you were coming. Who brought you, Verity or your dad?" I sat up, glad we were fully dressed.

Tru bounded in and sat on the couch. "Oh, I came by myself. Verity's phone has an app that brings me places."

"Oh, like a children's ride service?" I frowned, a little worried that they'd just drop her off at the hospital. Also, the idea that there was one for children so young made me a little nervous, even though it seemed useful for working families.

Certainly, Tru got points for ingenuity. Grabbing my phone, I texted Verity.

Me

> Tru just showed up at the hospital. She used your phone to order herself a ride. I don't want you to worry.

"Sometimes Verity uses it to pick us up when she's stuck at the lab. Mumsy and Mom don't like it, but sometimes they want her to miss class to get us. Can you believe it?" Her look went aghast. Today her curly, light brown hair was in cute little ponytails.

"That is scandalous," Spencer agreed, turning off the TV.

Verity

> I'm actually at the lab, so how... shit. I gave them my old phone to play games on. I must not have taken everything off. Thank you. I'm done anyway, so I'll finish cleaning up and come get her. I made you something and was going to drop by, anyway. Thanks for keeping an eye on her.

Me

> No problem. I didn't want anyone to worry.

I wasn't sure whose watch she'd slipped from. From the little I'd learned about the Thornes, Verity did a lot of the raising of the young ones. How she did that while getting a PhD, I wasn't sure.

I got up off the bed and sat down on the couch with her. "I let Verity know that you're here, so you have a ride home."

"Oh, okay, thanks." She grinned, kicking her feet happily against the couch.

"While you are always welcome, Tru, is there a reason for your visit today?" Spencer asked.

"You're leaving tomorrow. You haven't even come over and seen my room and met everyone yet." Tru sniffed.

"I know. I'm sorry. But we have to get back to Rockland. Everyone has work and school. But hopefully I will at some point." After all, I had two brothers that I hadn't met yet.

"Oh. Before I forget." She opened her hot pink plastic purse and got out a crumpled sheet of paper. "This is my application for the summer 'ship. Chance printed it out for me and helped me with some words, but we couldn't figure out how to send it to you because we don't have emails."

Tru handed it to me. I was pretty sure Chance wasn't even in middle school yet.

It was the Compass BioTek high school internship application and had been filled out in colorful felt-tip pens in mostly legible, but not always spelled right, baby scrawl.

"Don't tell Mercy I used her good markers." Tru grinned and ducked her head.

"Oh, thank you. I'll give this to the internship coordinator. But please don't be sad if you don't get accepted. I think you have to be going into your second year of high school." I looked over her application.

Why should you be chosen for this internship? *Because I'm going to be the second-best math scientist in the world when I grow up. My sister will be the best.*

My heart.

"I can handle it. They want me to be in a different grade, you know. But Mom says it's not fair to Pax for me to be ahead of him in school because we're twins." Her eyes rolled. "Pax doesn't care. His favorite subject is recess. Which is fine. But unsolvable equations aren't going to solve themselves."

"Very true. But perhaps he'll get inspiration at recess for something else?" Spencer told her.

"Maybe? Dare plays music and it makes my toes happy." She closed up her purse and set it next to her, giving it a little pat.

"I play the piano," I replied. "Music and math go together."

"I think the drums are pretty. If I get the 'ship, can I stay with you? I don't think Dad will let me stay in the dorms." Her head cocked.

"Of course. Just to let you know, Grace and I don't get to pick. Even Riley has to go through the same application process," Spencer remarked.

She thought for a moment. "Well, that sucks hairy balls. But Hale always mumbles that favoritism is shitty. I guess it is when you're not the favorite."

I put my hand over my mouth. Hale must do his share of babysitting. But I suppose they all did. After all, Dare, who was still in high school, had taken his two brothers to the park the day Hale, Mercy, and Tru came to the beach.

"But yes, if you get the internship, you can stay with us, as long as your parents are fine with it," Spencer assured.

"Thank you. It will be so much fun." Tru bounced on the couch.

"It would." I texted Wes.

I don't know if you've left the restaurant yet, but if you haven't, can you bring something for Tru? She called herself a ride so she could give me her application for the internship program.

We're getting ready to leave, so I'll see what I can do. She's the one who's five, right? Wow. But it makes sense your siblings would be geniuses like you.

Awww.

"What do you want to do eventually, after you solve Garamoci's Theory of Everything, of course?" Spencer asked her.

She thought for a moment. "I want to build spaceships."

Sure enough, there it was on her application, complete with a little drawing of a spaceship.

"I like that idea. Riley likes the idea of space travel, too." I loved how Spencer took her completely seriously and didn't wave it off as her being a silly little child.

"You'll hire me when I solve it, right?" Tru asked.

"Absolutely," Spencer agreed.

Yes, I was paying for her college so she could go wherever was best for someone like her. I might need to send her to the high school for geniuses that Evan's sister worked at.

"Do you want to color?" I asked her. Liz, the crisis counselor from the Omega Center, kept bringing Riley snack packs with coloring books in them, so we had a couple of them. She'd stopped by a bunch so that she and Evan could have long conversations about Blanket Brigade training.

Tru nodded. "That sounds fun."

I put away the application and got out the coloring book.

Tru and I colored while Spencer was on his laptop, wearing his slutty little glasses, occasionally adding things to our conversation.

Sweet baby Jesus, that man was going to make a great dad. Yeah, maybe I'd have three babies. Evan would get his first, because of what the doctor said about male omegas being good at making babies and getting my hormones going. Then Wes, and then Spencer.

While I'd take twins, I wasn't sure if I wanted to carry Spencer's enormous identical triplets.

"Hey, Babycakes. Heard you want to work with me this summer?" Riley came in.

"Riley! We'll have the funnest project!" Tru bounced as she carefully colored in a picture of fish.

"Oh, absolutely. Maybe my friend Hiro can be on the project with us? You'll like him. He enjoys using math to make models to predict things," Riley replied, grabbing a coloring sheet and joining us.

"That sounds good." Tru reached for the green. "But can Creed please be on another project? He's really bossy. Verity is bossy, but it's mom-bossy. Creed's just brother-bossy."

"We'll see," I chuckled, coloring in a hedgehog. "I don't know if Creed got in either."

Did I want him to get the job? Maybe? It might be nice to get to know him away from everyone else. Same with Verity and Mercy. Maybe I could plan a little girls' trip with Verity.

"How was whale watching?" I asked.

"A lot of fun." Riley started coloring a sheet with flowers on it.

"I brought food." Wes came in and gave me a kiss. "Tru, how would you like a brownie sundae? It's only a little melted."

Brownie sundaes for dinner? But I didn't tell him what to get her.

"Ooh, thank you." Tru's eyes lit up.

"Did you get some... rest?" Evan came in and kissed me.

"We did." I grinned.

"Jett and Bren went back to the hotel," Wes added. "Bren is having more work drama."

We cleared off the table so that Spencer and I could eat. Spencer even climbed out of bed and sat with us.

Tru dug into her sundae, which looked delicious. Not that my salmon with mashed potatoes and mushroom gravy wasn't tasty.

She and Riley started talking about skate smash. Apparently, Tru played in the little kid league, which had very different rules to make it safer.

"Hi, everyone." Verity entered, carrying a paper gift bag.

"Verity, this is so good." Tru, who had chocolate on her face, pointed to her almost-finished ice cream with her plastic spoon.

"It looks really tasty. Everyone was worried about you." Like what seemed usual for Verity, she was dressed in crisp pastels, with her accessories and makeup perfect.

Tru shrugged. "Chance knew I went to turn in my application."

"She's applying for the summer internship program at Compass BioTek," I explained to Verity.

"That makes sense. I could have helped you." Verity frowned.

"I wanted to be a big girl and do it myself. Bite?" Tru offered Verity a spoonful.

"Oh, that is delicious. Grace, I made you cake pops." She handed me the bag, which had ribbons on the handles.

"Verity." I pulled out an individually wrapped cake pop that had an equation carefully piped on it. "These are beautiful."

Tru nodded as she finished her ice cream. "Verity makes the best snacks. When we have parties at school, my treats are always the prettiest."

"Thanks again," Verity told us. "Tru, now that you're done, we should get home. It's a school night."

"Okay." She sighed. "Can I take my coloring page home?"

"Absolutely," I replied.

"Thank you for my dinner." Tru gave us all hugs. "Riley, I can't wait to work with you. Let's build a spaceship."

"That sounds great." Riley hugged her back.

Verity gave me a hug. "I started the book that you suggested. It's great. I think Dad gave up after chapter seven. It was a little much for him."

"I understand. The fact that he tried means a lot. Some of the titles you texted me sound like they'd be perfect for book club." The idea of him reading that book, the one Jett had made me read out loud to him back in the cabana, made me laugh.

"Have a safe trip back to Rockland." Verity took Tru's hand, and they left.

Riley held out her hand. "I want a cake pop. Mercy was telling me that Verity is one of those alphas that shows her love by baking."

I passed out cake pops.

"Spencer, we probably can't hire a five-year-old as an intern, right?" I asked as I cleaned everything up.

"I checked with legal, and we absolutely cannot. But..." Spencer got out his phone. "Rock Tech has a math day camp for kids her age. Maybe we could award her a special internship and bring her here for camp. I think I can get our education team to partner with the camp for that session and give them a special little project to work on. Like a *Future Intern* program."

"That would get a fuck-ton of good press from the sheer cuteness of it," Riley agreed. "They can have little shirts and badges and come for a tour and eat ice cream in the cafeteria."

"That sounds like a great idea, if we can get her parents to agree to letting her stay with us—and if the pack is up for a five-year-old."

Evan laughed. "Yes, have her stay with us. After all, we have to get the pack ready for when you have Spencer's identical triplets."

"Wait, are you pregnant?" Riley helped herself to another cake pop.

"No." I shoved Evan. "No identical triplets."

"One day we might have some kids, though," Wes added.

"Yeah, I kinda figured. Please wait until I can legally live in the guest house or let me move into the basement?" Riley asked, taking a picture of the cake pop.

I nodded. "That sounds like an excellent plan."

A nurse knocked on the open door. "Hi Spencer, we need to get some scans so we can see if you can be released tomorrow."

"Thank you, I'd like that very much." He stood, dragging the monitor with him.

I'd like that too. Because as nice as it had been to meet some of my siblings, I was ready to return to Rockland.

Chapter Eight

Brennan

Thank goodness we were back home. I enjoyed being here the best. Also, there was something to be said for a private jet. At the very least, we could bring Spencer home in a more comfortable manner than flying commercial.

The house was quiet as I went down to the kitchen. Spencer had been tucked in by Grace. Wes hauled Evan off to bed. Jett fell asleep watching a movie. Riley was playing video games.

I'd been catching up on work, mostly because I couldn't sleep.

Now I was in the kitchen. Should I have a snack? Maybe? Oh. My eyes fell on all the mail on the table. In the pile was the sheet music I'd ordered for Grace.

I took the music upstairs. Putting on my headphones and setting the piano to soundless, I got out the music for *Les Cloches de Mai* and started to play.

Theodosia's works weren't my favorite, mostly because they required a lot of subtlety and maturity. You didn't just play it with your fingers; you played it with your soul.

I didn't enjoy baring my soul to anyone, let alone a concert hall full of people that I didn't know.

At some point, I grew aware that I was being watched. I stopped playing and saw Grace standing there in some pajamas.

"Can't sleep?" I asked.

"I'm afraid that if I have a nightmare, I'll hurt Spence." She rocked on the balls of her feet.

"I don't think that you will. I'm also pretty sure that Wes and Evan won't mind if you crawl in with them." It felt like they were sleeping. Really, she should be with Spencer, but I understood; nightmares were no fun.

"What are you playing?" Grace eyed the music curiously.

"I ordered a couple of Theodosia's pieces for you. Would you like to try one?" I stood and got her headphones out of the piano bench. Handing them to her, I sat back down.

Putting them on, she sat next to me.

"Which one do you want to try?" I set them out. Besides the one Spencer had suggested and *Les Cloches de Mai*, I'd also looked up her mother and found the one she often played in competitions.

Grace studied them for a moment. "This one."

She'd chosen *Danser Dans La Neige*, Spencer's favorite. I played it for her, trying to focus on the notes on the paper and not her face. This wasn't a piece that I had memorized.

"It's haunting," she finally said as I finished.

"It is. Her pieces are complex in a very different way than Volkov or Kirkokov. Want to try?"

Grace studied the music for a moment, then started to play.

She was a good sight-reader, but a piece like this was difficult. Grace tried a few times. "Huh, maybe one of the other pieces?"

"Sure. It's okay if you don't like them. Really, they're not my favorite," I told her.

We tried the other two, then just ended up playing some duets.

"Thank you for getting me the music. I really like playing with you." Grace looked up at me with those big, blue-grey eyes.

I wanted to fall into them.

Her pink lips were right there. It would be so easy to lean in and kiss her...

"There you are. It's late. We all have work tomorrow." Jett stood there, shirtless.

Annoyance shot through me. Jett gave me an amused look.

"You're right. Back to work tomorrow." Grace stood.

"I got you some tea at the market. You might like it better than what Evan gets. It's in the cupboard," Jett added.

"Thank you, Jett." She smiled at him.

"I suppose we should go to sleep." I gave Jett a look.

She kissed me on the cheek. "Good night, Bren."

Taking off her headphones, she held them awkwardly. Getting up, I put mine and hers inside of the bench.

"Good night, Grace." I hugged her.

"Good night, Jett." She gave him a little kiss on the cheek, too, and went up the stairs.

"I wasn't trying to cockblock you, Honey. It's late, and I set off to find you." He put an arm around me.

I sighed as we went into our bedroom. "What am I doing?"

"Not her, apparently." Jett laughed as we went into our bedroom.

"Jett." I playfully shoved him onto the bed. "We're not like that. I just gave her the sheet music and was teaching her to play it."

"Sure." He gazed up at me, his long, dark hair loose.

I pinned him to the bed. "I'm sure."

Well, for now.

Leaning in, I kissed Jett.

No. I wasn't sure at all.

But that was a problem for another day.

Chapter Nine

Spencer

I stretched in my chair in my home office, careful of my injuries. It was nice to have all the comforts of home. While I was taking the rest of the week and working from home, on Monday I was going back into the office, more for my own mental health than anything else.

Really, I liked to leave work at work. When I was working in my home office, I was usually reading journal articles, watching documentaries, or researching new innovations in my industries, unless I was holding a meeting in other time zones.

Still, there was work to be done. Yes, I had good people helping me to run my company, and it would be fine without me, but I *liked* my work. Also, I didn't enjoy being behind on things–or letting people down.

But I was done for the night. Fatigue pressed down on me even though a glance at the clock told me it wasn't that late. Should I go see what everyone else was doing?

No, I think I'd take a shower. Yes, that sounded good. Perhaps Grace would come to snuggle with me later? She'd been tucking me in at night, which I adored, even if she usually slipped out at some point.

But, I couldn't keep her all to myself. Much or often. Taking off my glasses, I closed my laptop and left my office.

Going into my bathroom, I turned on the water in my shower, stripped, and climbed under the warm spray. Should I wash my-self? Yes. But I was more tired than I'd like to admit.

The door opened, and a naked little blonde slipped inside. "Hi. Can I wash you?"

"I'd like that more than anything, Darling." *Yes, please put your hands all over me.*

She frowned at my incision. "Can you get that wet?"

"Yes."

Her eyebrows rose. "Are you sure? Never mind, your company probably made the stitches."

"They did. You can wash it too. But you have to use the green soap." I nodded to the bottle of green soap next to my usual body wash.

Almost too gently, Grace washed my body. Bending down so that she could wash my hair was difficult, but the simple actions of her caring for me felt good. It made her feel good, too.

She got out and put on the robe I had for her, then got mine. "Come here."

"Thank you." I got out and let her put the robe on me.

Grace led me to the bed, sat me down, and got the hair brush I usually used on her. Climbing behind me, she began brushing my hair, just like I did for her.

Sometimes taking care of someone was more than the actual actions, it was giving them purpose and confidence.

Right now, I could feel that she needed to take care of me–and I was going to let her.

"That feels really nice," I told her, the motions almost hypnotic.

"I'd rub your back next, but I'm not sure if you should lie on your stomach," she said.

"You could just rub my shoulders while I sit here. That would feel nice." I pulled her in for a kiss.

Grace plugged in the oil warmer, peeled off my robe, and hung it up. Taking the warm, lavender-scented oil, she rubbed my shoulders.

"Oh, right there," I gasped.

Her strong little hands continued digging into the muscles, trying to soothe out the knots and stress.

Grace took off her robe and hung it up next to mine. Naked, she climbed onto my lap and kissed me.

"Would you like a happy ending now?" Her eyes gleamed.

"I would." I kissed her. Yes, I was feeling like much more than snuggles.

"On the bed. Get on your knees, Darling." I patted her ass.

Grace got on her knees, presenting for me beautifully.

I stroked her back. "You're always such a good girl for me."

"I like being good for you," she breathed, her scent flaring with desire.

That she was. I helped myself to her sweetness, making her nice and ready for me.

"Please, I need your cock," she begged as she orgasmed. "Please, Daddy."

How could I deny that?

"I'm all yours." Bracing my hands on her hips, I plunged inside her, delight shuddering through me as the room filled with desire and our scents.

That. That was what I needed to get better. I needed to be inside my baby girl.

Shifting my weight a little, I continued to plunge into her over and over, until I couldn't hold myself off any longer.

"Do you want my knot, Baby Girl?" I growled, knowing very well that she did.

"Please."

I thrust deep inside her, knotting her as I filled her up. My hand brushed over her stomach as I recalled our conversation about children. *Perhaps one day.*

Our bodies shuddered, and I carefully rolled us onto our sides so that I could hold my darling close.

"You take such good care of me." I peppered her face with kisses, then tracing them down to get to her bond mark, which was healing all nice and silvery.

"Same." Sleepy contentment flowed through our bond.

I was a lucky man in so many ways. Throwing the blanket over us, I closed my eyes, grateful that I was alive to hold her in my arms.

Chapter Ten

Spencer

"Don't overtax yourself, okay, Dearest?" Grace gave me a kiss as we went up the elevator at Compass BioTek.

"I'll take it easy, my good doctor." I squeezed her. Today I came into work with her and Wes.

It was Monday. Time to return to business as usual.

"Maybe your boss will let you leave early," Wes teased.

The doors opened on Grace's floor, and she glanced at me. "Join us for lunch?"

"I'd love that." I gave her another kiss, and she got off, the doors closing behind her as the elevator continued going up.

Usually, she and Wes ate lunch together, often with their work friends. I only joined them occasionally.

"Seriously, if you need to leave early, let me know," Wes told me.

"I'll be okay, thank you," I replied as he got off on his floor. Well, hopefully. I was feeling better, stronger. If I needed to, I could always shut my door, pretend I had a meeting, and take a nap on the couch in my office.

I really needed to talk to Mrs. K about so many things. I'd cracked the code on the documents I'd found in Dr. K's research, and while they were fascinating, and Grace loved reading them, they hadn't helped me with what I wanted to know.

Mrs. Katsopolis wasn't at her desk, so I made myself a cup of coffee on the fancy machine we had in the executive area and got my day started. While I had several meetings, there should be nothing too strenuous today.

"Spencer, really? Shouldn't you take another week off? You had *abdominal surgery.*" Mrs. K came in, frowning.

"I'm fine. I'll leave early if I need to. Perhaps I'll work from home tomorrow morning before coming in for my afternoon meetings," I responded.

"That sounds like a good plan. Are you sure that you don't want me to cancel the symposium?"

"No. Wes and I are excited about it." An email popped up with the subject *I love you.* I clicked on it, and Grace had sent me animated hearts.

"Okay. Are you bringing Grace?"

I shook my head as I emailed Grace back. "She wants to stay here."

Grace was also anxious that her co-workers would think that she wasn't doing her job. They wouldn't think that, but there was no need for her to come with us if she didn't want to.

"Also, can you try to get me on something at the Bay Area Genetics Symposium, the one that's usually in the fall?" I asked her.

"Of course." She made a note of it.

It would be an excellent place to look for people for some of the secret projects I had in mind. Ones that hopefully would eventually finish what Elaris had started.

No family should have to go through what Grace's biological mother did. It turned out that while most of the family were sigmas, none of them knew. Thora's father thought he was just an alpha that never fully awakened and never bothered going to the doctors about it because he didn't like doctors and was generally healthy.

Something that was pretty common.

"Spencer, what are you up to?" Mrs. K frowned at me.

"Close the door?" I said softly. I got the bug scanner out of my bag and waved it around. Nothing. Though the entire building was checked regularly.

She shut the door and sat down, concern in her beta scent.

"After our misadventures with the Office of Designation Management, I would like to resurrect Elaris' research. Though I understand the need for the utmost discretion." I laid out my ideas and cursory plans.

There were two parts to Elaris' idea. One was a pharmaceutical that would suppress 'dangerous' genetics to allow those with illegal genetics to function in society. The concept was not unlike alpha blockers. The other was to actually change the genetics of those who were illegal, making them alphas, like the pharmaceutical which pushed betas over to omega designations.

Of course, this was easier said than done. Breaking the push wasn't easy, which was why we weren't up to our ears in alphas—and why Mega-Push didn't work on all betas. The military had some projects, but they were more along the lines of making more deltas and alphas to be soldiers, not saving the lives of illegal designations.

"I'm happy to help. Perhaps we can reach out to Dr. Stonefeld again?" Mrs. K suggested, making more notes.

"Yes. Let's set up casual meetings, ones that look like they could easily be for less controversial topics. Also, we'll need cover projects," I commented.

We went over a few more things.

She smoothed the skirt of her outfit. "I'm so glad that you're doing this. I think it's time, and I'm so sorry Grace had to go through that. You know, for a moment, I thought that you were going to tell me you were, in fact, going to pursue your father's research and had found something helpful in what I'd given you."

"Actually..." I took a sip of my now cold coffee.

"Spencer."

"I'm not taking their research on. However, between the coded papers of Dr. K's, and my father's notebooks, Grace could probably do so if she wanted. But she's not. What I need is specific information that you might not have. Also, I'm about to tell you some very confidential things," I warned.

"You're scaring me, Spencer." Her brows furrowed.

"You told me that while my father and Dr. K wanted to send some of our illegal designations to other worlds for safety, it didn't go as planned. But some were sent, weren't they? If records exist, I need them. And if you know anything anecdotally, I'd like that information as well." I played with my coffee mug.

She frowned. "I need to know why. I'll keep your secrets, I always have."

Getting on my phone, I pulled up the dates that I'd gotten from Nate Thorne regarding Rosalind's appearance in Europe. "Sometime along these dates, did my father and your wife send a young sigma woman and an infant to another world? I actually have the world number if that helps."

Grace had written it down on her phone.

"I don't know about those specific dates, but to my knowledge, the few people that they helped were families." Her expression grew guarded.

"One of those children was returned to this world. That child is not a sigma, but their re-appearance is causing issues," I said carefully. The Office of Designation Management was continuing to push Grace for information on Rosalind. At least the Bureau of Investigation had backed off.

"What?" She jumped in her chair. "If they're returning people, lives could be at stake. And if they come for the ones here..."

"I don't think that's the case. This person was a witness in a weapons smuggling operation on their world of residence. Afterward, they were returned to their world of origin. That person didn't know that they were from here, have since been found by their paternal biological family, and it's an incredibly complex situation." I rubbed my temples as my inbox filled up with inquiries as people realized that I'd returned to the office.

"Oh. Did you speak to those temporal detectives or whatever you call them? Did you find out anything about your father and Demitra?" Her look went hopeful.

"That person did and discovered that my father and Dr. K were imprisoned, not executed, for their crimes. Though Dr. K has passed. I'm so sorry." I took her hand and squeezed it.

Her eyes teared. "Oh. But I figured long ago that she was gone. It was nice of this person to ask. How... how did they know?"

"It's Grace. She was the baby." I gave Mrs. K a very brief version of what happened.

"That poor dear. She ended up in a world with no designations at all? The people they were working with helped a couple of times mostly to appease them but wouldn't send many of our illegal designations over. They also wouldn't give my wife and your father the knowledge they needed to do it themselves. Really, we were just a receiving depot. Of course, they figured out a few things, but not enough. There were a couple of times they literally fired up the portal and pushed people through, hoping it was better than here. They just wanted to save lives." A hand went to her heart.

"I know." Exactly as I thought, and why the Temporal Authority might have objections.

Mrs. K frowned. "I'll see what I can find. But *only* because it's Grace."

"All we're trying to do is piece things together, mostly to stay one step ahead of the Office of Designation Management. Also, while we're talking about this. I'm not asking if there's a list of the omegas that were brought here. But, if you still keep in contact with any and know of one that's a therapist, Grace desperately needs someone to talk to, and we're at a loss as to what to do. People can't know about this. Also, rest assured, Grace isn't going to take up their research. She's actually been forbidden from doing so. Though that's not where her interests lie, anyway." I replied to a meeting request.

"I'll see what I can do. Just please, be careful?" Her look went stricken.

"Of course."

"What about your father? Did Grace get any news about him? It was sweet of her to ask," she told me.

I hesitated. "My father is still alive. The agent told her that he might be released for good behavior in his old age. I'm not holding my breath—and I'm sorry Dr. K didn't make it."

"For your sake, I hope he does come home. Even if you only get a couple of years with him, it's better than nothing." She shot me a sad smile. "Also, congratulations on your mating. Are you going to be having a party?"

"We are. Please work with Grace and the event planner that Evan found for her? I think we're just going to have a luncheon someplace. Maybe Zano?" I'd suggest Supressa, but we were banned.

She took some notes. "What about your club? They have beautiful rooms overlooking the golf course. Their food is good as well."

Oh, yes. My golf and tennis club hosted large personal events.

"If Grace is amicable, that works. That's all for now. And thank you."

Mrs. K stood. "Of course. Oh, the internship coordinator wants to put that adorable application in the employee newsletter. The education team is excited about this *Future Intern* program."

"Great." Now just to convince the Thornes to let little Tru stay with us for a week or two.

Mrs. K left, and I tried to get caught up.

There was a knock on my door, and Deb, who ran Special Projects, and was Grace's supervisor, stood there.

"Welcome back, do you have a moment?" she asked.

"Of course, is everything all right?" I looked up.

"We're selecting our fellows. There's a Creed Thorne on my short list. Since both you and Grace had inquired about his status, I wanted to check in since I wanted him for Narif's project," she replied, taking a seat.

"You can put him wherever you like. He's Grace's sibling. We just found this out at the conference. I don't know if this affects anything. Though you might check with Grace in case she wants him for her team," I answered.

Or if Grace wanted him here at all.

"I feel like Riley might create a project for herself, Tru, her friend Hiro, Grace, and Creed, involving space travel, and I'm a little frightened," I added with a chuckle.

A smile broke over her face. "Riley will be here? This summer is going to be fun. Also, I love the idea of us getting into space travel one day."

"There really are no limits as to what they can accomplish, and I'm happy to provide a place for them to do that," I stated.

"I'm impressed with Grace. Her ideas are extraordinary, and she and Blaise are already brainstorming. Thanks for bringing her to the team." Deb stood. "Also, welcome back. I'm glad you're okay."

She left, and I went back to work. There was a lot to do if I wanted to still meet Grace and Wes for lunch.

Chapter Eleven

Evan

"Iris wants me to come home for summer, but I don't want to," Rose blurted as we met in the lounge of her dorm at Finchley.

Today was a *school baby* afternoon, where I met with my students here at Finchley, going over exactly that—confirming everyone's summer plans. After all, not everyone had a home to go back to. I'd been doing the same with my students across the city.

After Rose, I just had one more omega. Then I could go home. I'd like a nice dinner, a cocktail, and some alone time with Grace. I even got us something new to try.

"That's fine. We've already got you enrolled in the summer semester here," I assured as we sat on the couch. The room was painted in relaxing colors, with soothing artwork, comfortable furniture for lounging, and tables for studying or collaborative projects.

Rose thought for a moment. "After our talk, I got in contact with my dad. He invited me to visit for the summer. While I'd like to see him, I don't know if I want to spend the entire summer there. Being enrolled in classes here, at least for one session, would give me a reason to stay for just a little bit. At the same time, he said that I could have a job as a stable hand for the summer. I know nothing about horses, but I love the idea of learning to ride. Then I could send half the money to Iris, and people would be less mad about me not going home because I'd be working."

"What do *you* want?" The fact that she even *had* to come up with this made my heart hurt.

"I'm leaning toward the first, even though it would make Iris angry. She wants me to work at the diner and help take care of our siblings. Though her interview went well and she's going to be starting as a receptionist at the car place, and then picking up diner shifts when she needs to." Rose added more tiny beads to her bracelet. Today she was making elaborate bracelets that looked like vines.

"I'm so glad." I was pretty sure their father had arranged that. He was trying to help, though Iris still refused direct assistance.

"Me, too."

"You should do what makes you comfortable, Rose. It's perfectly fine to want to get to know your father. I'm glad your reconnection went well. It's also fine to do it in small increments. Your idea of having it set up so that you have a reason to only spend a certain amount of time there is a good one," I praised.

"There were some things that my dad wanted me to see and do, so maybe we can figure out a schedule, so if I'm not doing one of the session's here, someone else can have my spot." She got out her phone. "Also, I have so many bracelets. Someone at the Center suggested that I sell them online. I could create a little store and send Iris the money."

"That sounds like a great idea. Though don't think you have to send the money to Iris. Having a little extra money is always a good thing. You can always get a summer job. Your school does job placements." With carefully screened omega-friendly places.

Her face lit up. "I want to work at CoCoCozy."

Every omega wanted to work at CoCoCozy. I should take Grace there. Usually, I didn't shop at the omega-only home store because I enjoyed going to the home store *with* my alphas. At CoCoCozy alphas weren't allowed past the alpha waiting area. But Grace should get a chance to experience it.

I pulled up a calendar on my laptop, and we started going through everything.

"My dad says that I can move in with them permanently, but he'll also support me wanting to stay here. I like Finchley," she told me.

"You can always finish here and then attend university near them, if after you get to know them you still want contact," I replied.

She thought for a moment. "I'll have to see what sort of pre-med programs are near him. Having a place to go on weekends would be nice. Especially if they let me bring my laundry."

"Yeah, that would be nice. Hey, those creepy alphas haven't come back, have they?"

The look on her face said it all.

"Just one. I thought I saw him yesterday when we went for coffee. But they haven't sent any more gifts." Her bubblegum scent went worried.

We were almost done figuring everything out when my phone rang.

"Jett, what's going on?" I frowned. He didn't call me when he was at work unless something was wrong.

"Yeah, so those bad alphas that were interested in Rose? They just had her uncle killed in jail. Apparently, the uncle owed them a lot, and he didn't make his payment deadline," Jett told me.

"Fuck." I eyed her as she added more dark green beads to the stretchy string. They *killed* Rose's uncle? That wasn't good.

"Yeah. But we knew he probably owed them money." Jett sighed.

"How much?" My stomach tightened. I had a feeling that it was a lot of money... enough that giving them a young omega in exchange might pay it off. My phone beeped with another call. "Hey. Detective Esposito is on the other line."

"You're at Finchley, right? Stay safe. I'll be there as soon as I can. I... I have a bad feeling. Love you." Jett ended the call.

Shit. Shit. Shit.

"Detective?" Taking the call, I stood and went to the other side of the lounge, lowering my voice.

"Rose's uncle is dead," she stated.

"I just heard. Is she in danger?" I looked over at her as another girl entered the lounge, and the two omegas chatted.

For a moment silence hung in the air. "What do you know?"

"Nothing. Just suspicions." Worry coiled in my belly.

"She was supposed to be the payment for his debts, and they got tired of waiting. But they haven't just taken her because she's sixteen. That's kidnapping. But they're also not trafficking omegas," she divulged.

"Maybe they want her for themselves. That's way more common, at least in my experience," I replied. "Also, if they were trafficking, they probably would have just snatched her, not caring about it being kidnapping. Instead, it feels like they're trying to keep it legal—like mentioning matching with Rose to the headmistress."

It all came together as I sucked in a breath.

"Oh, you're right. The mom thinks giving Rose Mega-push and turning her into an omega is for the good of the family, and then realizes Rose isn't being matched to rich alphas but given to gangsters. She drives Rose hours away to find *better* alphas, hoping to solve all of their problems while keeping Rose safe," the detective breathed, echoing my own thoughts.

"It makes sense." I'd half-suspected it, because as much as I'd like to think people wouldn't be that horrible to their own relatives, I'd been doing this long enough to know that sometimes they did.

"It's hard to prove and will be harder with the uncle dead. He admitted nothing. But for all we know, he was ordered by them to not speak of it. He's been trying very hard to bring her home, not because his family needs the help, but because if you don't pay your debts to people like this you end up dead. We need proof, but so far we have nothing concrete. Local police are rounding them up on suspicion of the death of Rose's uncle, which hopefully will keep her safe for the moment," she commented.

"Rose says that one of them was watching her yesterday. I'm with her now." I monitored her as she talked to one of her friends. Everything Detective Esposito said sounded right.

Of course, why Rose's mom took the blame for injecting her with Mega-Push when it was probably the uncle's idea, I didn't know.

"Stay with her for the moment? We're trying to get a hold of the headmistress to see what would be better, bringing Rose into protective custody or sending an officer. I've got to go." She ended the call.

Shit.

I called Jett back and told him everything. The friend had joined some others at a table to work on something. Rose was now on her phone.

"I'm on my way." Jett ended the call.

Rose frowned as I rejoined her. "What's wrong? Is it my mom? I worry about her being in jail."

"I'm so sorry to be the one to tell you this, but your uncle passed while in jail," I explained.

"Oh no." Her eyes grew misty. "I don't really like him. He's scary. He's always making us do things because he's an alpha–and what he did to Iris was just mean. But I love his mate and my cousins. What is everyone going to do without him?"

Um, thrive? Especially once her step-dad finished the job placement program and finally went back to work.

"We'll get it figured out," I assured. Oh shit. Rose's mom might be in danger, too. I texted Detective Esposito.

"How about if we get this schedule finished? I have another client coming soon, but maybe you can hang out here with me for a little bit?" I didn't want to scare her.

"Okay. But not for long. There's an end-of-the-year mixer happening today, and we get extra credit for going." She added more beads.

I nearly dropped my phone. "Rose, you're sixteen. Why are they having you go to mixers?"

"It's so we get comfortable with them, I guess. It's just a casual one. A warmup for the big graduation one, which I'm not going to. For this one, I'm just going to get a cupcake and my extra credit and leave." She shrugged.

A chill shot up my spine. No, we were in the dorms. Mixers kept to the public areas of the school.

"Rose, you're coming to the mixer, right?" Headmistress Nikita appeared in the lounge doorway, scent panicked.

Another scent hung in the air.

My phone rang.

A gun clicked. "Don't answer it," a male voice hissed.

Oh fuck.

Chapter Twelve

Jett

"What's going on today?" I asked the guard at the security booth at Finchley, as I came through in a squad car with Cam. There'd been a line of really nice cars.

"Mixer."

Shit.

"Hey, don't let anyone on this list in, okay? They're a direct danger to one of the students. If you have questions, contact Detective Esposito over at the Westside station." I showed him the list of the pack that had been bothering Rose, the one that had just had her uncle killed in jail.

We only knew about it because they'd had the audacity to brag, citing it as an example of why you needed to pay your debts.

They were a nasty lot. They were also a pack that had been through several omegas and had been banned from anything sponsored by the Omega Center—something that had originally been missed.

That could be why they might want a teenage omega as payment.

"Wait." The guard frowned. "Yeah, this guy, Carl, he came in earlier. He'd been to events before and wasn't banned, so I let him in."

"Thanks." My guess would be this was the pack member that they hadn't found yet.

"He wasn't alone. This guy was with him." The guy showed me the record.

"Thank you. Where's the mixer? The social hall?" I asked. Evan was in the lounge of one of the dorms. Still, that was a great way to gain access to campus–and a good way to get someone out.

"Yep." He nodded.

We drove off. "We need to let Detective Esposito know."

Cam, a blonde beta officer, whose hair was always up in an impossibly neat bun, nodded. "Already did."

There were *lots* of cars on campus and nicely dressed people milling about everywhere.

We parked by the dorms, and I called Evan. No answer. Panic shot through our bond. I texted the group chat.

Me

Evan might be in danger. Finchley dorms.

"Let's go." I got my gun out, and I led her toward the dorms, glad I was pretty familiar with the campus. *I'm coming, Evan.*

Security stopped us at the dorms. I flashed my badge. "I think people are in danger."

"Shit. The headmistress is in there. She was bringing someone to meet a student. Normally it's not allowed, but she's the head-mistress... Fuck." He pressed a button which hopefully set off a silent alarm. "They were going to the lounge."

I looked at the little map of the dorm and identified the lounge.

"She was asking for Rose? Was she with him?" I flashed a picture of Carl.

"Yes and I think so. I'll come with you," he said.

"He wasn't alone. Let's be on the lookout for him." Cam showed him a picture of the other guy.

"Okay. I've already summoned more security," he replied.

"Thanks. Backup should be coming." The fact that someone had already got into a place where they shouldn't, didn't give me confidence in him, though his logic made sense.

A scream echoed down the hall. We took off running. *Please let Evan be okay.*

"I will fucking kill her. This is how it's gonna go. I'm going to take Rose and leave. Headmistress Nikita signs the paperwork that Rose has been matched with us. No one fights it. And you, Mr. Advocate, will allow all of it and note that she doesn't need no advocate no more." Carl, who was a big, ugly alpha, had a gun pressed to Headmistress Nikita's temple in the doorway of the lounge.

"She's sixteen, you can't do that." Evan had Rose behind him. The entire room stank of burnt sugar omega fear as other omegas hid and cowered.

Some alphas got off on that. Clearly, Carl was one of them.

"We have a judge. We have lots of people. That's how we offed your uncle, Rose, and if you're not careful, your mama's next." Carl sneered at Rose.

"Police, drop your gun," Cam yelled.

Carl turned and fired at her, missing. Evan grabbed the headmistress. Cam shot Carl, and he crumpled to the ground.

"I said drop your gun. Fucking asshole. You give alphas a bad name." She kicked his gun away.

"Police," someone yelled as a bunch of officers joined us.

Hopefully, one of them was Detective Esposito.

"Is everyone okay?" I asked, going into the lounge.

"Jett." Evan ran to me.

I hugged him tightly. "I'm right here, Baby. I'm right fucking here."

"You came." He held on to me like a lifeline. While I knew he could take care of himself, I was glad I was in time–and that he was okay.

"Always." I looked over at the scared redheaded teenager with him. "Rose? Are you okay?"

"I don't know what just happened." Tears ran down Rose's face.

"It's okay, Rose. The police are here." Headmistress Nikita pulled Rose to her.

"We're here, Rose, and we're going to get this taken care of for good," a woman said. Detective Esposito.

"Thank you, Detective," the headmistress replied. "This is one of the men who'd been asking about Rose previously. I thought he'd been banned from campus. He forced me to bring him to Rose when she didn't arrive at the mixer."

"You're safe and I'm right here," I whispered to Evan, reassuring him.

"Where's the other one? Carl wasn't alone." Cam looked around, as other officers dealt with Carl. Another officer came in and checked with the rest of the students.

Thank goodness Cam was with me.

"We got him, he was waiting in the car," Detective Esposito explained. "You need better security, Headmistress. You shouldn't be able to bring him into the dorms. Now, let's get this piece of trash in jail. There's a special place for alphas that prey on teenagers, and you're not going to like it one bit."

Chapter Thirteen

Evan

"I've got you." Brennan held me tight, coating me in his pine scent and shooting love through the bond. We were all outside in a courtyard off one of the parking lots at Finchley.

The very injured Carl had been hauled off to jail. The mixer had been canceled, and everyone was sent home. People had been questioned. Reports had been made.

The entire pack was now in custody. Rose's mom was being watched, just in case someone came after her—same with the rest of Rose's family.

"You need better security," Brennan snapped at Headmistress Nikita as she came over to us.

"I know. About Rose..." Her expression went serious.

My belly dropped as I recalled what she'd said previously about Rose not being able to stay if her family continued to cause trouble.

"Please let Rose stay," I begged.

"What? You can't kick her out because of this." Detective Esposito joined us. "No, seriously. There's a law protecting omegas from being expelled from school or work because of alphas stalking them."

Headmistress Nikita frowned. "How do you know that?"

"I grew up at Redwood Academy, outside of Portland. My dad was assistant headmaster. I know the most random shit. Rose stays, well, if she wants. And I'm going to give you until the end of the school year to fix your security issues before calling in a tip to the National Association of Omega Academies–because you just failed a bunch of security benchmarks," Detective Esposito stated.

She nodded. "We did. But..."

"Look, I get it. Your full-paying fancy families will get their panties in a twist at things like this. But I guarantee you that they'll be more upset knowing all of your security breaches. Your security *let* an alpha into the dorms with a gun just because you were there. Fire that firm," Detective Esposito added.

"Will Rose be safe now?" I asked.

"Yes. We'll have an officer here for a few days to make sure. We'll get everything cleaned up and get out of here soon. Thanks for your cooperation." Detective Esposito left.

"Rose can stay. I do like her, and hopefully all of this can be put behind us," Headmistress Nikita said.

"Good. Come on, Evan, let's go home." Brennan wrapped an arm around me.

Jett was with Cam and some other officers.

I hugged him. "Thank you."

"That's what mates are for." He gave me a kiss.

"Thanks, Cam." I knew her from Jett's boxing gym.

She grinned. "Bring me more of those chocolate cookies with the powdered sugar, and we're even."

"Grace makes those, not me. But I'll see what I can do next time she makes them."

Jett gave me another kiss. "I have to finish up. See you at home."

"See you at home." I went and found Rose. "Are you okay?"

"I think so? The detective tried to explain everything to me. It's so scary." Rose hugged me.

"How about if we try to meet tomorrow or the day after and we'll talk through it," I told her.

"Rose, Rose, are you okay?" A man in a cowboy hat and boots ran over to her.

"Dad?" She looked over, brightening.

Colt Sterling, Rose's bio-dad, picked her up and hugged her tight. "Thank goodness you're safe."

"Dad." Her voice broke as she buried her face in his shirt.

"Are you okay, Rose?" I asked her.

"I... I called him. Um, I didn't think you'd come this fast?" She hiccupped.

"I'm in this area a lot this time of year. I was going to call you tomorrow and see if we could get some ice cream," Colt explained.

We talked a little longer, as I tried to gauge whether it was okay to leave Rose with him. In the end I let Brennan take me home on his motorcycle. Jett would drive my 4x4 back.

I spent the entire time holding Brennan tight. Fuck. That could have ended badly. My experience in the military was more being a blunt-force object with a large weapon and less facing an active shooter unarmed with civilians present.

But for some reason this kept happening. Maybe I should train for it.

Or, maybe for once we'd have something where I could actually use my skills. Not that I was in shape.

No. No. I would prefer things to be quiet and have to use zero of my skills, thank you very much.

Hopefully, Rose would be safe now, and all of this would be put behind her.

Finally, we pulled into the garage.

Brennan held me to him. "What do you need?"

"Evan." Grace ran into the garage, in one of her T-shirt dresses, feet bare. She threw her arms around me.

"I'm okay, Peaches." At this moment, I wanted her more than anything. I threw her over my shoulder, like alphas did to omegas in the movies.

Yep. *You. Me. Bed. Now.*

"Evan," she squealed.

"This second I need her. But then I need to spend tonight with you," I murmured to Brennan, giving him a kiss. "I might want some food later."

"Evan, I'm not a sack of potatoes." Grace kicked her bare feet. I tightened my grip.

"Be good for Evan, Little Butterfly." Brennan patted her ass.

I carried her straight up the backstairs.

"Evan, are you okay?" Wes intercepted me.

"I'm okay. I just need some peaches." Leaning in, I kissed him.

"Okay. My room?" He offered.

"I want some alone time, but I'll let you know if I need backup." I squeezed her ass.

Grace laughed. "I'm right here."

"Have fun." Wes kissed her, too.

Running up the stairs, I took her straight into my bedroom. I tossed her onto the bed and pounced on her.

Really, I couldn't explain it. But I needed my Princess Peaches under me. I needed to fuck her hard while she screamed my name.

My mouth sealed over hers as I kissed her, hard, pinning her to the bed. Her legs wrapped around me as she kissed me back.

"You're okay, Evan. You're home and safe, and I'm right here," she assured.

"Good. Because I'm going to fuck you." I kissed her again.

"Yes, sir." She grinned.

"I even got us a new toy to play with," I told her, attacking her neck with kisses as I tried to get her dress off.

She rolled out of my grasp and pulled her dress over her head and tossed it some place. My room, as usual, was a bit of a disaster. Were those Jett's boxers on the lamp?

Yes, yes, they were.

"No bra?" I helped myself to a mouthful, pushing her back down onto my bed.

Grace groaned as she stripped off her panties. "I don't like wearing bras around the house. They're uncomfortable. No one will mind, right?"

"Um, no. Feel free to go braless. If anyone complains, just start going topless." I gave the other one some attention so it wouldn't get jealous. We couldn't have sad breasts now, could we?

Satisfied that she was naked, I pulled off my clothes, then dive-bombed her. Holding her thighs open, I gave her sweet pussy a long lick.

"Mmmm," she sighed.

I lapped at her and sucked her clit, teasing her until her body bucked.

"That was delicious. Please, sir, may I have your cock now?" She blinked at me in that cute way of hers.

"It's all yours. Want to try? I got this just for you." I got the new toy out of the nightstand and held it up.

She eyed the hot pink, sparkly contraption curiously. "What is it?"

"It simulates a lady alpha's lock. They have a special set of muscles that clamp down on my dick and hold me tight. This toy mimics it." I got the remote and handed it to her. "This is the remote. So, when I beg you to lock me, you push the button, it locks me, and then gradually lets go. It's a shorter time period than a knot deflating."

"Is there a kill switch so that if I strangle your dick wrong, I can stop it?"

"Yes." Climbing onto the bed with her, I showed her how to work it. "Can we try?" I really wanted to try it.

"Yes." Grace nodded. "What's your safe word, Omega."

My dick shuddered with happiness at those sweet words. "Trampoline."

"We can both stop it at any time. I don't want it to electrocute you or anything."

I slipped the bands of the toy over her legs; they'd help hold it in place. Then, gently, I pushed it inside her. "How does it feel?"

"I barely feel it. But what I want to feel is you." Grace grabbed me and pulled me to her.

"Yeah, you want me." I blew a kiss on her stomach, which made her giggle.

"So much." She caressed my back.

I plunged my hard cock inside her. While I felt the toy, it was soft and not distracting as I thrust in and out of her over and over. Her breath came out in little pants as she moaned deliciously.

"You feel so good," I groaned, relishing the feeling of her under me as something inside me settled.

"Same." She made a happy noise as she squeezed my ass with the hand not holding the remote.

I increased my pace, bringing the both of us closer to our peaks.

"Evan," she cried as she orgasmed.

Finally, I couldn't hold it anymore.

"Lock me, Peaches," I cried.

"Okay."

I felt the toy squeeze down on me and came immediately, flooding her with my cum. The pleasure from the tightness of the lock rained down on me. Oh, I loved my Peaches, but this was a pleasant change, not unlike how I sometimes use the jelly knot on her.

My body continued to shudder.

"I've got you, are you okay?" She wrapped her arms around me.

"Oh, I feel amazing. I liked that so much. What about you? How'd it feel?" I flopped onto her, trying not to squish her.

"It does nothing extra for me, but it's not a turnoff in the slightest. Oh, do I like the way you smell right now. And if it makes you feel good?" Grace buried her face in my shoulder.

I rolled us onto our sides, so she was more comfortable.

"You always make me feel good." I kissed her, threw the covers over us, and tucked her small body into mine.

"Do you feel better now? You felt so scared." She buried her face in my neck.

"It was scary. We were lucky that Jett and Detective Esposito were on the way. And now, oh yes, you've made me feel so much better. Just what I needed." I kissed the top of her head.

"Rose is okay?"

"Yeah. She'll be okay." I held her tight until the toy unlocked and took it off her.

Her hand cupped my face. "How about we take a bath?"

"Oh, I'd like that." I was hungry, though. Hmmm, if I shot hunger through the bond, would someone make me food?

Yeah, that would be nice. No food in the bathtub, though. I'd hold firm on that.

But Graces? Yeah, they could always be had in the bathtub.

Chapter Fourteen

Wes

I waited nervously at the Motor Vehicle Division, glancing at the clock. She'd been gone a long time. But I got no worries from our bond.

Should we have waited? Maybe? But I'd been quizzing her on road rules at lunch.

This morning, she'd discovered that the MVD had a cancellation, and she could get a driving test spot today after work. While I'd made plans for a little date-night, a minor delay wouldn't hurt.

An alpha older than me waited next to me, fidgeting on the hard plastic chairs outside the testing area.

"My daughter's taking the test. I'm a little nervous. Yours too?" he said.

"My mate. She's got this." Really, Grace was an excellent driver, unless there was a roundabout. If she got her own car, I wasn't sure where she'd park it, but it would be good for her to have her license.

I wanted her to feel secure here. Having things like a license and her own money would help with that.

My truck pulled up. The tester got out of the passenger seat. Grace tumbled out of the truck and ran to me.

"You passed?" I hugged her.

"Yep. I passed the written and the driver's tests. They also let me take the written motorcycle test. Now I can practice with Jett and then I can take that one." Beaming, she dragged me inside so she could get her license.

Was I as excited for her to get her motorcycle license? No. But I wasn't going to stop her. I worried about the safety of Evan and the rest of the pack, too. I just didn't share my pack's love for motorcycles.

We went back to my truck.

"Can I drive?" she asked.

"Actually, let me? We've got our date tonight, and the roads are a little tight." I opened the door to the passenger side and helped her in.

"Okay." Her shoulders shook a little in excitement as she texted someone–probably Evan, who was out with Riley because it was Thursday.

"Hey, the symposium Spencer and I are attending is coming up fast. I can still cancel if you want me to," I told her.

She shook her head as she continued to text. "I know you're not big on travel, so the fact that you want to go means that I want you to go. I'll be okay with Jett, Bren, and Evan. You'll only be gone a couple of days."

"I know." I *was* excited. Not about Spencer making me speak in public, but for the keynote speaker and some of the hands-on workshops. I just worried about both me and Spencer being away from her.

Really, Spencer should stay home. He was still recovering.

"Also, I'm excited for the concert with Brennan." She bounced in her seat, still texting.

"I'm sure you'll have a great time." I left the freeway and started down the road that would take us to our date.

Grace looked out the window. "Where are we going?"

"I promised to take you to all the places we dreamt of. We haven't been to Starry Point yet." It was a lookout with a beautiful view of the city. We used to make out there sometimes in our dreams.

Delight flooded her face. "I'd forgotten about Starry Point."

Her phone beeped, and she looked at it.

"Everything okay?" I asked.

"Creed got the job offer, and he's accepting. I'm happy for him." She texted him back.

"He seems like a good guy. Bren won't let him stay with us. I think your sisters visiting us will be a lot for him as it is." I wasn't sure where we'd put them since they were too young to stay in the guest house. We had some rooms we didn't use much downstairs. Maybe we should make a guest room.

One of those rooms would probably end up as Grace's creepy doll room. But that could have a pullout couch. Ooh, we could put people there that we didn't want to stay for long.

Not that we had many guests.

"Compass BioTek can help with housing placements. Also, the professor hasn't agreed to Tru visiting us yet." Grace was still texting.

"What else are you worrying about? Is Margie still giving you issues at work? You said that Deb and Blaise loved all your suggestions from the conference." Something was bothering her.

"Spencer wants to have our reception at his club. He's going to take me there. Evan wants me to have two different wedding planners. It feels so privileged." She laughed. "Most weddings I went to growing up had their receptions in the church hall or at someone's farm."

Rich people shit. Got it. I knew she worried about it being elegant enough for Spencer. Something Evan's insistence at having a special wedding planner only ratcheted.

"Spencer's club is nice. I've been there. They'll probably make everything really easy for you. But that man is over-the-moon in love with you. You can have a cookout in the park with a bouncy castle, and he'd be all for it. It would be the fanciest one ever, though. Gourmet bouncy houses, and grilling champions flown in for it." It actually sounded way more fun than something at his club.

She laughed. "I love it. Still..."

"You don't have to have a wedding planner for your dinner. Mrs. K will probably have it planned in an afternoon, complete with things you never knew you needed," I added.

"She's nice."

"Yes, she is." We parked in the lot, which wasn't empty. Pity. But unlike in our dreams, outdoor sex was illegal here.

Tragic.

I got out the picnic basket and a blanket. Taking her arm, we made the easy hike. It was still a bit until sunset. But that would give us a chance to eat.

On the way up we passed families, several friendly dogs, and some couples.

"Are we still getting all the animals? Or are you waiting for your motorcycle license so you can go to the hardware store and buy chickens?" I looked for a suitable spot for us to have our picnic.

Grace laughed as she helped spread the blanket out. "So, Bren was wrong. We're allowed six chickens and no roosters. Should I order a coop and a bunny hutch?"

"As much as I'd love for you to start a petting zoo in the back-yard, you should probably bring it up to everyone first." I opened the picnic basket and got out the meat and cheese board I'd ordered.

We sat and ate as the sun set. Other people were doing the same.

"What do you think? Is it as you remember?" I put some cheese on a cracker.

She leaned in and kissed me. "It's more beautiful. Also, more people-y."

"True." After we finished our dinner and dessert, I pulled out four bottles of whiskey.

"How drunk are we getting?" She laughed.

I placed some glasses on the blanket. "Whiskey tasting. For our fountain. Your talk of menus and cake tasting made me think of it."

Pouring some for each of us, we tried the four bottles that had been recommended. As we tried them, the lights came on over the city.

"This one." She held up one.

"Oooh, good choice." It was one of the more expensive options, but Evan liked that brand.

Grace cuddled into me, leaning her head on my shoulder. "This is so pretty, thank you."

"You know, now that I'm sitting on this blanket, I'm pretty sure that having sex up here won't be as much fun as in our dreams," I admitted.

"But we can still make out, right?" Grace tipped her head up and caught my mouth with hers.

My arms wrapped around her, deepening the kiss. "I'll always make out with you."

I helped her out of the truck and escorted her back into the house. We'd had a delightful time, but all that making out made me ready for... other things.

By the sweetness in her peach scent, she was up for it, as well. If I pulled down her panties and touched her, would she be soaking wet?

Probably.

Picking her up, princess style, I carried her upstairs. "My room?"

"Please, Boo-Bear." Her voice went breathy, and her sweet need went through the bond right to my dick.

That nickname of hers from our youth always did me in.

"Whatever you want, Grace."

Evan was curled up in the sunken living room on the third floor, watching a decorating show. "Peaches, did you pass?"

"I did." She gave me a coy look, and from the bond I could tell exactly what sort of reward she desired–and it wasn't ice cream.

"I'm so proud of you. First your car license, next your motor-cycle license. I wish I could be your backpack." His gaze turned wistful.

Yeah, he wasn't going to fit on the back of that tiny motorcycle of hers. I wasn't sure how Riley would fit in that sidecar–certainly, I wasn't going to.

She thought for a moment. "I *can* ride Jett's. We could always take his for a spin around the neighborhood."

Getting up off the couch, he gave her a kiss.

"Our sweet peach deserves a treat. Will you stay with us for a while? I think she needs to be the filling." I kissed her forehead.

"Oh yes, please." Her eyes danced with delight.

"Don't need to ask me twice." Evan shut off the television and followed us into my bedroom.

I laid her down on the bed.

"You two smell like outside and whiskey," Evan said as he took off his shirt.

"We went up to Starry Point and tasted whiskey for the fountain and made out like horny teenagers." Grace kicked off her shoes and got undressed.

I did the same, my desire growing for them with every passing second.

Patting her bare ass, she got on all fours for me.

"Are you ready for me?" I swiped her with my fingers. "Oh yes, you are." I brought them to my lips. "So ready."

"Oh, I want to try." Evan licked her essence off my fingers. "Perfect."

That they were.

"Who do you want, where, Peaches?" I asked.

"I don't care," she replied.

"Ride me while Evan takes your ass?" I rolled onto the bed, needing to be knot deep in her.

"Mmmm, yes, please."

She climbed on top of me, holding my hands as she slid onto my cock. Oh yeah, she was so ready for me.

Evan grabbed the lube and got her ready as she rode me. Her cute little noises went straight to my cock. My knot was so ready to bury itself inside her.

Finally, he grasped her hips. "Ready for me?"

"Please," she begged.

I stilled as he slid inside her, and I relished in being able to feel him through her, in having both of them here with me.

We moved again, getting into a rhythm. Her eyes closed. Their pleasure washed over me through the bond as they came.

"Peaches, I'm going to give you my knot now." I pushed my knot inside her, her body shuddering with pleasure as I came.

I pulled them both onto me, sandwiching Grace between us.

"Everyone okay?" I stroked her hair as I kissed him.

"I enjoy being the filling," she said sleepily.

Evan kissed her temple. "I like you being the filling, too."

His look said he'd like to be the filling next.

Oh no, I'd need to fuck them again. Poor me.

Chapter Fifteen

Grace

Elation cut through me as I zoomed on my green motorcycle through our sleepy little neighborhood. Oh, it felt good to be on a bike again. What Spencer had ordered for me was a perfect fit.

"Hey, you're going a little fast," Jett said over the coms in our helmets.

"I like to go fast." But he was right. It was a Saturday morning. Kids could be out playing.

We returned to the driveway. Brennan and Riley were waiting. Evan and Wes had gone on a little date.

"How'd she do?" Brennan asked. He'd just come back from a business trip.

Jett took off his helmet. "Fine. It's not like she doesn't know how."

"It *is* pretty much the same." I rolled my eyes. This was my first time getting to test it out, since Brennan insisted I at least take the written test before using it.

Riley had her helmet in her hand. She looked at the two of them. "I get to ride, now?"

"Yeah, it's fine," Jett replied.

"Finally." Putting on her helmet, Riley climbed into the sidecar. "Let's test this fucker out."

"Let's go." I took Riley for a spin around the neighborhood. "Everything going okay?" I asked over the coms.

"I told my sister Sonja that I was going to change my last name. Evan made me. We talked it through, and she's okay with it. Which she should be, considering when she gets married, she and her doctor are changing their last names. You'll like her." Riley stated.

Right, she was a medical doctor and worked at the school Sonja was dean at.

"But..." I prodded, because I could feel a *but* coming on.

"She told Sasha, who then shit a cactus. Ugh." Riley sighed. "Evan's my guardian. Also, I belong to this pack. She can't do fuck-all. But the fact she's being a bitch about it hurts."

"Yeah, it hurts when family's mean like that," I agreed as I rounded a corner, noting how having a passenger in the sidecar changed things.

"Speaking of family, I really like Mercy. We've been texting. Is it weird if I make your sister my bestie? She and I just, I don't know, get along," she admitted.

"Go for it. I want to be besties with Verity." I loved Mercy and Tru, too.

"Are they coming to the party you and Spencer are having?" she asked.

I thought for a moment. "I'm not sure. Probably not? But I'll invite everyone to the wedding next year. Maybe some of them could even be in it."

"That sounds good. Mercy and Verity can be your attendants. Fuck, how boring is your and Spencer's party going to be?"

"Hopefully not boring at all. It'll probably be really fancy, though. We're not going to have much of a program. Cocktails and appetizers with mingling, then dinner and dancing. Probably no speeches." It sounded good to me. Also, Spencer wasn't up for much still, but his mother was pushing this to be sooner rather than later.

"Elegant is fine. I want good music," she agreed. "Speaking of music, can I take music off your laptop?"

"Yeah, take any music, movies, or books you'd like," I replied.

"Back to the reception. Can we rent out a fancy restaurant?"

"We could. Spencer's taking me to his club to see it." What Wes had said about grill masters and bouncy castles hit something. Could we make a cookout elegant? Spencer was the grill master, so it could make sense to have that theme.

I finished our lap around the block. Another motorcycle pulled up next to us. Spencer was on his, which was a larger version of mine without the sidecar.

Shit, he looked fucking sexy on a motorcycle.

He rode with us as we took another lap. Finally, we returned to the house.

"You look beautiful on that," Spencer said, taking off his helmet, as we parked in the driveway.

"Thank you." I grinned. It was the nicest gift.

"Ri, how was it?" Jett asked her.

"It's fine. Spence, can you add me and Grace to your club? Also, get us tennis lessons? Please? We want to play doubles with Kilroy and his mom. That's their club. It's not Hiro or Marco's though," Riley said as she climbed out of the sidecar.

"Of course. I was thinking of making it a pack membership, anyway." Spencer nodded and turned to Brennan. "I know you have your own club that you use for business, but considering your family also belongs to it, I thought you might like options?"

"Thank you. Yes, I'm unwelcome there right now," Brennan answered.

"The Queen Mum didn't like your terms?" he asked.

"Not at all. Really, it would be better for her to trade, since forcing the sale of my building won't get her the one she wants," Brennan replied.

"People are still really mad about the Morris Foundation cutting the omega scholarships," Jett added.

Spencer got out his phone. "Brennan, we should meet again about foundation things. How's your week?"

"What about tomorrow?" Brennan checked his own phone.

"That works because Grace can now drive, so after we go to the carnival meeting at Hiro's, she can drop me off at school." Riley looked smug.

Right. The one for *next* school year. It seemed like mom-politics were the same no matter what world you were in.

"You can take my car." Spencer nodded. "We should get you something. A pink convertible?"

"A pink pickup truck with a sticker that says *Silly boys, trucks are for girls*?" I grinned.

"I love it. If lessons are over, we should get going," Spencer reminded me.

"Sounds good, let me get changed. Thank you. I love my motorcycle." I pulled him down to give him a kiss. After putting our bikes away, I went inside. I had a text.

Have fun at the club. I'm familiar with their preferred vendors, so I can make recommendations. Also, if you don't like it, I'm pretty sure we can get Zano. There are other clubs, too.

Good to know. Zano was a fancy restaurant.

Thanks. Silly question. Could we make a cookout fancy? Like fly in grill masters? Serve nice meats? Perhaps have it outside? Spencer enjoys grilling, I'm trying to make it personal.

I sent her a little pin board that I'd made yesterday on my break at work. It had things like fairy lights, lemonade cocktails, and the most elegant picnic tables ever, covered in flowers, with real linens, fine dishes, and candles.

Oooh. Let me ponder this. The club lets you bring in your own chef if it's someone worth having.

Thanks.

I didn't know what that meant. But I had discovered an upscale wedding forum online and figured out that things like *that* were what fancy wedding planners were for. Want a gourmet chef flown in? Or a specific band that normally played amphitheaters? Need plates that matched the ones you ate off of on your first date?

Flowers from the farm he proposed at? *That's* the sort of shit they did.

Brennan came down the stairs. "Grace? Before I forget, I got you something from Italy."

He handed me a box. He'd gotten me something on his business trip? Last night we had delicious wine and chocolates, and he'd gotten Riley a leather jacket.

"Oh, thank you." Inside were glass earrings in the shape of quarter notes. I sucked in a breath. "They're beautiful." I kissed him on the cheek, then my own cheeks burned as I realized what I'd done.

"I'm glad you like them. You can wear them when we go and listen to Volkov being played properly." With a grin, he ruffled my hair and left the room.

Jett laughed behind me. "This is going to be fun."

"Is he courting me?" I blinked. He'd also gotten me piano music. At the same time, he hadn't asked me or announced it or anything.

"I think he is, but he doesn't realize it. Just go with it, Babydoll." Jett spun me around, then went into the living room.

What did that even mean? But I'd take nice Brennan over mean Brennan any day.

"What do you think, my good doctor?" Spencer asked, as we got a tour of the grounds at his country club. We'd already seen the ballrooms, which were lovely and had balconies.

"It's so pretty here. Do you have an outdoor space? It doesn't need to be tented," I asked.

"We do, but there's a party there right now. We can take a look, as long as we don't disturb them," the beta from the club told us.

She led us through a beautiful garden. "This area is perfect for pictures. You can also use it for a cocktail reception."

The sound of children greeted us as she led us into a tree-filled outdoor area. There was a tent, tables, and a bouncy castle.

Granted, it was the fanciest children's birthday party I'd ever seen. Yes, I could work with this. I took a couple of photos.

"We don't provide tents, but there's some on our preferred vendor list," she explained.

But I knew that already. I also knew that picnic tables were from another vendor, but the tent people had nicer linens. The fancy wedding planner was earning her fee and had been sending me all sorts of pictures and vendor suggestions.

We finished the tour, and she took us into the main dining room. "I'm here to answer any questions you or your wedding planner might have."

"Thank you. Shall we?" Spencer held out his arm.

I took it. Spencer wore a button down with rolled up sleeves, pressed khakis, and really nice shoes. I wore a floral dress and ballet flats.

A server led us to a corner table with a nice view of the golf course.

"What did you think?" he asked as the server handed us menus and brought us water.

"This place is really beautiful. I love all the trees." Yes, I could see why he suggested it.

I perused the menu, and we ordered.

"You have ideas, I see it in your eyes." He took a sip of merlot.

"How much is my budget? Because, yes, I do," I replied, taking a drink of my spiked lemonade.

He thought for a moment. "I try very hard to never do anything that might be considered wasteful or a spectacle. Elegant, not excessive. Would you be willing to share your ideas with me?"

"I know that you were thinking of a simple dinner in one of the ballrooms, but hear me out. These are also just ideas. I'm not even sure everything is possible." I got out my phone and started showing him photos.

"Oh. I do love that idea," he agreed.

"If we have kids at our party, we could have the bouncy castle."

"Let me see the list of the grill masters she suggested?" he asked.

I handed him my phone.

"Him. I actually know him, so if he's available it's not extravagant, it's a friend showing off what he's known for." Spencer tapped on a name. "See what I'm saying."

"Right, an old friend making food with a hometown flair. Wine from someplace someone owns?" I nodded and took notes.

"Precisely. My aunt has a vineyard with some decent vintages."

Our food came, and we went through everything as he made incredibly thoughtful suggestions.

"You'd be fine with all of this?" I added, worried a little it wasn't fancy enough.

"You're suggesting things that are us. A little of my home, a little of yours. It will be perfect." He leaned in and gave me a kiss.

That man.

"How about music? Should we fly in a band for dancing?" I grinned. While that seemed fun, it also seemed a little ridiculous.

"I'd like some traditional live music for dancing. You know, my cousins have a band." He took another sip of wine.

"Yeah? A famous one?" I took a bite of my pasta.

"More like infamous, because a bunch of Thanukos business tycoons have a band that plays traditional Greek music and keep being allowed to play because of their name. They're not awful. But they're not playing any music festivals." Spencer grinned over his glass.

"That sounds fun. Are we doing any special dancing?"

He leaned in toward me. "I'd like that very much–if you would."

"Only if you teach me in the living room. I miss our dance classes," I told him honestly.

"You just like excuses for me to touch you." His look went smoldering.

"Oh, I do, Dearest. You know... everyone's left for the afternoon." I looked at my phone. "While we could join them, we could also go home. How are you feeling?"

"Like if I don't take care of you soon, I'm going to burst." He squeezed my hand.

Check, please. Things with Spencer had been very gentle while he healed.

"No need to rush, though." He leaned back and took another sip of wine. "We have all the time in the world–just like we will when I get you home."

Oh? Heat flooded my core. I raised my glass. "Here's to it being well worth the wait."

Chapter Sixteen

Brennan

I walked into the courthouse. It had been a good day, and it was about to get better. We were finalizing our name changes today.

"Brennan?" Spencer joined me, wearing one of his fancy suits. "Can I have a word, quickly, before we join everyone."

"Of course." I hoped nothing had gone sideways–like my mother going after Compass BioTek.

She'd been very quiet; which worried me.

A giddy look lit up his eyes in a way I'd never seen before as he got out his phone. "I found it. Oh, she's going to love it."

"Grace's house?" It's all I could think of. Had I ever seen him this excited about something?

"Please excuse me for not running it through you, but it was perfect, and I knew that it would go fast." Spencer showed me a listing on his phone.

I read it. Then re-read it. No. He didn't.

Oh yes, he did.

"Spencer. This is an island." An island in Greece with an airstrip and a dock large enough for a substantial yacht.

"There's a house on it. It's also a tiny island." His look went self-conscious. "Is it too much? It's too much. It comes with the yacht. My jet's a little much for that airstrip unless we make some changes to it, but we talked about a pack plane, anyway."

"She'll love it. It's exquisite." It was a small island. But it wasn't a small house. When exactly were we going to visit this island? We barely went to Evan's cabin outside of his heats. Suddenly, were we going to not be a pack of workaholics?

Then again, would it be a bad thing? Really, both Spencer and I could step back from our companies, and they'd be fine. We just *enjoyed* being hands on. Wes and Grace had flexible jobs. Evan's training for the Blanket Brigade also opened him up to more options, which just left Jett.

Spencer looked at me expectantly. "Is it enough? The house just looked like her, and I know she enjoys the ocean, so it made sense. Hopefully, it should be settled so we can run the paperwork through the Center, get everything solidified, and she can be pack."

"It's perfect." Enough? Grace was getting her own fucking *island.* Who did that?

Never mind, this was Spencer, who was flying in a grill master, a band, and wine for his mating party because she wanted an elegant picnic.

"An island? Nice. I'll probably get my retirement island nearby one day. It's a good area, especially for taxes." Riley appeared, in black fishnets, boots, and a skirt, purple top ripped and matching her lipstick.

Spencer nodded. "You gave me the idea."

"I aim to please." Riley grinned.

"Are you okay with all of this, Ri?" I wanted to make sure.

She shot me a look. "Name me up. Tattoo me. You're stuck with me, fuckers."

I pulled her to me. "No, you're stuck with me."

"Get off me, you alpha fuck." She laughed, trying to push me away.

The three of us found the others. We met with the judge and changed our last names. Well, Spencer didn't have to change his.

Relief filled me as I signed the form. Wow, I never thought I'd be so happy to not be a Morris.

"All set. Also, I now formally declare you the Thanukos pack." The judge beamed at us. Okay, we still needed the paperwork submitted for Grace, but it worked.

"Thank you. I made reservations for us to have dinner, I thought we should celebrate," I announced. It was one of the restaurants we usually went to as a pack. Grace hadn't been to any of them yet.

"Are we all a pack, now?" Grace asked.

"For the most part. Though for you, some things need to go through Mrs. Beekman and the Omega Center before they're finalized." Which could happen now that I had the specifics of her property. "I'll meet you all there?"

I took my motorcycle and met them at the restaurant that was a pack favorite because you could cook your own food on the grill on the table.

"We haven't had a family dinner out in a while. This is nice." Evan's arm slid around my waist as the server took us to our table.

I frowned as we were led to the back room. "Wait, I didn't reserve a private room."

"We did. Surprise." Katie and her pack were there. A sign was taped to the wall. *Congratulations, Thanukos Pack.*

She did? I hugged my twin. "Thank you."

"We have an alliance, right?" Lexi grinned as she hugged her brother.

Wes' nose flared, and he sucked in a breath. "Wait..."

"Yeah. Not trying to hijack your party. Damn alpha noses." Lexi's smile broadened.

Grace blinked.

"Babies. The sister pack is bringing on the baby invasion," I explained.

She did a happy little dance. "Babies. Yay."

"Grace, I want to hear all about the PIIP symposium." Rami, Katie's omega, waved her over.

While I'd wanted to have a nice, quiet dinner with my pack, it was nice of the sister pack to do this.

We all ordered a ton of food and laughed as we ate and drank.

"Welcome to the chaos, Grace." Katie laughed. "Any other news, Bren?"

Oh. Right. "The courts have awarded me my assets. Which includes the Morris Foundation Building."

"Really? That was quick." Jett grinned. "Eviction notices all around?"

I shook my head. "Not yet."

Though I was considering selling the building. We'd see, after I liquidated some of the other things. Most of it was going into our family foundation, anyway. Did I need it? No. It was the principle of the matter. Also, I loved the irony of using the money from my mother's family to fund the scholarships we'd put in place to cover the ones that she cut.

"What about the State Street Building?" Katie asked.

I shrugged. "She had the opportunity to make the trade–which was a lot more advantageous to her. But that's passed. How's the new job?"

"I love it," Katie responded.

"Wow. Really?" My brother Liam, who'd head up the Morris Company one day, leaned in the doorway.

"Fuck off, Liam. I'm allowed to have dinner with my brother." Katie scratched her nose with her middle finger.

"I can't believe you did that." Liam looked at the sign congratulating our new pack.

Spencer stood, expression fierce. "Do you have an issue with my family, Liam?"

"Only that you had the poor taste to include my brother." Liam chuckled derisively.

"Don't be mean." Grace glared at him with an intensity that might make someone cower if they didn't know our mother.

"What do you want, Liam?" I growled.

"You're fucking up everything. We need that building to finish the State Street Project. Sell it to us, or else," he snarled.

"Bold of you to threaten him in front of two law enforcement officers," Lexi warned.

Liam laughed. "I'm so beyond that it's laughable."

"I'm willing to sell it for what I bought it for. The only reason I bought it was because you're fucking with my business," I spat.

"That dumb little event venue? Waste of money." His eyes rolled.

"Hey." Grace threw something at him. "I'm getting married there, you asshole. It's not dumb or a waste."

"Did you just throw a piece of zucchini at me?" Liam blinked.

Katie was trying not to laugh. Where once I'd tell Grace to leave it, I was super curious if he could take what our little gamma could dish out.

"You should be glad that I'm over here or I'd punch you in the tits. Bullies are not welcome. Go be a twatwaffle someplace else." Grace threw another piece of zucchini at him.

"Yeah, go away, Liam." Rami threw an onion at him.

"When's the last time you did something nice for your omega?" Evan added, tossing some broccoli.

"Go fuck a pineapple." Riley held a chopstick like a throwing knife.

Should I take it from her? Yes. Would I? No.

Liam stood there, incredulous, as the chopstick hit him in the chest.

"Arrest him, Officer." Grace laughed.

"Unfortunately, you can't arrest people for just being assholes." Jett sighed and shook his head.

"My job would be so much easier if you could," Lexi agreed.

"Look, he told you that he'll sell you the building. Fuck, I'm sure he'll sell you the other building, too. You know you can afford it, and honestly, you and Mom brought this on yourselves. As the courts ruled, you can't keep his shit from him, and you knew not to lowball that property owner, but you did anyway. I think the term is *fuck around and find out* and you just found out," Katie taunted.

The judge had literally laughed my mom out of court, too.

"You are going to regret this." Liam scowled and flicked some onion off his sleeve. "Also, you should teach them to behave."

"I'll teach you a few things," Grace grumbled as Wes practically sat on her to keep her from getting up.

"Are you threatening my family, Liam? I don't think you understand who you're dealing with here." Spencer strode over to him and growled, "This is *my* family. Mine. You don't threaten us. You don't threaten our businesses. Or it's you who will regret it."

Spencer growled again, the room filling with dominance. Sometimes I forgot who and what Spencer's family was, because he was so mild-mannered and his father was a professor. Leaders. Rulers. Ruthless business executives. Rich-ass motherfuckers who *expected* to get their way and had been doing so for a *very* long time.

"You heard him." I stood, joining Spencer. "This is a private party. If you'd like to meet, please call my office tomorrow and make an appointment."

A server came by. "Is there a problem?"

"Yes, please call security, this alpha is bothering us," Grace called.

"Please, he is most unwelcome." I glared at my older brother.

"I'll see myself out." Liam scowled at me and left.

"Thank you, Spencer," I said quietly.

"Always." He clapped me on the shoulder. "One of my cousins wants to take over the State Street Project and turn it into some sort of haven for the arts. I think I should encourage her. She'd eat the Queen Mum for breakfast."

"That's a woman I want to know," Katie said.

"Me, too." Grace raised her glass.

I wasn't sure how that would be possible, but at the same time, when you were stupid-rich, most anything was.

We finished dinner, and I thanked my sister and her pack for joining us.

"Can we all meet at home for a moment? I wanted to go over some things?" I asked everyone. "Riley, you too. We can always drop you off at school in the morning."

"Can I ride with you?" Evan asked me.

"Sure." I handed him my helmet and relished his arms around me as we drove home.

When we parked in the garage, I wrapped my arms around him. "Are you okay?"

"I'm fine. Other than Sasha's being bitchy about Ri and me changing our last name. My other sister decided on a wedding date and chose a location. We'll get it reserved for her?" Evan gave me a squeeze.

"Perfect. And just ignore Sasha." I took his hand, and we walked inside.

Grace was already in the kitchen making bowls of ice cream for everyone. She turned to me. "What room?"

"The living room is fine." I looked at the bar cart, then went down to the basement where we had a small area where we stored wine and liquor. My eyes fell on the bottles of bourbon Grace had bought at the distillery in Carolina. I glanced at the case she'd made with bottles inspired by us.

I grabbed one with my name on it. I was curious as to why she chose each one for us–other than the one from the year of Riley's birth.

When I joined them with the bottle and glasses, they already had the ice cream set out on the table of the living room. I didn't have a bowl, but I didn't really like sweets much and would just share Jett's.

"Grace, is it okay if we try the bourbon that you chose for me?" I asked.

"Yes." She fed Evan a bite. She, Wes, and Evan were on the couch. Jett had claimed the loveseat. Spencer had pulled over a chair, and Riley had a beanbag.

I poured glasses of it and passed it out. It was a beautiful color, like old oak. Taking a sniff, I got oak and brown sugar. I took a small sip. Yes, I got hints of oak, brown sugar, cloves, and maybe a little apple. I took another. Oh, that was smooth.

"Impressive," I told Grace as I sat next to Jett. "How did you select each one for us?"

"She brought out the special collection. I tasted them, and sometimes they made me think of each of you and that's how I knew it was yours." Grace took a sip.

"I can't wait to be old enough to drink and have mine," Riley added.

This bourbon reminded her of me? Spicy and sweet and going down smooth? I'd take it.

"I just wanted to go over all the changes in the pack charter before it gets run through Mrs. Beekman and then submitted for final approval. I was going to do it at dinner, but, well, that was nice of the sister pack," I explained.

"It was," Wes agreed, taking a bite of ice cream.

I started going over everything.

Riley blinked. "Was this clause about me always there?"

"It's new. It was Katie's idea," I replied.

"We wanted you to feel secure in your role here as our kid, especially if Grace ever, um, something about Spencer's identical triplets?" Jett grinned at Grace.

She tossed a throw pillow at him. "No triplets."

"I mean, if you all want to be saps, I guess I can tolerate it." Riley gave me a hug.

I hugged her back. Basically, it made sure that Riley would always have the same rights and protections any other children would have. The last thing I wanted was for her to feel displaced, or to end up not being as protected as we thought if anything happened to us.

"Grace," I turned to her. "When an omega, or in your case, a gamma, is brought into a pack, they're given assets of their own. We'd like to present ours to you for your approval. Spencer, would you like to do the honors?"

Spencer looked positively giddy. "I picked out a beautiful beach cottage for you."

Cottage? He called that a *cottage?* Sure. After all, we called Evan's house a *cabin.*

Grace sucked in a breath as she looked at it. "Spence, it's beautiful. But this is... this is too much."

"Nothing is too much for you." Spencer kissed her.

"Um, do I want to know?" Jett said softly.

"It's an island. I think we should have my excellent eighteenth party there," Riley declared. "We can take out the yacht and have fireworks over the ocean."

Wes froze. "What?"

"It's lovely, Spencer. You made a good choice. I wouldn't call that a cottage, though." She kissed him again.

Spencer's phone got passed around as everyone looked at the island he'd bought her.

I looked at Grace. "Do you accept?"

"I do." She crawled into Spencer's lap.

Spencer planted a kiss on the top of her head. "I'm so happy you approve."

I looked at Wes and Spencer. "Is everything set for your business trip?"

"Yep. Again, if anything happens, we can come back really quickly." Wes nodded, finishing his bourbon.

"Grace, do you still want to attend the concert with me? It's okay if you'd rather go with them," I asked. Again.

"Like I said, I'm looking forward to it," she replied.

"Go. Jett and I are going to spend some quality time together." Evan kissed her.

They hadn't gotten much alone time lately.

"Get a room." Riley made a face.

"Oh, Spencer and I booked a date for our party, it's on the calendar. We're getting the guest list together. We're keeping it small, but we can invite whoever you'd like," Grace said. "Sister pack gets included?"

"Yes."

"I have book club tomorrow. I hope they like me more than the carnival committee." Grace made a face.

"Hiro's moms don't like anyone. Kilroy's mom adores you," Riley assured.

We finished up, and I helped clear the dishes and glasses. Grace giggled as Spencer grabbed her and led her up the backstairs.

"You okay, Wes?" I asked as he poured himself another glass of my bourbon.

He gulped the drink down. "Spencer bought her an island."

"We said that he could pick," I replied. "But yes, I wasn't expecting that. Did you see that it comes with a yacht?"

Wes sighed and went to pour himself another glass. Taking the bottle away, I substituted another. This was *my* bourbon that Grace chose for me. He had his own in the basement.

With a shrug, he filled his glass with that. "I missed that. I got a little distracted that he got her a beach compound on her own island."

"Well, I think it's more of an estate than a compound," I pointed out.

"She deserves it, it's just a little weird."

"True. Weirder than the cabin we got Evan?" I asked, curious.

He thought for a moment. "Just a little. Though it's kinda sweet that he loves her so much that he got her a fucking island."

"Yeah, it is. Not to change the subject, but is it bad that I want to see Spencer's cousin steal my mother's project and turn it into an artist's colony? Honestly, I think downtown Rockland needs one." I poured myself a glass.

"I like that idea. Hey, take care of Grace while I'm gone, okay? I feel like all this party planning is making her cranky. Does Evan really need to drag her headlong into it? Can't he wait until her party with Spencer is done?" He took a sip of his drink.

"Evan's just excited," I assured. "I'll take care of her. Do you know if she has a dress to wear? It's not just a concert. It's a fundraising gala."

Wes blinked. "She has a wardrobe full of dresses."

Thought so.

Well, Spencer wasn't the only person who knew how to buy dresses.

Chapter Seventeen

Grace

"Are you okay, Grace?" Tish, one of my coworkers who worked for Margie, asked as I refilled my coffee in the breakroom at Compass BioTek.

"Spencer and Wes left today for the symposium." The box of pastries tempted me, and I grabbed a chocolate one.

"They'll be back soon," she assured. Several people had left, including Tish's mate, who worked with Wes.

"I feel shitty. I might walk to the drugstore at lunch because I have book club tonight." It was the kind of shitty that meant it was almost PMS time. Though considering how many hormones they'd shot me up with when I was in the hospital, I'd been expecting it.

"Feel better. Let me know if you need a walk buddy." She grabbed a pastry and got a mug.

I went back to my office. Yeah, I needed to see what this world's PMS relief options were. Hopefully, it wouldn't be awful this time.

With a new job, I didn't want to call in because I was doubled over in pain, crying and throwing up because the cramps were too bad.

Though considering I hadn't had a period since I'd gotten here, it probably wouldn't be fun.

I should also see what this world's feminine hygiene product situation was, too.

For a while, I worked and texted back and forth with the fancy wedding planner. Finally, I went to the executive area on the top floor, then went into Spencer's suite of offices to find Mrs. Katsopolis.

She looked up at me from her desk. "Hi, Grace, Dear."

"Hi, Mrs. K." I waved. She always looked so polished and pulled together.

"I have those lists for you; I'll send them over. If you need any help with the invitations, let me know. I'm happy to help with anything. Making favors, setting up, whatever you need," she offered.

"Tell me little things he likes that I should make sure are included?" I pulled a chair over. We were alone on the floor, except for perhaps an assistant or two.

We went over a few things, which was helpful.

"Wait, he plays what?" I blinked. Spencer was musical? I'd have to look up and see what a bouzouki even was.

"At some point he'll probably end up playing with his cousin's band, it'll be fun," she assured.

Huh. There was so much we still didn't know about each other. But that was part of the fun. And I had Mrs. K to make sure his favorite treats were included on the dessert table—like those chocolate orange pastries he'd fed me at the science dinner.

"Did Spencer and Elaris have a party?" I finally asked softly.

She nodded. "I wasn't there, but according to his mother, who I do speak to sometimes, it was exactly what you'd think a couple of university students would have when left to their own devices."

An upscale rager? "Sounds fun."

"You're good for him." Mrs. K smiled at me. "He... he told me about you."

"I know." I bit my lower lip.

"Grace, I hope you know how much I appreciate you asking about Demitra," she added. "Also, I'm glad you're going to move forward with Elaris' research. You're going to save lives. Not just those who are illegal. If you crack the push, you're going to bring hope to so many."

"How so?" The *push* referred to the degrees between designations, and that's why the illegal street drug that made betas omegas was called *Mega-Push,* though the legal version was called something else.

Her eyes went wide. "Oh, yes. You didn't grow up with designations. Sometimes people are born with ones that just don't fit who they are, if that makes sense."

"Oh, like with gender." It made perfect sense.

"Exactly. Only you can receive gender affirming care easily. Designation affirming care, not so much." Her look saddened.

I sucked in a breath. "Because they only have something that changes betas to omegas."

"Yes, and even though there's a legal version, it's still a process to be permitted to use it–and you have to have the right genetic markers," she explained. "But there's nothing to help betas or omegas who should be alphas, or the other way around. Not to mention all the others. Like iotas actually have larger percentages of designation dysmorphia than others, not that anyone pays attention to them."

Iotas. I think they were the ones that didn't have or smell scents and pheromones and didn't respond to barks.

"I don't understand why there's so much fear surrounding the idea of giving people control over their own designation.

Shouldn't people feel comfortable in their own bodies? Also, it would be nice for people not to lose their families. My birth mother didn't know she wasn't an alpha. Most of the family was executed." I looked away. It was just so sad.

"It is. I don't remember you, but Demitra talked little about that part of her work unless she really needed my help. She was trying to protect me and the children if they ever came for her." She patted my hand.

"That makes sense. Um, I have a sister who gave me an omega lily, and she was talking about mythology. Who's the patron Greek goddess of omegas?" I suppose I could just look it up.

"Hestia, the goddess of the home. Hera, as well. Artemis, too, though she's more their protector, going after alphas who dare lay a hand on them. It would be nice to have omega lilies at your party."

Those all made perfect sense to me, especially Artemis, who I knew as a protector of women and girls.

"You know, there's a temple of Artemis that is still quite active. Many young omegas in Greece visit there. You should have Spencer take you, though he'll have to wait with the other alphas in the welcome center. They have an amazing library. I was allowed there once. Sometimes they'll permit betas to do research in their archives." Her look went wistful.

"Oh, that sounds amazing. What's your field of study?" I asked.

"I worked in the university office. It's how we met. Demitra tried to convince me to let her meet with the Dean. When the children were young, I worked for a school. When they grew up and two of them moved to this continent, it made sense to take Spencer's job offer here. I'm close enough to them to visit often but not so much that I'm the overbearing mother," she laughed. "The one back in Greece is quite content there, and I see her when I can. But I digress."

The look on her face made me think there was more to her story.

"I was trying to help one of Demitra's students before she tried something rash, like going into the forest and invoking the wrath of Artemis. It's a bit of a joke, Dear. In mythology, Artemis would sometimes turn alphas into omegas as punishment, though more often it was deer or a tree," she said.

"Oh, I see. So, you were doing research at the temple to see if there was anything you could do to help her? She was a female alpha?" I asked.

Mrs. K nodded. "Yes, one that should have been an omega. I couldn't find anything helpful. No one has anything helpful."

The pain in her voice broke my heart.

"We'll do what we can, not that it's my area of expertise," I promised.

"It's not his either, but with the support of you two, who knows what's possible? Now, I should probably get back to work. Let me know what else you need," she added, in a clear dismissal.

"Thanks, Mrs. K." I stood, my stomach aching. Yeah, I should go back to work, too.

And perhaps visit that drugstore.

Chapter Eighteen

Evan

"You're making the right decision, Rose," I assured, as we made bracelets together at a table in the rec room at the Omega Center.

"As nice as my dad's offer is to move in with him, I want to stay at Finchley for the rest of high school. I only have one year left. I'm looking forward to my visit this summer so that I can get to know them. Maybe I can be closer when I go to the university." Today, she was braiding strings with beads on them.

"Exactly. Also, you're not that far as it is. You can visit on weekends and holidays." While there wasn't an ultra-bullet to where her dad's pack lived, there was still a pretty fast regional train that would get her close.

The pack that had been after her was in jail. She was now safe. It looked like everyone would be mostly okay.

We finished our visit. I grabbed my things, signed out, and left the Center for the day. My shoulders wiggled with happiness as I drove home. Grace had her date with Brennan, and I got Jett all to myself tonight. It had been way too long since we'd had quality time in the playroom together.

Yes, I wanted to be suspended from the ceiling and smacked and railed until I was an enormous pile of omega goo. While I loved Brennan, and my time with just him–and both of them–I enjoyed being with only Jett, too.

Grace needed a little time with Brennan. Would it be too much to hope that we could all spend the night together? Last night, after her book club meeting, she'd spent all night with just me. Which was delightful, but I really did sleep better with one of my alphas.

When I got home, a mauve pickup truck, with dark green detailing, and a bow on it, sat in the driveway. It wasn't a big, rugged pickup like Wes had, but a cute little one.

Please let that be something Brennan got for Grace.

The kitchen sat empty, though some ingredients littered the counter. I went upstairs to find Jett and Brennan.

Their bedroom smelled like pine, soap, and anxiety as I discovered a mostly naked Brennan shaving in the bathroom.

"You got Grace a truck?" I laughed.

"Who do you think had the truck delivered? It was Spencer. Now what I got her isn't going to seem like anything. I mean, it's not a courting gift. Because I'm not courting her. But, ugh. Okay, I can understand why Wes was so annoyed when I got you a car." Brennan examined himself in the mirror.

Wait. What did he get her?

My car had been a piece of shit held together with twine and duct tape. Wes was annoyed because he planned on using his signing bonus with Compass BioTek to get me a new vehicle. He was just waiting for a particular one to be in stock.

"We'll be home late. There's dinner first, then the concert. Jett said that you're having some *quality alone time.*" He gave me a look as he combed his hair.

That was code for using the playroom.

"Yep. We'll probably be done by the time you get home. He can send you pictures." I waggled my eyebrows.

"I'm a little jealous, but I really want to hear Kari play. Also, it will be nice to spend time with just Grace. She's doing okay with them being gone? She was a little grumpy when I picked her up from work." Brennan left the bathroom and went into the bedroom.

I followed him. "She wanted to drive Wes' truck to and from work by herself, not to be dropped off and picked up every day."

"Well, I suppose that she can take her truck tomorrow. Where are we going to park it? The driveway until we can extend the garage?" Brennan's tux was laid out on the neatly made bed.

"I guess?" While we had an enormous garage, we also already had four cars, several motorcycles, and dirt bikes. "And yes, spend all the time with her."

"Will you go check on her?" he added, combing his hair. "We need to get going."

"Okay." With one last glance at my mostly naked mate, I went upstairs to find Grace. She was doing her makeup in my bathroom.

"Hi." She smiled as she applied lipstick. Tiny music note earrings hung in her ears.

"That dress is *stunning.*" It was a black and white dress, with a ruffle.

"Thanks. You picked well." She twirled around.

I shook my head. "Not me."

"Oh. You didn't get it and put it out for me?" Frowning, she fluffed her hair.

"Wait, come here." Pulling her to me, I checked the tag. Vecci was one of Brennan's favorite designers, and most of his suits were from there.

"My guess is that it's Brennan." Awww. Was that the gift he mentioned?

She paused. "Oh. How kind of him. Is this necklace okay? It's something Spencer gave me."

"It's perfect. You look great. Speaking of great, you have a pink truck," I teased.

Grace ducked her head. "It's so sweet. It needs stickers."

"I'm sure Riley can help you with that. Are you almost ready?" I bundled her into my arms. She didn't smell quite right.

"Yes." She sighed. "I miss them."

"They'll be back tomorrow night. Wes' panel went well," I told her.

"Spencer sent me a video. He said that his panel went well, too." Grace struck a pose.

"Perfect." Really, she looked so cute and fuckable. Was Brennan going to fuck her tonight?

Could I watch?

"Are you nervous?" I asked.

"A little."

"Don't be. He'll be sweet with you. Also, you might get some in-the-dark snuggles during the concert." Really, it wasn't that bad. We just liked to tease Brennan because the music wasn't really to our tastes.

"You'll be okay with Jett. Date night in?" Grace got her purse and her shoes.

"Yep. I'm excited for some quality alone time with him. You know, if you want them to spend the night with us, we can ask. I'd love to watch Bren and Jett make a Grace sandwich." I grinned.

"Evan." She smacked me with her purse as she went downstairs.

"You know you want to," I laughed.

Grace paused as we got to the area on the second floor with the piano.

Brennan looked ultra fuckable in a black tux with white accents that matched her dress. A box with a bow sat on the piano.

Oh. That was the present.

"You look amazing." His eyes were on her.

Jett joined us, in only shorts.

"You too." She tugged on his white tie, straightening it. "Did you get me this dress? Thank you. I appreciate it."

"If you ever don't like my suggestions, it's okay. I know you're not used to all this, so I was just trying to be helpful. Also, apologies for going into your room without permission." His look went bashful.

"I don't mind. No really, thank you."

Jett chuckled. "I almost want to tag along just to watch those two act like they're at a school dance. Almost."

She pulled Brennan down and kissed him on the cheek.

"Oh, I got you something." He handed her the gift.

She unwrapped it and sucked in a breath. "You really got me the Theodosia doll?"

The doll wore a stunning dress straight out of the Golden France era. Oh wow.

He beamed. "I found one with a working piano. It doesn't have a box. But it's new. It was a store display." Reaching out, he tapped one key of the doll's ornate grand piano.

I put a hand to my face. "Jett, can you imagine when the triplets come?"

"We're so fucked," Jett whispered, grinning.

"I love her." She clutched the doll to her chest, sheer joy on her face.

"We're going to make you a creepy doll room. Wes and I figured it could also double as a guest room for people we don't want to stay for long." Brennan chuckled. "I'm happy you like her."

Gently, he set the tiny piano and the doll *on his piano.*

"She is. I love her little piano." Grace touched one of the tiny keys and it plinked a little note.

He offered her his arm. "We should get going."

"Bye." Grace kissed me, then hugged Jett.

They went down the stairs.

"Is he taking her on his motorcycle?" I asked. Usually, Jett drove us in his sports car, because Brennan was okay with the top down. When it was snowing, we could make my 4x4 work.

"In that dress? No, he's going to take my car."

We went downstairs, and I helped him chop up the ingredients for dinner.

"Are you okay with whatever this is between them? He says they're not courting. Which I believe, because he'd talk to us first before courting her. But clearly his inner alpha has other ideas." Jett grated some ginger into the sauce he was making.

"I'm here for it. Also, I think we should all sleep together tonight, even if we actually just sleep. Do you think we could do that?" I glanced over at him as I chopped vegetables.

"I don't have a problem with that. You know I like her. When I was getting some new things for tonight, I found some rope in a really pretty color that she'd like. Maybe one day she'll let me use it on her. I know it'll be a process for her. If she never gets there, it's fine. I just want to be prepared if she ever wants to try." He crushed up some garlic and added it.

Leaning in, I kissed him. "Thank you. You got things for me?"

Could we skip dinner and go right to it?

"Of course I did." Jett kissed me back.

Yeah, they could have their concert. I couldn't wait.

Chapter Nineteen

Grace

I rubbed my stomach. It hadn't been bad yet, but it was coming. I could feel it.

"Are you okay?" Brennan had been very quiet as we drove to the Performing Arts Center in Jett's convertible, top down, the radio playing.

It was probably because he didn't like driving cars. I offered to drive, but he insisted.

"TMI, but I think I'm getting my period soon. In the couple of days before, I'm often not just cranky, but sick. So, if I'm crying and throwing up, just get me a heating pad and tell me I'm pretty." I shrugged. The drug store had given me a few ideas–as had the omegas at book club last night. Kilroy's mom's friends had all been really nice. I was looking forward to the next one.

"Normal bodily functions aren't TMI. Also, that doesn't sound right. Have you talked to the doctor?" He frowned.

"They did some tests, but since I haven't had one lately, they said they'd wait and see how this one is. You know, every gamma is different and all that."

His look grew skeptical.

"It's not always bad. I hope it's not this time. I just started this job. It's always hard to explain to bosses when I need time off." I sighed.

"Why? That's what health days are for, and they shouldn't be asking you for specifics. Are your cycles more like alpha lady cycles than omega lady cycles? Like your uterus punishes you for not letting a sexy male omega put a baby in you?" he asked. "That's how my sister describes it. She takes something for it that she buys at the store. Well, she doesn't have to now because she let a male omega put a baby in her. But I can ask her what she takes."

I laughed. "Sounds about right. Yeah, though the punishing is mostly pre-bleeding for me."

Brennan frowned. "They just told you to wait and see? That doesn't sound right at all."

"It might be different now that I'm with alphas–and Evan. Apparently, omegas can influence gamma hormones, in a good way." If taking Evan to bed with me made my cramps disappear, count me in.

"Okay. Well, if we need to leave, let me know." His brow remained furrowed.

"I took something, I'm just waiting for it to kick in." Which hopefully would be soon. I wanted to enjoy myself tonight.

"Have they always been that way?" He frowned.

"Yeah. I mean, I didn't start having cycles until well into college. I'd already been a bit of a late bloomer, probably because of cheer. And well, apparently everything they did to me at wilderness camp probably disrupted them. It was part of why I was always brushed off. That, and they're irregular as fuck. The doctors just kept changing my birth control and told me they'd probably get better. But that hasn't happened. If someone here can figure them out, I'd like that a lot." I shrugged.

"Maybe you should see a different doctor?" he suggested.

"Maybe?"

We arrived at the Performing Arts Center, which was visually stunning. After valet parking the car, Brennan escorted me in, offering me his arm again.

Like the other dinners I'd been to with them, everyone was done up impeccably. It was fun to see everyone's beautiful outfits.

A cocktail reception was set up in the lobby. Music played as people drank and talked. Servers passed around trays of food.

"I don't really want to talk to people, if that's okay," he whispered, as we went straight to the bar.

"That's fine with me. Did you buy us an entire table, but it's only us, so we don't have to make conversation?"

"No. We're part of someone else's table, though I made a nice donation. But that's a brilliant idea though." He ordered a bourbon. I got a whisky smash.

Instead of mingling, Brennan showed me around the center, pointing out works of art and the architecture.

"You'll love the acoustics in the hall, they're spectacular," he added.

We returned to the reception.

"Oh fuck. I think that's Caroline and her pack," he muttered, pulling us behind a plant. "Makes sense. Her mom always buys a table for things like this."

"We just won't engage and hope she doesn't see us." Great.

"Bren, why are you hiding behind a plant?" A pretty Asian woman in a black dress grinned. She was probably Brennan's age and might be an omega.

"Because they frown upon throwing people in the fountain." He turned toward me. "Grace, this is Kari Jaroff. She's performing tonight. We used to compete against each other in piano competitions. Kari, this is my packmate, Grace. She needs to learn how to play Volkov properly."

Kari laughed. "You are so particular."

"He is." I giggled. "It's so nice to meet you."

"There you are. They're letting us in for dinner." A large man in a tux wrapped his arms around her. "Hi, Bren."

"Hi Sam. Sam and I played in a rugby travel league together as kids. This is Grace," Brennan introduced. "So, Kari became a famous pianist, Sam plays pro rugby, and me..."

Sam laughed. "Became a hotel mogul, is happily mated, and in a pack with Spencer Thanukos? I will punch anyone who says you're a slacker."

"Is my mother here?" He looked around.

I couldn't help but laugh. Oh, I loved playful Bren. That seemed like an old joke.

Kari laughed. "You're at our table, so you'll be fine. You'll just have to put up with my mom telling you how much more accomplished I'd be if I gave her grandchildren."

"Always with the grandchildren. Thanks for inviting us," Brennan added.

We went inside the room where dinner was being served. The decorations were impeccable.

"Three o'clock," I whispered, holding onto his arm as we followed Sam and Kari to our table.

I held my breath, and we walked past the table. Nothing happened. But it was hard to relax.

Dinner was fun, and not nearly as long as the other dinners, since here the main program was a concert. There were just a couple of speeches about the education programs for young musicians that the fundraiser supported–including ones from the kids. More music played as we ate.

Kari's pack, her parents and their pack, were really sweet.

"I'm glad you're doing Volkov, and not strange pieces like the one you did in Boston with the bubble machine," her mother said.

"That one was a little experimental," Kari explained.

Sam thought for a moment. "I liked the bubble machine."

Finally, Kari stood. "I have to go. See you out there."

Sam helped her up and offered her his arm. He and one of her other packmates went with her, probably so she could prepare for her performance.

The rest of us finished dinner, and then we were invited into the auditorium.

"The music program here launched Kari's career. Once, she was one of those young musicians getting free lessons, now she tours the world," Brennan whispered. "She was always very kind to everyone. She also kicked my ass at competitions. I set her and Sam up. Her mom didn't want her to date, so I manufactured reasons for them to get together. We had a lot of classical music appreciation parties and study sessions at my house that year. Wes knows them, too."

Brennan led me to a small private box with a magnificent view of her and the piano. He waved at Sam, who was right in the front. He waved back.

"This is beautiful." I looked around at all the seats, boxes, and the stage.

I checked my phone. Wes sent me a silly picture of him and Spencer at the dinner. I sent him one of Brennan and me.

Evan hadn't texted lately, but he and Jett were probably occupied. Actually, from what I felt through the bond, they might be getting ready to get *busy*.

I looked at the program, which listed what Volkov pieces that she was playing tonight. It wasn't a long concert, but I was really looking forward to it, especially since I knew some of the pieces.

She opened with my favorite–the one Brennan said I always played too fast.

He shot me a smug look, but I was focused more on her playing, which was mesmerizing. Oh yes, it did flow better the way she played it.

Kari's style was also completely different from Brennan's. Something about her interpretation made it almost... magical.

Brennan draped an arm over my shoulder. His pine scent wrapped around me. Oh. Was this a date?

Would I be sad if it were? No. Not at all.

"Yeah, she's good," he whispered.

"She really is." I'd heard a lot of pianists over the years, and she was extraordinary. I could imagine Brennan sitting in the audience, listening to her play as he waited his turn.

Had my mother's playing been like that? While I saw that there were a couple of recordings of her playing online, I hadn't brought myself to listen to them. I sniffed a little.

Kari played a few pieces, and I felt a little shot of pain through the bond. What? I reached out to everyone and got love back.

They didn't stop. My belly twisted. Something was very wrong. Brennan also didn't seem bothered. Huh. Even though you shouldn't text in a theatre, I tried to surreptitiously text everyone.

Me

Are you two okay?

Wes

I'm good. Did you know that Spencer will do karaoke for charity?

A photo followed.

I also tried Evan and Jett.

No answer. Those bits of pain, and my worry that something was wrong, continued. Bren frowned at me, and I tucked my phone away.

Brennan pulled me to him, rubbing the back of my neck.

Spencer and Wes were fine. Yes, I was definitely getting this through Evan. I sucked in a breath.

"Grace?" Brennan looked at me with concern as I tried to stand.

"Something's wrong with Evan. I can't get a hold of him. Something's hurting him. We should go, can't you feel it?" I whispered, my eyes pleading with him.

Panic rose inside me. I got it again, and this one made my eyes tear. My chest heaved as I grabbed my purse.

"Fuck." Brennan tried to pull me down. "Breathe, Grace."

Tears streamed down my face, and I struggled. "We need to save him, something's wrong."

Someone below us looked up.

"He's not being harmed, they're just fucking idiots," he whispered. "Shhh. Come on."

Brennan stood, arm around me and took me out of our little box into the hall.

Good. We needed to get to them.

"Relax, Little Butterfly." His body squashed me against the wall, as pine surrounded me.

Why weren't we going to the car?

"We need to save him." My fists pummeled against his chest. "Why aren't we calling the police? They can get there faster. Did someone break in? Why are you just standing there?"

"No one's being harmed or injured. They're completely fine and really enjoying themselves. Can you feel that part?" His voice was quiet as he let me hit him, not trying to grab my wrists.

I jumped a little as I felt it again, making me panic as I went to worst case scenarios. "What?"

"Do you know how to tamp down the bonds? I need you to breathe with me, okay? They're *fine.*" He leaned forward, increasing the pressure on my body.

"No, we need to save them," I sobbed, trying to wiggle out from between him and the wall.

"Trust me. Now tamp down your bonds with Evan. You don't need to shut them off, but let's turn them *way* down." He walked me through it, still keeping me squished between him and the wall.

I had no choice but to listen. But... but we needed to get them. *Deep breath. 3.1415926535.* I took another. *8979323846.* And another. *2643383279.*

As I breathed with him, following his directions. The pain lessened, but I still felt some pleasure... and happiness?

What? Was he okay?

"Better." Brennan purred for me. It was the quietest purr I ever heard.

"I'm so confused." I felt weird and buried my face in his chest.

"I'm sure you are. And I'm pissed. Not at you. No. Not one bit. But they're in fucking trouble." His head tipped down to mine. "Yeah, so sometimes some people might like a little pain with their sex. Evan's one of them. Jett *isn't* harming or injuring him. Everything is talked about beforehand, usually in great detail. There are safe words and limits. It's all completely consensual, and *no one is being harmed.* They're being a little rougher than usual, but Evan probably needed it. I can explain everything better later. But let me reiterate that everything in our house is done with love, care, and consent. It might hurt, but it doesn't harm or injure. No one's going to be left with permanent marks, I promise," he assured.

Oh. I suppose there was a difference between hurt, harm, and injure, but a lot of times it all blurred together for me.

His quiet purr calmed me as I mulled everything over. Evan had some bedroom interests that differed from mine. Really, I couldn't see Jett actually harming him.

"It... it took me by surprise. I know about the ropes, but I didn't understand what else was part of it." I was still trying to slow down my panic. *They're not in danger. They're safe.*

He kissed the top of my head. "Take a few deep breaths. They're fine and having a shit-ton of fun. Try to find that in the bond instead, okay?"

I sent some love through the bond and got love back. He was okay.

Brennan continued to hold me. "However, we also *warn* people that we have bonds with. I knew what they were doing, Wes knew what they're doing. Clearly, you didn't. Evan should have explained it to you."

I frowned. "I mean, he said something about *alone time,* and I figured they'd fuck, I just was surprised at *this.*"

"Shit. *Quality alone time* is code. But he should have explained it—and taken more care with you. It's not okay to give your partner a panic attack because they think you're being harmed. I'm sorry that they were idiots. It's not okay in our house, and I'll have words with them." His arms wrapped around me, pulling me to him.

"Oh, I don't want them to be punished." I started to cry again.

"Okay, okay," he soothed, pushing me back against the wall with his body. "I'll *just* talk to them, okay. But consent works all ways, and while you might be fine with feeling the average fuck, even during a meeting, *you* didn't consent to getting all that with no warning in the middle of a concert."

"Oh. I never thought of it that way. Now I'm all embarrassed for freaking out during the concert." My face burned. People probably saw.

I sort of enjoyed being squished like this. It was like a vertical man-blanket.

"Don't be." He kissed my head. "Would you like to leave, or do you want to stay and finish the concert? There's only a little left, but either is fine."

Wes and Spencer sent me some concern through the bond, and I sent reassurance back.

"I think I'd like to stay for the rest of the concert." I sniffed again.

He took his pocket square and wiped my face. "The last song is the one I really want you to hear."

"Thank you. For explaining, for not judging, I..."

Brennan's thumb traced my cheekbone. "I get it. Believe me. Now, let's go hear the rest of the concert, okay?"

He offered me his arm, and I took it. It wasn't just his arm I was taking. It was the trust and reassurance that it offered. While maybe Brennan would never be my mate, and I was okay with that, I really wanted, no, needed, him in my life.

Chapter Twenty

Brennan

"Did you like it?" I put my arm around her as I led her out of the box. As usual, Kari had given a spectacular performance.

"Very much. I need to learn that last piece. I've never heard it before." Grace tucked herself into my side.

She still smelled of salty, worried peaches, and had spent the rest of the concert half in my lap.

Which I didn't mind at all. Disruptions aside, our night had been nice. Yes, I think I'd be bringing her to more concerts. If I didn't have to go to so many silly dinners, I'd have more time to support the arts.

"It's a more obscure piece. Well, it was before she made it popular. I first heard it here. From her. We didn't know her and were all like *Who the fuck is she and what is she wearing?* We were such judgmental fuckers. You know what? She won. And now, we all know that she's Kari Fucking Jaroff." I grinned at Grace. I loved the piano. In another life, I'd play professionally.

Did I sometimes wonder what it would be like to play in some of the places Kari did? Yes. But I also loved my life.

Hmmm. Maybe one day Spencer would buy me an opportunity to play at an enormous concert hall for my birthday.

"I love that for her." Grace clutched my arm.

We went backstage.

"Well done, Kari, I think Grace gets it now." I kissed the top of her head.

Grace laughed. "I do. Your playing is magical. And that piano is *beautiful.*"

"Thank you." Kari grinned from her place in Sam's arms. "Do you want to see it?"

Kari dragged Grace off to go see the famous, expensive piano that had been brought in especially for her to play tonight.

"New mate?" Sam asked as we moved to the wings so we could monitor them.

"Packmate. She's Wes' and Spencer's, well, and Evan's. She at least appreciates classical music, and now I have someone to come with me." Honestly, Spencer would, and did accompany me to things, though he preferred the theatre.

Sam laughed. "She's yours, you just don't know it yet."

"Maybe." I didn't deny it, because he was right.

They sat down, and when Grace started playing her too fast Volkov, Kari stopped her and coached her.

A few people watched. But no one was going to tell Kari Jaroff that she couldn't give an impromptu lesson.

"What are you doing, you can't just play this piano?" a shrill, and familiar, voice came from in front of the stage.

Sam and I rushed over to them.

"They can if they want. Really, Caroline, haven't you done enough?" I frowned at her. My ex was a lot more pregnant than last time.

One of her mates came over to Caroline. "That's the pianist from the concert. I'm sure no one cares."

"But *she's* not. She's just some little nobody that stole–"

"I stole no one, Caroline," Grace snapped. "Keep your eyes on your own paper. Your life is pretty good, you know."

"Come on." The alpha started to hustle Caroline off. He turned and stared at Grace. "I was unaware that *you'd* be here."

"Sorry. Should I have our assistants coordinate next time?" Grace retorted, one hand wrapping around her stomach like it was hurting her again.

I put my arms around Grace. "Grace can go where she likes."

Kari laughed. "Still a bitch, I see, Caroline?"

"Don't talk to my mate like that," the alpha snapped.

"Don't talk to *my* mate like that," Sam snapped back.

Grace looked at her dead-on. "Just don't talk, Caroline."

"Ugh." Caroline made a face and allowed her pack to lead her away.

"I'm so glad that you didn't end up with that viper," Sam said. His arm snaked around Kari's waist. "We have a donor reception to go to. Are you coming to that, Bren?"

"We're going to head home, but thank you," I replied.

"Thanks, Kari." Grace hugged her.

Kari wasn't around a lot, but they'd be good friends, I was sure.

I took her arm. "Come on, Grace. Let's go check on our boys."

Because she wasn't going to rest until she knew that they were okay.

Chapter Twenty-One

Jett

"A re you sure you're okay, Baby? That was intense," I asked Evan as we cuddled in the bed we had in the playroom.

When we moved here after Caroline, we'd had the room custom built. Sometimes I missed the one in the basement of our old place.

Brennan enjoyed having it here in our suite to ensure that no one could get in but us.

"For the millionth time, I'm beyond good, Hot Stuff," Evan sighed. "That was so much fun."

"It was. Drink some water." I rubbed his arms and legs as he finished his water, contentment flowing through the bond.

Yeah, we both needed that.

We cuddled a bit longer, and I looked at the clock above the door. I had no idea what time they were coming back. Brennan felt a little annoyed. Maybe the Queen Mum was there? His family sometimes went to these things.

Well, I'd comfort him later. Right now, caring for Evan was my focus.

"How about a shower? Go turn on the water, and I'll clean up? Then maybe we can watch a movie and have some hot chocolate?" I asked him.

"That sounds perfect." Evan kissed me.

I quickly cleaned everything up and set Mr. Mopps, our little mop robot, to work. Later, I'd come back and finish. Grabbing my phone, I looked at the photos I'd taken. Really, it was a work of art—he was a work of art.

A text from Grace asking if we were okay made me frown. I'd text her later. I could feel her a little through Evan's bond, and right now, it seemed like she didn't feel good.

Locking the playroom door, which led directly into our bedroom, I went into our bathroom.

Closing the door behind me, I joined Evan in the hot shower. My arms wrapped around him. For a long time, I just stood there, holding him under the sprays, letting him know how much I loved him—and feeling his love for me through the bond.

Never, ever did he—or Brennan—make me feel like I, or our love, was lesser because I was a beta. I didn't feel like I was missing anything because I couldn't bond them back. Really, I didn't understand why that was even a thing people worried about. I could feel them, and they could feel me, just fine.

Gently, I washed Evan. The redness had faded, and there were no bruises, but that didn't mean he wouldn't be a little tender. I had some cream I'd use after our shower to make him feel better.

"Do you really think Bren will let Grace stay with us tonight? I'd like to be with you two tonight, but I don't want her to sleep alone." Grabbing the shower gel, Evan washed me.

"I can always stay with you two, and let Bren sleep alone for once, considering he always complains that I hog the bed." I laughed. "But I don't know what his plans are tonight. This feels like a date. He might want her all to himself."

I mean, I would.

"No fair. I wanna see." Evan pouted.

A powerful wave of irritation came through the bond from Brennan.

"Someone pissed in Bren's bourbon," Evan muttered.

"He probably ran into the Queen Mum at the concert." I continued to hold Evan.

"I hope Grace punched someone in the tits." He pressed his head to mine.

The bathroom door flew open as the scent of annoyed pine hit me. Brennan marched in, holding Grace in his arms, both fully dressed. Grace even still had her high heels on.

"See, they're fine," Brennan told her gently as he opened the clear glass door of the shower. "Look." His gaze shifted to us, blue eyes filled with irritation. "Evan, come here and turn around so that she can see all of you."

What the what? I didn't care if Grace saw me naked–it was what was happening.

What *was* happening?

"Yeah, okay?" Confused, Evan came to the edge of the giant shower and spun around in front of the open door.

"See. He's just fine." Brennan continued to hold her. "Do you need to touch him?"

Grace nodded and reached out and patted Evan's ass, her hand trailed up his back, getting a little wet from the spray.

"Evan, are you okay?" She bit her lower lip.

"Yeah, I'm delightful." He leaned in and gave her a wet kiss. "The concert was nice? I've heard Kari play before. She's good."

"It was. After I even got to play a little with Kari, until fucking Caroline showed up. Don't worry, I didn't punch anyone in the tits. Um, Jett, are you okay?" She peered around Evan.

Brennan made the *spin around* sign with his hand. I turned around.

"Can I touch?" Her voice grew small.

"You can touch my ass anytime, Babydoll." I got close to her.

Her manicured hand patted it, and her hand moved up my back, her fingers tracing my tattoos. She looked to Brennan. "You were right. They're okay. Sorry. I..."

"*Don't* apologize. You didn't know, and you were worried." He shot us another irritated look.

Her text. *Is everything okay?* Oh fuck.

"Come on, Grace. We'll let them finish up. I'll talk to them later." He carried her out of the bathroom.

Evan closed the shower door and blinked. "Why do I feel like I'm in trouble?"

"Did you tell Grace about tonight?" I held him, feeling his confusion through the bond.

"Yep, I told her that we were having *quality alone time.* Oh, I didn't tamp down the bonds. Wes doesn't care; and well, I'm still getting used to her and how the bond is different with her. Shit." His look became stricken.

"Did you explain to her what *quality alone time* means?" I gave him a squeeze. It was an honest mistake. But I also understood Brennan's annoyance.

Did she freak out at the concert?

"Oh. *Fuck.* She kept reaching out to me through the bond, so I thought nothing of it." Evan frowned, scent souring. "Shit. I... I fucked up."

"It's okay—and she'll be okay. Why don't we make her some hot chocolate, too, and she can watch the movie with us? Bren carrying her around like a stuffed animal probably means that she needs some extra reassurance." I brought Evan to me and gave him a squeeze.

Part of this was on me, I should have double checked.

Evan nodded. "Yeah, that's a good idea. But what about Bren? He seemed pissed."

I patted his shoulder. "Bren won't stay pissed at you for long. Let's rinse off, and you can go tell her that you're sorry."

Chapter Twenty-Two

Brennan

I held Grace in my arms as I carried her out of the bathroom. She'd panicked again in the car. We had the little touch tank session in order to reassure her that they were fine. While now she was a little damp, I think it did the trick.

"Your bedroom is smaller than the other bedrooms in the house." She looked around our bedroom.

"Yes. We had the suite gutted and rebuilt, and the other rooms were made smaller to make allowances for the third room in our suite." We'd also had Evan's room gutted and rebuilt, only they'd taken out the third room to add in his nest and expand the bathroom and closet.

Shifting her weight, I unlocked the playroom door.

"Secret room?" She eyed the numerical lock.

"No. The lock is for safety and privacy, not because it's secret. Grace, you *never* have to participate in anything that you don't want to in this house. But I don't want you to be afraid of what happens. Questions are always welcome. This is our playroom. No one comes in here without me or Jett. That's for safety reasons." I kissed her forehead and brought her inside and turned on some lights and the air filter.

"Okay." She looked around the room.

It smelled of Jett, Evan, lemon cleaner, sex, and desire. The walls were dark grey, with burgundy accents. We had both overhead lighting and recessed mood lighting that could change colors. That was all Jett. The floor was dark grey tile, and I heard Mr. Mopps running. I left the door cracked open.

"That's what Jett attaches the ropes to when he suspends someone." I pointed to the rigging on the ceiling. "It can hold the weight of two Evans. Though there are other places to attach ropes to." I showed her rings on the wall, then we went over to the bed, which was made haphazardly.

Carefully, I watched her for any indication that our tour wasn't okay. But she seemed curious, and I got no apprehension in her scent.

I sat her on the bed, hoping that their scents would calm her. "It's just a bed, Grace. There are surprises, like the rings in the headboard." Looping my finger around one, I showed her. "But they don't need to be used. Lots of cuddling happens here."

"Is that Evan?" She looked up at the black-and-white photograph on the wall above the bed.

"It is." It was one of Jett's more artistic ties that we'd had professionally photographed.

"Safe words still work here. Anyone can stop it at any time?"

"Yes. Also, we usually talk things out pretty clearly beforehand. Think of it like sheet music. We try to follow the music. Sure, improvisation happens sometimes, but there's always checking in. A lot of times a variation happens because of a check in—something's not working so we try something else. This is a spanking bench, but it's also good just for sex, and takes the pressure off things, like when Evan broke his wrist."

I brought her over to the spanking bench. Should I set her on it?

Her arms wrapped around my neck. "Oh. That makes sense."

That would be a *no*.

"When Jett first asked to tie me up, I was literally like, *What the fuck?* But we talked it through, and I tried it. Turns out, it was freeing for me. It won't be the same for everyone, and that's okay. If I didn't like it, Jett would never push me. No one will push you either. All that we ask is that you don't shame anyone for liking something that you don't. Not that you would."

"I understand that." She nodded.

"The same goes for you. Say, you're really into banging in your doll room, so the dolls all watch you, but Wes isn't. I'll make sure he doesn't make you feel bad about it." I grinned at her.

Grace laughed, body relaxing. "Thank you. I'm not sure that's on my list of things to try, but I appreciate it."

"It's all right if you never get to the point where you want to try anything here. It's also fine if you do. Or if you want a demonstration. If we try at some point and you change your mind in the middle, that's also perfectly okay. I just don't want you to be *afraid*." I carried her over to the wall where we had a small collection of floggers, paddles, and whips. We didn't have anything like what was probably used on her at that awful place.

"Oh." Her lower lip quivered.

"Jett and I know how to use them safely. Do you want to touch anything?" I brought her closer.

We also had a cabinet full of other things, including all of Jett's rigging gear, restraints, and plenty of toys.

"That one looks like a riding crop." She eyed a red one.

"I like that one. At some point, if you want to try using one on me, we can do that. I'd want Jett in here for safety, so that he can show you how to use it. In order to not harm or injure someone, everything needs to be done correctly, okay?" Shifting her weight to my hip, I smoothed her hair.

Grace looked up at me and blinked. "You'd let me use them on you?"

"Yes. I feel as if you'd understand better if it were me." Why did I even say that? It sounded so silly.

But it was true.

"Thank you. I appreciate you taking the time to show me everything so that I'm not scared. You're such a good boy." She gazed at me like I hung the moon.

What did I do to deserve that look?

"Only for you and sometimes Jett." I kissed her. Okay, I'd occasionally be her good boy.

"Are you two in here? Can I come in?" Jett asked from the doorway.

I looked at her. "Is that okay?"

She nodded.

"You can join us." I turned back to the wall.

Jett came in and stood next to us, in only shorts. "Grace is getting a tour?"

"Yes. I don't want her to be scared."

"Good idea." He cupped her face with his hands. "Hey, Babydoll. Everything here is done with love. I'll show you whatever you want. Now, this..." He picked up the purple cat-o'-nine-tails. "This is one of Evan's favorites."

Chapter Twenty-Three

Evan

Shit. I still couldn't believe that I fucked up like that. Seeing the way that she looked at me as she patted my ass hurt my heart.

Where'd Jett go? He wasn't downstairs in the kitchen, or the living room. I went back into their rooms. The playroom door was open, and I heard voices.

"This is one of Evan's favorites," Jett said.

I peaked in as he flicked the cat-o'-nine-tails in the air. Yeah, that one was nice.

Putting that one away, Jett picked up the red flogger. "This one's always fun. So is this one." He held a table tennis paddle in his other hand.

Brennan still held Grace tight in his arms.

Oh. Wow. He brought her in here? We'd been together for a while before he'd brought me into the playroom that he and Jett had at our old place.

"Are we having show and tell? If we're doing a demonstration, I volunteer." I came in, wearing only my briefs.

Brennan gave me a sharp look. Right.

"Peaches, I'm so fucking sorry that I didn't explain our plans to you." I wrapped my arms around both of them.

"She panicked, both at the concert and in the car. Grace was worried that someone had broken in and was hurting you. You scared her." Brennan didn't yell.

No, his voice was quiet and even. Scary stuff there.

"I'm also sorry for not checking to make sure that Evan had explained everything," Jett added as he hung them back up. "That's on me, too." Leaning in, he kissed her on the forehead.

"Thanks. I... I was scared." Her eyes teared.

"Oh, Peaches." I wrested her out of his arms, needing my mate close. "I'm sorry."

"Please be more careful next time. She didn't consent to feeling that during the concert. However, she's specifically asked that no one be punished. So just *please* remember," Brennan reminded.

"We'll make it up to you," I promised. Ugh. I felt *awful*.

"How about when we finish up here, I'll make us all some hot chocolate, and we can watch a movie?" Jett suggested. "I've shown you my ropes before. Do you want to see anything in particular first?"

Sure, we talked about hot chocolate. But now I was thinking more about taking her to bed and sandwiching her between me and Jett...

My eyes fell on the swing that hung in the far corner.

"Peaches, did they show you this?" I carried her over to it. This wasn't some flimsy door version. This was heavy-duty and hung from the ceiling. We didn't use it that much. But it was fun. They already had it when we started courting.

"There's no wrist or ankle straps, just places to hang on to. See." I put her in it, fancy dress, shoes, and all, showing her how to adjust everything.

"What?" She laughed as I tugged on a strap and got her at a very nice height for us to all take her.

"I've told you all my fantasies. If I stand here, and they stand there," I indicated the places next to me, "we could all have you at the same time. Bren and I could have your pussy, and Jett could have your ass. Or we could each have a hole. Or we could all be in your pussy. What do you think?" I grinned as I spread her legs as far as the dress let me.

"Hey, you're going to rip her dress. At least take her shoes off. May I?" Brennan asked, putting a hand on her ankle.

Grace nodded. Gently, almost sensually, he took her heels off and put them on top of the bench next to the mini fridge.

"It could be fun, Peaches. There are so many ways we could use this." Jett pulled something, making her legs go up.

She squealed deliciously. "Jett."

"If you want them to stop, tell them to stop," Brennan told her.

"I'm okay. This is fun, and well, I have heard Evan's fantasy about this a time or two." Grace smiled. She then looked at everyone. "But if this isn't okay, you don't have to stay. The safe word is *trampoline,* and anyone can use it."

Usually, I used traffic lights when I was with them. Green was *go,* red was *stop,* yellow was *check in*. But this worked.

My dick hardened in my pants. "Jett and I will absolutely make it up to you by showing you a good time in the swing. It doesn't have to go the way I told you. We can do whatever you want."

Sweet desire greeted me.

"Do you want us to close the door and take off that dress?" Jett ran a hand down her arm. "Or we can watch a movie. Your choice."

"Remember what I said, Grace. You don't have to do anything that you don't want to do. They'll understand and respect that. You can also try it if you want to–and stop in the middle if you don't enjoy it." Brennan positioned himself behind her upper body, which was tipped up so that she could see us.

"I..." Grace licked her lips, her arousal hitting me hard. It was strong, too, like when we'd taken her to my cabin for her birthday.

The room filled with Jett's amber, Brennan's pine, and my lemonade, mixing with her peaches, in a luscious cocktail of desire. I got all of their desires through the bond.

Even Brennan's. Especially Brennan's.

I knew it. It wasn't just lust, either.

"I..." Her head tipped back, and she looked up at Bren, as I got a huge shot of need and want with a bit of apprehension through the bond. "I want to try."

Oh, she didn't have to say that twice.

Chapter Twenty-Four

Grace

"I want to try." I trusted them. Loved them. And I could stop them at any time. Ever since Evan told me about this fantasy of his, I'd been so curious.

Brennan nodded to Jett. He also did something on his phone and put it by my shoes.

Jett closed the door. He tapped on the wall panel, and the lighting got softer, and some peach lights came on as well, making the room feel cozy.

"How do you want this to go? Evan has so many variations. Including some that he hasn't told you," Jett asked me.

I thought for a moment as Brennan did something else on the console and the little floor mopping robot scooted over to its base.

"Only dicks. No toys or restraints or blindfolds or anything. Just what the good lord gave you, and this swing, and I want you all as naked as the baby Jesus. All three of you." I needed to say it, because I'd heard too many stories in college from other girls who let their partners take control and they just did whatever they felt like, including things she said not to.

Not that I expected them to. But I had to speak it out loud.

"I mean, if you're okay with that. No one needs to participate. I want everyone who remains to be naked, but no one has to stay." I bit my lower lip. I wanted Brennan to stay, but I didn't want him to feel like he had to.

"Dicks only. No clothes. Got it." Brennan took off his jacket.

"I'll get naked for you, Babydoll." Jett stripped off his shorts, his single dick piercing winking at me from the tip.

"I enjoy seeing everyone in this room naked. Fortunately, your good lord was very generous to me." Evan, now naked, cupped his erect cock for me to see.

"That he was." I giggled.

"What are your limits and expectations," Jett asked, as he helped me out of the swing into a standing position.

"Orgasms," I blurted.

"Okay." Jett stood in front of me, completely naked.

I realized that his dark hair was down completely, something I rarely saw.

His brown eyes met mine, and I sucked in a sharp breath. Silently, he reached behind me and unzipped my dress; it slid to the ground. But I kept looking into those eyes. Those beautiful, brown eyes.

Jett's hand slid up my back and unhooked my black bra. Fuck, that was sexy.

He twirled it around his fingers and handed it to Brennan.

Jett got down on his knees while maintaining eye contact and slid my panties down my legs. "Well, Bren, she said that if we were lucky, one day we might see her in a thong."

Oh. I had said that.

As I stepped out of them, and the dress, Brennan picked them up and put them on the bench. He was now completely naked.

I eyed Brennan's ladder piercing. Yeah, I'd let him put that inside me. Just the thought made me gush. I always got really horny before my period. Nothing like puking from cramps while yearning to get railed.

"What else? Oral? How many dicks do you want and where? If you have any preferences, tell me." Jett took off my necklace and handed it to Brennan.

"Yes, to oral. Maybe we just make a sandwich to start and go from there? Um, I don't mind if someone fucks someone into me, either. And um," what was I forgetting? Oh. "Anyone can come whenever they want."

Yeah, that sounded good. I wouldn't mind two dicks inside my vagina at once again, that had felt good. Three... not sure I was ready for that. That was a whole lot of dicks.

Evan kissed me and looked at Jett. "Grace doesn't like mean words, being hurt, or anything rough. She likes it when you eat her pussy first."

"Okay. Does anyone have anything else to add?" Jett looked around.

"Here, Dear." Brennan came up behind him with a hair tie and pulled Jett's hair back. It was such a cute, tender little moment between them.

"Thanks, Honey." Jett nodded. "We'll just keep communicating. Go *slow*, she's not used to us."

Jett shot Evan a look. Evan smirked, picked me up, and put me back in the swing, making me squeal.

Brennan immediately helped me get into the swing. "We use *yellow* when we need to slow down or check in or pause. Just in case. Also, *please* talk to us."

He stroked my hair. *Good boy.* Ever since Evan had told me that I'd called Brennan that back in the hospital, I couldn't get it out of my head. I think some extra praise would be good for him.

Evan positioned me, opening my legs wide. Immediately, he was down on his knees, licking me. A happy shudder coursed through me as his tongue caressed me.

"Oooh, you taste so good." Evan looked up, face glistening.

And you look good on your knees.

"Yeah, Baby? I want to try." Jett joined him, and his mouth glided over me. "Delicious. I love how you're so wet for us. Such a good girl."

I gasped as he nibbled on me.

Brennan didn't move, he just continued to play with my hair, which was comforting. The other two took turns teasing me with their tongues.

Happiness shuddered through me. "Mmmm, so good."

Jett went over to a cabinet and came back with a bottle and a container of wipes. "I'm going to get your sweet little ass ready for me."

While Evan continued to eat me like an ice cream cone, Jett put something warm on my ass, then something cooler. I sucked in a breath as a finger slipped into me.

"Are you okay?" Brennan whispered, his thumb stroking my temple.

"So good," I sighed, as Jett's finger slid in and out of me.

I wasn't sure if I'd like being in this contraption, but right now I felt safe, not trapped. Brennan's being here with me, reassuring me, helped a lot.

Closing my eyes, I let pleasure flow over me as Jett and Evan continued to play me like a piano. The need for their cocks grew. But for now, I'd enjoy this.

"Yes, yes," I gasped as my body spasmed. "May I please have some dick now?"

Mmmm, yes, I needed those beautiful cocks.

"Their dicks are yours," Brennan murmured, stroking my face. "You're doing so well, Little Butterfly."

Jett patted Evan's ass, and he stood. Evan's beautiful omega cock was erect and ready, pre-cum dripping from the tip.

Leaning in, Jett kissed him and whispered something in his ear.

"You came so nicely for us. How about I take this cute ass and Evan has your pussy?" Jett repositioned me.

"Please," I gasped. "Make me the filling."

"Sounds good to me. You look so fucking beautiful, Peaches." Evan leaned in and kissed my nose. "You're doing okay?"

I nodded. "Yes. I... I like it."

"Good. I figured you would." He kissed my breast, then positioned himself between my legs.

Jett didn't stand behind me, but next to Evan. Okay, no sandwich, but I'd try something new.

Evan slid inside me, one hand on my thigh, one on Jett. "There you go, Peaches. Mmmm, I love my fantasy coming true."

Lubing me up, Jett slid that hard, pierced cock into my ass, and I gasped.

"I love your little lady ass, Babydoll," Jett told me as he started to thrust.

Both of them found a rhythm. Jett also stroked Evan's back and murmured to him, as well as to me. I hadn't seen them together outside of Evan's heat, and I loved how sweet Jett was to both of us.

"You can do more than pet my hair, but I like it," I said softly to Brennan.

"I don't want to overwhelm you." His fingertips brushed my face, and I tilted it up like a flower seeking the sun.

Those fingertips trailed my body. I gasped as they brushed my nipples, as Jett and Evan continued to fuck me. It felt so good. But something inside me wanted *more.*

Seriously, body? You're literally being fucked by two guys right now...

A whine escaped my lips.

"What do you need, Grace?" Jett came in my ass. "You are doing so well."

"Do you need a knot? I think you need a knot." Evan kissed me.

Want shot through me, along with another stupid cramp.

"Please? Bren, please fuck me, too, please?" It came out so needy, so desperate. My cheeks warmed. What if...

No. The man is naked, holding you, and making sure you're okay. He will absolutely fuck you.

Brennan leaned in and kissed me. "Since you asked so sweetly, I'll fuck you. Is that what you need?"

"Yes, please." A burst of want exploded inside me, and I gushed.

"Oh, yes, get wet all over my cock," Evan sighed as he came inside me.

I sucked in a breath at that beautiful, hard cock studded with piercings, knot inflated.

"This is what you want?" Brennan grabbed his cock. "Jett and Evan aren't enough. My greedy Little Butterfly needs a knot, too."

"Yes, please, please, Alpha." Why was he just standing there with it instead of shoving it in me?

"If you give me a moment, I can go again," Jett said as he cleaned me and himself up. Evan withdrew from me, and I whimpered.

Brennan's fingertips brushed my pussy. "Look at you, all nice and wet and full of Evan. How does he taste inside you?" He licked his fingers.

"Oh, I want to taste." Jett leaned over and licked Brennan's fingers. "So delicious."

A whine escaped my lips as the need to be dicked down hit me hard.

"Shhh, it's okay. You'll get some." Brennan leaned in and kissed me. He frowned. "You don't smell right. But it's okay. We'll make you feel better."

I'd feel better if you were inside me.

"I've got you." Putting his hands on my hips, Brennan slowly slid that beautiful, pierced alpha cock inside my empty, lonely pussy.

"Good boy," I whispered. Immediately I felt better.

Brennan smirked. "Only for you."

Evan came up behind me and kissed my temple. "You're right. She smells wrong. But she wasn't feeling good. Yeah, we'll dick you good, then we can have a bubble bath. That's always a cure for what ails you."

Slick fingers played with my ass as Brennan fucked me.

"That's it, just let go and relax," Brennan whispered. "Evan, slide into her."

My eyes closed as Evan's dick slid into my ass. Yes, that's just what I needed.

"Let go, stop thinking and let go," Brennan whispered. "We'll take care of you, Little Butterfly."

"Okay." It sounded good to me. With my eyes staying closed, I let wave after wave of pleasure wash over me as Evan and Brennan fucked me.

"Yes, yes," I cried as another orgasm racked me. Someone else, probably Jett, massaged my clit and played with my nipples.

"That's it, come for us," Brennan murmured.

"More, more," I breathed.

"Jett, come here. Little Butterfly, Jett's going to join me inside your pussy."

"Please." It felt so good.

Fingers joined Brennan's dick as Evan continued to fuck my ass.

"It's a little crowded in here," Jett whispered. "But let's give this a try."

My pussy stretched in just the right way as Jett slid into me with Brennan. All three of them fucked me. Jett continued to toy with my clit. Someone kissed my nipples.

"That's my good girl. Look at you," Jett cooed. "Yes, you're just getting wrecked and enjoying every moment, aren't you? Being in your pussy with Bren is nice."

"Knot, knot, knot," I sang. The need to be full consumed me.

"As you wish, Little Butterfly. Look at you, taking me so good." Brennan plunged his knot into me, wrapping his arms around me and holding me close.

"Such a good boy," I murmured as I pressed my face into his sweaty chest.

Someone fucked my ass, it might still be Evan, but it might be Jett. It didn't matter, I just kept my face pressed into Brennan, inhaling his pine scent over and over, letting go and feeling good as I came again.

Finally, they stopped, but it was okay. Brennan was still locked inside me, and I clung to him.

"There you go. See, I told you I'd make it up to you." Evan kissed my forehead.

Yes, he did.

"I'm proud of you for trying something new," Brennan murmured, kissing me.

Yeah, me too.

Chapter Twenty-Five

Jett

"There you go," Brennan murmured to Grace as he slipped out of her. "Let's get you out of there. You took me so well."

What had just happened? I mean, obviously, Evan got to act out one of his fantasies with Grace. Which was beautiful.

I needed to record her calling Brennan a *good boy* and make it one of my ringtones. Her calling him that didn't surprise me.

His allowing it, did.

Gently, Brennan got her out of the swing and carried her to the bed. I adjusted the lights, temperature, and air filter, because it smelled weird in here.

"Hey, I've got you." Evan lay down on the bed, and Brennan placed her on top of him.

Brennan climbed in next to them and hugged them. "Both of you did so fucking well."

I grabbed some water from the fridge. Yes, they did. Grace especially.

But again, what the fuck had happened? Something happened. It sort of felt like one of Evan's heat spikes.

It just didn't smell like it.

Yet it tasted like it. Well, what I'd think it would taste like. During Evan's heat, I noticed her taste change and get almost slick-sweet. The same happened tonight.

I handed Evan one of the water bottles; he drank half of it and then held Grace up and got her to drink.

Brennan stroked her hair. "That's it, drink up."

"Is everyone okay? That got a little intense." I took a long drink from the other bottle and then handed it to Brennan.

The end, where Brennan was locked inside her, but she was whining for more as we fucked her ass, was a little wild.

"Yeah, that was so nice." Grace sighed, and slumped back onto Evan.

Evan kissed her. "So fun. I knew you'd like to be in the swing with us."

"Are you okay, Honey?" I kissed Brennan, proud of him for making sure she got what she needed, and I let him know through the bond.

I felt him holding back the entire time. It was part of the reason why he let me take the lead. He worried that he'd be too rough with her, demand too much, out of habit.

But really, he'd been exactly what she needed.

"I am." He kissed me back.

I'd check back in with him later.

Grace looked at me and made grabby hands. I climbed onto the other side, so they were between Brennan and me and snuggled them. I was proud of Evan for letting the focus be on Grace. Usually, all the attention was on him.

We cuddled the two of them for a while, letting them know how loved they were. Okay, I was pretty sure that Grace was playing with Brennan's piercings under the blanket.

"It's getting late, should we take a shower?" I suggested. While this was amazing, I had work tomorrow.

"Evan, can we have that bath, and someone mentioned hot chocolate? Yes, I'd like that and then bed," Grace mumbled, eyes closed.

"I can make you hot chocolate. After the bath?" One of my hands found Brennan's, and I squeezed it.

"Evan, can we have hot chocolate in the bathtub? Please?" Grace batted her eyes at him.

"Oh, I like that idea. Drinks in the tub are okay." Evan grinned at me.

Hot chocolate in the bath. So spoiled. As they should be.

"Come, let's go take that bath." Evan carried Grace out of the room.

I rolled over and hug-attacked Brennan, getting him down on the bed, and smothering his body with mine.

"You did so fucking well with her. I love you so much." I hugged him tightly.

"It wasn't as hard as I thought it would be." He frowned.

"It's okay to love her." I leaned in for a kiss.

"Um, I do love her. I even laid there and let her use my dick as a fidget toy." His look went unsure. "Something is fucking wrong with her."

"It felt a bit like a spike. It just didn't smell like one," I agreed.

He nodded. "Yeah. She's not feeling good. In the car, she was telling me about her shitty cycles, where she vomits and cries, and how the Center doctor was like, *Wait and see.*"

My hand played with his hair. "I get that she has no baselines, and she's a gamma and they vary so much, but yeah, seriously."

"Yeah. I mean, I don't know what lady beta cycles are like, but I know what lady alpha and lady omega cycles are like. What Grace described is nothing like them." He sighed. "Hey, thanks for letting us take your car."

I kissed him again. "Anytime. I'm proud of you for driving a car. Though it would have been funny if you'd taken her pink truck. And really, you did fucking fantastic tonight–from actually bringing her in here, to everything in the swing."

"I don't want her to be scared."

"Good. I feel bad about upsetting her at the concert. Evan and I had fun. I'll show you the pictures later."

Brennan patted my ass. "I'd love that. Hey, you did great, too. Watching you undress her was so fucking hot. Why don't you go make them hot chocolate and I'll clean up."

"Sounds good." I sat up, running my hands across his chest.

I grabbed my shorts and put them on. Going down to the kitchen, I made Evan and Grace hot chocolate.

Balancing the mugs, I walked into Evan's suite. "I'm coming in."

"In the bathroom," Evan called.

I went into his bathroom to find the two of them in the tub, the water green, and the jets going. The room was dark, lit only by a large number of candles.

Grace was nestled in Evan's arms.

"Hot chocolate delivery." I gave them their mugs.

Grace took a tentative sip. "Perfect. Thank you."

"Yeah, it's so good. Thanks." Evan drank some of his.

I left them to their bath and went back down to the kitchen to clean up. Grabbing a beer for myself, I poured a bourbon for Brennan and went back upstairs. He wasn't in the bedroom, so I put them on coasters on the nightstand and went to go help him.

The room smelled of lemon cleaner, the air purifier on full blast, as he carefully made the bed. I patted his still naked ass.

"How can I help?" I asked.

"It's fine. I'm done, I just need to put Mr. Mopps back to work. Unless you want to wash the bedding because she was here with us." He stood up.

"I don't mind if they smell like her. We should wash them, but I was going to do it later. I'll still do it later." My arms wrapped around him.

"Okay. I have the air purifier on high not because of her, but because of that weird scent she had." He frowned and looked up at me.

"I brought up some bourbon for you." I tugged on his hand. Brennan didn't really like hot chocolate.

"Great." He got up and went to the wall and set Mr. Mopps back into action.

I grabbed Grace's dress and shoes, as well as his shoes and clothes, and his phone. Brennan turned out the lights, and we closed the door.

"Here, I've got that." He took all the clothes and his shoes from me and went toward our big walk-in closet.

Not knowing what to do with her little heels, I just put them in the other room by the door.

When I came back into the bedroom, he was sitting on the bed, holding the bourbon, staring into space.

There it was.

"Hey, I've got you." I climbed onto the bed behind him and pulled him into my arms, burying my face in the crook of his neck. Alpha drop hit him hard sometimes.

"You always do. I love you. You're my fucking rock, you know that?" His voice was rough.

"I love you." I kissed his temple.

For a long time, I just held him. Brennan was my everything.

"Shower and bed? Although we might get both of them in here with us. Unless we all sleep in Evan's bed," I said, thinking back to Evan mentioning that he'd like us to be together tonight.

"I mean, if they need us, they need us. But I can't sleep in Evan's room. The messiness exists too loudly." Brennan finished his bourbon.

The messiness exists too loudly. Yeah, that was the man I loved.

We got in the shower, and he told me all about the concert.

"Caroline was there? Ugh, sorry." I closed my eyes as he washed my hair.

"Whatever. I refuse to be annoyed by her anymore."

"Good. I'm glad you had fun with Grace." Warm water cascaded over me as he washed the soap out of it.

I told him about my time with Evan as we finished up in the shower and got ready for bed.

Brennan crawled into bed and got on his phone. I grabbed the book on my nightstand to read for a few moments.

"Grace doesn't feel good, can we sleep with you?" Evan stood there with Grace in his arms.

"Sure. Can you get her a heating pad? That might help," Brennan asked.

I got the battery powered one. When I came back, Evan was getting her into bed as Brennan made her take something.

"Here you go, Peaches." I turned it on and tucked it in with her.

Grace felt warm and smelled weird. A little sick, a little rotten, a little too sweet.

Brennan got in on one side of her, Evan claimed the other, and I got on his other side. Frowning, Brennan texted someone, probably Wes and Spencer.

I shut off the light, snuggling Evan, wondering how long it would be before he dragged me off to his room.

Chapter Twenty-Six

Brennan

A sense of wrongness woke me in the middle of the night. I sat up and heard sobbing. Climbing out of bed, I realized who was missing.

Just as I entered the bathroom, Grace threw up in the toilet. She wiped her face with toilet paper and curled into a ball on the rug, crying. That weird smell from earlier filled the bathroom.

"Hey, it's okay." I sat down and pulled her onto my lap. "You're burning up."

"It hurts so bad," she sobbed. "And the worse thing is that I want to be fucked. I hate it when I'm like this."

"Grace? Grace, what's wrong?" Evan stood in the doorway, worry on his face.

"She's sick. I think we need to take her to the Center clinic." This was most likely an issue for them, not the hospital. I cradled her in my arms as she sobbed. I could practically taste her pain.

"Shit." Grace bolted out of my arms and threw up again.

I got a thermometer and some anti-nausea medication out of the medicine cabinet.

"Here, rinse out your mouth." Evan put an arm around her and helped her sip some water. "It's okay."

Pressing the thermometer to her head, it didn't surprise me when it turned bright red.

"Let's see if this helps." I got her to take the medicine. "There you go. I'm so sorry that you're feeling shitty." I wrapped my arms around her.

Grace squeaked and flew out of my arms, barely making it to the toilet.

Well, that didn't work.

Jett joined us and handed me my phone. "Wes is calling."

"Hey." I leaned against the bathroom wall.

"Something's wrong." Wes sounded sleepy.

"Grace is sick. Fever, vomiting, and stomach pains that make her sob. I think we should take her to the all-hours clinic at the Center. Her scent is also really weird. Not just sick, but rotten and a few other things." My heart broke as she curled up on the rug again, Evan rubbing her back.

"Yeah. Do that. Um. hold on." There was muffled noise. "Spencer wants to know if we need to fly back now?"

"Why don't we take her in, and we'll call you. Just in case it's only a stomach bug or something." But I knew that wasn't it.

"True. I mean, I've been expecting her to get a cold or something. There's a good chance that she might not have resistance to things here. Yeah, bring her in and call us. The great thing about taking the company jet is that we can leave whenever we want," Wes said.

"I'll keep you updated." I hung up and turned to Evan. "We're taking Grace in. Um, I know she usually visits the Center in Midtown because she goes with you. But should we take her to the one down the street? I'm pretty sure it has a twenty-four-hour clinic."

"Midtown has a hospital and more resources than the one right here. They also know her there. This smell, it reminds me of something, but I don't know what." Evan frowned. "I'll get her some clothes and get dressed."

"Sounds good." I sat on the bathroom floor and held her as they got dressed.

Grace screamed.

"Evan, grab her while I put pants on." I threw on some clothes and grabbed my phone. "I don't think we have time to drive to Midtown."

Jett was on his phone. "There's one not that far from here with a hospital."

"Oh, right, the new one. I haven't been there. We'll take my car." Evan pulled one of her T-shirt dresses over her head.

We went downstairs and got in Evan's car. I sat in the back holding her as we drove through our nice, forested suburb into a newer, ultra-fancy one. We drove up to a very shiny and pretty Omega Center and were stopped at a gate.

"Do you have an emergency room or a twenty-four-hour clinic? My mate's sick." Evan showed his Omega Center badge to the guard.

"Yes, go to the left." He put something red on our windshield.

Grace had gone quiet.

"Grace, we're here," I told her. She didn't move. "Fuck."

We had barely parked the car when I was running for the doors that said *Hospital 24-Hours,* Grace in my arms.

A startled nurse in pink scrubs looked up at me from the emergency desk. Soft music played, and a few people sat in comfortable chairs.

"She's unconscious and sick," I called, Jett and Evan following me.

"I've got her Center card." Evan held up her phone for the nurse to scan.

"Found her, let's get her back," the nurse said, as another nurse rushed over.

"She has a fever, vomiting, cramping, and is in a lot of pain." I added as another nurse joined us.

A nurse led us back to an exam bay, and I sat her on the bed.

"Please, help her. She was complaining of her stomach hurting earlier tonight, and then she just started puking and sobbing," I begged.

A doctor ran in, looking stricken. "Is that smell hers?"

"Yes. There's something wrong with her. It shouldn't be like this," I pleaded, as the nurse started hooking her up to things.

"Please go wait in the lobby, we'll come get you," the doctor said.

"Can I stay?" Evan asked.

"Out." He scowled.

Shoulders slumping, Evan squeezed her hand, and we went out into the lobby.

"Look at this place. Wow. Evan, you should get transferred here." Jett looked around.

While Evan's Omega Center, being a regional center, was state-of-the-art, this was just as fancy.

"I like where I work. But maybe in a couple of years?" Evan got on his phone and frowned.

I went to the cart and got us some coffee and little bags of cookies, then joined them on one of the couches.

"What do you think is wrong? Have you seen anything like this before?" I asked Evan as I took a sip of coffee.

"If she was an omega that grew up here, I'd say it could be heat sickness. But she wouldn't get heat sickness because she has us.

And well, you'd have to have lots of neglected or unfulfilled heats for that. Years of trying to handle things yourself, badly, without ever going to a heat clinic or knowing what to do, or anything," he explained.

Horror coated me. "What if she wasn't having awful PMS? What if she's been going into heat for years but didn't know it? No one would know what it was or what to do, well, except for that awful woman who raised her, who could very well ignore it. Not to mention what they did to her at that camp fucked her up. Could that have something to do with it?"

"Oh fuck. You might be right." Evan put his hand to his mouth.

I got on my phone and called Wes.

"She's sick, isn't she?" Wes yawned. "Good thing Spencer has decided that we're leaving."

"Good. You need to come home now," I confirmed. "We think she's sick because she's trying to go into heat–and failing."

Chapter Twenty-Seven

Wes

"Wow, this place looks brand new," I said to Spencer as he parked his car at the Omega Center hospital Brennan said they'd taken her to.

"She'll be all right, she'll be all right," Spencer whispered.

I squeezed his shoulder. "She'll be okay."

Hopefully. It had been hard feeling her pain and being so far away. Especially for Spencer.

Worry burrowed into me. Failed heat? What the fuck? That happened when omegas didn't have the resources to be comfortable or safe. She had us. Everything was fixed between her and Brennan. Her room was cute and cozy again. Spencer tried to get her to eat right. Grace had everything she needed for her body to want to go into heat.

If she even could.

Oh. Maybe this was a gamma thing? Like when the process of becoming an omega was halted it fucked up her ability to go into heat?

We got out of the car and rushed into the hospital. Brennan, Jett, and Evan sat in a corner of the lobby, which looked like a living room.

"What's wrong with her?" Spencer asked.

"We've been trying to piece this together, mostly, so the doctor doesn't have us all arrested for neglect." Brennan looked up at us.

"Neglect, again?" I'm not sure I'd ever seen Brennan this rumpled in public. He was literally wearing a T-shirt from his university, sweats, and sneakers, hair unbrushed.

Spencer wore a suit, and I'd thrown on the pants and button down I'd planned on wearing in the morning.

"Don't worry, the advocate they sent to talk to me knows me *and* Mrs. Beekman. I think a lot of this isn't just Grace being a gamma, but what made her a gamma. Electrical current can fuck up a body's ability to go into heat," Evan explained. "I sort of forgot about that."

"Fuck. I remember what they did to her. She'd come to me in our dreams and cry and tell me about it, while I held her." I punched my hand. She'd clutch Mr. Hippo and sob into my shoulder.

"She told me that they gave her a fucking heart attack." Brennan looked like he wanted to rip someone's head off. Jett gave him a squeeze.

"Yeah, I remember that, too." My head bowed. The dreams had stopped not long after that–and part of why I thought that she *died.*

"I'm guessing that Grace has been having years of really shitty heats without knowing. I don't know if they got shitty because of heat sickness, or if they've always been that way because that's all her body could accomplish. She thought she was getting bad pre-menstrual cramps and sometimes vomiting and having a fever. But she was really in heat–and no one realized it. Not even her," Evan told us.

"I wasn't there." My hands fisted. "She was all alone, and *I wasn't there*. Fuck."

My poor Peaches. The idea of her suffering, and not knowing what was happening to her, wrecked me. Years and years of being all alone with her heat and no one helping her could fuck her up so bad.

Spencer squeezed my shoulder. "It wasn't your fault, Wes."

"I still feel bad. Though I'm surprised with everything that has happened to her, that her body could even go into heat. Not all gammas do." My brows furrowed.

The three of them looked at me.

"What?" My heart fell.

"She's mated. It was probably her body's way of looking for you. Every so often it would go, *Where is he?* And it would try to call you in the best way it knew how. Well, that's what we're guessing," Evan said softly. "Sometimes it happens. Also, you bonded young, and were very serious from a very young age, which can have ramifications."

True. They warned us about that in alpha class in school, but I always ignored it, because they were dreams–and she was my soulmate.

"Fuck." I wanted to punch something as anger at myself coursed through me. We *were* mated, and omegas could get sick when separated from their mates for too long. Just because she was a gamma, and I'd bonded her in our dreams, didn't mean it hadn't affected her.

"Hey." Evan got up from the couch and wrapped his arms around me.

"What happened this time? She has us now," Spencer said.

"She does. Grace has us, the right food, and a comfortable home. We saw her body respond well to Evan's heat. Also, the Center's been shooting her up with hormones. The hospital did, too," Brennan added. "We think it was earnestly trying, but given everything, it just... couldn't."

"Fuck." I clung to Evan. My poor Grace.

"What are they doing for her?" Spencer looked around.

"They're making her comfortable and trying to figure out the best way to fix it. This can't keep happening to her," Jett said.

Shit. Shit. Shit.

"I want to see her." Spencer paced the lobby like a feral animal in a cage.

So did I. But I also didn't want to get kicked out.

Brennan sighed. "They're making us wait. But maybe now that you're both here, they'll let us in."

"They think we're neglectful beasts, even though Evan was trying to explain things." Jett put an arm around Brennan.

I'd failed her. Again.

"Hey, none of that," Evan said softly.

"But it's all my fault. I... I bonded with her because I was trying to help her, and all it's done is cause problems for her." I winced.

"You obviously did it because you loved her. How were you to know?" Brennan said.

"You need to stop blaming yourself. It's getting tiresome and doesn't help," Spencer grumbled. "I'm serious. Every time you do so, I'm going to assign you a business trip with a speaking engagement."

I stared at him in horror. "You wouldn't."

"I would." Spencer glared at me. "Do you know how many people would *love* for you to present at their conferences, be on their panels, or speak at their universities?"

"What?" I laughed. "I didn't even graduate."

"You work in cybersecurity at one of the hottest companies in the world. No one has to know it's nepotism." Brennan laughed.

I sighed. "You're right. Please don't make me speak to people."

"That's entirely up to you," Spencer pointed out.

"Oh, there's the doctor." Brennan waved. "Her alphas are here."

The male doctor was tall for a beta. The older man scowled at us.

"Thank you, Doctor. I'm Spencer and this is Wes," Spencer introduced.

He looked unimpressed.

"She's stabilized and resting comfortably. For now," he stated.

"Can we see her?" I asked, the need to be at her side clawing at me.

"We need to make some choices," he told us. "Her body doesn't know how to fully have a healthy heat, and she can't take much more of this. We need to fix that."

"Okay, what do we do?" I'd do anything for her.

"The first option is that we medically induce a proper heat. Once it takes, we move her into one of the observation heat suites that we have here. You tend to her, and someone will observe the entire time to make sure it goes smoothly."

I didn't like that idea. Mostly because I wanted her first heat to be nice. Not have it forced on her and be in some hospital heat suite with doctors *watching*. The thought made me shudder.

"And the other?" Spencer asked.

"We give her medications that basically try to trick her body and reset it, in an attempt to break this cycle, hoping next time she goes into heat that it will be better," he said.

Spencer shook his head. "I don't like either of them."

"I know. They just seem... medically invasive," I replied.

"We don't have many options, unfortunately. We can't simply let her body continue to do what it's been doing," He glared at me and Spencer.

"The second seems better?" Evan nodded.

"What are the drawbacks?" Brennan inquired. "In my research on gammas, I found that sometimes they push back over to being an omega. Would either of these cause that? Grace barely understands being a gamma, as it is. I wouldn't want to give permission to anything that might alter her designation without her consent."

The doctor nodded, looking pleased at his question. "The obvious is that neither option may work. Even if they do, she still might have a future of medically supervised heats, both to make sure that she's okay and to help her body achieve a full heat until it can figure out how to do so on its own. The first is a lot easier to control, and we'll know sooner how best to care for her going forward. One issue with the second is that we won't be able to predict when her body will go into heat, if it ever does, and there might not be any markers. But," he scowled at us, "I'm sure a pack like yours has a heat plan."

"Oh, we do," Evan assured.

We did? Grace and Evan might have made one together. That seemed like something you'd do in an omega class.

"Good. It might not work. If she goes into heat again and it happens like it did tonight, then you'll have to bring her in, and we'll need to go forward with option one. Either way, you must make sure that she always feels safe and cared for and that all her needs are being met," he added. "Obviously, she's endured some trauma. Usually, I'd expect to see something like this while working with refugees or in a war zone, not here."

"Of course," Spencer assured. "While some of her past was unfortunate, she's with us now."

"As for your question," he turned to Brennan, "I don't expect either of those options to push her back over to omega. I'm not sure anything ever will. But who knows? Every gamma is different, and yes, some gammas can and do go into heat regularly. They're usually very short and far apart but can be healthy."

Well, then.

Spencer turned to me. "The second? I just can't see forcing her into heat and then having her have one with people watching in a hospital."

"Agreed." I looked at Evan. "Second?"

"Yes." He nodded.

"I support that," Brennan told us. "I don't like the idea of her not having a choice about going into heat. She had no idea what was going on."

"Agreed," Jett added.

I turned to the doctor. "We'll go with the second option. Wait, what does she have to say?"

The doctor gave me an approving look. "She's sedated and not in a position to make that choice. Which is why we're coming to you."

"But did you ask her at any point?" Brennan inquired.

"Yes. She said that she wanted chocolate chip cookie dough ice cream with extra fudge and a heating pad," he replied.

That was my Grace.

"We'll bring her that when she's awake then," Spencer said. "Can we see her?"

"We'll get her comfortable and administer the first series of drugs, then we'll bring you in–as long as her advocate says it's okay. I'm concerned about her," the doctor told us.

"Me, too. Especially the seizures, and, well, this. I feel like her other doctor isn't taking her seriously." Brennan frowned.

"Wait here until someone gets you." The doctor turned and left.

Evan turned to Brennan. "Dr. Davidson is a good doctor. They have no baselines for Grace. They're being cautious. No one, even I, thought *shitty cramps with puking* meant that she was going into heat and didn't know it."

"I just want her to be okay." I slumped down into a chair.

Spencer sat down next to me. "That's what we all want."

"We have a heat plan for Grace?" I eyed Evan.

"Sort of. I cleaned out the nest in the basement and scent bombed it a couple of times. Also, I got a few things in colors and fabrics she likes. It probably could use painting and new carpet. If it came down to it, we could use it for her," Evan said quietly.

Oh. The emergency nest. I sort of forgot that it was down there. It came with the house. Back after Caroline, when Evan's hormones got out of whack and his heats became irregular, we got it ready in case we couldn't make it to the cabin. We never used it much.

"Grace should have a space that's not mine, and well," he looked to Spencer, "we might not always be able to fly to Greece."

Brennan squeezed Evan's hand. "That's a good plan."

"It is." I nodded.

Spencer frowned. "She's going to be okay? I don't like all this."

"The doctor's right, there aren't many options," Evan confirmed.

"I'm going to get some coffee. Does anyone want some?" Brennan stood.

"Please?" I asked.

"I'll go with you." Jett put his arm around Brennan, and they headed toward the coffee station.

Spencer was on his phone, so I sat down next to Evan.

"Hi, Babe." I put my arm around him. "Did you have a good time with Jett?"

"Yes. I scared Grace though." He sighed.

I gave him a squeeze. "Bren told me. And that you all made it up to her. He... he was gentle with her, right?"

"He was perfect with her," Evan assured. "Did you know that Spencer bought her a pink truck?"

"Yes, he asked me for my opinions on models." It wasn't only really cute, but tough and we could actually take it off road.

Brennan and Jett came back with coffee.

Mrs. Beekman came over to us. The older beta looked tired. "Hello, boys."

"Hi, Mrs. Beekman." Evan waved.

She sighed. "Every time someone goes somewhere, something bad happens. How about if you all just stay home and remain together for a bit?" Her eyes flicked to me and Spencer.

"Of course, Mrs. Beekman," Spencer agreed. "We're still trying to get all this figured out. There's so much about her we just don't know."

"We really are trying," I pleaded. "We love her."

"I know." She sighed again. "Honestly, I didn't figure it out either when we were talking about it. Still, Grace is *delicate*. You need to take care of her like she's a fragile figurine, not a metal truck."

"We will, Mrs. Beekman," I told her.

She looked at us. "Do you have a heat plan for her?"

"I do. I haven't really talked to her about it, because I wasn't sure she could have a heat. But I came up with one just in case. When she feels better, I'll sit down with her and we'll go over everything, then she and you can talk about it further," Evan replied.

"Good." She rubbed her forehead.

"We appreciate you looking out for Grace," Spencer added.

She sighed again and left.

"Well, I'll be rearranging some business trips," Spencer whispered.

"I offer to not go on anything for business ever," I volunteered.

Evan fell asleep on my lap as we waited. Finally, the doctor returned.

"We have her set up in a room now. We'll probably keep her here for a couple of days. She'll be in and out of consciousness as we administer treatment. However, it would be advisable for someone to stay with her at all times. She'll do better if someone's there," the doctor explained, as he led us to a room.

"We will," I assured him.

She looked so small, asleep in the big hospital bed.

"Grace." I rushed to her side and took her hand. "I... I should have–"

"Wes." Spencer's tone went warning. "I meant it. Just because Mrs. Beekman doesn't want us to travel, doesn't mean that I couldn't have you speaking someplace tomorrow afternoon."

Yeah, I didn't want that.

I kissed her on the forehead. "We're here. And when you wake up, you can have that ice cream, okay? I promise."

Chapter Twenty-Eight

Spencer

I sat on Grace's bed, working on my laptop. Okay, it was more like I was texting my publicist, putting out fires, and answering ridiculous questions about mating gifts from relatives. Invitations had gone out, also, thanks to the entertainment news, the entire world knew that I'd taken a mate.

People were even sending random gifts for us to Compass BioTek.

What did I ask my family for? When Elaris and I mated, it made sense to let them buy us a home, furnishings, and all the things we needed to start our lives together, given we'd been living in the dorms.

But now? We had most everything. Would it be odd to ask for donations to our foundation?

Unless they wanted to buy us a jet that would not only get us to Grace's island but land on it. I mean, they bought my cousin a yacht. Or perhaps they'd expand our airstrip?

Possibly both?

"What do you think, Grace? Is there anything special you'd like?" I inquired, even though she wasn't going to answer. But I'd ask her again later. Just like I wore my glasses because I knew she found them sexy.

The doctors had finished administering the medicines; now it was up to her body to do the rest. The doctor seemed optimistic.

As was I. She looked better, smelled better. Soon enough she'd be fully awake and asking for that ice cream.

Right now, I was alone in her hospital room with her. Brennan hauled everyone else off for sleep and showers.

"Spencer?" There was a knock on the door. Mrs. K stood there holding a large container.

"Mrs. K. Come in. I wasn't expecting you." It was Saturday.

"I brought some soup. You all need to eat, and she might like something homemade." She came in and put the container on the table.

"Thank you so much." That sounded perfect.

Mrs. K glanced at the bed. "Is she awake?"

"She's still in and out." I got up and came over to my assistant. We sat at the table. Mrs. K wore her *I want to talk* face.

"I can't find any lists of anyone Demitra and Nick sent away when they were getting those with illegal designations to safety," she told me. "I know that they were working with an underground organization to help those who needed it. There weren't very many they sent, especially compared to the hundreds they took in, but that's it."

"That's fine. Thank you. I'd expect all of that was lost when the Temporal Authority blew up their research." And somehow they had all their backups erased.

But that made sense. It wasn't Rosalind who had the connection; it was someone in whatever organization she'd found to help her.

"I might be able to find Grace a therapist, though," Mrs. K added.

"Oh, there's a list of those brought here?" It would be interesting to see.

She shook her head. "One that survived? Not that I know of. But I've met a few. Also, most, if not all, of the male omega miracle births we've had in the past few decades were omegas that they smuggled in, coming from worlds where it's possible."

"I thought so. I appreciate it, Mrs. K."

Mrs. K glanced back over to her. "Should we postpone the party?"

"Not yet." I shook my head. I'd leave that for Grace to decide when she woke up. The doctor made it sound like she'd be fine in a couple of days.

"I'm logging all the gifts that come in so that we can thank everyone. There are a few that you should keep, but I'll let you and Grace sort through them. I'm sure we can donate the rest to the Omega Center or a shelter," she informed me.

"That sounds like a wonderful idea. Thank you."

"I should go, but please let me know if you need anything." She patted my shoulder and stood.

"I will. Thanks for the soup."

Mrs. K left, and I tried to get a few more things done.

The soup was still warm... and smelled delicious. Using an empty paper cup and a spoon left from dinner last night, I got some and sat down on the bed next to Grace.

I took a bite, letting the soup of lemon, eggs, rice, and chicken explode over my tongue.

"This will make you feel so much better when you wake up," I told Grace. I finished and put the empty cup on the bed table.

Grace stirred, and her hand moved in that way that meant she was searching for one of us.

"I'm right here. Do you want to wake up now?" I pulled her into me.

"Mmmm, dunno." Her face buried in my chest.

"Okay. I have soup. Such nice soup to make you feel better." I stroked her hair.

She made a non-committal noise. "Ice cream."

"Yes, Wes will bring you ice cream later." I looked at my phone. They were up, eating, and then going to Riley's school. The semester ended in a few days, so they were starting to move her things back to the house for summer.

"Okay." Grace snuggled into me and went back to sleep.

I went back to my phone, which was again full of mating party questions. But, my friend was all set to come and grill, my cousins would play the music, the rings were ordered, and the wine select-ed. Grace needed a dress, but that wasn't an issue. I'd just take her to Andre's shop unless she had something else in mind.

My grandfather even planned to attend, which surprised me considering his age.

Grace stirred again. This time she opened her eyes and looked at me sleepily.

"Hi, Darling." I stroked her hair again.

"Spencer, you're home?" She frowned and looked around. "Where..."

"Shhh." I pulled her back into me. "You're in the hospital, Baby Girl. You got sick, but you're going to be okay."

Her nose scrunched. "I have been spending way too much time in hospitals for my taste."

Mine, too. At least she was awake. Relief flooded me.

"Your body is literally adjusting to being in a different world. It's to be expected," I murmured.

"Where's Wes and Evan?" Her eyes teared a little.

"They'll be back. Should they bring you the ice cream with extra fudge you keep asking for?" I texted them that she was awake.

Grace nodded and snuggled into me. "Yes. What happened? I remember throwing up and…"

Embarrassment flooded the bond.

"None of that." Holding her tight, I explained what had happened–and what choices we made for her. "I hope it was the right one. The doctor asked you, and you said that you wanted ice cream."

"I'm so glad that you didn't choose the first one." Her lower lip quivered.

"Unfortunately, it might still be in your future. We have to do what's best for your body. But even if it's in a hospital, I'll make sure that your heart and soul are still taken care of, as will the others." I kissed her. We'd been shown the medical heat suites; they weren't awful, but it was still a hospital.

Grace made a face and then stared at her body. "Be good or else."

I kissed her temple. "That's my girl."

"I… I was going into heat and didn't know it? I thought heats were supposed to be magical. I'm fucked up." Her shoulders rounded in defeat.

My heart broke as her scent went salty with sadness.

"It's not you, it's everything that happened to you. Electrical currents can disrupt a body's ability to go into heat. Your body tried, but once you got to a certain point, it just didn't know what to do. But hopefully it'll be better now. Don't worry about it one bit. We *love* you." I pulled her, so she was on top of me, careful of all the monitors.

"Okay." She rested her head on my chest and looked up at me. "I love your glasses."

"I'm glad. Are you thirsty? For water," I added.

She nodded.

I got her some water and helped her drink. "Why don't we call the nurse?"

"How about if Wes brings me ice cream?" She pouted.

"I will absolutely ask him to. How about I feed you some of the nice soup Mrs. K made you, first? It's still warm," I suggested.

"She made me *soup?* Mrs. K is so nice." Grace nodded. "I want a bite. It smells good."

Getting my cup, I spooned some soup into it, trying to get mostly broth. I sat back down, and I fed her a bite.

"That's my good girl," I praised as she swallowed spoonful after spoonful of soup.

A nurse came in. "Oh, you're awake!" She looked at me and frowned. "What are you feeding her?"

"Homemade soup." I offered Grace another spoonful. Her mouth opened like a baby bird, and I fed her some more.

"At least it's not ice cream." The nurse sighed and went over to the monitors.

Grace made a face at her.

"You can have ice cream later. You should have a little food first. The soup smells nice," the nurse said. "How about if your alpha goes and gets some coffee and I'll get you checked over and taken care of?"

That wasn't an actual question.

"Oooh, coffee sounds amazing. Thanks, Spence." Grace smiled at me.

Putting the almost empty cup back on the bedstand, I gave her a kiss and stood. "I'll be right back."

"Are you serious?" Grace laughed as we looked at jets on my laptop. "They're going to buy us a plane as a mating gift?"

"Yes, which one do you want? These all will fit on your island, and these," I clicked to another tab, "will fit with a few modifications to the runway. These are not allowed on your island, but we could still have one. We'd just then need to keep another plane someplace to take to your island. Or get a helicopter." It was a little ridiculous, but my family in Greece was ridiculous.

My parents tried to give me what they deemed a normal upbringing. And they did. But I had plenty of experience with the finer things in life, too.

Also, in my family, the mating gift from the alpha's family to the new couple was usually substantial. My family was also very excited that I was taking a mate again. While they loved Elaris and knew that it would take time for me to heal, they also worried about me being lonely.

"We have a plane." Her eyebrows rose as she looked over them.

"The company has a plane. This would be for our family. Honestly, a pack plane is a good thing. It's about safety, and convenience. Brennan's business trips would be quicker and easier because he could just take the jet. Same with family vacations. Or quick business trips for you. Let's say that you get invited to speak at a university in New York. We could simply fly over, you could speak, we'd have dinner, and return right home," I explained.

"New York?" She laughed.

"The math department at the New York Institute of Technology has a speaker series. Narif has spoken to them. They'd love you.

Also, if we don't specify exactly what we want, my family will pick. That happened with Elaris and me," I laughed.

"What?" She laughed.

"We told them that we'd like a little house but were like, *Oh, we'll be happy with anything.*" With a laugh, I told her about our *little starter home*, the ostentatious decor, and the insanely expensive appliances.

"I mean, a house is a house," she laughed. "Did you sell it after she passed?"

"I gave pretty much everything to her family to do what they wished with it. They were lovely people who worked hard but didn't always have the resources to give their kids all the opportunities they would have liked." I hadn't heard from them in years. Which was fine. I understood if they blamed me.

Sometimes I blame myself.

But the investigation had been reopened, and perhaps we'd get justice for her.

Also, I had my sweet Grace. I kissed her.

"This is the yacht my cousin got. You'll love her. She and I were close growing up–she loved terrorizing Evan when he'd come visit." And was the reason he didn't like pizza. This was not the cousin who wanted to build an artist colony in downtown Rockland, but she was part of the cousin band.

I showed Grace some pictures.

"That is a floating mansion." She giggled at the ones of my cousin's yacht.

Leaning in, I touched my forehead to hers. "It's a floating eyesore. The yacht that came with your island is much better." My phone beeped. "Oh, look, my aunt is trying to send you the ugly jewelry that no one wants. It keeps getting passed around."

I'd probably be forced to wear the horrid cufflinks we all wore for our mating parties.

"They're a lot," I added. "But they're good people. My grand-fathers taught me as much about business as my father taught me about science. More even. I attended Rock Tech because they have one of the few science business programs in the world. You see, I wanted to combine what I loved with what I was good at–and I did. I know some people question why a biotech company has special projects like we do, but I never set off to actually do biotech or even pharmaceuticals. All I wanted to do was to find brilliant people who could change the world and help them carry out their work."

"The *Thanukos Incubator for Interesting Projects*. We will change the world. If I ever actually work," she laughed. "Margie is going to complain that I'm never there."

"You and Blaise are forming your team for the simulator. It is fine. You're doing a great job," I reassured her.

I had a feeling that I might need to create an additional campus just for Special Projects so that they could do what they wanted without the zoning limitation we had in our current building.

Especially if they ever got into space travel.

My phone beeped, but it wasn't from one of my relatives. It was a warning from Wes. However, Grace was dressed, and we weren't in any compromising positions.

"Incoming. Someone is bringing you ice cream." I nuzzled her, making her giggle.

"About time." She laughed.

"Fuck of the morning, bitches. We have ice cream." Riley came in holding a bag.

"We also have food," Evan added. "And more things for you."

"I'm so glad you're okay." Riley gave her a hug, her anise scent a little worried.

"I'll be okay. The doctor says I might even be able to come home tomorrow." Grace smiled. "Which is good. I have a lot of work to do."

"Grace, Darling." My voice went warning.

"I can work from home, Dearest. Thinking about all the stuff I need to do is making me anxious."

That was something I understood.

"I'm so relieved that you're okay." Wes rushed over to her. "I was so worried."

"I'm okay," she reassured. "Really, I am."

"I'm glad you're okay, too." Evan also gave her a hug.

"Give me some of that, Babydoll." Jett joined them and kissed her.

Grace looked at Brennan and made grabby hands.

Silently, he rushed over and looked at her like she was everything. He leaned in and kissed her so deeply that Riley cleared her throat.

"There are children present, you dumb fucks," Riley grumbled. "This is why I like to live at school."

Brennan looked right at her and turned and kissed Grace again.

"Well, then." Riley laughed.

But it wasn't like we didn't all feel that way.

Chapter Twenty-Nine

Grace

I'd been working from home in the library on the second floor. It was a nice space, and about the size of my bedroom, with the same view only a floor lower. They'd made me my own workspace. But I was also bored.

So bored.

The guys were treating me as if I were made of spun sugar, doting on my every need since I'd been released on Sunday. While they weren't making sure someone was always home, they were sending me lunch, calling me, and finding random reasons to drop in.

While I didn't mean to scare them, I hadn't felt this good in some time. Not to mention they'd done tons of tests on me at the hospital, not just trying to address what had happened to me, but everything else, including the seizures.

I was okay.

"Hi." Jett came into the library.

"You're home early. Please tell me that you're teaching Cam's class and you'll steal me, then we'll go out for noodles. I need to get out of here," I pleaded. Okay, I had a truck and a motorcycle. I could go anywhere I wanted.

But it wasn't the same.

Jett laughed. "Her class is on Tuesday. It's Wednesday. But we can go on a date. Wear those boots and the jacket I got you. You can pick the rest of the outfit."

"Thank you." I hugged him to me, inhaling his amber scent.

"Anytime, Peaches. I think we're due for some alone time."

Yes, please.

I went into my room and changed. Yes, Jett and I needed a date. As far as I knew, no one had anything planned. No date nights, no family dinners, no game nights. Evan, Wes, and I were going on a date tomorrow night, even though it was Thursday. Tomorrow was Riley's last day of school, complete with an end-of-the-school-year dance that Evan had gotten her a new dress for.

She was going with *Hiro.* Okay, she was going with Marco, Hiro, and Kilroy, but I spoke subtext.

A lot of what I'd been doing while working from home was figuring out the project Hiro and Riley would do with me for their internship, as well as other activities for the special projects interns.

Okay, and helping Creed with the logistics of his moving here now that he'd graduated from Natty. Verity and Hale were also done with classes and had been texting me a lot. The professor had agreed to let Tru come for a week so that she could go to math camp. Mercy would come for a different two weeks to do the Rockland Raider's skate smash camp with Riley.

I texted Wes, Spencer, and Evan.

Me

> **I hope no one has anything planned for me because Jett is taking me on a date.**

Wes

> **Are you feeling up to it? I thought we could watch movies again.**

Evan

> **You've got your motorcycle test next week, so yeah, go practice with him. Have fun.**

Spencer

> **Enjoy. Call me if you need me.**

I took a picture of myself and sent it to Riley. She was done with class for the day but was studying for finals with her friends.

Me

> **Going on a date with Jett. Cute?**

Riley

> **Not slutty enough.**

That made me laugh. Hmmm. We'd probably take his motorcycle. I switched out the jeans for some tight black pants, and a sleeveless top, and used redder lipstick. I sent another photo.

Me

> **Better?**

Riley

Much. Can I ask you math questions before you go?

Jett came to the door as we were finishing up.

"Does that help?" I asked them.

"Yes," Kilroy's voice said over the speaker. "Thank you."

"Yeah, that helps a lot. Thanks. Laters." Riley ended the call.

I looked over at Jett, who was wearing all black and looked delicious. "Sorry, math help. Their test is tomorrow."

"It's fine. Wow." He eyed me. "Very nice. This is a casual date, not a formal one. Is that okay?"

"Perfect." I took his hand.

We went down to the garage.

"Ride with me? We'll practice more for your test this weekend. Okay?" Jett handed me my helmet.

"I suppose I'll make the sacrifice." I laughed.

Jett looked at my little green motorcycle. "It's perfect for you. The only problem is that you have to worry about it getting stolen given the brand."

"That makes sense." I got behind Jett and wrapped my arms around him. We took off, and I enjoyed the ride as we went to the market where the noodle shop was.

Oooh. Spicy noodles. My mouth watered. The people who worked there were so nice, too.

He parked and put an arm around me. "Come on. I've been wanting to take you here. This is my favorite of the outdoor markets in the city. Though the one over by Wes' old place is fun."

I looked around at the bustling market, which was filled with permanent and temporary stalls and shops. Right now, we were in an area full of fruits, vegetables, and flowers.

"I like to buy things here when it's my night to cook. Also, I get most of our spices here." He pointed out a stall.

"Are you cooking for me tonight?" That sounded adorable.

He grinned. "Not tonight."

Jett led us to a booth that had lots of colorful containers. He bought two and handed me one. "Try it, it's lychee."

It tasted like jello, though there was an enormous chunk of fruit in it. "That's good."

We turned down a street that was full of clothing stores and booths of accessories and makeup.

"Are we getting manicures?" I asked as we passed a nail shop.

"Not today." He grinned as I paused at a place with cute hair accessories.

I held up a clip. "My hair is getting so long."

"Is that good or bad?" Jett asked as he held up a headband with bear ears.

"I don't like the awkward stage where it's long enough to be a bother but not long enough to really put up." I put the headband on and posed.

"Cute," he told me. "We can see if they have time to trim it, if you want."

"I... no one will be mad if I cut my hair, right?" I put it back. Growing up, I hadn't been allowed, though later my dad, who raised me, apologized and said it was silly of them.

Jett cupped my chin with his hand. "Grace, it's your hair. While they can have opinions, it's your choice. Sure, I prefer Bren clean shaven but I'm not going to stop him from growing a grizzly beard."

Oh, that hair clip was pretty. I held it up. "I think you should all grow grizzly beards. The winner gets an uninterrupted night with only me."

No matter who won, I was the real winner.

"Don't tempt me. I'm not good at growing a beard." Jett snuck a kiss and paid for the barrette.

"Oh. Thank you."

"Of course." Leaning in, he put it in my hair, lips brushing my ear. "Perfect."

My core tightened.

Putting an arm around me, we continued. "Honestly, Wes usually has a grizzly beard. He only shaved it because the Queen Mum got mad at him for it. I've never seen Spencer with a beard, but Evan looks pretty delicious in a goatee. I can manage that. We just have to be very neat about it for work."

"We're getting our hair done? You have such very luscious locks. I'm a little jealous." I gave him a squeeze.

"Have you ever been to a head spa?" he asked.

"Is that where they wash your hair for an hour? No, but I've heard of it. Is that what we're doing?" Giddiness rose up inside me.

He nodded. "Something fun but also relaxing. They cut and style hair too, so we can ask if they have time for you if you'd like them to trim it up."

"Why not." Better to let someone do it now than for me to get mad because it's itchy and trying to chop it off myself at work using my phone as a mirror and whatever scissors we had lying around.

Not that I'd ever done that.

We walked into a little shop that smelled of herbs. Bottles and containers filled the walls, making it feel like an apothecary shop in a novel. Jett greeted the woman at the desk in Mandarin. I caught some of it as he asked if they had room for us.

She led us through a curtain and into a salon-type area. Soft music played, and everything was in relaxing greens with lots of plants.

We went through another curtain. The light was much dimmer here and very quiet as people lay in reclining chairs with masks over their eyes as uniformed staff rubbed their scalps, or water rained down on their heads from curved waterfall fountains.

We were seated next to each other, and as I laid down, he reached over and squeezed my hand.

"Hi, first time?" A young woman asked me.

I nodded. She told me what to expect and then asked me questions about my hair.

"It's okay if you fall asleep." She put a little warm eye mask over my eyes and got started.

Fall asleep. No, I was going to enjoy every minute.

"Wakey, wakey," she teased, as she handed me a bottle of something.

"I didn't mean to fall asleep." I drank a cool bottle of tea.

"It's fine. It happens all the time." She laughed and handed me some sort of little cookie crackers.

Hair wet, I was taken into the other room, and someone trimmed up my hair, dried, and styled it.

"That was fun, wasn't it?" Jett asked, putting the clip back in my hair.

"It's very relaxing," I agreed.

"The hair mask they use here is the secret to my luscious locks," he confessed. "Also, it's a great place to decompress after a bad day. Especially when I'm not fit to be around people. Go to the gym, come here, get a spicy snack, and then I'm ready to face the world again."

"Good plan," I agreed as we went back out to the desk, and he paid for us. "Spicy snack time?"

"Yes," he replied as we went back outside into the bustling market.

I perked. "Noodle shop?"

"Today, we're going to have a delightful multi-course feast, that, while not as fancily presented as any place the others might take you, will be extraordinary. And it's fine if you don't like things. Just try?" He led me into an area filled with food stalls and shops.

The delicious smells made my nose twitch with delight.

We had scallion pancakes, skewers of meat, and fried tofu. He fed me big buns filled with meat and tiny ones with red bean paste, along with crispy dumplings, little rice balls, and so many other delicious things.

"Everything was so tasty," I told him as we ate candied fruit on a stick.

"I'm having a great time. Did you get enough to eat?" he asked as we walked through the bustling market. There were lots of little lights and the occasional musician.

"I'm so full," I told him as he led me back to his motorcycle, throwing my empty skewer away.

"Great, come on. Time for the next stop." He patted his motorcycle, and we took off and went to some sort of...

"We're going to karaoke?" I asked over the intercom in our helmets as we parked at a bar.

"Yes. I'll have a beer, but I won't drink enough that I can't get us legally or safely home. Feel free to have a few, Evan usually does."

"Is Evan coming?" I got off and looked around.

He shook his head. "You're all mine."

"Yeah?" I giggled as I took off my helmet, and he led me inside.

"Yes. Um, Bren will be here in a moment. He's been trailing since we got food. Don't worry, he won't crash our date." Jett led me inside.

I frowned. "I'm not so fragile that I need an alpha with me always."

"I know. It's a very normal thing in most packs. If it were me and Evan, he'd do the same. He's just making sure we're okay," he assured

"We should make him do karaoke." Hmmm, would he do it for charity like Spencer?

The place had a stage, lots of tables, and a bar.

"I'm having fun," I told him as a server brought us beers.

"Me, too. This weekend I want to take you and Riley to the gym, and start teaching you some things," he said.

I nodded. "I'd like that a lot."

"You know, we should ask Brennan to add you to his fancy executive language subscription. It not only has all sorts of recorded language lessons, but you also have access to live tutors, people who will check your translations, and even coaches to do mock business meetings with you," he suggested.

I took a sip of beer. "That sounds great. I want to practice Mandarin more. Also, I should learn Greek. You know, one of my little sisters was telling me they have language nights where they all speak another language at dinner. We could do that and all practice Mandarin and Greek?"

"I like that idea. Riley already knows some phrases in Mandarin. Okay, they're mostly swears." He grinned over his beer.

"I wouldn't expect anything less." I peered through the crowd trying to find Brennan. "Huh. I don't see him."

"You won't. I told you because you're still getting used to how things are here. Let me show you." Jett pointed out couples and throuples to me, along with an alpha, or in some places more than one, that might sit at the bar or another table in order to keep an eye on the others.

"Okay, it'll take a little getting used to." I shrugged.

"Yeah. It will. Evan grumbles about it sometimes, too. But it's just because we love you."

My belly leapt. "You love me?"

Jett leaned in and kissed me. "Yeah, Grace. I do."

"I love you, too," I breathed.

"Good," he smiled. Someone called his name. His look turned conspiratorial. "I hope you feel that way after I sing."

I watched as he went up. The person there seemed to know him. Music played, and Jett started to rap. Well.

Grabbing my phone, I shot a video clip and sent it to Evan.

Evan

I'm jealous. Wes and I are at the home store.

I got a picture of Wes lying sexily on a display bed.

Me

Have fun.

Turning my attention back to Jett, I enjoyed the rest of the song.

"That was so good," I praised.

He got out his phone. "Thanks. Here, let's choose a song together."

I looked at the list. "Sure. But I think I'm going to need another beer."

Chapter Thirty

Jett

"Thank you, I had so much fun," she said to me as we got on my motorcycle.

Even though she didn't know many songs in this world well, she'd still dragged me up there three times. While Grace wasn't drunk, she was feeling pretty good.

"Babydoll, I had a great time," I told her as we drove home.

"Um, do you want to come back with me to my room?" she asked, breathily over the coms.

"I'd love that, very much." Some alone time with Grace? *Yes, please.*

"No one's spent the night in my room. I haven't even really spent the night in my room," she confessed.

I'd believe that. Evan didn't sleep much in his room either.

"Yeah? But someone's fucked you in it, right?" I added.

"No. Evan and I will make out, but when things get hot and heavy, he drags me to his room. Well, Wes has eaten me out in it, but there's been no dicking in the bed."

I exhaled sharply. "I'm very excited to be the first. Though the bed isn't going to get used right now."

Not with what I had in mind. No. I had some promises to keep from our time in the cabana. Fuck, it had been hot when she'd read to me from her book.

"Please?" Her voice was a near whine.

"I can't wait." Yeah, I'd give her everything she needed.

We arrived back in the garage, and I hung up my helmet. A moment later, Brennan came in and parked his motorcycle.

"Thanks, Honey." I gave him a kiss. Lowering my voice, I whispered in his ear, "Grace has invited me to her room. No one has fucked her in it. I'm going to fix that."

"Have fun. And anytime, Dear." Brennan kissed me back.

"Thank you for making sure we were okay." Grace pulled him down to her and kissed him.

Brennan kissed her on the nose. "Be good for Jett."

"Why do people keep telling me that? I'm always good." She pouted, her scent souring.

Oh, I could see why she might not like that.

"You're right. I guess I should tell you something else, like, *Have fun*." He ruffled her hair. "Oh, I like it."

"Thanks."

It looked cute.

We went inside and took off our shoes. She took my hand and led me up the back stairs to her room. Flipping on the small light, she shut the door.

"I have a man in my room and the door's closed. Scandalous." She giggled, throwing the clothes on her bed into the laundry basket in her wardrobe.

"So scandalous." I pushed her against the wall and kissed her hard, pinning her between me and the wall, her peach scent flaring with desire. "I think someone needs to be fucked. Hard."

"Mmmm, yes, please," she whispered. "Fuck me hard and fast into the wall."

"Beautiful," a voice said.

Annoyance flickered through me. I looked over and Evan stood in the doorway between her room and his bathroom, wearing nothing but a pair of boxers with blue monsters on them.

"Not sharing tonight." I shook my head and held onto Grace. *Mine.* I wanted my own time with her, too.

Evan smirked. "Door was open."

Grace mumbled something about socks.

I rolled my eyes. "Close it on your way to spend your night with Wes or Bren."

"You go in late tomorrow, right? Morning bath time?" She waggled her eyebrows at Evan for emphasis.

"It's a deal. But I can't believe you went to karaoke without me." Evan pouted.

"Another time, Baby," I promised. No, not feeling bad that I got some solo time with Grace.

"Okay." Blowing kisses, Evan went back into the bathroom and closed the door behind him.

Now... where was I?

My eyes met the blue-grey eyes of the sweet girl in front of me. I caged her with my arms, my palms against the green wall on both sides of her little blonde head.

"Now where were we? Oh yes. Now, I seem to remember us talking about me railing you against a wall while I call you a good girl with my hand around your neck? Does that still sound nice to you? We can try something else if it doesn't."

She should have options, just in case she wasn't feeling up to that. I'd make sure she came no matter what she wanted to do tonight.

"Yes, please." Her eyes sparkled as sweet arousal surrounded me.

"Done. Are you feeling okay?" I added, wanting to be cautious, given everything she endured in the hospital.

While I was happy that she was feeling better, I still remembered how sick she'd been, how worried everyone was–and how helpless we all felt.

She rolled her eyes. "I'm still feeling fine, other than I would like to be fucked now, please and thank you."

"Okay, then. It will be a lot easier with you naked." I pulled her over to her pink daybed and sat her down on it. It didn't seem like it had been chosen for fucking, especially because it was small. No, this looked more like it was for solo naps.

But it would work just fine. One of the alphas would probably not be comfortable in it for long. Oh, what I'd give to see Brennan wrapped in her pink sheets.

Maintaining eye contact, I slowly undressed her, putting her clothes in a pile, until she was naked and laying on the bed like a goddess.

"Mmmm, beautiful." I took off my pants.

Before I could take off my shirt, she took the hem of it. Looking into my eyes, she unbuttoned the shirt one button at a time.

With every button I felt the heat grow between us. She was just too fucking adorable.

I grinned. "Such a good girl. You know what to say if it's too much, right?"

"Yes. And I tap you twice if it's too tight."

"Look at you remembering." I licked my lips.

My hand gripped her collarbone, and I pushed her to the wall, just like in the passage from the book she'd read to me back in the cabana. My pierced cock sprung to attention, ready to bury itself deep inside her.

Touching my forehead to hers, I grinned. "Good girl."

Peachy sweet arousal blossomed from her. If I touched her I knew she'd be wet. The fact I could do that to her made me so happy.

"I love your body's reaction when I tell you that." My lips crashed into hers, my hand lightly gripping her throat. Without warning, I plunged into her, with one hand bracing myself against the wall.

So wet for me. So beautiful.

A gasp escaped her lips, but I swallowed it with my kisses.

"You feel so good," I whispered as I pounded her into the wall so hard it made a thumping sound. "I love how my good girl lets me fuck her against the wall. So fucking perfect."

Her pussy fluttered around me.

What a good, sweet, responsive girl she was. Like a little doll. *My babydoll, to play with and treasure.* I might not be an alpha, but I could still spoil her, take care of her.

Love her.

I kissed her again as I continued to fuck her hard against the wall. "Oh, you take my cock so well. My hand looks so beautiful around your throat. No one ever needs to tell you to be good because you always are such a good girl."

Orgasms shuddered through her.

"That's it, don't hold back. Come all over my cock." My free hand toyed with her clit as I continued to thrust into her hard.

I loved that I could shatter her like this.

"Mmmm, come for me, so I can shoot my cum inside you and fill you up," I directed.

"Yes, please. I love the way your pierced cock feels inside me." She kissed me back.

I broke off my kiss and gazed into her eyes, my forehead touching hers.

"Jett," she gasped as she came again.

Pulling out almost all the way, I slammed into her again, filling her with my cum.

"I love having you like this." My hand left her throat. For a moment, my sweaty body pressed into her, keeping her trapped against the wall as my cum dripped down her thighs.

"You make me feel so good," she breathed.

"I'm glad, Peaches." I brought her over to the bed. "Can we lie in the bed sweaty, or do we need to shower?"

"Either's fine. But my shower is Evan's shower." She laughed.

"Right. Sweaty it is." Yeah, if we took a shower in Evan's shower, or my shower, Evan would probably climb in with us. I wanted her to myself for as long as I could.

Pulling down the covers, I placed her on the bed and crawled in with her. Wrapping my arms around her, I pulled her to me.

"Mmmm, I like this." Her hand found my cock, and she traced my piercing with her finger. "Is that okay?"

"Very. Though I'm not going to be ready to go again as fast as them. Maybe next, I'll bend you over the bed and fuck you?" I kissed her nose.

She nodded as she cuddled into me. "I'd like that very much."

Chapter Thirty-One

Evan

"Rise and shine, or you're going to be late," I sang from the doorway between my bathroom and Grace's room.

Before me was the most beautiful scene. Jett laid in Grace's cute, ruffly pink, daybed, naked, the pink sheets only partially over him. Grace was curled into him, head on his chest. The fairy lights on the canopy over the bed glowed in the dark room.

He'd stayed the whole night with her. So stinking cute.

Jett's eyes opened, and they flickered to the alarm clock on her nightstand. "Right, my alarm clock is in my room."

"Spencer is making breakfast," I added.

"Fine. I'll get up." He kissed Grace's forehead. "Thanks for an amazing night, Babydoll."

"I had fun." She gazed up at him sleepily.

Getting out of bed, Jett went to the door.

"You know you're naked, right?" I smirked, lounging in the doorway.

He looked down. "Yep. I am."

Jett picked up his clothes and threw on his briefs and a shirt.

"Can I come in, Peaches?" I asked.

Sitting up on her elbows, she gave me a coy look. "I suppose."

"Morning, Baby." Jett kissed me.

"Morning, Hot Stuff. See you at breakfast." Smirking, I crawled into bed with her right where he'd left.

Jett hurried out of the room to get ready for work. I was going in later today, so I didn't have to rush.

After all, someone promised me bath time later.

I pulled Grace into me. It smelled good in here–a combo of her peaches and his amber.

And sex.

"Did you have fun?" It felt like they'd had a great time last night, and I loved that for them.

"Yes."

I stroked her hair. "I'm so happy that you had fun. Your new haircut is cute. I was teasing you last night, you know. You're allowed to have alone time with him."

"I know you were. Did you and Wes have fun on your date?" She looked up at me.

"We did." I'd show her what we got at the home store later.

She made a little noise as she cuddled me, and I felt a longing through the bond. But it wasn't *I want dick* needy.

"What do you need, Peaches? I think Wes is still getting ready, do you want him? Spencer's in the kitchen. I think Jett's going to take a shower. I could take you there. Or I can cuddle you until someone gets us," I added, holding her tight.

She thought for a moment. "Wes."

"Okay." I picked her up, naked, and walked her straight out of her room.

"Evan." She squealed and kicked her feet.

I shrugged and walked down the hall. Though with Riley coming home for summer, I should probably remind everyone about our general *Living with a Teenager* house rules.

"Incoming," I yelled from Wes' doorway. I carried her through his sitting room and into his bedroom.

Wes looked over at me as he put his pants on. "Good morning."

I tossed Grace into his bed. "It's nearly time for breakfast."

Giving her another kiss, I went to finish my rounds.

The shower was running in Jett and Brennan's bathroom, and it seemed like they were both in it. Mmmm.

"I hope you don't mind that I stayed all night with her," Jett said softly. "I thought about coming back to bed, but I didn't want to leave her alone. She was really cuddly. And well, we haven't actually talked about bringing her to bed regularly."

Oh? I liked this conversation.

"I'm glad you stayed with her. I don't mind you bringing her in sometimes," Brennan replied.

Wow. Brennan had made so much progress going from, *Don't come to bed smelling like Peaches* to, *Sure, Peaches can come in the bed.*

Could I cum in Peaches in the bed?

"I like that idea." I walked into the bathroom.

Brennan was holding Jett as the water rained down on them.

Jett looked over at me. "You know that I still love you even though I went on a date with her alone, right?"

"I know. I want my mates to date my mate." And fuck her so hard against the wall it shook. I took off my briefs and climbed in with them.

Jett wrapped his arms around me. "I don't have time for a shower party. But you're getting some bathtub time with Grace later."

"I just need cuddles," I replied.

"We can do that, Love." Brennan sandwiched me between him and Jett.

Ahh, that was the stuff.

"I actually came to remind you that breakfast is almost ready. Spencer's cooking," I added. Which was something he'd been doing more lately.

His cooking was delicious, so I didn't mind.

"Then we should get dressed so we can go eat what he made us. See you down there." Brennan gave me a kiss.

Getting out, I grabbed a towel and went up to my room and threw on some clothes.

When I came downstairs, Grace, in one of Wes' shirts, was sitting on his lap at the kitchen table as she drank coffee from one of the tiny cups that Spencer always put her coffee in.

Did he know she'd just have more after he left? Probably.

I grabbed some coffee and sat down. Spencer started putting food on the table.

"Fuck, you made crepes." I wiggled my shoulders happily.

"Yes." Spencer kissed Grace and went to get something else.

Jett and Brennan came into the kitchen dressed for work.

"Crepes? Thanks, Spencer." Brennan grabbed him and Jett coffee.

We all sat down for breakfast.

"Who's coming to help me get the rest of the stuff from Riley's room today?" I asked. She had her last final exam today and the dance tonight, but we were going to get most of what's left so that when we check her out tomorrow morning there were just a couple of things.

"I'll leave work early if you need my truck," Wes replied. "Or we can take Peaches' truck."

Grace made a face. "I actually have to go in for a staff meeting this afternoon."

"Oh, right." Spencer nodded. "How about if I get a ride with Wes, then you can drive me home?" He looked to Wes.

"Works for me." Wes shrugged and stuffed some crepe into his mouth.

"That sounds perfect." Grace leaned over from her spot on Wes' lap and gave Spencer a kiss.

"I can if you need me to, but there's not really that much left," Brennan replied.

We had gotten the bulk of it over the weekend.

"I have work," Jett sighed. "Sorry."

"It's fine, I know we've really disrupted your work schedule," I assured. "We don't need to owe Cam and Lexi more than we do already."

"We're still on for our date?" Wes asked Grace and me.

Grace nodded. "Yes."

"Can't wait." We were going to take the paddle boats at the lake under the bridge since I'd never been and Grace liked it, then out to dinner. I'd done a little research, and if we got a swan one, I should be able to fuck her without anyone knowing as long as she wore a dress.

"On Saturday morning I want to take Riley and Grace to the gym." Jett took a sip of coffee. "Also, Peaches, we should have more motorcycle practice."

"We can do that." She nodded.

"I can practice with you, as well. Oh, on Saturday afternoon I'm taking Grace and Riley to tea at the Everydoll Boutique." Spencer looked at Grace. "Do you have a dress in mind for our party? I can make an appointment at Andre's."

"Riley wants to look at dresses with me, but if we don't find anything, can we go to Andre's shop?" She ate another piece of crepe with strawberries, powdered sugar, and whipped cream.

He nodded. "Of course."

"At some point, we should talk about your dress for our wedding," I told her. "If you want someone to make the dress Wes drew, we should start on that."

Grace giggled. "I don't know. Maybe I'll get some ideas when Riley and I are looking."

"Great."

Wes nodded. "I love the idea of you doing that."

Jett looked up. "My grandmother has opinions about whatever date you choose for your wedding next year."

She usually did. But I didn't mind.

"Like choosing an auspicious day?" Grace asked.

He nodded. "Yep."

"I love it." Grace took another sip of coffee.

"Having a set date would be good so I can make sure the renovations are finished," Brennan agreed. His crepes just had butter and a little jam on them. "Everything seems to be going well."

We hadn't heard from Brennan's family since his brother crashed our dinner party with the sister pack.

"Riley's coming home for the summer. Most of her activities are here. Boxing camp. Skate smash camp. Tennis camp. Her internship with Grace. I think she's going for one week with Grandma and a long weekend or two with Sonja and Sasha and that's it. So please make sure when you do the walk of shame down the hall you're clothed appropriately." I grinned at Jett.

Jett rolled his eyes. "Noted. Though I was mostly dressed. Is it really the walk of shame when you live here?"

We finished breakfast, and Grace and I cleaned up so everyone else could get to work.

"Come on, let me show you something." I took Grace's hand and opened the door in the kitchen that led to the basement.

"Where are we going?" She blinked as I led her past the laundry room, gym, and the areas we used for storage.

"Wes and I were fixing this up for you last night." I led her into a little suite that smelled of paint. "This is the nest that came with the house. We don't use it much, because we usually go to the cabin. But, like the doctor and Mrs. Beekman said, you need a heat plan. Given it might be hard to predict them, and we might not have time to fly to Greece, we have this."

The walls were a very pale mauve. It was basically a large bedroom with a sitting area, a small anteroom with another sitting area and kitchenette, and a bathroom.

"We replaced the mattress. Though we just got new covers for the couches and chairs. We bought all the furniture when we moved in here and, like I said, we barely use this, but we can change it." I looked down. "We can replace the carpet or put in wood floors. The chaise is new."

Grace looked around. There was a very large, low bed, a giant couch, and a chaise. We'd put some pretty bedding in it. There were no windows, but there was a lot of nice mood lighting, and a separate air filtration system.

"We also picked out the art on the walls. But again, we can change everything. I was just trying to be prepared," I told her. Also, I'd brought it up twice, once in the hospital, once since, and she sort of ignored it.

"I like it. But am I really going to go into heat?" She made a face and flopped down on the bed.

"Possibly. Gammas can go into heat." Though her body might decide during the reset not to, which was fine. The point wasn't for her to go into heat. It was for her body to go into heat *correctly* if she ever did. Her not going into heat didn't necessarily mean she couldn't have children, either.

I laid down with her and curled her to me. "We need to actually come up with a heat plan. At the very least, who do you want in here with you?"

"Everyone, of course." She nodded, then bit her lower lip. "I can do that, right?"

"Yes, but you'll probably want to talk to Jett, Bren, and Spence. Not sure what everyone's comfort level is. However, we can always trade off. Here, let me show you the rest." I showed her the anteroom and the bathroom. Someone could always sleep in the anteroom or have a snack while other people fucked her.

"I like it. Thank you."

"You are so welcome." I kissed her. "Now, I have other rooms to show you." I led her back to the first floor, but instead of taking her upstairs, I took her past Riley's room.

I opened the door. It was a pretty room with lots of windows that looked into the backyard. It was near the downstairs bathroom we hardly ever used.

"This is what they call the *omega room*, it's a living room where the omega might have her friends over for tea and gossip. We never use it." Which was why there was literally nothing in here other than a couple of boxes.

She nodded. "That's what the room we had book club in felt like."

"This would be an option for the creepy doll room and or a guest room for people not old enough to stay in the guest house," I suggested. "Let me show you the other one."

I led her to another room off the main living room. While it had a window, it also had wood paneling and lots of shelves.

"The alpha study for cigars and brandy?" she laughed.

"Exactly. We were going to put a pool table in here but never did."

She looked around. "This could be a nice guest room. I love all the shelves. Right, we're going to need a place for Tru and Mercy to stay."

"Yep. We should buy shit for it before they come." Though we had a little time–and they wouldn't be here at the same time.

I put my arm around her. "So, about that bath?"

She grinned, her scent flaring. "I thought you'd never ask."

Chapter Thirty-Two

Grace

Friday morning, I pulled up in the dorm parking lot of Hadley Hall in my pink truck. The parking lot was full of well-dressed people loading things into fancy cars. My phone beeped.

Riley stood there in fishnets, combat boots, a black skirt, and a band T-shirt. Her braids had been taken out, and today her hair was in a style that I could only describe as 'anime girl' buns with green clip-ins. The last few things from her room sat beside her–like her bedding and a few personal items.

Rolling down the window, I yelled, "Get in the car, fucker, we're going shopping."

Wait. We were at her school. Should I have said that? Probably not.

"You're speaking my language." Riley beamed and threw most of the stuff in the truck's bed, then got into the small, two-seater truck with her backpack.

Someone came over to us, and I signed Riley out, glad no one called me out for swearing.

"I love this truck. It just fits us and some dead bodies. Perfect." Riley grinned. "Um, can we actually go shopping?"

"While I have a couple of things that I need to do today for work, we can if you'd like to. How was the dance? The pictures made it look fun." I started driving.

"It was great, but…" Riley got quiet. "Be cool, okay?" Her anise scent flared with anxiety.

"Of course."

"Hiro and I kissed last night. I… I really like him," she confessed.

"I'm glad. Will you be okay working with him for the internship program?" It was only four weeks, but four weeks could be a very long time with someone you're awkward with.

"Fuck yeah." She nodded.

"Okay. What do you want to do right now, then? We're going to the mall with Spencer tomorrow." I was looking forward to it.

"We can go to a different mall. Go get manicures, have bubble tea, maybe look for clothes for the party? If you'd like to buy me some work-appropriate clothing, I won't be sad." She grinned as she set the navigation on her phone.

"Is there a movie theatre there? That new rom-com you were talking about opens today," I stated.

"Yes. They have enormous screens there, and nice chairs, but they don't bring you food," she replied.

I nodded. "Sounds great."

We drove to the mall and got our movie tickets and then went to get manicures. Riley had already made us appointments. I texted the group chat and sent them my location.

I looked at Riley. "Wes wants to join us."
She shook her head and texted.

"Someone might just show up," I said to her as we went to the food court to get bubble tea. I'd been to this mall before with Evan and Riley to buy things for the PIIP conference.

"I know. It's so fucking annoying," Riley huffed. "Possessive shitheads."

"Yeah, but they're our possessive shitheads." I added our manicure and movie times to the chat.

We sipped our bubble teas and had our manicures. I got hot pink, Riley got dark green. Riley filled me in on all the gossip from the dance and some end-of-school drama.

After we finished and I paid, she dragged me off to a popular teenage store.

"Can I get clothes for work here?" She batted her eyelashes at me.

"Maybe?" I looked around and started assembling some things that were her style but fit the Compass BioTek *scientist professional casual* dress code well enough.

Riley tried on some outfits, and I got her a few. After all, I had a paycheck now. I also found a couple of cute swimsuits since I'd thrown out the ones I'd gotten for the PIIP symposium.

"I need stickers for my truck," I added. Yes, I wanted to put fun stickers all over my brand new truck.

"I know just the place." Riley took me to a shop with a lot of obscene stickers that I wouldn't put on my truck, but I picked up a few to stick on the e-reader that Spencer got me. We went to another store, where I found a few good ones.

She then led me to another shop. "Here, this is where Sonja found her dress for her elopement."

The shop was filled with wedding and formal dresses. While Eunice the fancy wedding planner had sent me ideas of what to wear for my party with Spencer, as had Evan, I still wasn't sure. A lot of brides wore gold, but that also varied by culture and preference.

Riley found some things, but nothing I tried on was quite what I wanted.

"I like." Riley came out in a flowy green dressy romper that had long pants but was sleeveless. The party's colors were mauve, green, and lavender to go with our fancy summer picnic theme.

"You look great. I'm not sure about this one." I looked down. The sleek minimalist dress was lovely, but it wasn't quite what I was looking for.

"You're not doing something poofy?" Riley asked.

"For the one with your brother and Wes, yes. For this one, I was thinking of something simple and elegant."

"Okay, I see that," she agreed.

We finished up, bought the pantsuit, looked in another store that didn't have what I wanted, grabbed some lunch, and found some shoes.

She checked the time. "You know we're being followed, right?"

"By which one?" I checked the location app on my phone. "Never mind. It's Brennan."

"We're going to ignore him." Riley took me into a really nice department store. "This is where I got my black dress that I wore to the other dance."

We looked through all the racks of dresses. I tried some on. But nothing was *right*.

"We have time. Maybe the fancy mall will have something. There's a store I have in mind, but this was fun," she told me as we went to the theater to see our movie.

"I'm having a great time." I bought popcorn, soda, and candy.

"Need help?" Brennan stood there in one of his work suits.

Riley eyed him. "We can go to the movies ourselves, you overprotective fuck."

"I know. I wasn't going to see the movie with you, because I have an online meeting with one of my overseas properties. But I was in the area, so I just thought I'd stop by to make sure that everyone was okay." He gave me a kiss.

"Thanks." That was sweet.

"Sure." Riley rolled her eyes.

"Are you going to shop more after this?" he asked me.

"I actually need to get some work done today. So probably not. We'll be safe. And I can carry the snacks. Thanks." I got the snacks. Riley and I went into the theatre, which had stadium seats and a gigantic screen.

"Such a sap." Riley snorted. "You know he's probably going to do his meeting from the work lounge here or something."

"Probably." I texted him.

We watched the movie then Riley and I got cupcakes.

"Sadly, we need to head home," I apologized, as I finished my chocolate cupcake.

"That's okay. I'm on dinner duty anyway. This was fun. I enjoy having time with just you," she replied.

"Me, too."

I frowned when we got to the car. A bag from a department store lay across my seat.

"You have a stalker." Riley put her purchases in the small space behind our seats.

There was a little note. *You deserve something pretty, Bren. Also, stop and get you and Riley a treat on the way home.*

"A stalker named Bren." I laughed. Inside was the blush dress and the green dress. Warmth flowed through me.

"Nice choices," Riley said. "Such a sap though."

Maybe. But that sap was mine. They all were.

Chapter Thirty-Three

Spencer

"We have reservations for three for tea under Thanukos," I informed the hostess at the restaurant inside the Everydoll Boutique. We'd already been through the store so that Riley could choose a doll to bring for tea. Though I'd promised that we'd go shopping more afterward so that Riley could get some outfits for hers and Grace's doll could have her hair done.

"Would you like doll seats?" the hostess asked.

"Three, please. Spence, you're getting a loaner doll." Riley grinned and pointed to a wall of dolls that diners could borrow for the duration of their meal.

"You choose," I replied.

Riley, who was wearing a long black lace-up dress and clunky shoes, chose a doll as the hostess grabbed three doll seats and three menus and brought us over to a table.

Grace held my hand, the doll the professor gave her clutched to her chest. Her blue T-shirt dress complemented her eyes. It didn't really match her slip-on sneakers, which had peaches on them. Maybe I should get her slip-ons that coordinated with all her T-shirt dresses, since that's what she primarily wore outside work.

The restaurant was crowded with families, most with multiple children. Many of them wore party hats, as this was a popular place for birthdays. But there were also tables full of only adults, having a good time, some of them also wearing party hats. Everydoll had an almost obsessive following.

I pulled her close to me. She had her *I'm overwhelmed* face on.

"Oh, is that a Gracie doll? She's in impeccable condition other than her hair. She looks like she just sat on a shelf," a random omega asked as we walked past.

"Yeah, it is, and old doll hair gets like that," Riley retorted.

We took a seat. The hostess affixed seats for the dolls so that they could sit next to us. We put our dolls in them so they could join us for tea. Riley had chosen a boy doll in a tennis outfit for me to borrow for the duration of our meal.

"Someone will be back to take your order," the hostess told us.

I turned the menu over to the beverage list and handed it to Grace. "Riley, what are we getting today?"

Afternoon tea had several options, but it was for the entire table.

"Oh, we should get the special-tea, since that has the most food. Also, a pot of jasmine green tea?" Riley asked.

Grace nodded. "Sounds good. Now, do I get a beer or a cocktail with a silly name? Perhaps a mimosa?"

"The champagne here is mid, but they have a very nice wine list," I replied.

Grace ended up with a beer, I got a glass of merlot, and Riley ordered a blinking mock-tail.

"Did you have fun at the gym today, Grace? I love that place." Riley took a sip of her drink.

The two of them had gone with Jett to the boxing gym this morning. I'd played a little golf, since I was healing up fine.

"I like it. Next weekend I'll have my motorcycle license, and we can take my bike?" Grace took a drink of beer.

Oh, how I love the way my good doctor's pink lips looked wrapped around the neck of the bottle.

"Perfect. You looked good when you were practicing earlier. You'll pass your motorcycle test no problem," Riley agreed.

"Yes, you've got this," I assured. Once again, I'd joined her on my own motorcycle, and it was fun going around the neighborhood with her.

"Here's your tea." The server brought a pot of tea and put it on the table. She gave each doll its own tiny teacup. "I'll be right back with your food."

Riley looked at Grace. "We're allowed to take the doll teacups home."

"I think we should build a blanket fort and make the guys have a tea party with us in it." Grace took a picture of her doll with the teacup.

"Which guys?" Riley laughed, doing the same.

A grin spread across Grace's face. "All of them."

"I'm there," Riley agreed.

"I'd do it," I told them. Evan, Wes, and I played tea party with Riley many times over the years.

Grace leaned over and kissed me on the cheek. "I know."

The server brought over a tower of sandwiches, savory pastries, fruit, and treats and set it on the table. "Enjoy."

We started eating. Riley kept feeding her doll and taking pictures.

"Spencer, you haven't fed your doll anything. So neglectful." Riley laughed.

I pretended to feed my brown-haired loaner doll some sandwich. Grace snapped a photo. A moment later my phone buzzed, and I saw that she put it in the group chat.

"Are you enjoying yourself, my good doctor?" I gave her a fond look as I took a sip of merlot.

Last weekend had been frightening, but all week Grace had been in good health and was only occasionally grumpy because she felt smothered by the others. She was looking forward to returning to the lab.

"I'm enjoying the company. Do you think Tru would like to come here and have tea? I know she'll be in camp most of the week, but I'd like to do a few special things with her." Grace bit into a savory pastry. "I love bacon."

"I can't think of a better place to take her. She'd love it," I assured.

Everything for our *Future Intern* project with Rock Tech's math camp was going well. Our VP of Communications was excited about the positive press that it would bring. I was excited because it made Grace happy. She couldn't wait, not just to spend time with her little sister, but to nurture Tru's love of math and sense of wonder.

"Yeah. Ooh, you can make an appointment for the doll lab, and she can create a custom doll. You come and have tea, do a little shopping, then go get your doll," Riley suggested.

"That sounds fun. But other siblings might be jealous if she comes back with a fully custom doll," Grace said softly, plucking another treat off the tray.

"Probably just her twin and the little one. You can pick out dolls for them together. Oooh or make sister dolls." Riley took a picture of her drinking out of the doll cup.

"That sounds expensive; this place is insane." Grace looked around the crowded dining room.

I squeezed her hand. "I think it would be a fun treat, and a nice way to make some memories with your sister."

After we finished eating, I paid the bill, and Riley took us back into the shop. The store had many levels, each one divided into different areas. We dropped off Grace's doll at the doll spa.

"Oh, you have Gracie," the omega doll stylist cooed. "Original outfit and everything. I'll get her hair fixed up and perfect for you."

Riley got a skate smash outfit for her doll as well as some other things. Grace just quietly took everything in, clutching a basket as she wandered around.

"Let's look at the accessories, maybe they have a motorcycle." Riley pulled my elbow.

"Where's Grace?" I looked around.

"Spencer. Look." Grace held a pink foil, crystal-studded box, with a blonde doll wearing a crown, a pink dress, and gloves.

"Would you like another doll?" I asked her. It was clear from her face that she did.

She nodded. "The one from Bren is really special, and apparently so is the one from the professor. I think I'd like just a doll so that Tru and I can play dolls together. It was hidden behind some dolls in another section. She's adorable. Look at her dress. Even the box is pretty."

"The one from the professor isn't special, she's just old, and you can't buy her anymore. They do that a lot, so people will buy more dolls thinking they're collectable. I mean, go amass a doll army if it makes you happy, but it's not going to fund your retirement island." Riley looked at the box. "But she's really pretty. You're getting her that one, Spence?"

"You can choose another doll if you'd like, Riley. That doll is lovely, Grace. Of course I'll get it for you." I hugged her to me. Anything for her. Between my knife wound and her getting ill, I just wanted to give her everything.

"It's so silly, but I absolutely want to make up for never having dolls like these as a kid. And, well, the toys I had that she gave away." Her peach scent went salty with sadness.

I kissed the top of her head. "I'll get you as many dolls as you wish."

We went downstairs where there was an entire selection of transportation options for your dolls–from cars to horses to bicycles–even remote-control trains.

"Spence, do you want me to distract Grace when you pay?" Riley whispered. "Not sure how one of those ended up on the main floor. Pink foil boxes mean limited special-edition, and they're kept in glass cases in a room on the first floor. That one isn't just foil, it *sparkles*. I only know this because girls on my floor in the dorms collect these fuckers. Anyhow, Grace might want to put it back if she knows how much it costs, and she should have the fucking doll. Honestly, we should take her to Stuff-A-Stuffie, too. Let's buy her all the toys."

"I agree. That's a wonderful idea, though we might need to do that another time if we're still going dress shopping. Wes and Evan are making dinner tonight," I reminded her. Last night it was her and Jett.

Riley made a face. "And that's a good idea, *why*?"

I laughed. "They're trying."

We finished shopping, Riley adding a remote-control doll motorcycle to the basket.

"Look, they're having cookie decorating. Let's make a cookie while Spencer buys our stuff," Riley said as we saw a bunch of people sitting at small tables.

"Are you done looking? We haven't seen everything, though I'm okay with making cookies and checking out," Grace replied.

Riley nodded. "Yeah, we can go through the doll museum and look at the fancy dolls another time."

Grace glanced over at me.

"Go on. Make a cookie for me." I kissed her and got in line for the register.

"Oh wow, we still have these? Someone is very lucky," the omega at the register said as he rang up my items.

"I'm the lucky one." As the price flashed up, I saw what Riley meant. But honestly, it was nothing in the scheme of things.

I found them finishing up decorating sugar cookies.

"Thank you, Spence." Grace gave me a kiss. "Here, try." She fed me half a cookie and then ate the other half.

We collected Grace's doll from the doll spa, hair looking fresh and styled.

"Let's go. Okay, so, dress shopping for Grace," Riley said as we entered the main part of the mall.

We strolled past the upscale stores. Grace browsed in a few but found nothing she wanted to even try on.

"Oh, Faun. At book club, the ladies were talking about their flats and how comfortable they were for dancing. They also like their purses," Grace said as we passed the Faun boutique, which was an upscale accessory shop known for its leather goods, scarves, and purses.

"Yeah, Spencer, can we please go shop for purses at Faun? I'd like a mini backpack, please." Riley grinned.

"They have nice shoes. I'm partial to them myself. Let's see what they have." I ushered them inside. I'd never bought a handbag here, but they were quite popular.

We walked in and started browsing.

"Oh, the scarves." Grace touched the display of silk scarves.

"My mother collects them. I often get them for her as gifts," I replied. "Their ties are nice as well. I should get one to match whatever color you're wearing for our party."

Grace squeezed my hand. "I love that idea."

We headed toward the shoes. I was a little surprised that no one asked if we needed help. Usually, I had an appointment.

"I think these are the shoes, oh, for the love of baby Jesus," Grace whispered, as we went to a display of leather ballet flats in many colors, the price on a tiny sign.

"Their shoes are worth the price. Impeccable craftsmanship, and they last a long time," I assured her.

I looked around and waved over a bored looking associate, who sighed and trudged over.

"Can I help you?" She looked disinterested.

"Yes, I'd like to try on the white ones." Grace gestured to the shoes.

"We'd also like to see some purses. I'm looking for a mini back-pack, and Grace is looking for some sort of cute everyday bag," Riley told her.

She sniffed. "I can get you the shoes to try on, but I don't think we have time for a purse appointment today."

"Purse appointment?" Grace's brows knitted.

The sales associate smirked. "One simply doesn't walk into Faun and buy a purse."

She left without asking Grace's size and started talking to some-one else who was also looking at shoes.

"You don't? Is this not a store?" Grace frowned.

"Let me see if the person I know is in today." I texted Emil, the sales associate I usually worked with.

Me

Are you in today? My mate wants to look at purses and get some shoes for our mating party.

"Grace." A small, impeccably dressed Asian omega, and another Asian woman who smelled of alpha, came over to us, carrying a bunch of bags.

"Hi, Yui." Grace smiled at the smaller one. She waved to the taller one. "Hi, Sara."

"Hi, Hiro's moms, is Hiro here?" Riley looked around.

Ah yes, Hiro's moms, the ones mated to Councilman Nakamura.

Sara shook her head. "No. But he's so excited for his internship."

"We're so glad that he could join us," I replied.

"Councilman Nakamura, the two of us, and our boys are very excited to attend your mating party," Sara said as the sales associate gave us a look.

"We're so happy that you're coming," Grace added.

"Did you get a dress?" Yui asked. "I can't believe you don't have one yet."

Grace shook her head. "That's why we're shopping today. We just stopped to look at shoes. I was thinking of something like this."

Leaning in, she showed her something on her phone. My phone buzzed.

Emil

> **You have a new mate? Congratulations. I was going to text you tomorrow about the new scarves we're getting in. We have some with matching ties. That might be fun for you and your new mate.**

Me

> **That sounds lovely, perhaps I could have an appointment this week?**

"That's very simple, Grace," Yui said. "While I'm all for being understated, you're mating *Spencer Thanukos*."

I'm not sure anything about Yui was understated.

Sara frowned. "I do see what you're going for–elegant and unfussy. Pity you didn't think to have someone custom design something for you ahead of time. It's too late to get anyone worth having. Not to mention, I hope your tailor is speedy. You're cutting it close just getting your dress now."

"Can she have those designers' names, anyway?" Riley interjected. Sara's frown deepened. "Hear me out. She and my brother are having their *Enormous Fantastic Wedding* next year. Grace has this sketch of her in a dress that one of her other mates drew. And well, Evan's mate *bought* an estate and is making it into an event property, just so they can get married in the garden like they're in a Tea-Time Era British Drama. So, I think she needs a custom dress based on that sketch."

Yui clapped. "I love that show. And Sara loves those dramas. Oh! I'm on the planning committee for the Rockland Ballet's gala, and our venue fell through. I really don't want to have it at the Performing Arts Center, and if I have to go to something else at the HighTower or the Hotel Gladiola, I will just be beside myself. A garden, you say? That sounds *perfect*."

"I'm not sure if it will be ready, but maybe you can work something out? Ballet under the Stars sounds beautiful," Grace agreed.

I took Brennan's card out of my wallet. I carried them because I often had reason to send business his way.

"Here you go. If it's possible for him to help, he will, though I'm not sure where he stands in the renovation process." I handed it to her.

A ballet gala was exactly what Brennan needed to introduce his venue to Rockland society. Yui's friends would all buy tables for her gala, and her friends probably served on committees of other organizations that also held galas.

"Back to the dress. The one in the photo looks like a Ferrel by the neckline. Just take it to their shop on the second floor. I'm sure they can help you," Sara added. "Though I'll send you my contacts."

"Thank you," Grace replied.

The sales associate who had brushed us off was staring, and I suddenly realized that they weren't actually too busy. It was about appearances. Riley, Grace, and I were dressed quite casually compared to the Nakamuras. She started to walk over to us.

"Yui, I found it." A blonde omega associate that I recognized came over holding a scarf box.

"You're the best, Christine." Yui beamed.

"Of course. Oh, hi, Mr. Thanukos." She beamed. "Emil told me that your mate wants some shoes and a bag. Let me get Mrs. Nakamura rung up and I'll help you."

That other associate froze.

"Christine will absolutely help you upgrade your purse collection," Yui gushed

"Pam, can you get them some champagne, oh, and a lime soda. Get shopping room number three ready, please," Christine called over her shoulder.

The associate nodded, looking unhappy. "Of course, Christine."

"I'm looking for a mini backpack," Riley told Christine. "Preferably black with silver spikes."

"I'll see what I can do." Christine's eyes flickered to our purchases from the Everydoll boutique. "Would you like to see what we have in the Faun for Everydoll Collection? We do have matching backpacks, but I'm not sure what colors."

Riley sucked in a breath. "My doll needs a backpack."

"One of the ladies at my book club has a really cute tiny pink purse. Something like that in green would be fun. Or maybe a big work tote?" Grace suggested.

"Or all of them," Yui laughed. "One can never have too many bags. If you're talking about Ansley, she has an entire collection of mini-Heathers, though she did get a mini-Gwen recently. They're very rare, though I'm not really into bucket bags."

"Oh, you're in *that* book club? Must be nice to have the time to read fiction." Sara rolled her eyes and checked her phone.

Yui turned to Grace. "It was so nice seeing you. I'll be in touch about our next committee meeting for the carnival. Also, you should buy a table for the ballet gala."

"Sounds fun." Grace waved as Yui, Sara, and Christine went to the register.

"Spencer, you absolutely don't need to get me a mini backpack. Really, I just want to see if she actually brings me one. Sasha keeps trying to get one, and so far no one has bought her one. Now one for my doll would be fun—or at least one of the little keychain ones? A lot of the girls at school have them as zipper pulls on their backpacks. They're perfect for keeping your earbuds in," Riley murmured.

Pam came over with a tray with three champagne glasses, all had strawberries, but one drink was clear like it had soda in it. She wore a glum look. "Your drinks."

"Thanks. You two can have whatever you want," I told Grace and Riley, feeling slightly petty. "Grace, I think you and your doll should get bags as well. Really, let me spoil you."

"Thank you, Spence." Grace ducked her head and grabbed a glass. "Thanks."

"Yeah, thanks." Riley grabbed her glass, whipped out her phone, and took a selfie.

"Um, is this one of those stores where they have to deem you worthy of the privilege of buying a purse that's as much as a car?" Grace's voice went soft as she took a sip.

Riley nodded. "Yep. And you don't even get to really choose. They're like *Here's the purse we think you deserve. Do you want it or not?* Personally, I think their main bag is fugly. But some of their things are cute. I really want a mini backpack, and only partially because it will make my sister jealous."

We sipped our champagne, which was quite decent, and looked around. Grace was texting someone, she also waved at Yui and Sara as they left.

Christine came back over to us. "Let's go into the shopping room. I think I have some things you'll really like."

Chapter Thirty-Four

Grace

I sat in a private shopping room at Faun surrounded by beautiful things, as we sipped champagne and had little cookies with the store's logo on them. All the items had been carefully selected and brought over for us to choose from. I'd never experienced anything like this before.

This was surreal. My phone buzzed.

Yes, I'd asked my new little sister for advice on purses. Because who did I even ask? I did like the tote. The messenger bag from

Evan was cute, but sometimes I needed a bag that I could fit more things in. My phone buzzed again.

Kilroy's Mom

All of them. Get them all.

Okay, I'd asked Kilroy's mom, Ansley, too, since she had so many purses. I actually liked all three bags and didn't know how to choose.

"You're shitting my dick, I can actually get it?" Riley gave Spencer a look as she clutched the silver mini backpack. Christine had found a matching one for her doll.

I sent Verity a photo of a doll purse that matched the dark green one.

Me

My Gracie doll needs a Grace purse?

It was ridiculous. This entire store was ridiculous.

So was the fact that I was going to let Spencer buy one for me. They were well made. If I got something I was truly happy with and took care of it, it would probably last for a long time.

Verity

I think she does.

Spencer ran a hand down my cheek. "What are you going to get, my good doctor?"

"The white shoes." If they didn't go with my dress, they'd be good for work, or other occasions where I wanted to be comfortable but couldn't wear sneakers.

"You should get them in black, as well. Very practical, especially for walking around at symposiums," Spencer recommended.

"Sure. And the tote. Oh, and the doll-sized Grace purse." There. Mostly practical, but a little ridiculous.

Spencer's eyebrows rose. "Not the dark green as well, so that you can match your doll? You should get these scarves, too."

He pushed over a couple of thin scarves Christine had brought for exactly what Verity had suggested–tying on the handle of the tote.

"If you insist." I really wanted the dark green purse as well. It just seemed a little greedy.

"Perfect–we'll take the pink, too. Oh, and that small wallet." Spencer leaned in and gave me a kiss.

"Thank you, Spencer." I leaned into him. Absolutely ridiculous.

He kissed the top of my head, then gestured to all the other things piled on the counter. "Riley, did you want a wallet or anything else?"

"I'll take this one." Riley pointed to a black coin purse. "Oh, and I'd really like a black keychain backpack, please."

"Perfect. I'll grab you a keychain backpack at the register. I've noted all of your preferences. Next time you need something, just text me or Emil," Christine told me.

Riley dragged me off to look at stuff as Spencer paid.

"That was ridiculous." I giggled.

"Yep," Riley agreed with a chuckle.

I took his arm as he joined us, bags in hand. "Thank you."

"Anything for you. Though I might have shown off a little." He smirked at that sales associate who wouldn't help us as we left.

"Should we go to that store on the second floor that Sara recommended?" I asked. Actually, the fancy wedding planner had mentioned that brand, too. Verity might have mentioned it as well.

"Sure," Riley said.

We went into the store. Everything looked elegant and understated. Soft music played.

"Are we shopping for something specific today?" an associate asked us as we browsed.

I showed her the photo. "My event coordinator suggested something like this for my mating party."

"But a little fancier," Riley interjected.

The associate found me a room, and I tried on some beautiful dresses. I sent pictures to both Evan and Verity. It felt a little weird to text her about dresses when I wasn't inviting her to this party. But she'd started texting me first, offering advice since she'd heard from Mercy what Riley and I were doing today. Maybe I should invite her. The more I got to know her the more I wanted her there, too.

Verity

> **Ferrel? They're just so elegant.**

Me

> **They are. Some of them are itchy, though. None of them are The One.**

They were also too long; even the ones they had in shorter lengths.

Verity

> **I get that. You might try Vecci. I've done a few of their shows, and they're my favorite designers. One day I'd love to have all the Vecci dresses.**

I sent her a photo of me and Brennan at the concert.

Me

> **I think that dress is a Vecci. Wait, shows?**

I sometimes do a little modeling. I've gotten lucky and done a few runway shows. I don't do much now because I'm so busy. But I have one coming up in Paris, and I'm excited.

She added photos of her wearing different outfits.

"Wow." I turned to Riley, who was trying on dresses for fun. "Verity is a model. Like a runway model. And she's getting a PhD."

Riley nodded. "Mercy told me. Verity's pretty amazing. Probably why they don't want her to date—so she doesn't find a pack and leave them."

Yeah, I knew exactly the kind of girl Verity was—that responsible daughter everyone depended on to the point where they couldn't function without her.

You're so hot. Some omega is going to be all over that.

I can only hope.

She added some laughing emojis.

Evan also texted.

Very sexy.

We changed, and I looked at Spencer. "Some of them were pretty, but none of them were *The One*."

He squeezed my hand. "That's okay."

"I know where to take you." Riley grabbed my hand, and we set off.

But they didn't have anything. Neither did the other shop she took me to. No one had *The One*. Not even Vecci.

"It's all right, Darling. We'll set up an appointment with Andre," he assured me.

"Why don't we go to Stuff-A-Stuffie. It'll make you feel better." Riley shot Spencer a pleading look.

"Why not." Spencer pulled me close, and we walked to a store where you made stuffed animals.

"My world has this, too," I whispered as I looked at all the stuffed animals you could choose from. "Oh, I want to make a hippo for Wes." I still had Mr. Hippo in my room, even though I had both the teddy from Evan and the bunny that Wes had won me.

I stuffed a hippo and recorded a message, then made her an adoption certificate. *Mrs. Hippo.* Riley made a bear in a Rockland Raiders outfit, complete with skates.

"You can make one for yourself, Darling." Spencer wrapped his arms around me and gave me a kiss.

"It's fine. I got a doll and purses, I'm feeling nice and spoiled. Even if I didn't find a dress." I squeezed his hand. This had been quite the amazing shopping trip.

"Spence, I think you should make her one. I'll make Evan and you one, and Grace can make Brennan and Jett ones, and then we'll all have one," Riley suggested.

"I love that idea." Spencer gave me a kiss and hurried off.

That was a cute idea. Hmmm. Jett was easy--the shop had boxing gloves. But what about Brennan? Maybe a suit? I picked out a tiny bear suit. I wandered over to an area that said *Club Stuffie–Adults Only.*

"Wow, today I learned you can buy lingerie for your bear," I muttered as I looked at all the very interesting things.

Should I get Brennan's bear a thong? We hadn't ever really talked about the night of the concert–or what happened after. But then, Brennan didn't seem like a *talk it over* sort of guy.

Something caught my eye, and I held up a pair of bear-sized briefs that said *Good Boy* across the ass. Was that overstepping or was it funny?

Mmmm. I texted Jett and sent him a photo.

Me

Am I overstepping if I put this on the bear I'm making for Bren? They'd be under the suit...

Jett

I love it. Not overstepping.

Me

Thanks.

Hmmm. Should I record Brennan a message? Yeah, I should. I put it in the foot so it would be harder to find. I wouldn't tell him either. I finished up, and we checked out with our stuffed animals in their little boxes. Spencer looked smug.

"We should probably head home," Spencer told us.

"I suppose." Riley thought for a moment. "Can we get candy first?"

He glanced at his phone. "Sure."

Riley took us to one of those shops where you filled a bag with whatever you wanted, and they weighed it. I had fun getting a little of this and that so I could try all of this world's sour candies. Spencer got some chocolates. Riley got all sorts of fun-looking treats.

Finally, we headed back through the mall toward where we parked.

I stopped short in front of a store. An elegant dress hung in the window under a bunch of lights. It was a slightly off the shoulder, A-line dress with a beaded sweetheart neckline. The satin skirt was full-ish but still sleek–not straight but not puffy. No train. It said *I'm* the *princess,* not *I'm* a *princess.* It could be pale gold, it might also be pale pink, or even off-white. I couldn't tell with the way it was lit.

But I knew it. This was *The One.*

"Spence, I need to try that on," I breathed, consumed with an overwhelming desire to have that dress. *Please don't be itchy.* I'd cry if it were itchy.

Or had a low back.

"You found it." Spencer wrapped his arms around me. "Let's try it on."

"Wow, you have good taste," Riley whispered. "The girls at school covet these. They're peak excellent eighteenth party goals when you're stupid-rich."

We went inside. Soft music played. Like Ferrel, it was sophisticated, but it had more of an elegant princess undertone.

"Oh, that's pretty," I breathed as we passed another mannequin in a pale pink, puffy dress.

"My mate would like to try on the dress in the window," Spencer told the associate.

"Which one?" he asked.

I pointed to it, since there were two windows, one on each side of the door. "That one."

"Lovely choice. That's part of our Sapphire Collection. Why don't I bring you over to the modeler? Not all stores have it, but we do." He led me over to an area that said *Dubois Sapphire Collection,* and there was a kiosk and some sort of photo booth.

"Can't I try on the dress?" I blinked.

"Step into the scanner and it takes a complete 360-degree photo of your body. At the kiosk, you can see how you'd look in any of our Sapphire Collection dresses. You order what you'd like and pay at the kiosk. They're made to measure and will be here at the store for you to collect in about eight weeks," he informed me.

My heart fell. "I don't have eight weeks."

"I'm happy to show you a couple of lovely dresses that we have right here in-store that are similar," he offered.

"Why can't she try on the one in the window? It looks like it's the perfect size," Riley questioned.

My thoughts exactly.

"Um, I have to talk to the manager. Usually we don't do that," he replied.

"Darling, why don't I talk to the manager, and you look around and see what else you can find? They do have lovely dresses here," Spencer said.

"Okay." I followed the associate, telling him about the party we were having. He pulled out some exquisite dresses. I had to admit that some of them could work if I couldn't have the one in the window.

He led Riley and I back to a beautiful dressing suite and brought us pink lemonade and little pink cakes.

"Just try," he suggested. "If none of these from the special occasion collection work, we still have the rest of the store. We *will* find you the perfect dress in time, even if we need to order dresses from Paris or New York and have them overnighted here for you to try on."

"Okay, thank you." I appreciated his positivity.

"Would another store have that dress in a different size?" Riley asked.

"The Sapphire display dresses are returned orders. Each store has different styles and sizes. It's not that we wouldn't sell it to you, but they're a pain to take off," he confessed. "But the manager will have the measurements, so if it's close, maybe she will?"

Did Spencer know my measurements? Never mind, he'd bought me dresses before, and if he didn't know them exactly, Andre probably had them from my fittings.

I tried on a pale gold dress that was a very similar style but with a different neckline and a hint of a train.

Oh? I took pictures and sent them to Evan and Verity.

Verity

That is beautiful. Very elegant and under-stated. Where are you?

Me

House of Dubois.

Verity

Goals. Modeling their bridal collection is something I've always wanted to do.

Me

I'd come see you do that.

I came out. "I like it."

"You look incredible," Riley agreed.

I tried on another. The tulle skirt was puffy, and it reminded me of the silver one I wore to the Morris Foundation gala. Riley had picked it out. I was a little lost in its largeness.

I sent more pictures.

"So?" I spun in front of the three-way mirror as Riley lounged on the chaise with her glass of pink lemonade.

"You look like dandelion fluff," Riley told me.

I was on the last dress when I heard a voice. "Darling, we have it."

My heart sped. "We do?"

"Just to warn you, it might be too short to wear with heels," he cautioned.

"We're going to be outside, so I can wear flats." I came out in a gown with a beaded bodice and lace skirt.

"Oh, that's lovely, indeed," Spencer told me.

I went back into the changing room, and I took that dress off, then stepped into the new one. It was fully lined and not itchy at all. The back was high enough that it mostly covered my scars.

"Perfect." I looked down. Yep, not wearing heels with this. Whoever had originally ordered this must be even shorter than me. But it would be fine with flats.

"Let me see?" The manager asked.

I opened the door. The manager looked me over and straightened the skirt. "It's very elegant and doesn't overwhelm you. You still might want to have it tailored."

I looked at myself in the mirror and sucked in a breath. "I love it."

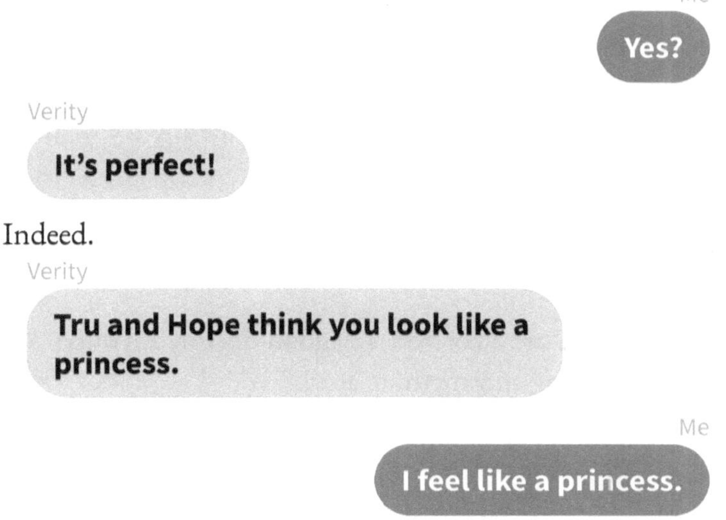

Indeed.

"How does it fit, Darling?" Spencer called.

"Incoming." I came out and stood before him, feeling like the prettiest princess ever. "I say yes to the dress."

For a moment he was speechless. "Oh, my good doctor. You're a vision."

"You look fan-fucking-tastic," Riley breathed, taking a photo.

"Please?" I looked up into his eyes. It was probably expensive. Since it was the display could we get a discount?

"Yes." His reply came out quick and breathless.

That look in his eyes made me want to take him into the dressing room. I adored that all five of the guys loved all of me–even the imperfect parts.

"I told you that it would fit her," Riley said to the associate.

"You did. Would you like to see anything else today?" he offered.

"I think I'm good," I told him.

"Yeah. So, Evan's blowing up my phone because they want to start dinner even though he knows we're over here doing important shit." Riley rolled her eyes.

"Oh, yes." Spencer checked his watch. "Let him know that we're on the way."

"So, you'll take it?" the manager asked.

"We will." Spencer looked at me. "How about if you take that off, we'll get you your dress, then we'll go home and see what Evan and Wes are making tonight?"

Grabbing his shirt, I pulled him down and kissed him.

"Thanks for making my princess dreams come true," I whispered.

Spencer kissed me. "For you, my good doctor, anything. I will give you everything and anything at all."

Chapter Thirty-Five

Brennan

"You know, this actually might work," Terrance murmured as we went over the numbers for the estate project. "Now we just need people to book it. Once it's ready to book."

"They'll come. Evan's going to have a big-ass wedding, people will see it, and they'll book events." Renovations were going well. The gardens were already beautiful. We were on track for our liquor license and permits.

And my mother hadn't fucked with any of my contractors or suppliers. While I dared not think I'd won, I'd be happy for silent treatment.

My phone rang. "This is Brennan."

"Hi, Brennan. This is Yui Nakamura. We lost our venue for the ballet's gala, and Grace told me that you have a brand new space with a garden, and we would like to have our gala there," she said.

"That sounds amazing. Thank you for thinking of us. Unfortunately, we're still under construction. Depending on when you're looking at and what you want, we probably could accommodate you in the gardens. But we won't be able to cater it. We might not have a liquor license by then. But if you're willing to bring in everything, we could probably work something out. After all, I love the ballet," I replied.

Okay, Katie loved the ballet, not me, but a lot of times it had delightful music.

"Oh. I see. The other place was going to provide the food. But I think we can pull this off. Have your event coordinator call me this week, and we can go over vendors, and I can see the grounds, and we'll get it all set. This is going to be perfect, because I just can't attend one more event at the High Tower. Have a good evening." She ended the call.

"Did you just book an event for our venue that's a year out from being ready?" Terrance's eyebrows rose.

"Councilman Nakamura's omega needs a venue for the ballet gala. I can't say no–it might affect our liquor license. But now I need an events team, or at least a coordinator with vendor connections, by Monday. Something like this could make us." I sent off an email about that. Then I sent another. We should get the website up too.

Usually, I had someone handling this for a new venue, but since I bought this for Evan, I was doing a lot of it myself. Too much. It was probably time to delegate.

"It could also break us if it goes badly. You know how those society omegas talk. How did she even know?" Terrance asked.

"Grace is on the Hadley Hall Carnival committee with her–Riley and her son are friends." I sent another email.

"That makes sense. My wife is very excited about going to Grace and Spencer's mating party," he stated.

"It should be nice?" At least it felt like Grace was trying to plan something enjoyable. "Spencer took her and Riley shopping. From the pictures Riley keeps dropping in the group chat, it looks like he's buying them whatever they want. Why do dolls need designer purses?"

"I think the answer would be *because you can*." Terrance chuckled. "Oh boy. What is he getting her for a mating gift?"

"I'm not sure what he's getting for her personally, but his family is buying them a plane and fixing the runway at her beach house, and she gets some family jewelry. However, I let Spencer buy her asset for being brought into the pack, and he bought her an island with a beach estate and a yacht." I sighed. How could I compete with Spencer? Was this how Wes felt when Jett and I were courting Evan?

"Ooh, you like her." Terrance smirked.

"I care for her a lot. We went to Kari Jaroff's concert, and it was fun." What happened after had been nice, too.

Terrance looked at his phone. "Well, I have to go. I think we're done anyway."

"We are. Thanks for going over everything. I'll see you later." I cleaned up, and there was a knock on the door.

"Hey, Bren." My dad stood there, dressed casually in a T-shirt from his old rugby team and shorts.

Once he'd been a professional rugby player and had been traded to Rockland. He met my mother at a bar. She wouldn't talk to him, and he hunted her down. Eventually, they fell in love and had us. He'd taken her last name and supported her and her career. Though he enjoyed running the foundation—especially the program that provided athletic opportunities for underprivileged children.

My parents had never formed a pack. Mother always said they hadn't met the right people.

It was probably about control. Well, for her.

How did my father even know that I was here? Probably Katie, who, like my mother, always seemed to know everything.

"Um, hi, Dad." I looked around, hoping this wasn't a family ambush.

"It's just me. I had lunch with some of my old teammates at the restaurant in your building's lobby. I saw your motorcycle in the garage and figured that you were getting some work done. Do you have time for a beer? Nothing serious, I just miss you." The earnestness in his face and voice made me pause.

I missed him. Once we had a good relationship, nicknames and teasing aside. It was fun coaching youth rugby with him and watching games with him and his friends. It just felt like we had less to talk about as I got older.

"We can do that. Though I have to be home for dinner. Wes and Evan are cooking," I told him, grabbing my things.

He chuckled. "Is Wes allowed to use the oven now? I remember when he burned the cookies, and your mom banned him from using her kitchen."

Laughing, we left my office, and I locked everything behind me.

"I have no idea what they're cooking or what inspired their desire to make dinner. Grace has been teaching Evan to bake, though," I said as we took the elevator up to the rooftop bar.

The weather was warm, and a lot of people were out enjoying the weather, some watching a race on one of the big screen televisions. We grabbed a table in the shade with a great view of the city below us. A server came over, and we ordered beers and a basket of onion rings.

"Is everything going okay?" I asked, a little worried there was an ulterior motive to this.

"The summer sports programs have started, and everything's going well. A few of my buddies want to donate and help increase our reach. Yeah, it was a working lunch." He chuckled. "Though the idea of all-omega rugby teams is a little frightening."

"Skate smash has an entire semi-pro all-omega league that's hugely popular. We have the Rockland Bathrobes." The names of the teams were all silly, and the rules were closer to what they used for the children's teams than in the PSSL, but it was a fun time. I'd brought Riley to a couple of games.

The server brought our drinks. My dad took a sip of his.

"I'm not against encouraging omegas to play contact sports. It's just that most of our programs are aimed at younger kids, not high-schoolers. I'll have to look at everything to see what would be the best, strategically," he said. "You didn't hear from me, but we have lost donors."

"Considering the backlash over cutting the scholarships for omegas, perhaps you could bring the scholarships back in some other form. Sure, my pack's foundation is covering all the students that lost theirs, but I'm sure there are other omegas that need scholarships? Maybe omegas-in-sports would align better with the foundation's mission? Need-based omega scholar-athletes?" I missed talking to my dad about shit like this.

"Oh, now that... that could work." He sent a text. "I miss this."

"Me, too. Just because I'm not interested in talking to Mother, Troy, or Liam, doesn't mean I don't want to talk to you," I admitted.

"Thank you. I'm glad you and Katie are still talking to me. Your mother is really torn up about Katie not talking to her, especially with her expecting. It's making her act a bit out of character." His brow furrowed with worry.

"Mother has been a little less careful." I took a sip of my beer. *Katie?* My mother was upset about not talking to Katie, but not me?

Wait. I didn't want to talk to her, anyway.

"It makes me worry. I do love her." Conflict crossed his face.

"I know, Dad."

He picked up his glass. "You took Grace to Kari Jaroff's concert? It's nice that you and Kari stay in touch."

"We had a good time. Grace competed in piano in high school, too." Also, I'd listened to some recordings of Grace's mother playing. If she'd lived, she probably would have been famous.

"Grace mated Spencer and you're having a party?" He had a drink. "Not fishing for an invitation. Your mother was grumping about not getting one when Councilman Nakamura did, and we know you just *love* him," my dad teased.

"I don't like how Councilman Nakamura seems to enjoy fighting wage equality while finding ways for businesses to cheat their taxes. It's Spencer and Grace's party, not our pack's. However, the Nakamuras were invited because their son and Riley are friends, and Spencer let her invite a few people." I ate an onion ring.

Including her friend Kilroy, whose father was some sort of professional fighter. Though it was his mom that Grace was in a book club with.

"I see." He nodded.

"Spencer and Grace are angry with Mother. That's why she's not invited. I'm happy to have you, Dad. But only you, not her or my brothers. I also understand if you wouldn't attend without her," I told him.

He brightened. "You want me there?"

"I do."

"I'll think about it. I like your pack. You did well. Thank you." His look grew concerned. "Are you okay with all of this? Things are moving fast with Grace. Too fast according to your mother, but alpha-omega relationships can move quickly. Caroline hit you hard, and I know how much you love your mates and pack."

I took a deep breath. "I've been trying to handle my shit. Grace isn't a bad person. The fact that Evan loves her with his whole heart tells me a lot about her. So does Spencer mating her. She fits so well, which, yes, is scary. But unlike Caroline, this is inevitable. Even Jett has a crush on her."

As do I.

He patted my shoulder. "I'm proud of you. I drove past that venue you bought. It has so much potential."

"Right? Terrance can't see it. But he will."

We talked more. I kept waiting for him to bring up the buildings or the State Street project.

But he didn't.

"Well, I should go," he finally told me.

We walked down to the parking garage.

"Thanks for taking the time to meet up with dear old dad." He looked wistful.

"Anytime," I replied "Maybe we can make this a regular meeting? We don't work that far from each other."

My dad beamed. "I'd like that a lot."

I got on my bike and drove off. Glancing in the review mirror, I saw him continue to stand there, longingly.

I walked into the kitchen to find Evan, wearing a pink apron, standing over Jett as he sat at the table, eating a cookie.

"Is it okay?" Anxiousness filled Evan's lemonade scent as he watched Jett eat.

"It's good, Baby, really." Jett pulled Evan to him.

I looked at the rack of cookies on the table. "You made chocolate chip cookies?"

"All by myself." Evan beamed. "Try one?"

"Absolutely, Love." I took a bite of the cookie. I preferred mine soft and thick, not thin and caramelized, like these were. But they were very good, all things considered.

"They're great." I kissed him. "No Wes?"

"Wes was doing something with his dad, then grabbing what we needed for dinner," Evan said.

"I'm here, Babe." Wes burst in with bags of groceries.

"Good. Let me text Riley. I thought that they'd be home by now." Evan looked at his phone and texted something. "Oh, shit."

"What's wrong?" Immediately, I went to his side.

And saw a mirror selfie of Grace in an *incredible* dress. "Oh."

"Wow," Wes breathed from over my shoulder. "I knew they went dress shopping, but that..."

"That dress looks like you can't leave it on the floor," Jett said.

No. I wasn't sure where they were, but everything about that dress said *expensive.*

Evan texted her. He looked through other pictures, passing his phone around. They were all exquisite.

"That one. She chose that one, right?" Evan showed us another photo. This one was even more beautiful than the first. It also fit almost perfectly, where most of the others were too long.

"I really like this one." Wes went back to the one where Grace was swallowed by tulle and flounces.

Evan took back his phone and sent another text.

"I... I was thinking of drawing her a grown-up version of the wedding dress I drew her in back in high school," Wes said softly. "Especially since she was talking about getting it made."

"I love that," Evan said. "I don't know why Lexi thinks it's not pretty."

"Probably because it's fluffy. Lexi likes simple things," Wes replied.

I looked at the bags. "How can I help?"

"We've got it under control." Wes took things out of the bags.

"What are you making?" I eyed the ingredients. There was a lot of cheese.

"Something I used to make for Grace in our dreams. Yes, we dream-cooked. Yes, I woke up starving." He set out some bacon.

"Oh, Riley says they're buying a dress and leaving," Evan said to Wes. "Should we get started?"

"Yeah." Wes got a pot and a pan out, while Evan got down a baking dish,

Evan looked at Jett and me. "Why don't you take your cookies to go?"

"Oh, you made cookies." Wes' eyes lit up. He shoved a whole cookie in his mouth. "Mmmm." He kissed Evan's forehead, mouth full of cookie.

I grabbed a cookie, Jett took two, and we went into the living room.

"They're going to dirty every dish in the kitchen, aren't they?" I sighed, as I settled onto the couch.

"Probably." Jett curled into me and told me about his day. He and Evan had gone for a motorcycle ride this afternoon.

I mentioned meeting up with my dad. "The entire time I expected him to deliver a message or ask something of me, and he didn't."

His talking about the party didn't count because I knew when he was fishing and that wasn't it.

"Wow."

"Grace, it's fine, you can show them later. They just want dinner to be a surprise." Riley came into the living room from the kitchen, arms laden with packages.

Defeat crossed Grace's face. "I know."

"Dinner's soon, bitches. I'm going to put these down and set the table," Riley called as she disappeared down the hall.

Grace stood there, clutching her purchases, looking like the world was ending.

"Come here." I took the bags out of her hands and put them on the table, though the dress bag went on the chair.

Pulling her to me, I motioned for Jett to hug her other side. Together we hug-squished her tightly.

"That was a big day at the mall, wasn't it?" I started to purr for her, trying to calm her down. I don't think she was upset with Wes and Evan. She was overwhelmed.

Ever since the hospital, she'd been so much more sensitive. It could be the sounds, the smells, or so many other things.

"I found the perfect dress. Spencer bought me a doll. And some purses and shoes." She buried her face in my shirt. "I love your purr. It's so much quieter than anyone else's."

"Your guys could probably do it, too. It just takes a little practice," I told her, stroking her hair.

"It's the baby purr, so you don't startle the baby." Jett chuckled.

I shot Jett a look. "Thank you."

"Like you're purring while you're rocking the baby to sleep? Love it." Grace's arms tightened around my waist.

"Yeah." I had experience from helping with Terrance's kids. Sure, my brothers had kids. But I wasn't that sort of uncle to them, sadly. But Katie? I'd be there for her pack's kids.

"I like this," she whispered.

"I love holding you," Jett said softly.

Me, too.

"Dumb question, since we're alone. Mrs. Beekman is making me actually fill out a heat plan worksheet. If I ever have one, which I don't think will happen, you'll both be there, won't you? Even with Spencer? I asked him, and he said he'd do whatever I wanted. I mean we could trade off and stuff if you're uncomfy, but for part of it at least?" She looked up at me, scent anxious.

She wanted me there? Happiness bloomed in my chest.

I leaned down and kissed the top of her head. "If you want me there, I'll be there."

"Me, too." Jett squeezed her.

"Thank you."

It would be interesting, but at the end of the day, we were a family.

"Have you started going over the pack contract with Mrs. Beekman?" I asked. Once they went through it, we'd sit down with her and our lawyer and get things finalized.

"Not yet, but she went over the mate agreement Spencer had made for us, and we signed it," she replied.

Spencer had me read it first, which was nice. Wes didn't have me read over the one he and Grace signed, but it was a standard one drawn up by Katie. Also, Spencer's family had different traditions.

"Do you want to show us what you got at the mall?" Jett asked.

Grace nodded and wiggled out of my arms. "Look. Spencer got me an Everydoll. I love the one you got me. But she's special. So is Gracie. I wanted an ordinary one so I can play dolly tea party with my little sisters."

She took a hot pink foiled and sparkly box out of a bag.

Yeah. I was pretty sure that wasn't your basic Everydoll. But I wasn't going to tell her that.

"She's beautiful." I took a photo and sent it to Katie.

Me

> **Grace wanted an ordinary Everydoll to play dolls with her sisters. Spencer got her that.**

"We're going to be making your creepy doll room, aren't we," Jett teased.

Grace nodded. "Yes."

Katie

She didn't take it out of the box, right? That's from this year's limited edition excellent eighteenth doll collection. All their dresses were designed by Vecci.

Right, because dolls needed Vecci gowns the same way they needed Faun purses.

Putting down the doll, Grace showed us her purses. Though she was most excited about the work tote and the doll purse. She had no idea what she'd just gotten.

Not to mention they'd just *walked into Faun and bought purses.* So spoiled. My eyes fell on the dress bag. *House of Dubois Sapphire Collection.*

Me

She literally got the doll to play tea party. What is the House of Dubois Sapphire Collection?

Katie and I had a joint excellent eighteenth party. She had a Dubois gown in dark green. She'd also gotten a crown from a popular high-end jeweler. I wore a Vecci suit but had a tie and pocket square to match her. All our attendants wore a lighter shade of green. Lexi had been one of them. We'd rented out a popular rooftop club, and a good time had been had by all.

"Here's the dress." Grace unzipped it and took out the very last dress we'd seen. "We literally got it off the mannequin in the window. We have to take it to be altered."

"It's beautiful." I gave her a kiss.

"It is. How many stuffies did you make?" Jett eyed the three boxes on the table.

"Here, these are for you." She shoved a box into each of our hands. With a squeak, she took her things up the stairs.

"I didn't know she made me one." Jett opened the box to reveal a stuffed bear in a boxing outfit, complete with little gloves.

Katie

The Sapphire Collection is their semi-custom line. Wow. I had to get one off the rack.

Me

Oh, poor you.

"Open yours." Jett nodded to the other box.

"Wait, she made it for me?" I'd actually never been to Stuff-A-Stuffie.

"Yeah, like you pick a stuffie skin, stuff it, make a wish on it, dress it, and create a birth certificate for it. Okay, I know where we're going to make Lexi and Katie their baby gifts," Jett teased.

"That actually sounds pretty special." Opening the box, I took out a bear in a suit, with a watch and sunglasses. "I love it."

My heart warmed. Grace made me a stuffie.

"Pull down the pants." Jett laughed.

"What?" I did, and briefs that said *Good Boy* on the ass peaked out at me.

He kept laughing. "Sorry, she asked me if it would be overstepping if she did that."

"And clearly you told her to do it. I... I think it's cute. I'll put these away." Taking the boxes, I put them in our room. She made me a bear. My heart swelled.

When I came out, Grace was coming down the stairs.

I grabbed her and kissed her. "Thank you. No one has made me a stuffie before."

"You're welcome." She smiled.

"I can't believe you gave it to them early. We were supposed to do it after dinner." Riley pouted, joining us. "Food, fuckers."

Grace bit her lower lip. "Spencer gave me mine early."

"It's okay." I kissed Grace again. "Let's go downstairs and have dinner."

We sat around the table. There was a big pan of cheesy noodles, lumpy rolls, and some sort of green beans with bacon in them.

"Wes, is this…" Grace brightened as she took her seat.

"Yes. My grandma's lobster bacon mac and cheese. Just like we used to make. I also called and got her cheesy bay biscuit recipe." Wes practically burst with pride.

"And I got my grandma's green bean recipe." Evan beamed.

"I'm all over that shit. I love you assholes, but I miss Grandma's cooking." Riley took a big scoop of green beans.

I gave Wes a look. "You made lobster mac and cheese in your dreams?"

"It's the ultimate comfort food. Usually, my dad makes it with canned crab. But in our dreams we had actual lobster. Sometimes the lobsters would go all over the place, and we'd have to chase them." Wes beamed and took a scoop.

We started to eat. I took a bite. "This is pretty good, Wes."

Very cheesy and rich, but not bad at all.

"Oh, it is." Grace nodded. "The green beans, too."

"They're fantastic, Evan," I praised. "Grace, you're booking my venue?"

"Yui called you? Doing my part to make you profitable." Grace laughed as she put butter on a biscuit.

"Thank you. We'll see if it works out. What's going on this week?" I asked. "Riley has boxing camp, right? I have a business trip."

Grace looked up at me like I had kicked her puppy. "You're going away?"

"I'm just going to Asia." I was going to see both my properties there.

Spencer frowned over his glass of wine. "I thought we were all staying together."

"Sorry. I have to do this. I've put it off too long."

"Fine." Grace's shoulders slumped. "I have my motorcycle test this week. The professor is coming to town for a conference. I'm going to give him a tour of Compass BioTek and have lunch with him. He's also moving Creed into his new place. Creed is unamused by that. Are brothers allowed? I know sisters are, but what about Creed?"

"*Assholes* aren't allowed. It just happens that the sisters who live locally are not assholes, and the brothers who are not assholes aren't local," I clarified. "As long as your siblings are not assholes, they're welcome."

Instantly I regretted saying that as I remembered Hale *throwing* Grace like a ball on the beach. However, *train wreck* and *asshole* were two different things. We'd have to childproof the house when he came to visit.

"Okay, thanks," she replied.

"My internship starts next week. I need more shit." Riley gave her brother an imploring look.

"How about tomorrow after boxing camp?" Evan asked.

"Sure." Riley piled more green beans on her plate.

"I'd like to bring up the chicken army," Grace said. "According to zoning, we can have six hens. I would like to put a coop in the backyard and get some. We can't have goats, but I think we can have ducks. Bunnies, too."

Jett thought for a moment. "I'm all for bunnies, but we should probably wait on a duck until we have a pond and a garden. Next time I go home, I'll find all my stuff from the landscaping classes I took back when I was a scout."

Um, what?

Grace nodded. "I like that."

"Chicken coops are not very attractive," I blurted.

"Some are. I mean, one that looks like a spaceship would be fun," Riley interjected, getting more green beans.

"Who would take care of them when we're gone?" I added. Her look hurt my heart, and I regretted saying anything.

Evan looked at me, then Grace. "Brennan has never had pets, and the idea scares him. Jett has wanted a pet for ages."

"Pets are a lot of responsibility." The idea of caring for one more living thing was a lot.

Grace nodded. "True. I can take care of chickens, but we would have to find someone to care for them when we're away."

"I want a dog," Wes said. "We had one when I was little, but my mom took him in the divorce."

Oh.

"I didn't know that. Um, maybe after the summer? Since we'll be away for a bit." Both for our vacation and for Evan's heat.

"Fair. I will have a chicken army," Grace agreed.

"Sadly, we are not zoned for mini tigers," Riley added sadly.

I was happy for that, because Jett was right, a tiger the size of a dog was still a tiger.

Everyone talked about what they were doing. But my mind went back to the bear Grace had made me—and how sad she looked that I was going away.

...you'd be there, wouldn't you?

Yeah. I would do whatever Grace wanted, anytime.

Chapter Thirty-Six

Grace

Nerves coursed through me as I went down to the Compass BioTek lobby. Why was I so nervous? I literally wasn't this nervous yesterday when I took my motorcycle test, which I passed.

Creed, Pippa, and Nate walked through the door. Pippa was here. Yay. Not. She might seem on the surface to be the voice of reason, but she was very critical of Verity, which I didn't like one bit.

I waved them over.

"Sis." Creed picked me up and hugged me.

"Creed." I hugged him then turned to Nate. "Thanks for coming."

The professor gave me an awkward hug. He wore suspenders with beakers and flasks on them. "Thanks for inviting me."

"Pippa, hi. You're joining us?" I hadn't expected it, given she disliked Compass BioTek and called Spencer *that Greek man*.

"Sadly, no. I have a meeting. But I'll be back." The stately British alpha female gave Nate a kiss. "Have fun, Dear." Pippa looked at Creed. "Good luck." It felt a little forced.

Creed was just going to go to human resources and meet with a few people before he officially started next week. But his parents hadn't been thrilled about the job. Fortunately, no one had actually tried to stop him. My brother also was an adult who'd finished engineering school, so there wasn't much they could do about it.

"Thanks, Mum." Creed gave his mom a hug.

I got their badges and took Creed to HR. "Have fun."

"I'd rather go on your tour. Oh, Verity sent you cake pops." Creed handed me a little handled paper sack.

"Oh, she did?" Inside were pink heart-shaped cake pops. Immediately, I texted her my thanks.

"See you later." Creed grinned and left us.

"So, this is where you work?" The professor looked around.

"Yep. Let me give you a tour. I've been practicing so I can help with the interns," I told him. "Let's get started."

I showed the professor around, telling him about Compass' programs and products.

He frowned. "I can't believe you have such a complex in the middle of the city."

"Manufacturing and the warehouses are elsewhere."

"Do you like it here?" Nate glanced around.

"I do. They gave me a chance, Professor. If we can do this, it will be extraordinary," I replied.

The professor nodded. "Chances are good. I know that sometimes we don't get the ones we should. Still, what *are* you doing here? What is Creed going to do here?"

"Let me show you. I got permission. You're speaking at a conference here in Rockland?"

His eyes shone with excitement. "I am. It's a little silly. It's literally a chemistry professor conference that Rock Tech is hosting. I'm presenting on teaching best practices."

"That's amazing and not silly at all. From what I hear, you're everyone's favorite professor." I led him out of the elevator.

He beamed. "People say that?"

"They do." I took him down a warren of halls and locked doors as he told me about the conference, what he was presenting on, and what he hoped to see.

"Welcome to Special Projects. This is less biotech and more like *The Thanukos Incubator for Interesting Projects.* Let me show you our particle accelerator." I swiped my badge.

I showed him around, telling him about some of our projects.

"Oh, I've heard about the nano-computing project from one of my students in the Daedalus Society chapter I'm advisor for," he mentioned.

"Maybe they should apply for an internship next year. Would you like to see?" I took him through that lab, introducing people, and showing him the work. "This is where Creed's going to be working."

"That is incredible," he breathed. "Creed's on this project? Are you?"

"Not me." I waved to everyone, and we went to Margie's lab.

"Awww, is this your dad? Hi Grace's dad!" Tish waved.

"This is Professor Nate Thorne. If you think we look alike, you should see my brother. He's joining Narif's project," I told her. "This is Tish."

We finished our tour and ended up at my little office-lab.

"When the project officially kicks off, we'll have a bigger space, but here's my lab for now." I brought him inside. There were equations and papers and boxes everywhere. "Sorry, our new super computer was delivered. I'm making my interns put it together."

Like particle accelerators and super colliders, super computers were *much* smaller here.

Blaise, who'd started back from parental leave part-time, was going to teach them about quantum coding. We also had some simulations to run. It would be fun, even if Creed wasn't going to be working with us.

"What is your job here?" Nate looked around.

"We're attempting to make a virtual super collider. That's why I was interested in the modeler at Marquess University and was seeing it that day that I ran into you at the cafe," I explained.

Nate whistled. "That's incredible."

"If we can do it, it will be." I grinned. Excited by the prospect.

We finished our tour and ended up in the cafeteria and grabbed our free lunch. The professor updated me on my siblings.

"I'm so excited to see Tru. Thank you for trusting me with her." We sat at a table with a window to the courtyard. I'd understand if they didn't.

"Harry is beyond nervous. They've never really been away from us other than a weekend with grandparents," Nate confessed. "The other parents worry that it would be unfair for Tru to get a special trip and not Pax, but honestly, he doesn't actually care, he just wants a new toy truck."

"Oh, I don't want anyone to feel left out. I just know Tru and Mercy a little better," I agreed, making a note to get him a big truck.

"When I saw the program, I pushed for it. The fact that they have something like this for kids as young as Tru is astounding, and I know she's going to love it," he told me.

And if she didn't, we'd find something else for next year.

"Spencer found it," I said. "The camp and Compass BioTek are really excited to do the Future Intern program, too. We're going to run it for a couple of sessions, not just hers."

He beamed at me. "Thank you for encouraging her. While of course we nurture academics in our house, her love of math is very strong for her age—even more than Verity and her flowers, and it's hard for everyone to understand that she is serious."

Oh, she was. I loved her messages.

"I just want to do for her what no one did for me. What I would have given to go to a camp like that." I took a bite of salmon and spinach salad.

"The alpha parents are still a little wary, though. I mean..."

"You don't know me. I get it. Feel free to send Verity as chaperone." We'd started getting a guest room ready.

Nate thought for a moment. "I can suggest it, but we need Verity for the summer to help wrangle all the kids. I'm leading research and teaching summer sessions, and well everyone else has work..."

And Adriana was in jail.

Honestly, from what Verity told me, she could use a week with us. Not to mention, I wanted to spend time with her. Maybe it was the guilt I felt at having a poor relationship with my three brothers growing up, but I just wanted to love all my new siblings.

"In fact, I think we're going to have to make her cancel a modeling thing she's doing. We just can't figure out coverage for the kids without her." He took a sip of his iced tea.

"No. Don't do that. Let her go. Just send them all here. There are lots of camps and things," I offered, horrified they'd make her cancel a *job* to help them.

But Tru said sometimes they wanted her to miss class.

"I don't think they make camps for kids Hope's age," he chuckled.

"We have an onsite daycare. We saw it on the tour." That's where Blaise's baby would be when they came back to work.

Given everyone in my pack seemed to want a stack of kids, maybe we should borrow some and then see what they thought.

"I'm sure we'll figure it out. It's just tough with Adriana in jail. We now have one less income, one less adult. I don't regret what I did, but it's affecting us more than I expected, and it hasn't even gone to trial yet," he explained.

"Is it going to trial?" I didn't know how things worked here, and I'd been letting Spencer and Brennan handle both cases—me being trafficked and her stabbing Spencer.

He nodded slowly. "They found Thora's mom. She turned over the *contract* and all the details in exchange for a lighter sentence. It was her, Rosalind, and Adriana who did this."

"Shit." I hadn't realized that Thora and Rosalind's mom was part of this, too.

It could have been her idea. She'd already lost one daughter, so why not save the other?

"Was she surprised that you found me?" I was still curious about who the contact was.

"She was more interested in how her daughter was. Not how I'd expect a grandmother to behave. My parents and siblings send their love. One day they'd like to meet you." He frowned as he poked at his food.

"Okay. I... I'm trying here, Professor." This was a lot. Today was a lot.

"I appreciate you trying so much, Grace. What did Rosalind do to you? Those scars..." Pain clouded his eyes as he took a sip of his drink.

"Do you really want to know?" While part of me wanted to spare his feelings because he'd been through a lot, another part of me wanted him to fully understand what his pack did to me. It felt so much worse now that I knew the truth.

I understood Rosalind's hatred of alphas and her fear I'd upend her life. But still, how could she dislike me that much? Okay, I wasn't her daughter, but I was her niece. I never asked for that life.

Nate nodded slowly. "She did that to you? Why?"

"Technically, she sent me someplace, and they did it. It was because of Wes. I started dreaming of him when I was ten. I was seventeen when she found out about it and got upset that I was convinced that I had an alpha soulmate out there. That was how they made me forget him." My voice was quiet as I toyed with my food.

"You and Wes are scent matches, right? She made you forget him?" He sucked in a breath.

"Yeah. For a long time I thought he was a childish fantasy."

Nate frowned. "Wes didn't try to find you?"

"He did. But when we stopped dreaming of each other, he thought I was dead." I took a sip of my drink.

"But you found each other, eventually." Worry creased his brow.

"We did. Sometimes I wonder what it would have been like if we'd found each other sooner." It was a pointless thought. If she hadn't made me forget him, we wouldn't have found each other sooner, I just would have had him to keep me company.

And if I'd grown up with the professor...

My childhood would have still been shitty, because I would have been 100% parentified and there would have been resentment from the other parents.

"I don't understand why she would make you forget him. Dreaming of your soulmate is a beautiful thing. Pip and I didn't even do that. Yes, Rosalind wasn't the best person, but how hard would it be to take you to a Center and have them help find him?" Anguish rolled off of him.

"It was a threat to her existence. I don't think she gave much thought to what raising kids would mean. Until we grew up." I was glad my brothers were in another world and didn't have to worry about illegal genetics.

"Oh." Nate nodded. "I can see that. It's still awful."

"Yeah. Did she even love me? Or was I always just a tool?" I sniffled. I'd been wondering about that. Maybe when I was little?

"Honestly, I'm not sure she's capable of love. I'm sure marrying, having kids, and everything else was just all part of the construct she made to protect herself without thinking about how her actions affected those around her," he admitted honestly.

"True." While she didn't seem as harsh towards some of my brothers, I wasn't sure that she loved them, either. As for the man who raised me, she was kind to him in a way I seldom saw her be to anyone else. Sometimes I saw them being flirty and having little stolen moments.

She could have loved him—or lusted.

"Wow. This looks cheerful." Creed stood in front of us. "All the food here is free? And you can get whatever you want, whenever you want?"

"Yep. Hot food service opens at ass-crack for breakfast and closes around five. But it's open twenty-four hours for drinks, snacks, and grab-and-go. Ice cream machine flavors change on Wednesdays," I added.

"Amazing." He disappeared.

"I'm sorry," Nate said softly.

"The fact that you didn't stop looking for me means everything—so does you letting me get to know my siblings. Riley is so excited to go to camp with Mercy." I pushed away my food, done with it.

Nate smiled. "It's silly, but I'm hoping Riley's academic drive will rub off on Mercy. I mean, Riley's a year behind her in school and already is thinking of things like internships."

Yeah, I wasn't going to pop the professor's bubble.

Creed plopped down with us with his food. "This is going to be great."

As he ate, he told us how his meeting went.

Nate's phone rang. "I'm going to get that."

He grabbed his phone and went out to the courtyard.

"That went okay? As much as Mum wanted to be close, Harry thought that you needed some time with him." Creed shoveled food in his face.

"Yeah. I... I don't know how much I can do, Creed. I mean, the woman Adriana sold me to literally made me forget my soulmate. But I want to love all my siblings. Even the ones I don't know." I'm sure they were getting overlooked in one way or another. I could already see it with Verity and Mercy.

Okay, and the fact Tru could just *leave* and come visit me without anyone noticing was alarming.

They all needed a sibling who didn't give a shit what their parents thought.

Creed hugged me. "It's enough, Grace. You just made him so happy. And Tru is so excited about her special trip."

"Verity can come, too. We'd have a lot of fun." I swirled my drink cup, like it would magically refill by doing so.

He laughed. "Oh, you will. We'll get her out here for visits."

"How's move in?" I finished my drink.

"They didn't move me into the dorms when I went to Natty. I don't know why they suddenly want to be all parental." He rolled his eyes. "For now, I'm sharing an apartment with some other Compass BioTek fellows. They seem okay. At least I have my own room. You know, that's what I liked about Natty–at home I shared with Hale for years."

"That sounds chaotic." I looked out the window at the professor.

"Dad's fine. It's probably just Mum." Creed continued to eat. "I didn't realize what an incredible project they put me on. I thought I'd be in R&D building medical shit."

"You sort of are. Just tiny." I grinned.

He nodded. "True. But as interesting as Dr. Terik's project is, I sort of hoped to be working with you."

"I'm also part of Special Projects. You'll see me around, though our projects don't cross over, like yours will with Margie's," I explained.

Creed leaned in. "What are you doing? Did you show Dad?"

"I told him about it. I can show you my lab when I walk you to Special Projects so you can meet with Narif," I replied. "And we can work together at some point. After all, we have to start the framework, so when Tru solves Garamoci's Theory of Everything and Spencer hires her, we can build a spaceship."

The professor came back in and joined us. "I have to go but thank you for the tour." He hugged me. "I'm so proud of you. Both of you."

"Thanks, Professor. Let me walk you out?" I offered.

He shook his head. "Stay with Creed. I'll see you later."

"Bye, Dad. See you for dinner," Creed waved.

Grabbing his tray, the professor threw out his garbage and left.

"We should go watch him give his presentation at the conference," Creed told me. "It's a thing we do."

"Right, sit in the back until he notices you. I remember when Verity suggested we sit in on his class. But I'd rather wear a Compass BioTek polo and sit in the front row," I replied.

Creed laughed. "I love that. Usually, we're sneaking in. But you, *Dr. Thanukos of Compass BioTek,* can probably contact any conference and ask if you could sit in on a single panel, and they'd probably let you."

"We should do it." It seemed like an easy way to support him.

"And hey." An anxious look crossed his face. "Don't feel like you have to hang out with me."

"Brothers are allowed as long as they're not assholes," I replied. "I plan on inviting all of you to my big wedding next year. I'd love for the little ones to be my flower children, and maybe Verity and Mercy could be attendants. But I'm not inviting everyone to the party I'm having with Spencer the weekend after next. I hope no one's feelings will be hurt. He's still recovering from what happened at the beach, and we're keeping things simple. That being said, you're invited, and so is Verity if we can get her away from kid duty–maybe Mercy can come with her."

I'd decided I'd really like them there.

"It's fine; no one is expecting it. Though it would be super funny to see Mum try to make nice with *that Greek man*. But I guess we'll see that next year. I'd love to come, thank you. Verity would like to attend, I'm sure. She just loves weddings. Well, mostly. But I think that's when her modeling thing is," he said.

I groaned. "The one they want her to cancel. Fine, we'll just bring all the kids over so she can go. I can have a bouncy castle at the country club."

We hadn't ended up getting one because there weren't that many kids.

"Hale's not allowed in a bouncy castle, just to warn you," Creed laughed. "We'll figure it out."

Did I want to know?

Creed finished eating, and we cleaned up, and I led him over to Special Projects.

"I can get myself back to my place, you don't have to worry about me. The public transportation seems good here, and I should get used to it. But you probably get chauffeured by your alphas," Creed teased.

"I have a truck, sometimes we take that. When Riley starts, we'll probably take my motorcycle. Also, Evan said something about going on a date tonight," I replied.

As we entered Special Projects, Tish and Jordie were leaving.

"Awww, it's Tall Grace," Jordie joked.

Tish waved. "See you later, Grace, Tall Grace."

"Yeah, that's not going to get old," Creed chuckled.

I'd have to tell Verity about that.

"Here's my lab." I showed him and told him about the project.

"That is fucking cool shit," he told me. "But it makes sense, considering what you saw on your field trip and your being at the PIIP Symposium. Can I tell Ina?"

"Absolutely. Maybe one day she'll work with us, too. Let me take you to Narif's office." I led him down the hall and knocked on Narif's door. "Special delivery."

Narif looked up from his laptop. "The resemblance is uncanny. Creed, I am so excited for you to be joining the team."

"I'm happy to be here." Creed shook his hand.

"That's my cue to go." With a wave, I left. Then I went into the office and shut the door.

That was... a lot. Sitting on the floor under my desk, overwhelmed with too many emotions, I brought my knees to my chest and cried.

Chapter Thirty-Seven

Wes

There was a knock on my open office door, and a familiar blonde stood in the doorway of my office.

"Peaches. Did everything go okay with the professor?" I'd felt a little conflict there–and a lot of sadness.

Honestly, if my mom wanted to be part of my life again, I probably would refuse–even if I desperately wanted answers. But I wasn't as good-hearted as Grace.

"I guess? Oh, I brought you a cake pop. Verity made them." She closed the door of my office and climbed onto my lap. Grace put a pink heart-shaped cake pop on my desk and buried her face in my button-down.

"No, it didn't go okay, did it? I should have joined you." I wrapped my arms around her. Both Spencer and I offered, but she'd wanted to do it herself.

"It went fine. I'm the one who's not okay. It's a lot to grapple with." Her voice broke.

My arms tightened around her as I rocked her in my rolling chair. "It is a lot. Especially with your brother working here."

"That doesn't bother me. I like my siblings." She kept her face hidden.

"That's great. But the moment you don't, it's *okay*. You don't owe them anything." I kept rocking her, trying to soothe her with my pheromones. While I understood her wanting to get to know her bio-dad, she didn't have to go beyond the basics.

"I know."

"Personally, I'm proud of you for trying." I kissed the top of her head. "I think you deserve a reward." My hand went down the back of her pants and squeezed her ass.

I needed to settle her before my alpha ended up fucking her against the wall—or on the desk.

"Wes, what are you doing," she whispered as my fingers caressed her through her panties.

"Give me a moment." Leaning forward, and taking my hand out of her pants, I went on my computer and blocked out my calendar. I didn't have much time before my meeting, but I had enough—and this way no one would bug me.

Lifting her up off my lap, I set her on the chair, then went over to the door and locked it. Just in case.

Moving the chair with her still in it, I got between her and the desk. Kneeling down, my eyes met hers.

"Now, where were we?" I murmured as I removed her shoes.

"Wes, we're at *work*," she whispered.

Yep, and her being unsettled needed to be taken care of. While she still didn't smell quite like an omega, her scent had gotten more pronounced since the hospital.

"I know. Ooh, we were here. Sit back and relax while your alpha makes it all better." I tugged off her panties and pants.

What a sight—her naked from the waist down in my desk chair.

My hands spread her thighs, and I buried my face in her pussy.

"An alpha on his knees is always sexy," she breathed. "Worship me, Alpha."

Worship her I shall.

"Oh, Wes," she gasped as my tongue caressed her clit.

"Shhh. Now let me reward you. We don't have a lot of time," I whispered, going back to my worship.

Her hands tangled in my hair, but I could still feel her anxiousness through the bond.

"You're still thinking. No one is going to bother us. Not even Spence." I continued to toy with her–kissing and sucking and lapping. I felt her let go, and I continued showing her all my love so that for one moment she could just feel, as I rewarded her for meeting with her dad today.

She was close, and I tickled her with my tongue just the way she liked.

"Wes," she gasped, as an orgasm shot through her.

"That's it, come for me, Peaches," I murmured. Finishing, I got up and pulled her to me, so we cuddled in my chair. That was all I had time for right now.

"I like seeing you on your knees." She kissed me.

"I'll get on my knees for you anytime." My arms tightened around her. "Do you feel better?"

"I do. I don't suppose I can have your dick?" She batted her eyelashes at me.

"I wish. Tonight, after your date with Evan." An alarm went off on my computer. "You should probably put on your pants. I have a meeting in five minutes."

Standing, she pulled on her pants and panties. "Thank you for taking time out of your busy day for me."

"What's the point of working with your mate if you can't have her in your office once in a while?" I gave her a kiss, and she left, our bond feeling much calmer. Yeah, a mid-day orgasm would do that.

My dick strained against my pants. There was nothing I could do about that. Though I'd much rather fuck her than go to a meeting.

I eyed the treat on my desk. Well, at least I had a cake pop.

Chapter Thirty-Eight

Evan

I parked in the garage under Compass BioTek and made my way into the lobby. Unlike Riley, I didn't have a badge, but I was on the *always allowed* guest list.

Grabbing a pass from the front desk, I took the elevators up to Spencer's office. I also texted Grace.

Me

> **I'm visiting Spence. Come up when you're ready.**

"Evan, Dear. He's free. Is he expecting you?" Mrs. Katsopolis beamed.

"I just thought I'd pop in while waiting for Grace. We're going on a date." I figured she'd need it after seeing the professor today.

She smiled at me over her computer. "How fun. Go right in."

I walked into Spencer's office, and he looked up from his laptop.

"Evan! Wes is in a meeting. Do you want me to walk you over to Grace?" He smiled. Spencer was wearing his glasses, something he'd been doing a lot more lately.

Probably because Grace thought they were sexy.

"I came to see you." I gave him a hug. "We don't seem to hang out much nowadays, so I thought I'd stop by until Grace is ready."

The last thing I wanted was for him to think our friendship wasn't important anymore.

He hugged me back. "I'm sorry. I didn't mean to neglect you by mating Grace."

Laughing, I sat down in the chair on the other side of his desk. "I think *I* neglected you by mating Grace. You can come with us, if you want, it just won't be fun for you."

"I appreciate it. But I have a meeting tonight."

"Is everything going okay with the party? Grace just shrugs and tells me it's all handled," I asked.

Spencer nodded. "The planner you recommended is excellent and has it under control. Even Mrs. K is impressed. Everything is set, people have responded. At some point we will need to go through those unsolicited gifts. Work went all right? You seem down. Is it Rose?"

"Rose is great. She has a campus job, is taking summer classes, and is doing a course at the Omega Center to learn how to sell the bracelets she makes online." I sighed. "It was a rough day, but it was just more of the usual. I love this job, but sometimes..."

Spencer reached across the desk and squeezed my hand. "If it doesn't make you happy anymore, you don't need to stay."

"It does make me happy. Some days are just better than others. I'm looking forward to the training this fall. When Grace has your triplets, I can stay home with them then do crisis work on-call to keep up my license and benefits," I explained.

He chuckled. "You could always work for the foundation. While Mrs. K found us an admin, and we're looking for a scholarship coordinator, it would be nice to have your expertise," he suggested. "Not just with the omegas but with our science scholars."

"Sonja is really excited about having your first Starbright Scholar at Darthmore," I added. They'd gotten that set up quickly.

"Me, too. Our scholar for Rock Tech is set up, too. Hadley Hall wants to wait until next year so we can actually have proper applications," he replied.

"Sounds good. I know we're giving our scholars laptops and allowances, but can I make them care packages? Sonja said the boy who's getting the scholarship for Darthmore is literally living in a shelter right now. There's no way he can afford all the things he'll need for the dorms. We could give him gift cards, but his mom doesn't have a car," I said, looking at my phone to see that Grace was on her way.

The idea of making our scholars custom care packages made me really happy. I wanted to do that for our omega scholars, too. The comfort cupboard didn't always have what they needed, and the Center usually didn't have the funds to buy anything special.

"I love it." Spencer nodded.

"Is your mom coming to the party?" It would be nice to see her.

He nodded. "She's excited and has booked her hotel."

"She can stay in the guest house," I offered.

"Mama likes her independence. Also, some of her family is coming, too, not just my father's."

"It'll be nice to see everyone." Though I knew his dad's family in Greece much better than his mom's family from New York.

We talked for a little longer.

"Hi." Grace came in. She kissed my cheek and went right for Spencer's lap.

"Hi." Spencer kissed her and held her.

She grinned at me. "I'm ready for our date."

"Good." It was a surprise. Hopefully, she liked it.

"Have fun. If you're going shopping, get whatever you want. Both of you. I'm serious." He gave her another kiss.

"Thank you." Grace got off his lap and took my hand, leaning into me. For a moment I just savored holding her.

"Okay, I'm ready." Wes stood there with his stuff.

"I don't have a problem with you coming with us, but you're going to be bored," I cautioned.

Wes blinked in surprise. "Nothing is boring when I'm with you."

Awww. Though I did warn him.

I nodded. "Okay, let's have a date."

"Oooh, where are we?" Grace asked as we pulled into the *giant* CoCoCozy that was on the fancy side of town.

"Come see." I opened the door of my 4x4 and helped her out.

Wes got out and looked around. "I don't think I've ever been here."

"Nope. Usually, I come here with people from the Center." Though Brennan took me on a shopping spree here when we moved into our new place.

I brought them inside, where there were a couple of help desks. Behind them were signs: *Alpha Waiting Area, Shopping, Cafe,* and *Item Pick Up.*

"Checking in?" an omega asked us.

"Yes. Two for shopping." I showed my ID. "Grace, show your ID."

Confused, Grace did.

The associate looked at Wes. "One alpha for check-in?"

"Yes. Wes, show your ID," I instructed.

Wes did, also confused.

"Here you go." She printed off three stickers. "Do you know where to check him in?"

I put one on me, one on Grace, and one on him.

"Yes, I do." I grabbed Wes' arm and pulled him toward the sign leading us to the alpha waiting area.

There was a large area with glass walls and lots of TVs, some showed sports or news, others broadcast feeds from the store. Some people worked at tables, others played video games or pool, a couple read or were on their phones. There was also another section with a soft-play area for children, along with an art table, and a reading corner.

"One alpha for check-in?" The employee, in her yellow and pink uniform, beamed at us.

"Check-in?" Wes blinked.

"This is the omega-only home store. We shop, you sit in the waiting area. I told you that you'd find our date boring," I teased.

"All snacks and beverages are complementary, and you can order food from the cafe on the kiosk," she told him as she scanned my name tag and his.

"Have fun! Play nice with the other alphas." Grace giggled, pulling him down for a kiss.

"Yeah, play nice." I kissed him and pushed him inside. I grabbed Grace's arm. "Let's go."

"So, he stays in the alpha play area while we shop?" Grace laughed as we went up the escalator.

"Yes." I grabbed a scanner. Grace headed one way, and I took her arm. "No, this way, we have to follow the arrows. Soft goods and home goods are on this floor, furniture is upstairs, downstairs are home essentials, the snack hall, and the cafe."

Grace took everything in as we walked past the art. The air-filters were top-notch here. Everything was de-scented regularly. Soft music played, and it smelled vaguely of vanilla. The entire store, from the colors to the way things were laid out, was designed to be relaxing. All of the employees here were omegas, except for the delta security and stockers, and possibly a couple of betas.

It was also very fancy.

"Let me know if you see anything for your nest or the guest rooms or anything," I said. "Spencer told me three times that we can get whatever we want."

She looked at a painting of a ballerina. "I like this one for the creepy doll room."

"Great." I scanned it as a couple of omegas walked by giggling.

"This is an omega home store? I love the alpha day care," she giggled.

"Right? There are cameras all around the store so they can watch us and know we're safe, but we're free to shop. You can also check on your kids. It's one way some omega parents get a little time for themselves. They can smell some candles and have coffee in the cafe for an hour. There are cameras in the play area, and you can watch them on your phone," I said as we looked at rugs. We'd put hardwood floors in the basement nest, but she might want rugs.

"This one for the nest. This one is for the other guest room." She indicated two different rugs.

I scanned those. Most things you scanned, then picked up or had delivered so they weren't contaminated with scents. Though the home essentials section downstairs was an exception.

"Are you doing okay?" I asked as she looked at throw pillows. They had all sorts of sizes, colors, and textures.

Grace frowned. "I feel fine but today was a lot. Also, I feel *more*. I smell more. I hear more. Sometimes it's overwhelming."

I pulled her to me. "Sounds like it. If you need something to take the edge off, we can get that for you."

Certain types of blockers could make it a little easier for her. There were also a few simpler things we could just grab at the drugstore.

"I should learn to deal with it." She snuggled into me.

As she told me about her meeting with the professor, we scanned some pillows, chose bedding for the creepy doll room and guest room, and bought some things for her room, my room, the bathrooms, the kitchen, and the basement nest.

"Let's go upstairs and look at the furniture," I suggested, following the arrows toward the escalator.

The furniture was grouped by room type as we sat on couches and lay on beds, and I told her about my day.

Delight lit up her face as she pulled me down on a demo bed, laughing. I kissed her, hard. Yep, this was exactly what she needed.

"Toys," she gasped as we walked past another area. "Beautiful wooden toys. Oh, and look at those dolls." Grace led me into the nursery area, which, unlike the others, you didn't have to pass through to get to the next section.

There were both things for babies' and kids' rooms. But she didn't care about that.

No, she sat herself down at a tiny table. "This. For tea parties in the creepy doll room."

"Absolutely." I scanned it, along with some toys, a toybox, and a beanbag. "We can come back here when we need a nursery," I offered, as we passed a bunch of ridiculously fancy cribs.

"Where will we put the nursery?" She picked up a doll with little ponytails and a pacifier. "I had a doll like this one, once."

"We might need to remodel or move. Spencer mentioned wanting to move us to that new development by the fancy Omega Center where we took you. Something about a backyard tennis court." I laughed.

Grace thought for a moment. "I liked my first tennis lesson. Our house is nice, but it is laid out weird. It might be a while, Evan. With everything that happened, I don't..."

"I know." I hugged her tightly.

We finished on this floor and then took the elevator to the first floor since we had to go through home essentials and the snack hall to get to check out.

"Anything here we can just put in the cart," I explained as we grabbed a basket and wandered through a giant display of candles. "They also have a kiosk where you can review everything you scanned."

"Okay." She smelled a candle and put it in the cart.

"Look." I led her through a curtain into a room full of every kind of fairy light imaginable.

We got some lights and continued on. There were a lot of things we didn't need down here, like pans and dishes. We got a kettle and some teacups so we could have tea in the bathtub. I got a few cute things for Riley.

I added some bath stuff to the cart along with a new bath pillow. They had high-end bath products, including a fancy version of the green fizzies that she liked.

Finally, we got to the snack hall.

Her eyes lit up as she took in all the snacks, treats, and gourmet food for sale. "The candy wall is better than the candy store Riley took me to at the fancy mall."

Grabbing a bag, she happily filled it up with candy. I did, too.

"Oooh, let's get some samplers of instant drinks for our kettle?" Grace added them to the cart.

"Perfect. Hey, let's review what we're going to get and decide what we're going to pick up and what gets delivered," I said as we went to the kiosk.

We reviewed everything and then went to check out with all our goodies.

"Wow," she whispered at the total.

"It adds up fast, doesn't it? But, Grace, we mated rich. I think we should just give in and let them buy us shit when they offer, like when Spencer bought you purses." I draped my arm around her, as we got our bags and our pickup ticket.

She leaned into me. "I know."

"Mostly, I brought you here because I thought that you could use a nice, calm place to decompress after a hard day." I hugged her close.

"Thank you. Mostly, it's a lot to process." Her arms wrapped tighter around me.

"It is. Should we collect Wes and eat at the cafe?" I asked. "Alphas are allowed there if accompanied."

She looked up at me and smiled. "I love it. If he played nicely with the other alphas he can even have dessert."

Chapter Thirty-Nine

Jett

"Anyone home?" I called as I entered the kitchen. It was pretty late. Today had been a hard day at the station, so after work I'd gone to the head spa, gotten a spicy snack, grabbed a few things at the market, then spent hours at the gym.

I put the food away and went upstairs. The bedroom was quiet. Even though Brennan wouldn't be home until tonight, this morning I'd still made the bed the way he liked it. Well, I added the stuffies from Grace and put them on the pillows. He'd done that the first day we'd had them, before he had to leave for his business trip.

It made me smile that Brennan had gone from wanting her out of the house to giving the stuffie she made him the place of honor on the bed.

The idea of her, Spencer, and Riley making everyone stuffies had been a fun one. Riley had given Spencer one in a tux, and Evan's wore a shirt that said *I Love My Little Sister*. Grace had made Wes a girl hippo with a recorded message. Spencer had made one for Riley in a goth outfit, complete with a backpack with bat wings. Grace had put away hers without showing anyone, but I had it on good authority from Evan that hers wore lingerie and had a spicy recorded message from Spencer.

Had Grace recorded Brennan or me a message? Huh. I grabbed my boxer bear and squeezed every limb—and the ass. No message. I did the same for Brennan's. When I squeezed the left foot, I was rewarded with her soft voice saying, *You're such a good boy.*

Amazing. He probably didn't even know it did that. Should I tell him? Hmmm.

I showered and changed. There was a text from Spencer.

Spencer

I have to rush off to take care of a production facility emergency. I'll be back.

Oh. So, he wasn't home. Grace was probably with Evan and Wes. Evan was going to stay with Wes tonight so I could have Brennan to myself when he got here. Okay, so I could have him for a while. Evan would probably crawl in with us at some point.

Riley was upstairs in the third-floor sunken living room playing video games. I waved; she waved back but seemed very busy shooting zombies.

I went downstairs and found Grace trying to drag an enormous cardboard box across the living room.

"Grace." I went to help her. "You're not with Wes and Evan?"

She shook her head as we dragged it outside, where the recycling went. "Alone time. I was with Spencer, but he had a work emergency."

"I'm sure you can join them," I remarked as we went back inside, not seeing a scenario where she wouldn't be welcomed by those two.

"Later, after they're asleep. I don't want to interrupt them. All the stuff Evan and I ordered from CoCoCozy yesterday came today. I was just working on getting the guest rooms set up." Grace frowned. "Should we freshen up the guest house? Just in case?"

Just in case of what? Honestly, we should probably turn it into an art studio for Riley.

"Maybe, but not tonight." I followed her into the creepy doll guest room, which had a hutch for her dolls, a daybed covered in shopping bags, a little table with small chairs, a toybox, a bookshelf, and a beanbag. Okay, the toybox was in pieces, and not all the chairs were put together.

No more cardboard, though. She seemed anxious, flitting around the room, gathering up trash and putting it in a sack. I should help her, but I wanted to have the food ready by the time Brennan came home.

"I'll help you assemble furniture tomorrow. Hey, how would you like me to teach you to make something? You can have some," I offered. Considering she'd worked in a bakery, she'd probably find it interesting.

"You're going to cook this late at night?" She nearly tripped over the furniture pieces and did a little hop to keep her balance.

"It's a good way to occupy myself when I'm waiting for Bren," I replied.

Taking her hand, I led her into the kitchen. She washed her hands and put on a frilly apron with peaches on it while I started getting everything out and putting it on the counter.

"We're making pork buns. Well, not from scratch, I bought the char siu at the market." I got the barbecue pork from the fridge.

"Oooh, I'm excited." She grinned.

We chopped the pork, and I showed her how to make the filling. Then we started on the dough. I wasn't sure why Evan had bought a stand mixer, but it sure made some recipes a lot easier. I'd never suggested it because Brennan was anti-counter-clutter.

Taking out a pot and the bamboo steamer baskets, I started boiling water so we could steam the buns.

"Next step." I showed her how to make the buns, pleating them like my grandmother had taught me.

"Like this?" Grace asked, showing me her handiwork.

"You catch on quickly," I praised.

We lined the baskets with parchment paper, placed the buns inside, and then put them over the boiling water to steam. My phone buzzed.

Brennan

On my way home.

I texted him back.

Me

I can't wait to see you.

"He's on his way." I couldn't help but grin as I loaded the dishwasher.

"Thanks for teaching me," she said as she wiped the counters.

We cleaned up, and I grabbed us beers. Grace told me all about her dress alteration and preparations for the party next weekend.

"I'm nervous about meeting Spencer's mom. Have you met her?" Grace took a sip of beer.

"She'll love you. Ilena's a force of nature but considering she's an artist with a professor husband and raised *Spencer,* she has to be," I chuckled. Oooh, would she cook for us?

"Okay. What about everyone else?" Grace frowned.

"I'm sure it will be fine, Grace," I assured.

The door from the garage opened, and Brennan stumbled in, looking tired and a little worse-for-wear, his suit a bit rumpled as he pulled his rolling bag behind him.

"Jett." His face brightened as he put his briefcase on the kitchen chair and pulled me into his arms.

"Bren." I let his pine scent swirl around me, comforting me, and sent all my love through the bond. For a moment I let myself melt into his arms, savoring a quiet moment together.

The timer buzzed.

"The buns are done." Letting go of him, I went over to the stovetop and checked the buns.

"Hi, Grace." Brennan hugged her, and I didn't miss how he melted a little as she snuggled into him.

I set the steamer basket on the table. "I made pork buns."

"Ooh, you did? I thought I smelled food." Riley popped up behind us, reached in, and grabbed one. "Ooh, hot." She bounced it between her hands.

Grace handed her a paper towel.

"Thanks. Hey, Bren." Riley added another to the paper towel.

"Hi, Riley." Bren smiled at her. "Yes, I got you something. But you'll have to wait until the morning."

"Sounds good to me." She added one more bun to her pile. "Laters." Riley disappeared with her food.

"I'll take mine to go. Good night." Grace pulled Brennan down to her and gave him a tentative kiss.

"Good night, Little Butterfly." He held her to him for a long moment.

"Thanks for the baking lesson." Grace kissed me, grabbed her food, and left.

Brennan washed his hands, poured himself some bourbon, and sat down at the table. "That trip was a lot. But I got a lot accomplished, and I'm here now."

"I think it's time that you and Terrance start training people to help you," I said as I took a bun.

"It's the personal touches that make this company." He frowned and grabbed one.

"Then train them to do all the other things, so that you can handle the things only you can. You have amazing people who've been with you for a long time. People you trust who would love, and probably deserve, the promotion. Also, no one blinks when Terrance handles things instead of you. You and Terrance should each have someone, or someones, that you slowly bring in to do the same. You two are no good to the company burned-out," I replied.

I'd seen Terrance burn out before, back when he was keeping the company from sinking after Brennan's car accident.

"These are so good." Brennan reached for another. "Thank you." Leaning over, he gave me a kiss. "You're right. It's time. I know the company could handle it if I step back, so I should make sure everyone is in place if I should choose to do so. Step down? Never. But step back a little eventually so I can do more with our family foundation? Yes."

"I'm so proud of you for saying that." I gave him another kiss. "How did everything go with the estate? Didn't you just land your first event booking?"

"Speaking of people who deserve promotions, yes, our new acting manager for the estate and acting event coordinator were perfect. The ballet will be hosting their gala in the gardens in September." He took a drink of bourbon.

As we demolished the buns, he told me more about his trip, and I told him about my week. He helped me clean up.

"I love it when you stay up for me and make me food. It's so silly, and a little antiquated, but it's so nice to come home to that." Brennan pinned me against the refrigerator, his lips smashing to mine.

The thing was, he did the same for me after a late night at the station or making me food after a tournament as I took a shower. It was nice to come home to someone–and it wasn't even about the food, it was about thought and care.

Kissing him back, I told him all those things with my lips.

His kisses were that of a starving man, as he pressed into me, letting me know just how much he missed me.

"Sweet baby cheeses, get a room." Riley came back into the kitchen. "Any food left?"

"No, sorry, we ate them all," I replied. We hadn't made that many.

"Oh, okay." She took a bag of chips and left.

"Mmmm, should we get that room?" Brennan continued to keep me trapped against the fridge as he kissed me again and again.

The heat building between us was all-consuming.

I kissed him back, adding a little push as I grabbed his chin. "I'd like that very much."

"Mmmm, I'm glad to be home." Brennan's head lay on my chest as we cuddled in bed.

"I'm glad to have you back." I stroked his hair. Evan was *still* busy. There was also some underlying anxiousness in the bond.

Brennan rolled over and checked his phone on the nightstand. He sighed. "Would you like to retrieve the tiny ball of anxiety or should I? Why is she so anxious? Why is she not asleep in some-one's room?"

Tiny ball of anxiety. Good one.

"You feel her?" I put my chin in my hand as I leaned on my elbow.

"Sometimes. Again, why is she playing the piano at this hour and not under someone?" He put his phone down and sat up.

"How do you know she's playing the piano?" I blinked.

"Back when I didn't want her to play, I set the piano to alert me whenever it was being played. Someone is playing it right now, and it's not me." He sat up and went to the dresser, giving me a good view of his tight, pale ass, even though the room was dark.

"I think she's anxious about meeting Spencer's family. Also, Spencer had to deal with something for work. She didn't want to interrupt Wes and Evan and was waiting until they were asleep. I don't think she enjoys sleeping by herself. I don't mind if you just throw her in between us. She'd probably like to play with your attached fidget toy until she falls asleep." I laughed as he pulled on some glow in the dark boxers Evan had gotten him as a joke.

He gave me a look. "Don't encourage her."

"Why not? It's funny." I grinned at him from the bed.

Chuckling, he left the bedroom. A moment later, he came back in with Grace slung over his shoulder, as he kicked the door closed. Her hair was wet, and all she wore was a big T-shirt. He tossed her into bed.

"Go the fuck to sleep. I'm exhausted." Brennan turned off the light and climbed in, squashing her between us.

"Jett, is this okay?" She snuggled into us, her head on Brennan's chest, her ass rubbing against me.

"It's perfect." I kissed the top of her head. Closing my eyes, I went to sleep.

A soft growl made my eyes fly open.

"Grace, my dick is not your personal fidget toy," Brennan growled.

"You don't mean that. Why have little buttons on it if you don't want them touched?" There was a challenge to her voice, and the tiniest bit of hurt, her scent going a little salty.

It was hard not to laugh. I'd never really thought of his ladder piercings as *buttons to push*. She certainly enjoyed pushing his–and not just the attached ones.

Brennan growled again. "Don't tease me or you won't like the consequences–and yes, I know it's not intentional, but I'm too tired to play. Nap on it or take my knot and go the fuck to sleep."

"Oh, Sorry. I... I can't sleep. Can... can I... please, Alpha?" Her scent went sweet with need.

"Fine." Brennan's growl was tired. "You're in our bed, so we're in charge. Don't try me, Little Butterfly. Safe words still apply."

He rolled over, pinning her to the bed with his body as he ripped her panties off. She made a little noise of protest as he tossed them off the bed.

"Words, Grace," Brennan growled, his nose pressing to hers. "Also, if you want to be fucked in our bed and don't want your clothes ruined, then *don't wear any.*"

"Okay... Oooh." She sighed as he entered her.

"Feed her your cock, Jett. Just smack his ass if you need to say something." Brennan started fucking her hard and fast.

Just smack my ass? "Thanks, Honey."

"Anytime, Dear."

"Here you go, Babydoll." I put another pillow under her head and lowered my cock toward her mouth.

Her little pink tongue darted out and teased my piercing.

"Don't play with fire, Peaches," I warned as her lips wrapped around my cock.

She blinked at me in the darkness as if to say, *What? I'm such a good girl.*

"Little balls of anxiety get fucked until their brains shut off and they go the fuck to sleep." Brennan pounded her, the air going thick with the scent of her desire and his pheromones.

"That's it, take it like the good girl you are," I praised as she sucked on me. Her scent flared at my words.

Clearly, this was what she needed. Brennan's want for her, and his satisfaction at being able to give her what she needed pulsed through the bond. My own desire rose, not just from that sweet little mouth around my cock, but because my husband looked so fucking sexy as he fucked her.

Just like she looked so beautiful in our bed.

"I'm going to come," I warned, wrapping my hand lightly around her throat, as my cum shot into her mouth.

Eyes widening, she swallowed me down.

I stroked her hair. "That's my babydoll. You take us so fucking good. I love seeing Bren wreck you."

"You're taking me so well," Brennan added, leaning down and kissing her as I removed my cock from her mouth. "I love tasting him on you."

An orgasm shuddered through her as she continued to fill the air with her heady, peachy scent.

"That's it. Now take my knot, like a fucking good girl," he muttered, pulling out and slamming into her.

"Alpha," she moaned, as his lips crashed down on hers.

Fuck, that was hot, as I let my own arousal and desire continue to shoot through the bond.

"You fucked her so well, Honey." I kissed him.

"I love you, Dear." He kissed me back. "I love you, too, Little Butterfly. Now go the fuck to sleep." Brennan kissed her and then slumped on top of her, keeping her pinned to the bed.

"You do? I love you both. I am adding you to my collection of husbands," she mumbled.

Well, consider me collected.

"I love you two, as well," I replied. Shit, Bren told her that he loved her. Wow. I sent love through our bond.

I threw the blankets over us as Brennan let out a soft snore.

Well, he was exhausted.

"Are you okay, Babydoll?" I kissed her temple, unsure if his weight on her like that was too much.

"Perfect." Her voice was a whisper as her eyes closed.

Good. "Good night, Peaches."

She didn't answer, eyes closed, expression content. Well, I was glad we could give her what she needed. It felt like Evan and Wes *still* weren't asleep. Fucking shit, that was some aspirational action right there. Maybe they didn't have to work tomorrow?

Certainly, I did.

Curling into Brennan and Grace, I felt his arm drape over me, keeping me close, flickers of love going through the bond. Fucking shit, I loved that man. And I loved the little blonde pinned underneath him.

I closed my eyes and let sleep take me as well.

Chapter Forty

Spencer

I got back from my latest meeting and was trying to finish up a few things so that I could leave. My mother had arrived from Greece yesterday since our mating party was tomorrow. I joined her at her hotel for breakfast, and she was coming over for dinner tonight so that she could meet Grace. Riley and I were going to cook.

Glancing at my phone, I realized that I missed a bunch of texts from Grace along with pictures. She was working from home this afternoon since the interns had an activity day that she wasn't a part of. Though she'd come in this morning. At lunch, she helped me sort through some of the presents that we'd gotten, like we'd been doing at lunch all week.

Grace

> **Your mother arrived with bags of food and just went right to the kitchen.**

> **She's been cooking all afternoon. The house smells amazing, and the stuff she's making is delicious.**

> **Also, she brought me an omega lily that's in a pot as pretty as the one Verity gave me.**

How had I missed that? Oh, I'd been in meetings.

The pictures were of all sorts of familiar dishes as well as of her and my mom. Yes, my mother had made the pot the omega lily was in. I'd know her work anywhere.

Me

> **Are you okay? Is she being nice?**

While my mother showing up and cooking even though we'd planned to cook for her was perfectly normal, this also felt 100% like a test for Grace.

Grace

> **I love her. She's teaching me to make your favorite foods. It's fun.**

Relief coursed through me. Not that I expected her to dislike Grace. My mother had also loved Elaris, even if she was a disaster in the kitchen.

"Let's go home and cook for Yiayia." Riley stood in the doorway in black pants and a silver shirt, badge around her neck.

I wasn't sure when Riley had started calling my mother *Grandma,* but she loved it—even though Evan and his other siblings had always called her *Auntie.*

"We just need Wes. Warning, she's been at our house cooking with Grace." I put my laptop into my bag.

"Oh. Okay. I could live with that. I hope it's good, because I could eat a polar bear."

Grabbing my things, we went down and collected Wes. All week Wes had been coming with me, so that Grace and Riley could take her motorcycle. Maybe next week I'd take mine and ride with them. Wes could get to work himself.

Wes grabbed his stuff. "Did you know that Grace has been alone with your mom all afternoon?"

"Yes. I hope Grace passes. Not that her failing means anything." I shrugged as we went down to my car.

"Your mom is pretty nice. Also, considering your father was a physicist, Grace probably won't confuse her too much," Wes agreed as we got into the car, Riley scrambling for the front.

"I want to talk to Yiayia since I'm taking ceramics next year," Riley added as she changed the radio station.

I started to drive. "She would love to discuss ceramics with you. Maybe when you visit, she'll give you a lesson. We probably still have the pottery wheel that she taught me on."

Her face brightened. "I'd love that. Question. Grace said lots of worlds were real and full of all types of people. Do you think there are worlds with magic or shapeshifters or superheroes?"

"Probably. Why?" That was an odd subject change.

"So, Grace said the Greek gods we have here are similar and have stories a lot like the ones in her world. I know there's only so many ideas in the universe, and things are bound to overlap. But... do you think there's maybe a world of them and they know how to travel from place to place. So, like they're real and lived here, but eventually got bored and left for another world? People like that probably don't give a flying fuck what the Temporal Authority thinks and do what they want," Riley rambled.

"It's an excellent theory. That's also a horrifying thought, and I hope to never encounter a world such as that or those who reside in it," I replied as I drove us home. Yes, if Greek gods existed, I hoped to never, ever run into them.

When we got home, Jett and Brennan were already there, as was Grace. The entire place smelled like my youth. My mother loved to cook—especially when she needed to work out her latest art project in her head. I often came home to delicious things on the stove and her humming away in her studio. We'd also often have people over for dinner, mostly my dad's family, or Dr. and Mrs. K, or students who could use a good meal.

"The boys are setting the table, wash up." My mother's eyes fixed on Riley. "Look how much you've grown. Come give Yiayia a hug."

I kissed Grace. "You're okay?"

"This is so much fun. We made baklava for dessert. I've never made phyllo dough from scratch before." Excitement danced in her eyes.

Now two omega lilies sat in pots in the window that looked out into the backyard next to the glass doors that led out onto the porch.

"Go." My mother shooed us upstairs.

When I came back down, changed, I went down to the basement and got one of the bottles of bourbon Grace had chosen for me.

I came back up and saw a sumptuous feast of *all* my favorites from childhood were on the table—and it wasn't just Greek food.

"Is it okay if we try my bottle of bourbon tonight?" I asked as I got the glasses out of the hutch.

"I'd like that," Brennan replied.

"I'm so curious about the tiny sausage octopuses in the mac and cheese," Jett joked as he took a spoonful.

"The macaroni is the ocean." Evan shrugged as he took some. "I haven't had this in forever. It's perfect after a day at the beach."

I poured all the adults a little bourbon so that we could try it. "Grace chose this bottle for me especially."

Brennan went through his whole process of observing the bourbon, sniffing, and tasting it. "Leather and chocolate with a hit of orange." He took a larger sip. "I think this is even smoother than mine, but fuller-bodied."

Wes took a sip. "It tastes like booze. Expensive booze."

And this was why Brennan got annoyed when Wes drank his high-end liquor.

I took a sip, making note of what Brennan mentioned. I looked over at Grace. "Thank you, my good doctor. I feel like this suits me perfectly."

"I'm glad you like it," Grace replied.

"It's quite nice," my mother agreed.

"Mama, this is amazing," I praised, starting with a bowl of meatball soup.

"It's nice to have a competent helper." She gave Grace a fond look. "Cooking is lonely with no assistant."

I'd been her helper so many times, especially after we moved to Rock Springs. Evan's family was over a lot, too. Though I had plenty of fond memories of my father cooking with her.

A little bit of loneliness crept through me. How I wished he were here.

"Ilena, this is delicious. Thank you. We could have cooked for you." Brennan took some marinated lamb and roasted artichokes.

"No, no. It's fun to cook for a family again." She waved us off.

"How was your activity?" I asked Riley, adding some macaroni and cheese to my plate. Personally, I thought the tiny sausages sliced to look like octopi were a sweet touch, something she used to do in order to tempt me to eat as a small child.

"It was fun, very chemistry-oriented, but it was nice to get to know some of the interns in other departments. I like the internship. It's almost as fun as punching people all day." She picked up a dolmas and stuffed it in her mouth.

"Boxing camp. She was at boxing camp last week, Auntie," Evan corrected, taking some roasted artichokes.

"Does everyone have everything they need for tomorrow?" Grace looked at everyone anxiously as she took some souvlaki.

Wes squeezed her hand. "We're all set."

"Good. We were able to squeeze in our unexpected guests. Oh, right, so we have some additional guests, one will be staying a couple of nights. The other guest room isn't done, so she'll have to sleep in the creepy doll room," Grace added.

Brennan sighed. "Tru booked herself a plane ticket?"

"Verity is flying to Europe tomorrow for a modeling job. She managed to re-book her ticket with a long enough layover to attend our party. Mercy is coming and staying with us for a couple of days. I'm surprised her parents let her come, too, since who's going to watch the kids with Verity gone? Hale?" Grace shook her head.

"That sounds disastrous." Brennan shuddered.

"Grace recently found her biological father, and she has nine siblings. It's a complex story, but her siblings are very nice. Hale is simply... rambunctious," I told my mother.

Brennan snorted.

Grace glanced at her phone. "I think Tru assumes that she's coming with them. She keeps sending me pictures of herself in different dresses."

"I mean, she thinks she's your favorite sister. I just love her. She has no filter, and I get rambling video messages with all the gossip. I think she thinks she's making insta-chat videos like Mercy does. Did you know that Hope stuffed a rock up her nose?" Riley laughed.

"I sort of want to know why Hale isn't allowed near bouncy castles," Grace added.

Brennan shook his head. "No. I don't want to know."

"Well, I'm looking forward to your visit this summer," my mother told everyone.

"I can't wait." Riley started talking about ceramics, and she and my mother had a lively conversation about it. We finished up dinner, and had coffee, baklava, and tiny orange and chocolate cakes. Grace also made slushies out of the peach bourbon.

"So delicious, Ilena," Jett complimented. "Really, thanks for making such amazing food for us."

She waved him off. "My pleasure. Grace should know all his favorite foods. Just like you should know all of hers, and how to cook them, or at least where to buy them."

Her eyes narrowed as she looked over us.

"Of course, Mama," I assured her.

"Wes and I just made something for her the other day, Auntie," Evan added.

We tried to help her clean up, but she kept shooing everyone out of the kitchen. Finally, I just started doing dishes.

"Thank you." As she worked, she told me about all the plans she had made to do things with the various relatives coming to town. Besides the party tomorrow, some of my father's family was hosting brunch on Sunday, and my mother's family was hosting a lunch, so that we could spend more time with everyone.

"Do you like Grace?" I asked as I loaded the dishwasher.

"Yes. Very smart. Very kind. So very small. Your father would have made her his assistant and brought her everywhere because she's travel-sized," my mother laughed as she rinsed dishes and handed them to me.

I laughed, picturing it. "Yes, I could see them getting along. But that would mean either you moved to Rockland–though Rock Tech would love him–or we moved to Greece."

And, for my father to be here. I wasn't going to hope that the Temporal Authority ever released him. No. That was too dangerous. If it happened, then it did.

She gave me a look as she handed me another dish. "They have schools in Greece. They have Omega Centers and police in Greece. They even have places to open company offices in Greece. You can move some of your company. Your hotelier can buy a hotel in Greece so that you can visit more often."

"That is a very thought-out plan." No, I don't think we'd be moving to Greece anytime soon. However, she seemed lonely. We should make more visits. Maybe I should see if there were any symposiums coming up near her.

"I'm getting nostalgic in my old age." She shrugged. "While I like my quiet days in my studio, I enjoy traveling with my friends, and I love touring the world with my art, sometimes I just want my family."

Noted.

"Well, hopefully we can visit more often," I assured as we finished up the dishes.

She looked at me. "Is everything all right? Something feels... unsettled."

Her words sent shivers down my spine. The last time she'd said that to me was right before Evan's parents died. While she hadn't said it before Elaris' death, she had the night before the super collider blew up.

"I hope it's nothing," I said softly as I put a soap pod in the dishwasher.

"Me, too." Her look went worried.

Indeed. With Grace, who knew what could be coming?

Chapter Forty-One

Grace

I glanced at my phone and sighed.

> **I'm so sorry, but I can't find anyone on such short notice. But it's okay. Deep breath. You'll still look amazing.**

The person who was supposed to come over and do my hair and makeup for the party had canceled at the last minute. Literally, I should be getting ready right now.

Spencer and Evan were with a bunch of Spencer's family at a house they'd rented for the weekend. They'd meet me at the club.

It really wasn't that big of a deal. I was fine with it. But, I needed to get started. Verity and Mercy should have been here by now. I looked at my phone and all I had was a picture of Mercy's face. *Well, then.*

The doorbell rang. Oh, that was probably them, and the selfie was an *I'm coming* text.

I went downstairs. Riley, who wore a long black robe with feathers on it, makeup half done, beat me to the door.

"Get the fuck out of here, Agent Ass-face." Riley stood there, hands on her hips.

"Who's there?" I rushed over and saw Agent Weigmier there in a dark suit. "Hell no." I went to close the door.

He caught it. "Please, Dr. Ellington, a moment?"

"I didn't take the cat," I snapped. While there were a few things I still didn't recall from my time at the Temporal Authority, I did remember that black cat with the blue eyes. Yeah, I wish I had brought him back with me.

"I have what you requested," he said quickly.

"What?" I'd requested something?

Puzzled, I looked past him to an older man in slacks and a shirt, standing in the middle of the walkway, looking at the house, confused.

"Oh." I sucked in a sharp breath. "Riley, go get someone right now. *Anyone.*"

"Um, sure." She scowled at Agent Weigmier. "Touch her, and I'll rearrange your insides."

Agent Weigmier nodded. "Noted."

"That's..." I gazed at the man with grey hair, olive skin, and Spencer's eyes.

"Yes. He was released recently. Per protocol, he recalls nothing after leaving for work the morning that the Temporal Authority Enforcement came. He thinks that he'd been unconscious this entire time, as a John Doe, and we just recently figured out who he was, and now that he's awake, are returning him to his family. Nick knows that many years have passed, but I don't think he grasps it," Agent Weigmier said softly. He turned. "Nick, don't you wish to be reunited with your loved ones?"

"This isn't my home. Where are we?" Nick Thanukos stared at me. "I don't know you. I want my son and wife." His Greek accent was much thicker than Spencer's.

"Hi, Nick. You're in Rockland. I'm Grace. We'll see Spencer and your wife really soon," I explained.

Shit. They did it. The Temporal Authority had actually released Nick Thanukos and brought him to me.

"Oh. But who are you?" Nick frowned at me. He looked so much like Spencer.

"I'm Spencer's mate," I replied.

His brows furrowed. "He's not that old, is he? They say it's been years, but has it been that many? How much have I missed?"

So much. Did they really have to punish him like that for saving omegas? He and Dr. K probably didn't even fully understand what they were doing and why it was considered wrong.

"He'll be so excited to see you. Your wife, too," I assured.

"Why are they in Rockland? Kim is in Rock Springs." He rubbed his forehead.

I was pretty sure that Kim was Evan's mom.

"Spencer lives here now. Ilena lives in Greece, but she's here for a party. Please, come inside." I opened the door wider.

Evan came running down the stairs. "What's wrong?"

"I thought you were with Spence?" I looked at him, he was wearing a tux.

"He needed me to get something that he forgot." He gazed at the doorway. "Uncle Nick? Uncle Nick. Is that you?"

Nick glanced at Evan, head cocked as if trying to place him.

Evan crossed the living room in a few steps and threw his arms around him. "It's me, Evan. Kim's son. I'm so fucking happy to see you. Spencer and Auntie Ilena are going to be so happy. They've missed you so much."

"Evan." Nick held him tight. "You're such a big boy. Did you and my son mate?"

Evan laughed. "We just formed a pack together. Spencer and I are mated to Grace."

Agent Weigmier focused on me. "If I might have a word?"

"How old are you now? How much did I miss?" Nick sniffed.

Evan put an arm around his waist. "Hey, why don't I make you some coffee, and then we can go see Spencer."

I stared at Agent Weigmier, still not convinced he wouldn't stuff me in his car and take me some place.

"In private?" he prodded.

"Okay." I brought him inside and led him to the creepy doll room, which was ready for Mercy. All three of my Everydolls stared at us from behind the glass of the cabinet. Someone had placed a sign that said, *Please help me, I'm trapped* in the hands of my Gracie doll. By the handwriting, I was pretty sure that it was Wes.

Shit, I hoped my sisters would arrive *after* Agent Weigmier left.

"Thank you for bringing him," I told Agent Weigmier.

"He is your husband's father. I assumed some sort of familial relationship." Agent Weigmier nodded.

"Yes. The father of one of my husbands, not Fade. In this world I can have all of the spouses," I said. "You won't need to take Nick back for any reason, will you? Does he have to meet with a parole officer? I don't know how any of this works."

"Someone might come to check on him, but unlikely, especially if he gives no cause for it. I tried to reduce his footprint, as I did yours. He *can't* resume his research, Dr. Ellington. Certainly, he can't hide more omegas. If he does, I won't be able to help him, and he'll die in jail like his colleague," he implored.

"I'll do my best. Hopefully, he'll just want to travel with his wife and enjoy life. You... said something about things still not being set right after all these years. You're not going to return the omegas to worlds where they're illegal, right?" The very idea sickened me.

He shook his head. "There are very few good reasons for us to do that. Even if there were, omegas fall under Precious Population Protection Protocol, and a case can usually be made. However, not all designations sent elsewhere have all those protections–especially when their crimes have nothing to do with their designation."

I snorted. "If the woman who stole me from this world and raised me in the other wasn't dead, or of an illegal designation, I'd have you extradite her here to stand trial for what she took."

Agent Weigmier paused. "You were *stolen,* or do you mean it colloquially, since I am assuming you were small and had no say?"

"She's my mother's identical twin. I was stolen so that she'd look like a single mom." Anger surged through me. Rosalind took so much from me. If she hadn't robbed that vault, they wouldn't have come after my mother. While sure, Thora might have had to raise me by herself, I would have been here.

I could have gotten to Wes, because I would have been able to find Rockland on a map. Thora would have taken me to the Omega Center, and some nice advocate would have helped me locate him. Tears pricked my eyes.

"Oh my. Do I need to recite equations with you?" His voice became soft.

"I'm okay. You can't change the past. It was a mess because of people being sent to incompatible worlds." I rubbed my temples.

"It's a mess because of tenacity and people thinking that doing good absolves them from breaking the laws—or that they're above them. And yes, sending people to incompatible worlds is an even greater headache than sending them to compatible ones," he admitted. "It was eventually taken care of, with much effort, but as I said previously, we're still cleaning up."

"But the omegas here are okay?" That was a relief because I worried about them since it had been so long and they all had established lives now.

"Yes, those who have made their homes here should be safe."

Good.

"What about other people like me?" I couldn't be the only one.

"As in young people who ended up in biologically incompatible worlds through no fault of their own? Usually, I try to return you," he explained.

He tried to return them. Not *they*. Huh.

"Are only omegas under the Precious Population Protection Protocol?" I vaguely recalled that being mentioned when I was slated for relocation.

"No." He shook his head.

"Are you going to tell me what you do for the Authority?" I asked. He didn't seem surprised that I remembered everything, but he also struck me as being very deliberate in his actions.

"I fix things." He shrugged as if that explained everything.

I paused. "Am I the only person you've returned?"

"To this world? Yes. From your world, no. At least you blend in and don't cause urban legends." He grimaced.

"Oh." I sucked in a breath. "Like shapeshifters? I think I met a wolf shifter at the Authority. So, Sasquatches are really shifters smuggled from someplace and dropped into my world to be safe? Or was it just werewolves, maybe vampires?"

He shot me a look that clearly said he'd said too much as it was. Huh. Of course, werewolves and vampires could have just visited our world and went home.

"Okay, well, if you ever return someone else to this world, will you please let me know? Maybe I can help. I was lucky that I had someone here waiting for me. But not everyone is so fortunate," I suggested.

Brennan would just love that I made this offer, but I'd hate for some to be just left here with nothing–no record, no money, no memories.

"Oh. Thank you for that kind offer. It's difficult for me to operate in this world, and that would be quite helpful to me." He nodded. "You're very interesting, Dr. Ellington. Please be careful. Interesting people seldom live quiet lives."

"Isn't that a curse? *May you live in interesting times?*" I countered.

"I believe it is."

"Grace, are you in here? Why–" Brennan stopped short. "Fuck no."

"I was just leaving," Agent Weigmier said to Brennan.

"You're not leaving with her. Grace, *eight* of your siblings are here?" Brennan looked baffled.

"They are? I didn't even hear the doorbell. Eight? Only two were supposed to come, but I expected a third." I checked my phone.

There was a picture of Hale getting kicked off the baggage conveyor belt; Tru and Pax being pushed in a baggage trolley by who I was pretty sure was my brother Dare; and Verity carrying Hope and multiple suitcases.

I sighed. "Let me finish here? Also, Nick Thanukos is here, he's with Evan."

"Spencer's dad? Oh." Brennan looked at Agent Weigmier. "He kept his promise."

"It wasn't a promise, but I'm happy that I could do it," Agent Weigmier clarified. "I should go."

"Let me move them out of the living room? If Tru finds out other worlds exist, we're done for," Brennan told me.

I sucked in a breath, seeing it. "Let's keep her focused on unsolvable equations and space travel for now."

"I would agree that minimizing those who see me is a sound choice. Nick thinks I'm a social worker from the hospital," Agent Weigmier said.

Brennan left. Eight siblings? I texted the wedding planner.

Me

> I know the party starts soon, but how difficult would it be to get that bouncy castle? Also, to add six more people? The rest of my siblings showed up. They're mostly children. Feel free to make them a kids' table, but you can keep my other siblings where they've been seated. Thank you.

Hale could be in charge of the kid's table.

Fancy Wedding Planner

> On it. Can it be any inflatable?

Me

> Anything that will help entertain them.

I texted her their names for the table assignments. I'd probably regret putting Hale at the kids table, but I wasn't sure where else to put him without rearranging things. The teenager table was full.

"Sorry. Is there anything else I need to know about Nick? Is he sick?" I asked Agent Weigmier.

"No. He's in good health. Just with his age, the fact that he was a model prisoner, and giving him leniency for his world of origin, the judge decided to release him early. I think I told you everything else. Have a delightful party," Agent Weigmier said.

"Thank you. If only Dr. K were here for the same. I don't agree with such a long sentence for something they really didn't understand." I walked him out to the empty living room, though there were a bunch of bags piled on the couch and floor. "Thank you. This will mean everything to my mate."

"I'm happy for that." With a nod, Agent Weigmier left.

I texted Creed.

Me

Did you know that Verity was bringing everyone?

Creed

Yes, because I'm taking the boys to the adventure park tomorrow. I can take everyone if you want. Tru will probably want to stay with you. Hopey's a little shy with me since I've been away at Natty and might like you better. I think Mercy and Riley have plans.

Fuck, did Dad not tell you?

Me

No. I thought it was only Verity and Mercy.

How long?

They're leaving with Mercy tomorrow night.

I thought it was weird that you would have houseguests tonight other than Mercy, but I didn't know they were all coming until yesterday.

Well then.

I went into the kitchen and saw my siblings in the backyard with Brennan and Riley. Where were Evan and Nick? I went upstairs.

Spencer's door was open, and voices drifted out.

"Okay, we need to get going. Don't worry, Uncle Nick. Everything's fine," Evan soothed.

"I... don't understand. I missed so much." Nick's voice broke as he came out in one of Spencer's suits.

I wrapped my arms around him. "Don't think about the years you didn't get. Think of what you have. You still have your wife and your son, and you'll have many happy years together."

"Thank you." He hugged me back.

"Evan, all of my siblings are here. I think I'm going to make all of them but Mercy go with Creed to the adventure park tomorrow." Not that I had any idea what that was.

"Good plan. Fuck. I'm late. I'll see you at the party." Evan looked at his phone and then kissed me.

"See you there." I waved and went down to the backyard in time to see Hale throw Pax to Dare.

"Hi!" Verity came over and gave me a hug, Hope on her hip. "Sorry we were late. We had issues with security." She looked at Hale and sighed.

Did I want to know? Probably not.

"Hi, Hope." I waved at my tiny sister, her blonde hair done neatly in little braids. Her dress was the same blue as Verity's. I realized they were nearly all wearing something blue–probably so Verity could easily find everyone in the airport.

Hope waved back as she sucked on her thumb.

"Dare, Chance, come meet your sister," Verity yelled as Dare threw Pax back to Hale.

Two boys who looked a lot like Verity, with her dark hair and golden skin, ran over. One was older than Riley and Mercy but not as old as Hale. The other was in elementary school.

"This is Grace, you didn't get to meet her last time," Verity introduced. "These are your brothers, Dare and Chance.

"Sister, nice place," Dare, the older one, said as he looked around. He wore black jeans with a chain, a blue band shirt, and had his eyebrow pierced. He was in high school if I remembered correctly.

"Hi. You could play so many games in this backyard," Chance agreed, wearing a blue shirt for some sports team.

"Yes, they play flying disc sometimes," I told them.

"That guy, what secret agency was he from? He *has* to be an agent, between that car and his suit," Dare said.

"Dare." Verity gave him a look.

"Oh, come on. I looked up Compass BioTek after the parents shit a pumpkin about Creed applying. I absolutely believe that you work with secret government agencies." Dare grinned at me.

"Shhh." I eyed Tru, who was on the porch swing with Riley and Mercy. "It's not an agency that Tru needs to know about, at least not until she's old enough for a work permit."

Verity and Dare laughed.

Chance looked puzzled. "She got the internship, right? I had to look up a lot of words to help her fill that out."

"Thank you for that," I said. "She did. I'm teasing. Tru is so smart, but we don't need her taking over the universe yet."

Chance blinked. "I thought she wanted to solve an equation no one has solved and go into space." He sucked in a breath. "Are you working with the Agents in Glasses?"

"That's a *movie*, Chance," Verity reminded.

"If we are, I can't tell." I grinned.

Chance nodded. "Understood."

"Well, thank you for having us all. Dad's sorry that he couldn't make it. I have something for you from him in my bag. Where can we get ready? Wait, why aren't you ready? Shouldn't you be in hair and makeup?" Verity appraised me.

"They're not coming, so I have a slight hair and makeup emergency." I sighed, knowing we were now behind schedule. "Um, the boys can use the guest house. The girls can use the creepy doll room, and you can be with me? Wait, the little ones probably need help."

"I've got them," Mercy assured. "Hi, Big Sis."

"Hi, Mercy." I hugged her. Her hair was up in a messy bun, her blue shirt with a skate smash team on it.

"Grace." Tru ran over and hugged my leg.

"Hi, Tru."

"Please, let's not go in the—" Brennan winced as Hale threw Pax into the pool. "Pool."

"Hale, get the boys, girls, you're with Mercy," Verity yelled. "Hopey, baby, get dressed with Mercy, okay?"

Hope pouted as Verity handed her to Mercy.

"You, too, Tru," Verity added.

"Hey, Babycakes." Riley joined us. "I love your hair. We're going to have a getting ready party. I've got the perfect music."

Verity turned to me. "Let's go."

"I didn't know you all were coming," I murmured. "It's totally okay, but I might make Creed take them all to the adventure park tomorrow."

Where were they even staying tonight? Here?

"He's *supposed* to take them all to the adventure park. I literally gave him money to cover the tickets." She sighed. "Hope is very shy with him, so he probably figured he'd just leave her with you. Typical. Tru wants to stay with you, but she's going to love the adventure park. Don't worry, Creed *can* handle them, he just doesn't want to since Mercy won't be there to help. Dare and Hale are capable."

"Maybe we can meet them at the adventure park for dinner and fireworks?" Riley suggested, her and Mercy joining us, the little ones in tow.

"Possibly? It would be nice to see everyone, though I have a brunch and a lunch tomorrow. We'll figure it out," I assured.

"Come on," Riley told Tru and Hope.

Tru tugged on Riley's feathered robe. "I love it."

"Thanks. Let's go." Riley grabbed some bags and herded them down the hall.

Verity grabbed a purple suitcase and a purple, sparkly, wheeled makeup case. "Good thing I know how to do makeup quickly. We'll have you ready in no time."

"Thank you. Um, let's go upstairs. Warning, I don't have my own bathroom. I share one with Evan."

"The giant omega." Verity giggled. "Sorry."

"Oh, I know. He's delicious," I laughed as I led her up the stairs. "I went *home* with him when I first met him."

"Do tell?" She grinned.

We went up to my room, the dress already laid out on my daybed.

"Your room," Verity breathed. "This is the prettiest room. The painting on your door is beautiful."

"Riley painted it. She and Evan did a lot to make this room ready for me." I went into the bathroom and got my makeup and the curling iron someone had gotten me, but I'd never used it.

When I came out, Verity was taking a dress out of her bag.

"I think I can get away without steaming it?" She smoothed the lavender dress.

"I'll ask someone to bring up the steamer." I texted the group chat, not actually sure where everyone was.

Verity went over to the bed. "This is the dress? I'm a little jealous that you have a Dubois Sapphire gown."

"Whose show are you doing? It's for Paris Fashion week, right?" I asked.

"The main one I'm doing is Ferrell. A few of my friends are going to be there. I think we're going to try to sneak into a party at Surpressa." She started digging through my makeup.

"Ooh. That sounds fun. We got kicked out of the one here," I told her as I pulled over a chair.

"You did?" Her blue-green eyes sparkled. "Sit. I want to hear all about it."

Chapter Forty-Two

Evan

As I drove us in my 4x4, Uncle Nick looked nervous, scent sour and anxious.

"It's okay, Uncle Nick. Um, I let Spencer know that we're on the way. He's so excited to see you," I soothed. "We are all so happy to have you back."

I'd called Spencer as I made coffee for Uncle Nick, because I wasn't showing up with his dad unannounced. Also, I wanted to ask before letting Nick wear one of his suits. Uncle Nick didn't fit in mine, and if we were bringing him to the party, he needed to be dressed accordingly.

Shit, how was Auntie Ilena going to take this? Good, I hoped.

"Oh." Nick frowned. "Nothing makes sense. I wasn't even in this country. How did I get here? The last thing I remember is leaving for work and reminding Spencer to be on time so that we could run some experiments. How could I have been unconscious and unidentified for so long?"

Uncle Nick looked a lot like I remembered, just a little older, and completely grey-haired. He seemed fit and healthy, just a little haunted.

If I'd lost over twenty years of memories, I'd be haunted too.

"Do you remember your research?" I asked, glancing over at him as we drove.

"Why wouldn't I? Oh, I need to call Demitra. She probably won an award for our work, didn't she? Does Spencer help her now? Did he become a scientist, or does he work for his grandfather? Though I suppose it would be one of my brothers. My parents are probably gone." He frowned. "So many people are gone. And you, you're all grown up."

"Your father is still alive and here actually. Very spry for his age. Your mom passed away only a couple of years ago." This made me hopeful that Uncle Nick and Auntie would still have plenty of time together. Though his other parents passed years ago when Spencer and I were young.

"Oh?" His hand went to his heart. "And Ilena is well."

"She made us so much food last night," I chuckled, recalling our feast. "I think she's a little lonely. She travels a lot."

"Oh. I didn't mean to leave her alone." Nick's brow furrowed.

"We know, Uncle Nick. Spencer has a biotech company. Basically, he took what your fathers taught him about business and what he learned from you about science and uses it to fund projects that will change the world. Grace, and my other mate Wes, work for him," I told Uncle Nick, going back to the topic at hand.

He remembered his research. Huh.

"I still don't understand how I got here." His fingers tapped nervously on his thigh.

"Um, Uncle Nick, do you want to know what happened?" I didn't want to hide this from him.

"What happened?" He sucked in a breath.

"There was a super collider explosion. Almost everyone thinks that you died in it–including your wife. I went to your funeral," I admitted. "Many people died that day. Spencer had left right before it exploded, and he was fortunately okay."

"Thank goodness for that. Oh." That stricken look reappeared, then went thoughtful. "The super collider *exploded?* What were we doing that day? I don't remember. Did we rip a hole in time and space and somehow I ended up someplace else? Was there a time push? I never asked them exactly *when* I ended up in the hospital, and they didn't tell me how many years I'd been there. That would explain it."

I didn't know what a time push was. But I was guessing he thought a super collider explosion could somehow make him go forward in time and possibly move locations?

"What about Demitra?" he added.

"She was there with you that day. Um, do you remember your other research?" I asked. "We know about the omegas, well, we being my pack. Spencer also knew that you didn't die in the explosion and eventually shared that with us."

Nick froze. "You know about the omegas? That's dangerous knowledge."

"Yeah, though not everyone knows. Auntie doesn't. Beyond the barest basics, there's a lot our pack doesn't know about what happened. One thing we are aware of is that the super collider didn't explode because of an experiment. The Temporal Authority made good on its threats to shut down your project. They took you and Dr. K away, exploded the super collider, and not only did many people die, it made people afraid to carry on your type of project," I said as I drove.

He swore in Greek.

I continued, "You haven't been in a hospital unconscious for all these years. You've been in Temporal Authority prison for your crimes. I think it's stupid that they did that. Helping omegas is really noble. They let you out for good behavior, but they took all your memories because it's one of their rules. While we knew that there was a possibility of you coming back to us, we weren't expecting you, because we weren't sure if they'd actually let you go."

"This is a lot..." He was quiet for a moment. "You're telling me that those temporal agents, the ones we were told not to worry about, arrested me, imprisoned me for years, then took my memories?" His eyes teared as he looked at me.

"Yes." My heart broke. I loved Uncle Nick. He'd taught me so much over the years.

His head bowed. "What about Demitra?"

"She was taken too. We were told that she had died in prison. Mrs. K will be at the dinner. Also, she knows about the omegas. But I'm not sure what else she knows," I said.

"Yes, she would help a little sometimes. Thank goodness she's all right. Spencer keeps in touch with her?" His look went tentative.

"She works for him. When he started this company, he lured her out here," I added.

Nick went quiet again. "Demitra didn't make it. She was a talented scientist. I was also the one who kept pressing her to continue every time we were told to stop. Though some of it was because the others told us not to worry about it. We... we trusted them."

His scent went salty again as he looked away.

"You saved lives, Uncle Nick. And as far as we know, they're still here, safe, and living happy lives," I assured him.

A heavy sigh escaped his lips. "Will your parents be at whatever this party is?"

I shook my head. "They passed away a while back in a car accident."

"Oh, I am so sorry to hear that. They were good people."

"Thank you. My sister Sonja will be here with her fiancée, but Sasha won't. Riley, my little sister that you've never met, lives with me and my pack. Which is me, Spencer, Grace, Brennan, Jett, and Wes. I'm not mated to Spencer, but I'm mates to everyone else. Spencer's only with Grace."

"The tiny one." Nick nodded. He frowned. "Why did they bring me *here* and not to Ilena?"

"Short version? Grace was a witness to something for the Authority. It scared the fucking shit out of us when they took her, and we were afraid she wouldn't come back. The guy who brought you to us is an agent of some sort. While she was there, she asked about you and Dr. K, and when he mentioned that you might be released, she asked him to bring you to us. And here you are. Just in time for Spencer and Grace's mating party. They bonded a few weeks ago." We stopped at a stoplight, and I used voice-to-text to send Spencer a message that we were almost there, and he should come out.

I wasn't sure how Spencer wanted to do this. Especially since so many people were here, including Uncle Nick's dad. We wouldn't want to give Spencer's grandfather a heart attack.

Or Auntie Ilena, for that matter.

"Their mating party? She knows about the Temporal Authority. You said that she works for my son. What does she do?" Nick asked.

"Grace is a theoretical mathematician. She works with qubits and string theory. Right now, your son has her trying to make a virtual super collider," I told him. "You're going to like her. And not just because she's also Dr. Thanukos."

He beamed. "I love it. You're an omega? I didn't expect that."

"Me neither. I was in my twenties and in the military when it happened," I laughed. "I'm an advocate for the Omega Center now."

His head bowed again. "I missed so much."

"But you're here now, Uncle Nick. Um, I'm pretty sure that the Temporal Authority won't let you take up your old research. I say this because Grace isn't allowed to do hers. But now, you can travel and do all sorts of things with Auntie," I said. "She's been working her way through the list of places that you were going to visit when you retired. You could start with that."

"Oh. My poor Ilena, alone for so long. I suppose I could. I'm not sure I have the taste for my research anymore now that I know so many were lost because of it. Traveling with her sounds nice. I was always too busy to do so before..." He grew quiet again as we turned down a street full of very fancy old homes, many with hedges and fences. "They'll be happy to see me, won't they?"

"Spencer looked for you. He saw you taken and tried to find you. He's so happy to have you back. Auntie will be, too," I added as we drove through an open gate.

"Prison." He swore again in Greek. "They took so much from me."

We pulled onto a massive brick circular driveway. Spencer stood in front of the giant home, looking nervous in a suit. His tie, vest, and pocket square matched Grace's pale gold dress.

"There's your boy, Uncle." I turned off the ignition. "Yeah, it's awful that you lost so many years just for helping people. But you're back with us now. Your son and wife are well. Get your revenge on the Authority by making the most of your life."

Uncle Nick's face lit up. "Oh, just look at him. You're right. Now, I need to go hug my son."

Chapter Forty-Three

Spencer

My heart pounded as I ended the call. Hand shaking, I went to put my phone in my pocket. I missed, and it dropped to the floor. Bending down, I picked it up and dropped it again.

He was here. My father was *here*, in Rockland, with Evan.

I dared not hope, but here he was, just in time for my mating party.

That *everyone* was here for, including my elderly grandfather, who never completely got over my father's death. Sure, my father was the odd one, preferring to be a scientist instead of a business-man, but he'd definitely been a favorite.

And my mother...

...no, she'd be so happy. She missed him. She was lonely. I saw it last night.

Something feels... unsettled.

I sucked in a breath. Oh. We had him back.

"Spencer, are you all right? Where's Evan?" My cousin, Zoie, ducked into the room, looking like a garden goddess in her floral gown.

"That was him; he's on his way." I stood, putting my phone in my pocket. I'd sent him to get Grace's ring because in my nervousness I'd forgotten it at the house. Thank goodness I had.

"Yeah, you're not okay. What happened?" She leaned against the doorway of the luxury mansion my grandfather had rented for the weekend.

I have my father back.

"I got some unexpected news. Not bad news, just unexpected. Everything will be fine," I assured her.

"Okay." Her look said that she didn't believe me.

They'd all gotten in yesterday. I'd brought Grace over for breakfast to meet them. Just as I'd thought, they loved her.

"I'm nervous," I admitted.

"It's okay to love again, Spence." Zoie came into the room and hugged me. "Honestly, I'm so happy that you found someone. What happened to Elaris was awful, and I know you miss her. You always will. But it wasn't your fault. You're a good man and worthy of love."

"Thank you." I hugged her back. We'd always been close. My omega cousin now had a powerful pack of her own and an excellent position in one of our family's companies.

"I also adore Grace. She's a little odd, but I love her. I can't wait to take her and Evan to the Temple of Artemis this summer." Zoie smiled.

"Grace is quite excited to make that pilgrimage with you," I told Zoie. "I should finish getting ready."

"Here." She brought out a box. "You're supposed to wear the cufflinks."

The box contained the hideous cufflinks that we all wore for our weddings and mating parties. Here I hoped to get away with not wearing them this time.

Zoie replaced my cufflinks with the family ones. I got out the vest, tie, and pocket square I'd bought at Faun to match Grace's dress.

"You look perfect." Zoie straightened my tie and smoothed my shirt.

"You do. You know, after doing some research and seeing the area, I think I really am going to take over that State Street project and make it a multi-use artist colony." My cousin Daphne appeared in the doorway, in a stunning purple dress.

"I think you should," I replied. While Zoie was small, curvy, and soft, my theta cousin Daphne was tall, muscular, and angular. She was a real estate developer, focused on projects that created more spaces for art–both studio space for artists and performance spaces, and was a force of nature. I was looking forward to introducing her to Riley.

I still wasn't sure how exactly Daphne would take over the project, but this was a woman who somehow convinced the Greek government to let her renovate a historic theatre so that plays could be held in it once again. If anyone could do it, it would be her.

My phone buzzed. I sucked in a breath. Evan and my father were almost here. Also, it looked like *all* of Grace's siblings had come for the party.

"What's wrong?" Daphne demanded.

"Evan's here." I put my jacket on.

"Something's wrong, but he won't tell me." Zoie pouted.

I shook my head as I looked in the mirror and fixed my hair. "Nothing's wrong. The news wasn't bad, just unexpected."

We'd need a cover story, of course. What, I was unsure. Also, I didn't know what my father recalled, and what he'd been told.

"I'm going to go outside and wait for Evan." Yes, we needed a story quickly. Also, my mother was with Mrs. K. I should absolutely tell her immediately.

Should I tell her now? No. We needed to get our stories straight. Someone like my father coming back from the dead would be noticed, especially if he showed up at my party. My publicist had even invited a few select members of the press.

Shit. I should tell my publicist too.

After my mother. Yes. One step at a time. I'd meet my father. Get my story straight. Tell my mother–

"Spence, are you *good?*" Daphne frowned.

"I'm going to meet Evan." I went outside the mansion. The June sun made the stone driveway sparkle.

Evan's 4x4 pulled into the massive circular driveway. My heart pounded as I saw my father sitting in the front seat, looking older and bewildered, his hair entirely grey.

His eyes met mine and lit up, making my heart skip a beat.

Baba.

The car door opened, and my father got out. Relief coated me, yes, he looked older, but he seemed okay.

Of course, who knew what mental and emotional tolls his imprisonment had taken on him? Even if he couldn't remember, I'm sure they'd be there.

"Baba." I ran over and hugged my father as if I were still fourteen. As I embraced him, he still felt muscular and fit. My suit was a little big, but that's because I was a little taller and broader. The smell of neutrons clung to him.

"Spencer, my boy," he sobbed in Greek as he hugged me tight.

"We're going to need a story, fast. Zoie's looking out the window at us," Evan muttered.

"I think what they told me, about me being an unconscious John Doe, will have to work. We can blame it on the super collider explosion," my father murmured in English. "I still don't know how it didn't rip apart space and time."

Me neither.

"That will have to work." I hugged him tighter. "We can talk later, but I'm so happy you're here. I... I didn't want to hope they'd actually keep their word and bring you to me, and I'm overjoyed to see you."

Tears filled his eyes. "I'm sorry."

I tapped my forehead to his. "Don't be. We have you back, and that is the greatest gift that I could ever ask for."

"Okay." For a long moment he just continued to hug me.

"Incoming," Evan told me. "Hi, Zoie."

"Evan," she squealed, giving him a hug. Zoie looked at us. "Theíos?" Her voice went small as she used the Greek word for uncle.

"I told you, it wasn't bad news, just unexpected. Please, hold off for a moment, I need to tell my mother. She doesn't know." I reluctantly let go of my father.

"Sure. Theíos! It's Zoie." She gave my uncle a big hug.

"Zoie! Look at you." My father hugged her. He looked around. "Where is Ilena?"

"With Mrs. K," I replied. "I'll call her and have her meet us at the venue. This isn't where the party is. It's just the place Pappous rented for them to stay in for the weekend. He's here along with most of your siblings and their packs."

The door opened, and Daphne ran out. "Theíos? We... we thought you were dead."

"It's quite a story, Daphne, and I'm not sure how much he even recalls." Taking a step away, I called my mother.

"What's wrong? Something isn't right, I feel it," she demanded.

Did she feel it? Or did she feel *him*?

"It's the opposite," I said as Daphne hugged my father tight. "We have been given the best gift. Are you with Mrs. K?"

"I am. Grace is pregnant?" She perked.

"No, she's not. I... I don't know how to say this." My voice shook.

"Just say it," she demanded.

"They found Baba. Something happened in the blast, and he didn't die. He was unconscious in a hospital, and they didn't know who he was this entire time. He was literally just brought to the door of my home, and Evan drove him straight to me. Right now, he's hugging Daphne and Zoie. I wanted to tell you before we take him inside to see Pappous," I blurted, worried about how she'd take it.

"He's alive. Nick, my Nick isn't dead?" She swore in Greek. "He probably blasted himself into another universe. I told him that messing with reality would make people grumpy."

She had? I didn't know that.

"He seems okay?" Her voice wavered.

I lowered my voice. "He's feeling guilty about how much he missed. The last thing he remembers is leaving for work. Be easy on him?"

"I suppose. Can I see? Please?"

"Of course." I took a photo of him with Evan and my cousins and sent it to her.

She swore again in Greek. "It's him. He's back. I... I have him back. I knew I felt him, and sometimes I would feel him even though I shouldn't. Do you know how many times I wished that he was really alive, since we never found a body?"

"Your wish just came true, Mama. I'll bring him to the party, and you can meet us there? You might need to shield him from everyone. But there are many nice places at the club that you can run off to and talk," I assured her.

"Yes. Oh, if I'm seeing Nick again after all these years, maybe I should wear the other dress I bought." For a moment she sounded self-conscious.

"He doesn't care about your dress, Mama. He just wants *you*."

"I... I don't know how to feel about this." Her voice wavered.

"Happy, Mama. We have him back. You can now travel the world with him just like you wanted and do all the things you regretted never doing." I saw the door open, and Pappous peered out.

"What are you all doing out here?" he called, leaning on his cane.

"I need to go. I love you. We'll see you soon." I ended the call and ran over to my pappous, my grandfather. The patriarch of the Thanukos family.

"Pappous, we got the best present," I explained. "They found Baba. He wasn't dead. Just missing."

"Nick?" He looked startled.

As he should. *Please don't have a heart attack from the shock.*

It was a lot. Not only had he and my yiayia mourned the loss of their son a lot, but they'd taken care of my poor battered heart as I struggled with what I'd seen versus what everyone told me, as my mother grieved losing her bonded mate and the love of her life.

They like to say that betas don't feel the loss of a bond mate like alphas and omegas do. That was pure bullshit because I saw what she went through. Just like I grieved losing the beta I'd bonded much harder than the 'experts' thought I 'should.'

"Baba." My father's voice broke as he ran over to him. "You're still alive, Baba."

"I should be saying that. Nick. You're here. How?" Tears streamed down Pappous's face.

"I don't even really know. I was unconscious for a long time. But I'm here now. I'm here, Baba." He hugged him tight.

"What is going on?" Ari, my dad's brother, came out. "Nick?"

"Ari? You look old," my father teased as he let go of his dad and hugged his brother.

"Fuck, man, we thought you were dead." Ari hugged his older brother.

"I'm here." My father sniffled. "As are all of you. Tell me, when can I see my wife?"

"Do I look all right? Here I am acting like it's our first date all over again," my father said in Greek as he paced the small room the club had made available to us to store things and get ready.

"You look perfect," I assured. My father, Evan, and I headed over to my club early. Not just to see to any last-minute issues, but so that my parents could have their reunion in private.

I could tell that my father was getting overwhelmed with all the questions our well-meaning family pelted at him. Evan had also told him the truth, which was a lot of him, I was sure.

Not to mention, all he really wanted was to see my mother.

"Here." I poured some champagne that the club had left for us in an ice bucket, along with some snacks. I handed my father the glass, then poured one for myself. Right now, the two of us were alone.

"Thank you." He sipped it. "You're doing very well for yourself."

"I am. The road hasn't been without heartbreak, but I have my company, my pack, Evan, and now I have Grace. You'll love her," I told him.

"It's a lot. Everything feels muddled." He made a face. "Nothing tastes right."

"I think that's a side effect of something they use. Grace was like that, too," I replied.

There was a knock on the door. "Spence? Uncle Nick?"

It was time. My heart pounded, and I hoped that my parent's reunion was everything they hoped it would be.

The door opened, and Evan came in with my mother.

"Nick." My mother flew into my father's arms. "It's really you. You're alive."

"Ilena. I'm so sorry. But I'm here now. I love you. I'm sorry." Tears streamed down his face as he held her tight.

My mother looked up at him, defiant. "Don't you dare be sorry, Nick Thanukos. Or I will make you do dishes for a month. You're here. You're home. You're *mine.* Which means your focus is on *me.* Not what you missed out on. *Me* and *your son* and *now.* Understood?"

"Understood." My father kissed her more deeply than a son wants to see his parents kiss.

"We'll leave you here. I need to check on some things. Help yourself to the snacks." Finishing my champagne, I grabbed Evan, and we left the room, closing the door behind us.

"They're going to bang, aren't they," Evan joked.

"Probably. Not that I want to think about that," I replied. "How did she seem when you got her?"

"Cautiously optimistic. Mrs. K wants to talk to you," Evan added as I led us outside to where our party would be.

"I'm sure she does." That would have to wait. Reunion accomplished, and publicist contacted, my focus was now getting us through the party.

The grounds of my club that we reserved had been transformed into the ultimate upscale picnic. Tiny lights formed swooping canopies. Underneath sat white picnic tables, topped with brocade tablecloths, candle lanterns, sumptuous floral arrangements from a local farm, and tiny boxes of handmade candies brought in from the candy shop that I'd always gone to growing up in Greece. Two smaller tables had battery-operated lanterns, along with some coloring pages and colored pencils.

More lights hung over the dance floor and the area for my cousins' band. A long buffet table was set up, along with a wine bar, a customizable lemonade station, and a table that would eventually be filled with desserts.

Evan whistled. "This is amazing."

"It's all Grace and the wedding planner you found, with some help from Mrs. K and the coordinator here at the club. Grace wanted an upscale barbecue, and here we are." I looked around at all the potted trees and flowers...

...and the giant white bouncy castle with a slide and ball pit. The balls matched the colors Grace had chosen for the decor–mauve, green, and lavender to go with the summer picnic theme. Flowers and balloons of the same colors decorated it, with more lights over it.

"That is the fanciest bouncy castle I've ever seen. When did she add a bouncy castle?" Evan asked, looking around.

"That's what she wanted, isn't it? We didn't have much time, and it's what the approved vendor had on short notice. I wanted better flowers, but it's what I could do." The wedding planner, named Eunice, came over to us, dressed elegantly but understated in a floral maxi dress. She had on a headset and held a tablet.

"It's beautiful."

"Oh, good." Relief flowed through her scent. "I had the children's table set up as well. I'm so glad we could accommodate those last-minute changes."

Shit.

"We have one more addition. I'd like him to sit with my mother. We can move them if needed. I'm so sorry," I apologized.

Looking a little frazzled, she tapped on her tablet. "One more. If I can move them, I can absolutely do that. Can I move some of the other children to the children's table? That would help."

"Of course."

She set off.

"I'm guessing the children's table and bouncy castle are for her siblings?" I told Evan as I spied my friend, who'd flown in to grill for us tonight. He was with some chefs and massive grills.

"Yes. Her siblings arrived right after your father did, while Grace was talking to Agent Ass-Face. Hale was talking about how nice his car was." Evan sighed. "How are you? Your dad coming back is huge. While we knew it was a possibility, it being reality is a whole separate thing."

"My heart broke last night when my mother said that she was lonely. Now she has him back. He's no longer in prison. My father is back... I..." So many emotions overwhelmed me.

"I know, old friend." Evan hugged me tightly. "I know."

"Hopefully, we can keep him away from his research." The idea of them coming back for him made me nervous.

"I'm pretty sure that your mom is going to make him stay re-tired. He's got years of traveling with her ahead of him. If he gets bored, maybe he can teach again–not resume his qubit research but just teach, after all, his students loved him," Evan responded.

"True. Maybe at some point he can tell us more. Perhaps we can even figure out what happened with Grace. It is curious that they let him remember all that. Why make him forget prison and the trials but let him recall what got him put there?" That, too, bothered me.

Evan thought for a moment. "I'm guessing it was deliberate, like Grace having all of her notes on her phone. Grace could also probably tell us more."

"Spence, where do we set up?" Zoie held up her bouzouki case, some of my cousins trailing, all dressed colorfully and carrying instrument cases.

I was excited for them to play later when it was time for dancing. We had a DJ while everyone was eating, and string music for the reception. Grace and I had made the playlist together, which had been fun.

"Ah, your cousins." Eunice came over to us. "Welcome, I'll show you where to go. Spencer, I got the seating fixed. The reception is being set up. Also, I think your grill master wants a word."

"Perfect. Thank you," I said as she led my cousins off. Yes, I should go greet my friend. Today was already wonderful, and having my father here made it even better.

Chapter Forty-Four

Grace

"Are we ready?" I asked, surveying everyone dressed and ready in their finery in the living room. Well, everyone except me. I'd put my dress on at the club.

"Yeah, um, how are we getting there?" Wes looked at everyone.

Verity held Hope, who napped on her shoulder. Tru was braiding Jett's hair.

"Hale, please don't touch that," Brennan said through gritted teeth as Hale picked up a small statue.

"Grace, I think Hale, Chance, and Dare should go with you, Mercy if there's room," Verity said.

There was something about the way she said it that made me think that perhaps some of my siblings needed to talk to me. Which was fair.

"Okay, we can't fit all four of us in my truck legally. But Spencer already said that we could take his car..." Mentally I counted. How were we going to do this?

She started unfolding some rectangles that were with their luggage. "I have the car seats for Tru, Pax, and Hope."

Oh. They would be in car seats. I loved how they just folded up like that. I suppose when Tru visited us, they'd be sending one for her.

"Do we have cars we can put car seats in?" Wes gave us a baffled look.

"Jett's the police officer; ask him. Also, since you three seem to think that I'm going to have triplets, you can figure out where to put them." It came out cranky. We were behind schedule because Pax had gotten stuck in a vent, and then we had to get him changed.

"Triplets?" Verity looked startled. "Are you pregnant?"

"Not pregnant. But twins run on both sides of my family apparently, and the guys all seem convinced that I'm going to have Spencer's triplets." I rubbed my temples.

Hale thought for a moment. "I think the world needs that."

No. The world did not.

"I think the only car we can put three car seats in is Spencer's. Well, and Evan's. But Evan isn't here." Jett rubbed his chin. "We can't put those car seats in the trucks, and we can only fit two in my car."

"Okay, so Wes, Verity, and the car seats go in Spencer's car. Jett, can I drive your car?" I mentally counted.

"Um, I guess. Who does that leave?" Jett looked around.

"It means that you and Bren get to take Mercy and me on your motorcycles." Riley, who wore the elegant green jumpsuit from the mall, struck a pose.

"Okay..." Brennan nodded. "I'm supposed to take Spencer's motorcycle, anyway. Riley, Mercy can wear your helmet, and you can wear Evan's?"

Mine was with the things I was bringing with me to the venue, since Spencer and I were leaving the party on his motorcycle.

"Oh, that sounds amazing," Mercy agreed, looking stunning in a similar jumpsuit, only in a leaf pattern. It might be a popular style right now.

My guys all wore suits with green ties and pocket squares that matched Riley.

"I'll take a motorcycle," Hale offered.

"No. I think we're set?" Brennan looked to Verity.

"Um, okay." Verity bit her lower lip.

"Jett could also take Mercy and Riley in one of the trucks," I offered.

"Oh, come on, Ver," Mercy pleaded.

"Fine." She sighed.

Hale laughed. "I mean, you rode a motorcycle in a bikini."

"It was for a photo shoot, and we weren't going fast. Okay, let's get everyone packed up. Here, take this." Verity handed Brennan and Wes each a car seat then grabbed the third car seat and the diaper bag, while still carrying Hope. "Okay, you know who you're going with. Everyone load up and mind your buddy."

"Got mine." Mercy grabbed Riley's hand and raised it. "This is going to be amazing."

Verity and Wes started leading everyone to the garage.

"Breathe." Brennan held me to his chest. "It'll be okay. Creed *is* taking them after this, right?"

I sighed. "No. They're staying here. Spencer and I will just cancel the hotel. In the morning, Creed will pick them up, except for Verity, who is leaving tonight, and Mercy, who has plans with Riley, and take them to the adventure park. We'll go to brunch with Spencer's family from Greece, after that, Mercy and Riley have their own plans. I have lunch with Spencer and his mother's family from New York. Then, whoever wants can go to the adventure park for fireworks and dinner. After that, they're all going on a late-night flight home. Mercy's visit has been cut short so that she can return with them." At least she was coming back soon.

"Absolutely not." Brennan shook his head. "I'll book them a family suite at the adventure park hotel, and Creed can take care of them all, well, except for Mercy. I can handle one well-behaved, self-sufficient teenager over for a sleepover. But all of them... no. And I'm not the one teasing you about triplets."

"I know." I hugged him tighter.

"You and Spencer should have your night together. We'll meet you for brunch. I probably will opt out of fireworks at the adventure park. But Wes, Evan, and Jett fucking love that place." He sighed.

"Grace, are you okay?" Wes came back in.

"She needs a hug." Brennan let go of me.

Wes pulled me to him. "We're not having eight kids."

"Agreed." I closed my eyes.

"Sister, are you coming? Can I drive?" Hale yelled.

I sighed. "I'm coming, and no. We're not putting the top down either."

"Well, no, it'll mess up your hair." Hale stood there, looking like trouble even in his suit, wearing fancy cowboy boots and a dressy cowboy hat. Chance and Pax also had on their nice boots, hats, and bolo ties.

"See you there." I gave Brennan and Wes a kiss.

I got into the car with my three brothers, and we started driving to the country club, my dress and everything in the tiny trunk.

"Hey, um, can you explain why and how you put Mom in jail?" Chance inquired from the back seat. "No one will tell us anything."

"Yeah, even Verity and Creed are being assholes about it." Dare shrugged and looked at his brothers. His suit was very Victorian rake. He had on more eyeliner than I did and looked amazing.

"I mean, I know she stabbed your mate. I was there, but there's more to it, right?" Hale's brow furrowed.

"What is baby trafficking, anyway? Babies can't drive." Chance frowned.

"It's when you sell a baby." I sighed. "Short version, you know I'm your dad's from before he met your alpha moms, right?"

Heads bobbed. How did I explain this gently?

"One of your moms didn't want me around after my mom died and gave me to my mom's mom. But, she didn't talk to your dad about it first. She then gave my aunt money to take me far away so that your dad would never find me, which in the eyes of the law is selling me, and is what got her arrested." My gut churned. "There's more to it, and I can tell you later."

"Oh. Okay. That is weird. Mom likes kids more than Mumsy but not as much as Mama." Chance frowned. "But you found us, and that's why the parents are mad?"

"No one told me that I wasn't supposed to find you. Though I wasn't looking. I'm sorry. I didn't mean for your mom to end up in jail. Truly, I didn't know about any of this. Meeting Creed at the conference was a surprise. I thought that my dad abandoned me; of course, I also thought my aunt was my mom," I added. "She stabbed Spencer because she was mad at me."

Chance frowned. "Okay. I don't know if Mom should be in jail because it makes everyone sad, but selling babies sounds wrong. Not telling Dad things is very wrong and usually ends with much yelling. Stabbing people is also wrong."

"I wasn't trying to wreck your family. I'm sorry." I sniffed.

"No one thinks you are, Sister," Hale said gently. "You were a baby, and none of this is your fault. But the parents aren't telling us shit, and Verity and Creed are like, *This isn't our story to tell,* so we wanted to ask you."

"I'll answer everything I can," I promised.

"Are you rich?" Chance asked. "Your house feels like a rich person's house. I love the little house your big house has."

"She's mated to a billionaire. Of course she has a nice house." Dare smacked his younger brother in the head.

"Oh. I thought she mated to *that Greek man.*" Chance blinked.

"Yeah, a Greek billionaire who runs a biotech company that works with secret government agencies." Dare rolled his eyes.

As we drove, I answered their questions, which were less about their mom and more about why I didn't have any pets, and the sports and video games I liked, and what exactly I did for Compass BioTek. I tried to learn about them, too.

"You play the cello?" I asked Dare. Right, Tru told me that he was a musician.

Chance rolled his eyes. "All the time."

"It's called *practicing.* I play a few different instruments, but mostly the cello. I'd like to do more with it, but the parents are about as excited at the idea of me majoring in music as they are at Mercy becoming a professional athlete." Dare sighed.

"I play the piano, and while I never wanted to major in it, music is so helpful for so many reasons. If you want to do it, go for it," I encouraged. "I support doing what you love. For me, it was math—and no, my parents didn't want me to study math."

Hale started laughing. "Yeah, you didn't grow up with us. That would be an acceptable major."

"What did they want you to be?" Chance asked.

"A teacher. Teachers are great, I just didn't want to be one," I said as we drove through the gates of the country club.

"This is where the party is? What is this place?" Chance asked.

"Spencer's golf and tennis club. Hale, why aren't you allowed around bouncy castles?" I asked as we turned into the parking lot.

"What? I am so allowed around bouncy castles. Ugh, you fill *one* bouncy castle with helium borrowed from the university chem lab." Hale made an exasperated face.

Yep. This was my brother, the chemistry major.

We parked. Eunice, the fancy wedding planner, waited for me, looking stressed.

"There you are," she said as I got my dress and things out of the trunk.

"Sorry, we're running behind." I saw Wes drive up in Spencer's car, followed by the motorcycles.

"It's your party. They can wait for *you*. Everything is in place. People are already arriving, but don't worry, we're sending everyone to the gardens for the reception. We've got the string quartet playing, and the canapes and drinks are being passed. It's okay." She eyed my three littlest siblings getting out of the car.

"Show me where I can get ready? I need five minutes alone. We have two rooms, right?" I asked.

"We do." She smiled. "Let me show you where to go."

"Grace?" Evan's voice came through the door as there was a soft knock.

"You can come in." I sat on the chaise in the pretty little room that Eunice showed me to. Mostly dressed, I was just taking a moment to drink my champagne and compose myself.

Okay, and eat a bunch of the beautiful pastel macarons off the ornate tiered tray. I'd never mastered baking macarons.

Evan slipped in. "You look beautiful."

"Hi. I just needed a moment." I stuffed another macaron in my mouth.

He shut the door and sat with me on the lounger. "Take all the moments you need."

"Did you need to put anything in here?" I rested my head on his shoulder.

"No. Everyone and everything is in the other room eating all the snacks. Oh, you have nicer snacks. May I?" Evan eyed the macarons.

I handed him the tray. "Try one, they're so good."

"Mmmm. Delicious." He sighed happily, eating one of the pastel cookies.

"Try this." I handed him the bottle of champagne.

Evan chuckled and took a swig directly from the bottle. "We're so classy."

"Yep. Especially with the back of my dress undone and no shoes." I took another cookie. "I'm probably getting crumbs all over it."

"Doesn't matter. Spencer will still adore you." Evan snagged a kiss, which tasted of macaron.

"Is Spence okay? Thanks for handling everything with Nick earlier." I put my head back on his shoulder.

"I'm happy that I was there to help. Um, I told Uncle Nick everything. He remembers his research and the omegas. They didn't take that away." Frowning, he took another sip.

"Huh." I hadn't expected that.

Evan looked at the closed door. "Spencer will probably be here soon. He's having a drink with his dad; they haven't had a chance to really talk alone yet. After I brought Uncle Nick to the house, we came here, he and Auntie got, um, reunited, then the three of them had a talk. Now Auntie is absolutely entranced with your little siblings–and I'm here with you. Brennan and Jett went to get all of your siblings' things and are going to store them in the other room. Something about them all going with Creed to stay over at the adventure park?"

"Sounds good." I took another drink. "So, Spencer and I will do the individual photos his publicist wants so we can send out formal mating announcements, followed by a pack photo, then we'll take our places and welcome everyone to the party?"

"Hey, if any of this is stressing you out, screw the formal photos. The photographer can get candids during the party and be done with it," Evan assured.

"I'm okay. It won't take long." I took another drink of champagne. "Who are the *Agents in Glasses*? My brothers think that's who Agent Weigmier is, and Compass BioTek works with them."

"I mean, if it existed, you'd probably need to work with them for any advanced space travel projects." Evan grinned. "It's a movie franchise about agents who help keep aliens and other planets a secret. So, I guess Agent Weigmier could be part of it?"

"Oh, I suppose if we create warp engines and create faster-than-light travel or perhaps harness this world's equivalent of Einstein-Rosenberg bridges to travel across the universe, we might run into someone or something." I nodded. *Makes sense to me.*

"Grace, are you ready for me?" Spencer knocked on the door.

"No, but you can come in," I replied.

The door opened, and Spencer walked in, holding a large bag. Heat rushed through me at how sexy he looked.

I held up the bottle. "We're just day drinking."

Spencer kissed me. "I'll have some of that."

Taking the bottle, he took a sip and sat down on the other side of me.

"Hi, Darling." His look went smoldering.

"Hi, Dearest." I sent a heated look back.

"Fine. I'll do up her dress and leave." Evan grinned. Handing me the macarons, he stood.

"Would you like one?" I offered Spencer the tray.

"I would. They look almost as tasty as you." Winking, he took a cookie and bit into it suggestively.

So smooth.

"Save it for tonight." Going behind me, Evan zipped up my dress.

"Oh, I will." Spencer waggled his eyebrows and leaned in and kissed me.

Evan shook his head, laughing. "All done. See you for photos."

"We'll be out soon," Spencer replied.

Evan hugged him and kissed me on the cheek. "Congrats, you two."

He slipped out the door.

For a moment, Spencer and I just sat there, eating cookies and passing the champagne bottle back and forth.

"How do I look?" Verity had curled my hair and done my makeup. I had on the peach blossom necklace and earrings that he'd given me for my birthday. Riley had loaned me a beautiful headband to wear.

"Perfect. And me?" Spencer asked.

"Like I want to kiss you." I kissed him. "We're having our mating party."

"We are." His forehead touched mine. "And my father is here."

"Agent Weigmier has great timing." Quickly, I told him what happened as I leaned over and got a couple of things out of my bag that was on the floor by the chaise.

"That works with what the three of us came up with. We had to tell everyone something." Spencer added in the gaps.

Nick remembered his research? That was surprising. But it could be useful. I was still curious about Rosalind and me going to another world.

However, I'd ask him about it another time.

I smoothed Spencer's hair with my hand. "How are you doing?"

"I have my father back." His eyes went misty. "Oh. Before I forget. Your shoes."

Spencer handed me a box with a brand-new pair of pale gold ballet flats that matched the dress.

"Thank you." I kissed him and sat down on the chaise as he slipped them on my feet. His eyes met mine, and my core warmed at the sheer devoted sexiness of the motion.

"I got this for you." Still on his knees in front of me, he pulled a little ring box out of his pocket and opened it, revealing a gold band with three emeralds and several smaller clear stones. It was big and fancy, but at the same time, classy.

"Spencer, it's beautiful," I breathed. We ordered rings for each other but kept them a surprise.

"Just like you." He slipped it onto my right hand.

We talked about which finger I wanted to wear it on. I liked how here you wore your rings on whatever fingers you wanted. It made sense if you had rings from multiple mates.

"Here." I handed him a box. "Evan helped me choose it." It was a titanium wedding band engraved with the Greek key design, set in a larger gold band. I slid it onto his finger.

"Darling, I love it." Spencer leaned in and kissed me.

"Um, I have something else." I handed him a box. Inside was a tie tack that matched my necklace. I pinned it on his tie. "Perfect."

Spencer kissed me again. "I love it. I have something for you, too. Though you don't have to wear any of it today. I think your jewelry choices are perfect. My grandfather brought it, per our mating agreement."

He got out a beautiful carved box and opened it. I sucked in a breath as I took in all the pieces of jewelry in it, some quite lovely and others...

"A family as old as ours had a lot of heirloom pieces. Some are more interesting than others," Spencer laughed. "We keep them in the family by passing them around. It's not an insult. It actually means they accept you, because they might be ugly, but they're part of our heritage. One day you can pass some of them on as gifts to other family members."

I held up a hideous bejeweled broach that looked like it should be in a museum. "Like this?"

"Yes." His eyes crinkled as he smiled.

A blue stone caught my eye. I fished out a delicate bangle with blue stones. "This. I'll wear this."

Because I needed something blue. I meant to get a blue thong and had forgotten. Not to mention, Evan had surprised me with a beautiful gold bra and panty set.

"A lovely choice. This was my yiayia's, and it means a lot that it was included." Spencer slid it onto my arm.

"Thank you." I kissed him. I'd look through everything later. "You know, I think it's a little silly that you give me all these things and I don't give you anything other than a ring and a small piece of jewelry. I'd like to get you a hedgehog, when you're ready," I offered. What else did you get the billionaire who had everything?

Okay, I knew it was about transferring assets and tradition. The alpha showed they could take proper care of a mate, and the gifts were supposed to let the mate know that they were wanted by the alpha's family. Jewelry was historically a way to amass money of one's own. But still...

Leaning in, he gave me another kiss. "That sounds perfect. I think I'd love a pet hedgehog. I actually wanted to get you something special, just from me. What do you think of this?"

Taking out his phone, he showed me something that looked a lot like a small version of our guest house.

"Is that a chicken coop?" I asked.

"Yes, this company makes chicken coops that match your home or guest house so that they're not eyesores. Since Brennan brought up chicken coop appearance, I thought this would be the perfect compromise. I admit, the spaceship ones are cute, though they seem difficult to clean," he explained.

A chicken coop. "I love it."

"There's a service that will care for our chickens when we're away. I should see if they'll take care of hedgehogs," he added. "They're called *Chicken Tenders.*"

I giggled. Chicken Tenders. So funny.

"Perfect." I kissed him. "Now I can go buy those chickens. Um, the professor gave us something." I took the rectangular wrapped gift out of my bag. The professor was also apologetic; he thought he told me that they were *all* coming.

"Oh, that was kind. Should we open it?" Spencer asked.

We unwrapped the gift, and inside was a framed piece of art. The numbers of *Pi* formed a heart going around and around, the calligraphy numbers getting smaller and smaller, until they disappeared in the center. Our names were inscribed on it, and it was accented in watercolors of mauve, green, and lavender.

"That is beautiful," I breathed. I sent the professor a text thanking him.

Someone knocked on the door. "Are you ready for photos?"

I looked at Spencer. "Ready?"

He helped me up. "Yes."

We left the room, arm in arm. Eunice stood there with her headset and clipboard. "Let's go."

First, we went off to a part of the gardens for some beautiful formal shots of just us. His publicist was there to oversee.

Brennan brought in Spencer's motorcycle, and we took a couple of silly shots of us on it, for fun. Eunice fluffed my dress, and the photographer used a fan to make it more dramatic.

"What do you think?" The photographer showed us some of them.

"They're perfect," I replied.

"Hey, since *all* of your siblings are here, do you want to get one with everyone?" Brennan asked me, as he walked with Spencer, me, Eunice, and the photographer to the area where we were taking pack photos.

"Oh, I love that." I turned to the photographer. "Do we have time to take one?"

"Of course."

Eunice nodded. "I'll collect them for you."

"Perfect."

The rest of the pack was waiting for us.

"Fuck, you look *perfect.*" Riley rushed over to me.

"Hey, that's my line." Evan laughed.

"No, it's mine." Wes grinned, giving Evan a playful shove.

"We all know she looks great." Jett looked me up and down suggestibly.

Brennan's eyes met mine. "She does."

"Yes, I made a good choice." Spencer kissed me.

The photographer positioned us and took the photos.

"Here they are," Eunice said, herding all nine of my siblings over. Verity was holding Hope.

"You want pictures of us?" Creed blinked.

"Since all ten of us are all together, I thought it would be nice. It was Brennan's idea." I laughed.

Verity smiled. "I love it. Okay, Hopey, let's put you down."

Hope shook her head.

"We could work with that," the photographer said.

"Yeah, uppies for everyone." Hale set Pax on his shoulders.

"Oh, we could do a silly picture," the photographer suggested.

Honestly, even though I didn't know them well yet, it seemed like it would be more *us* than a formal one.

"Grace, hold me?" Tru asked. She wore a cute purple dress, which had been one of the photos she had sent me.

"Let's just make sure your shoes don't get dirt on her skirt," Riley said, helping me pick up Tru.

Dare put Chance on his shoulders, though it looked like they'd topple over any second.

"Incoming." Mercy jumped on Creed's back.

"This is great," the photographer said. "So cute."

We got a couple of shots. I'd have to send one to the professor.

"All right. I guess we'll go through the garden reception, then head over to the party area to greet everyone?" I asked Eunice.

"Um, Grace, can I play something for you, first? The cellist in the quartet said I could." Dare's voice was soft.

"I'd love that. Thank you, Dare." Awww.

We entered the garden, where friends and family mingled and ate. Riley grabbed Mercy and dragged her over to Hiro, Kilroy, Marcos, and Rose.

Dare went over to the string quartet and when they finished their song, whispered to the cellist.

"Hi, I'm Dare, and I want to play something for my sister." Dare took the cello from the cellist and sat down.

Spencer put his arm around me. "I'll make sure they get an extra good tip."

"Thank you." It was nice of them to do that.

Dare closed his eyes and started to play. A beautiful melody that reminded me of the Prelude from Bach's *Cello Suite in G Minor* enveloped us. You could feel his passion in the music and see it on his face.

"Fuck, he's good. That's a piece that isn't technically hard, but difficult to play well," Brennan said softly.

"Dare's talented. I really hope the parents let him study music," Verity said quietly, joining us.

"Your family is into science, right?" Brennan asked. "Boston Institute of Technology has one of the best collegiate music programs in the country. He could pretend to study something parental-approved and actually major in music. It's difficult to get in, but a possibility, if he's up for the deception."

I squeezed Brennan's hand. I was guessing he'd investigated that at some point for piano.

Verity thought for a moment, still holding Hope. "Huh. That's a thought. The parents would have a lot of difficulty saying no to that, even though we can study for free at Briar and Marquess."

My attention went back to the music. Yes, that should be encouraged, just like Mercy's passion for skate smash. It was a pity their parents didn't see it.

Well, it was a good thing they now had me.

Chapter Forty-Five

Spencer

Grace's idea of an upscale barbeque was *perfect*. As darkness fell, tiny lights glowed, illuminating our outdoor picnic area. Dinner finished, my cousins' band played Greek music, as people danced and chatted.

Dare was playing an oud. I wasn't sure where the instrument came from, but he seemed to be having a great time playing with them. My parents had disappeared at some point. Right now, Grace danced with Wes and Evan.

The bouncy castle also seemed to be quite popular, especially with the teenagers in attendance.

"Spencer, have you been avoiding me?" Mrs. K came over to me.

"Not at all, it's just been busy," I replied. "My father is back."

"He is. Spencer, I have questions."

"I might have answers. Walk with me?" I nodded toward a path.

We walked back toward the garden where the cocktail reception had been.

"We didn't know he was coming. Literally, he was dropped off on the doorstep this afternoon. He remembers his research, but he remembers nothing past leaving for work that morning–including the explosion. Evan told him what happened." I filled her in.

She squeezed my hand. "I'm so happy that you have him back. Spencer, I know you want answers, but perhaps go easy on him?"

"I will."

We returned to the party.

"There you are." Zoie grabbed me and pulled me over to the musicians.

Yes, it was the part of the evening when I played the bouzouki. My mother had brought mine per my request.

Zoie handed me the beautiful stringed instrument that my yiayia had not only given me but taught me to play.

"I suppose that I can play a song for my good doctor–my incredible mate that I am so fortunate to have in my life. She and my equally wonderful pack who have supported me through so much," I announced.

My publicist looked startled, and I saw her run to get the photographer. I started a song that was one of my yiayia's favorites, the rest of the band joining in.

People danced, and I saw my pappous take Grace's hand. I'd given her some living room dance lessons to prepare. My mother and father had returned and joined in. Even Brennan seemed to be having a good time, but one of my aunties had decided it was her job to make sure he had fun. Daphne danced with my friend, whose grilling duties had now finished.

Brennan's father had even shown up for a bit, without the Queen Mum, which had been surprising.

My heart burst with love for everyone. Yes, this was just what we needed. A nice reason to get together and have a good time.

"Thank you so much for coming," Grace told the Nakamuras as we made the rounds to greet everyone before sneaking off.

"Your dress is perfect. This was an excellent party," Yui complemented. "I'm going to need the name of your planner."

"Of course," Grace replied.

"Thank you so much for attending, Councilman," I stated.

Arm in arm, we moved on. The band was still going; the drinks continued to flow, and dessert had been set out.

"We're going to sneak out," my mother said with a giggle, arm around my father. "I suppose you'll be doing the same soon?"

When had I last seen her this happy?

"We will. Will I see you at brunch tomorrow?" I asked.

"Yes," my father assured me. "I do hope that we can spend time together, soon."

"I told you, his whole wonderful pack is coming to visit us," my mother said. "Oh, those little siblings of Grace's are so cute."

"They are, I'm glad they came," Grace replied.

"And you, my dear, are lovely. I can see why Spencer chose you," my father added. The two of them had been engaged in a very spirited discussion about qubits earlier.

They left, and Grace and I continued to make sure we talked to everyone.

Evan came over to us. "Getting ready to go?"

"Yes." Grace hugged him tight.

"You two have fun. See you at brunch." Evan hugged her, then me. "Congrats, old friend. This was quite a party. Our wedding will be better though."

"As it should be." I laughed.

We looked around to see if we needed to talk to anyone else. Verity had already left to catch her flight.

"Sneaking out?" Hale stood there, grinning. "I've got you. Don't worry about it."

"Thanks, Hale. I'll see everyone tomorrow at the adventure park for fireworks and dinner," Grace reminded him.

He left with a wave.

She turned to me. "Should we make a run for it?"

"We should." Though that really meant going back to the main building, so Grace could change and grab her bag. The pack would make sure the rest of our things and all the gifts got back to the house.

Suddenly, heart-shaped *fireworks* went off over the lake.

"You planned for fireworks for our departure? How lovely," I remarked, as we left the party.

"No..." Grace looked at her phone. "This is Hale's distraction so that we can leave. He and Dare smuggled fireworks onto an airplane. It's their gift to us. I wonder if that's why they had issues with airport security."

Of course it was them.

"Let's just go, and we'll worry about the club being angry tomorrow. There are other clubs if they kick us out," I assured.

We went back to the room where I'd originally collected her, and I helped her change. We'd be taking my motorcycle to the hotel. Evan had already made sure our things were there.

I handed Grace her helmet and grabbed mine. "Ready."

Eunice was waiting for us. "Where did the fireworks come from? It was a pretty display, but I'm unsure we have a permit."

"My brothers." Grace sighed. "I'm sorry."

"We'll pay a fine if we need to," I apologized.

I led Grace out to my motorcycle. Our pack was waiting, along with Mercy.

"I didn't let anyone attach anything to it or deface it, though your cousin tried," Brennan told us. "Have fun, see you tomorrow."

"Thank you, Brennan." I hugged him. It was probably Daphne who made the attempt.

"Don't add to the population, subtract from the population, or end up in jail because I don't have bail money." Mercy hugged Grace.

"Same," Riley added.

"See you tomorrow." Wes kissed Grace, and Evan did the same.

I helped Grace onto my motorcycle and got in front of her, putting on my helmet. With a wave, we took off.

We drove to a luxury hotel that I had booked for the night.

Evan had already checked us in and given me the key, so we went directly to the mating night suite, where champagne and chocolate-covered strawberries awaited us.

"Spencer, this is beautiful," she breathed, as she took in the lovely sitting room and the view.

"Almost as beautiful as you." I kissed her long and deep, trying to tell her how much she meant to me, how perfect she was for me.

After all, how many people would be all right with your presumed-dead father being dropped off on your doorstep?

"You planned the most wonderful dinner. Everyone had so much fun," I added. "It was nice to see everyone. My family *adores* you. I think my cousins want to keep Dare."

From my business associates, to my friends and colleagues, to my family, everyone seemed to enjoy themselves and was impressed. She'd been nervous about meeting my family, but they were excited for her. Just like they were pleased that we became the Thanukos pack, and everyone had taken my last name.

"It was fun. You know, I think we need to help Dare study music." She popped open the bottle of champagne. "Creed wasn't happy about going with them *all* to a hotel at the adventure park, but oh well. Brennan got them a nice family suite with bunk beds. But we'll worry about my siblings later."

Her look became coy as she poured us some. "To us, and all the science we're going to make."

Taking a glass, I tapped mine against hers. "Mmmm, I think I'd like to make more than science tonight."

Grace giggled. "I think I'd like that. And perhaps some room service after. While dinner was delicious, I barely got to eat."

"Same." I picked her up and took her into the giant bedroom. "Yes, we'll make a little... science, then have something to eat, then enjoy a bath?" The room had an extra-large tub.

"Perfect," she murmured as I gently placed her on the bed.

I undressed her, placing her cute departure outfit onto the dresser, along with the even cuter underthings, then removed my own clothes. She'd changed, but I was still in my tux–putting the cuf-flinks and tie tack aside so I wouldn't lose them.

"Hi, Darling." I put my phone on the bedstand and hopped onto the bed with her.

"Hi, Dearest." She smiled back.

Taking the massage oil off the nightstand, I put some in my hand. "Roll onto your stomach."

"Gladly." Eyes closing, she rolled over.

Straddling her, I started massaging her back, trying to get rid of the tension in her shoulders, using the self-warming oil.

Today had been a lot for both of us, and I wouldn't be surprised if she fell asleep. Though our stay here came with a late-night feast, since so many didn't get to eat much at their mating parties.

"Too hard?" I asked.

"Not at all," she hummed.

My cock grew hard as I continued to knead out her tensions and stress.

"Yes, that's it, Baby Girl, just relax for Daddy and let go." I felt her tension ease in the bond and be replaced with contentment. With every touch, every stroke, I reminded her of how much I loved her and how happy I was to have her in my life.

How she filled cracks in my soul I didn't know were there. I was looking forward to the happy life we'd have together.

That our pack would have together.

I kissed her temple. "Turn over for me?"

Grace flipped over.

"Good girl." I planted a kiss on her nose.

Once again, I straddled her, as I massaged her arms, my hard cock teasing her in the way I knew that she liked, my fingers brushing her nipples but never doing much more. Seeing her delight, smelling her want, feeling her desire was *everything*.

Oh, that desire built within her. My hands worked her thighs, and I teased her just a bit, then moved down to get her legs and feet.

"Are you still doing all right, Darling?" I started working my way back up her legs.

"So good, but I would very much like your mouth to do a bit of massaging soon." She smirked at me.

"Soon." My hands worked up her thighs, gently caressing and exploring her but not doing more than that...yet. The air grew cloying sweet with her desire and arousal–not quite perfume, but ever so delightful.

"Please." Her hips arched. "Please, Daddy?"

"Mmmm, does my baby girl need her pussy eaten?" Leaning forward, I flicked her nipple with my tongue.

She gasped. "Yes, please."

"You ask so sweetly. Of course, I will." My tongue traced patterns down her body until it came to her clit. I circled with my tongue, teasing her as my fingers entered her.

"That feels so good," she sighed, eyes closing in contentment.

"You feel so good; come whenever you want to." I ate her with abandon, trying to bring her to her peak with both my mouth and hands so that I could knot my sweet love.

Her thighs trembled, and her scent got even sweeter as she orgasmed.

"Such a good girl, coming on Daddy's face. So pretty," I cooed, continuing to tell her how much I loved her with my mouth, my fingers working to get all the special spots that made her squeal.

"Please, I need you inside of me," she begged.

Oh, I loved it when she asked me to knot her. Though having her like this was hardly a chore. She tasted so sweet and delicious. It was even better than the chocolate and orange pastries I knew she'd included on the dessert table because I liked them.

"Absolutely." I slowly sank into her.

Gazing into her eyes, I made love to her nice and slow, taking my time, my lips savoring her lips, teasing her breasts, licking my mark on her.

"You always look exquisite taking my cock," I praised. Over and over, I thrust inside her, sending her all my love, as I made her come several times.

"Spencer," she screamed as another orgasm shuddered through her body.

Such sweet music. I adored that face she made.

"Are you ready for my knot now?" I leaned in and kissed her again. My knot was ready to be inside her.

"Oh, yes, Alpha, please," she begged.

"So sweet, so good," I told her as I pushed my knot all the way inside her, rocking her so she still got pleasure as I filled her with my cum. My lips captured hers as she came again in my arms.

So perfect.

Still joined, I rolled us over so that we were on our sides. I caressed her face.

"Are you all right?" I asked her, even though I could tell she was just fine.

"Divine." She pressed her face into me. "Just what I needed. Now I think I'd like some food... and I think you mentioned a bath."

I kissed her. "My darling, I will give you anything you want."

Just like I'd given her my heart and soul.

Chapter Forty-Six

Wes

Taking a sip of excellent coffee, I looked around the chaos as we had a lovely catered brunch in the giant mansion Spencer's family had rented for the weekend. Our house was fancy, but this was just ridiculous. Though honestly, if we ever got a new place, I wouldn't mind a pool with a waterfall.

While I wasn't hungover from the mating ceremony, I'd been up late as Evan bounced between my bed and Brennan's, both of us getting Grace's lust and desire through the bond as she and Spencer enjoyed themselves at the hotel last night.

Okay, that was a bit of an understatement.

Fuck, I got so worked up last night that I'd been tempted to join Brennan, Jett, and Evan. Yeah, usually Brennan and I didn't fuck outside the nest, but he'd let me in, right?

All around me, people chatted and joked. A few people played music in the corner.

I hadn't met much of Spencer's family other than his mom. I'd expected them to be like him—serious, reserved, a bit shy. While his father was like that, most of them were exactly the opposite. Especially his cousins Daphne and Zoie. They'd all grown up together.

And no one would tell me how Zoie made Evan dislike pizza. He knew most of Spencer's family, even if he hadn't seen a lot of them in some time.

Everyone wanted to talk to Grace, and it was nice that they liked her, especially since she'd been nervous about it.

They also wanted to talk to Spencer's father. He arrived this morning with Spencer's mom, looking like they'd had a very happy night of their own.

Fuck, Spencer's dad was back. Wild. At least Spencer was happy about it. If my mom showed up, I'd probably kick her out and refuse to talk to her. If Grace's not-mom showed up I'd kick her ass.

I was curious if Nick remembered sending Grace and Rosalind to another world.

"Eat, you haven't had enough," an auntie of Spencer's told me as she gave me another plate of food.

"Thank you." Was there anything else to say? The food was delicious, though I couldn't eat much more.

The entire pack was here at the brunch Spencer's family had organized. The house had a piano, and Brennan played along with the musicians, occasionally laughing as he tried to improvise to an unfamiliar style. For once, he looked relaxed and happy. Huh, was that the secret to his having fun at large functions?

Sonja and her fiancée were also there, talking to Evan in the kitchen.

Grace walked past me, and I pulled her down into my lap. She wore a blush dress that made her look like a princess going to a garden party in a story.

"Hi, Peaches." I kissed her, hoping I could get her alone before we had to go to the adventure park. Last night made me think about how amazing it would be when she, Evan, and I finally had our wedding.

"Hi, Boo-Bear." She leaned her head on my shoulder. "Ugh, I wish that I didn't have to attend a lunch after this. I need a nap."

"Oh, I'd gladly put you to sleep." I kissed her, holding her close.

Spencer's mom had some family in town, too, and they were having a late lunch. Fortunately, I didn't have to go to that. I'd need a nap before the adventure park.

"Get a room." Riley appeared before us in a skirt, shredded shirt, and boots. Mercy, in a Capitol Crushers T-shirt, shorts, and sneakers, was with her.

"You're off? Have fun. We'll pick you up on our way to the adventure park." Grace climbed off my lap and gave them both hugs.

"Thank you for inviting us," Mercy said. "We had so much fun. I can't wait to come back, Tru, too."

"Hale's fireworks were the best distraction," Riley added. "We're out of here, laters, fuckers."

The two of them left.

"*Hale's* fireworks? You didn't plan that?" I pulled Grace back down onto my lap.

"Hale and Dare's present," she laughed. "According to Verity, having some sort of elaborate distraction so that the couple can sneak off is a big thing in the South."

Fireworks. And Hale tried to float the bouncy castle in the lake. Spencer's club might not have us back.

"Oooh, food." Grace took my plate and started eating.

"Here, have some coffee." I offered her my cup.

"Thank you." She made a joyful noise and ate my food.

Spencer came over to us. "Grace, my father would like to speak with us. My mother is busy talking to Sonja. Wes, you can come as well, if you'd like."

"Sounds good." I lifted Grace off my lap, and we followed Spencer up the stairs, Evan, Brennan, and Jett joining us.

Nick was waiting for us in what looked like a TV room. Spencer shut the door as Evan pulled Grace down onto the couch, I sat down with them. Jett and Brennan took the loveseat. Spencer sat with us.

"Oh, I didn't think you'd all be here." Nick frowned, looking a little nervous.

"We all know, Baba, both about you and Grace," Spencer explained.

"Oh, I see. Grace, I wanted to know about your time with them, the Temporal Authority. I don't remember anything, and I'm quite curious," he said.

"I'd like to know about your encounters with them as well," she replied. "I've seen some of your and Dr. K's notes for your dimension mapping and how you found parallel worlds. It's so different from what I was doing."

Nick's eyes lit up. "Did you bring yourself here?"

"No. But I wanted to." Grace looked over at me and squeezed my hand. Going light on the bad things, Grace told him about dreaming of me, her research, forgetting me but still being driven to prove parallel worlds, ending up seeing the wrong things, her time with the authority before she came to us, which I knew little about, coming to us, the trial, and returning here.

"Oh, that is quite an adventure," Nick replied. "Thank you for asking them about me. If you hadn't, perhaps I wouldn't have been let go at all. I wish I could remember."

"You may never. It could also just take a really long time. It depends on what Agent Weigmier gave you. I got too much on accident the first time, the second time, I think I got too little on purpose. My notes helped, but I eventually remembered almost everything," she assured.

"You dreamt of your soulmate while in another world?" His hand went to his heart.

"We did," I said, giving her a squeeze. "I'm so glad."

He thought for a moment. "Why did the Authority bring you here? Because of your soulmate? That would be the decent thing to do, but also generous for them, not that I know much about them."

"I think I fall under their Precious Population Protection Protocol. That's what Agent Weigmier does for the Authority—help omegas and others. I think," she replied.

Oh. I hadn't really understood that. "Agent Asshole is the literal legal omega distribution system?"

"I think that's actually Gloria in Processing who relocates people. But..." Grace sucked in a breath through her teeth. "Why I'm *here*, that's the second part. There's a good reason why he brought me here—and why I dreamt of Wes."

Grace explained everything about Thora and Rosalind.

"We don't know everything," Grace added. "The only thing that makes sense is that somehow Rosalind contacted an organization that hides sigmas that was also in touch with you. She turned on her charm, and you sent her and a baby to a world without designations. I don't blame anyone for anything. Well, other than Rosalind. All I want is information as I try to piece things together."

I pulled her off Evan's lap and onto mine, sending her love through the bond.

"Huh." Nick thought for a moment, then spoke to Spencer in Greek. There was frowning and counting on fingers.

"Wait, you hadn't been doing it that long, had you?" I breathed. "Huh. I never really considered that. I mean, if you were, good for you, but..."

Grace exhaled sharply. "It wasn't you."

Spencer squeezed her hand.

"It wasn't us," Nick said slowly. "We worked with an organization in Europe that smuggled illegal designations–and we placed families. I will admit, there was a family or two we literally pushed through and hoped for the best. But it wasn't us, I'm so sorry."

"I'm curious. There were others?" I asked.

"They were tenacious. Huh," Grace muttered.

"Dr. K and I weren't the first," Nick told us. He looked at Spencer. "We really discovered the existence of parallel worlds–with no help from them. That discovery, and the paper Dr. K wrote, came after they first came to us. But it was just that, a theory. We did it partially because we wanted to prove it for ourselves and save people without their help. Of course, that discovery was just a small step compared to actually bringing people to our world, but it was an important one."

"Of course it is," Grace assured. "It's further than I got. And you're right, proving something and reliable travel are very different things."

His eyes pleaded with Spencer. "I never lied to you. The day we proved it, and I shared it with you, the excitement was genuine. But I kept things from you, and if you saw us taken, I hope you understand why?"

"I do, Baba. Also, I'm pretty sure that the paper that Dr. K wrote isn't around anymore. After the explosion, research in your field was discouraged. Especially given that you weren't the first or last project in your field that went awry. Though once a month Mrs. K thinks I'm starting it back up again." Spencer shook his head.

"Perhaps it's time for me to start at the beginning." Nick took a sip of his coffee.

"Please?" Grace asked.

"It was perhaps three years before we were taken that they first appeared. We made some very significant progress in our qubit research. They said they'd noticed us and pitched the opportunity to help. At first, we thought that they'd help us with our research and share their science. Who wouldn't want that? Quickly, we realized that we were just a drop off point, and they didn't want to keep their promises to share their knowledge. That led to us pushing ourselves with our other research. We knew it was possible, so we proved it," he stated.

"I'm so proud of you for both those things, Baba, both discovering other worlds exist and saving all those omegas," Spencer said.

"It was why we kept doing it, even when they didn't help us in return much or often. We saved hundreds of omegas, many of them male," he continued. "Most of their stories broke our hearts."

I could imagine.

"How did you manage that? Even over three years, creating identities for that many is a lot for one Center. You were using the Center's Omega Protection Program, right?" Evan asked.

Nick nodded. "Oh, yes, it was too much. We actually had to confide in someone at the Temple of Artemis. They assisted us, both by placing omegas themselves and sending them to Omega Centers all over the world to be relocated. We didn't want to be noticed."

"I didn't even know the Temple of Artemis did that," Spencer said.

"Alphas aren't supposed to know such things. But we couldn't have done it without them."

"Where was the equipment? Was there equipment?" Spencer asked.

"There was. We kept it in a closet, and they'd message us when they were making a delivery, and we'd set everything up and make sure no one was around. Sometimes we needed Mrs. K to help," Nick said. "Ilena knew little about this, mostly because she didn't want to know about our research. She was afraid we'd anger someone or blow up the world."

"Fair." Jett nodded.

"We also tried to hack the equipment so we could use it to send people ourselves. Their reason for not helping us much was that they said our illegal designations were also illegal in many other places and getting them to those safe worlds was difficult, which made sense. Also, I think that something happened previously which made them wary regarding sending our designations elsewhere, but I'll get to that in a moment," Nick added.

Spencer looked thoughtful. "Huh. I never found the equipment."

"Oh, you did. I don't recall what Dr. K told you it was. Possibly a particle charger?" Nick looked amused.

"I remember that now." He started laughing.

"It was a very coordinated effort, and it wasn't always the same person reaching out to us or bringing the omegas. We were one of several worlds that they brought omegas to," he stated. "Though toward the end, we were getting groups quickly, large ones as well, often with omegas that were ill. The Temple was getting frustrated with the load, but no one was going to turn them away."

"Do you have records of them?" Grace asked.

"We did—both of them and the people we sent over, complete with world numbers," he replied. "I had hidden backups. I'll see if they survived. The first time an agent visited us was right around when we'd figured everything out. We thought it was a courtesy visit, a bit of a congratulations. Yes, there was a thinly veiled warning about rules, but they never explained everything."

Well, that tracked. They didn't seem like they'd give you a handbook and gift basket.

"Then we got an actual formal warning, telling us that we couldn't continue to accept these omegas because it broke the law. Again, no explanation of consequences, and they wouldn't tell us what to do with them, just not to do it. We let our contacts know, and they said to ignore them, and that no harm would come to us because of our type of world." Nick looked away, scent souring. "We believed them, trusted them. The agents kept coming and warning us, but never actually explaining anything–and we kept ignoring them. If I had any idea that they'd take us away, imprison us, and blow up our super collider, I would have taken them more seriously, despite all the lives we saved."

Spencer squeezed his father's hand and said something in Greek. Nick sniffed and nodded.

"Why did they blow up the collider if the other people provided the equipment? Was it to hide your qubit research?" Grace asked, still snuggled into my lap, though she held Spencer's hand.

"Possibly. But we used the super collider to power the device," he replied.

Spencer looked at her. "Did they do that at your old place of employment?"

"No. They used super computers, I believe. I never got much information on all the logistics since I was just a witness," Grace replied.

"You did good work saving those omegas, Nick," Brennan said. "It's shitty they took you, but everyone is glad you're back."

"I am, too. I just wish I could remember the trial–and being in prison with Demitra." Nick's head bowed. "Do you know if it was just us?"

"I think they eventually took down the entire operation, since Agent Weigmier said it was a large, multi-world, person-smuggling ring. He also told me yesterday that it had been taken care of, though he also said more than once there was still a mess to clean up. I don't know what that means. He also mentioned that they were tenacious." Grace looked at Nick. "You weren't the first that they were working with in this world?"

"No. Though I didn't know that until close to the end. They let it slip that they'd worked with someone else, but something happened, which was why they were so happy to have found us. All I knew was that they, too, were in Europe and engaged in similar research. I'd meant to figure it out, after all, there weren't too many people doing what we do. But that didn't happen. I'm so sorry, Grace. I'm sorry that I don't have the answers for you that you wanted," he apologized.

Grace shook her head. "It's okay. You've helped me to understand so much."

"And now I can comprehend why the people we were working with who smuggled sigmas were so quick to accept our very vague help. They may have been working with our predecessors and guessed what we were doing. For all I know, they also worked with whoever came after us, if there was anyone," Nick added.

All this information was a lot to take in, and I gave Grace another squeeze. But at the same time, I was glad for it.

"I don't know if it continued. But I do know that people from other incompatible worlds besides this one were left in the world I grew up on—and I know that world number," Grace said. "I think sasquatch legends are because they're really refugees from shifter worlds."

"What, Peaches?" I blinked.

"Think about it. We never hear about packs of sasquatches, it's one or two. I know that you have those legends here, too, because you literally have a hockey team called the Portland Sasquatches, which I only know because they're Tish's favorite team," Grace added.

Evan gasped. "That actually makes sense. Fuck. Now I want to go bushwhacking through the Pacific Northwest with a blanket brigade tote and offer services to the poor scared omega sasquatch refugees."

"I'd go with you," Jett offered.

Nick looked a little bewildered by all that.

Spencer turned to her. "Agent Weigmier was chatty yesterday?"

"He was. I mean, he didn't answer all my questions, but he told me a few things. Um, oh, I told him that if he ever returns anyone to this world to let me know so we can help. So far, I'm the only one from this world returned here. I turned out okay, but it could have gone so badly. Like what if the Sergeant didn't call Lexi? I could have ended up in a homeless shelter, and you may have never known that I was here." Grace looked at Brennan, pleading.

Fuck. I never thought about how bad that could have gone. Yeah, we might have never found her, with her being *right* here.

"Well, we have the foundation now. I dislike the idea of someone suffering because Agent Weigmier's good intentions aside, they are assholes," Brennan said.

"Agreed," Spencer said.

I didn't actually have a problem with that.

"Did he tell you anything else, Peaches?" Jett asked.

"Only that I was interesting, and that wasn't a good thing." She shrugged.

"Do you have any other questions for me?" Nick asked. "I can feel my mate's impatience."

Spencer and Grace asked him a few more questions. I sort of dozed off.

A phone ring woke me up.

Frowning, Spencer answered it. "This is Spencer."

I felt awash in sheer emotion and realized I was getting it from Spencer through my bond with Grace. She climbed off my lap and onto his.

"Yes, I see. Thank you. Yes, I do. I'll do whatever you need." Spencer was practically shaking. "Thank you again. I appreciate it. Please keep me updated."

"What's wrong?" Grace asked, hugging him tight.

"It's not bad news, just unexpected," Spencer told us. "The police are re-opening Elaris' case—and they have a confession."

Chapter Forty-Seven

Spencer

Finally, after all these years. So much had happened in the past two days. Overwhelmed, I clutched Grace to me, and buried my face in her shoulder, inhaling her peachy scent.

I'd hoped that the information we found would actually lead to someone being prosecuted for their crimes against Elaris.

And here we were with a confession. The day after I got my father back. My mind wouldn't stop spinning, as Grace held me tight, reassuring me through our bond.

"That is fantastic," Evan replied.

"I'm so glad," Jett said. "We had some significant evidence. And a confession? Fuck."

"They're going to send me more details. I don't know who confessed or why. Perhaps Adriana gave names, or they used what we found. But I'm happy to get justice for Elaris," I replied.

"Good. I looked the organization up and they seemed like rat bastard assholes," Grace added.

"Who's Elaris?" My father whispered.

"Oh. She... she was my mate. We met at university and started a company together. While her death was ruled a vehicular accident, I always wondered." Briefly, I told him about her, what she'd been doing, and my suspicions. "Knowing what happened is a comfort."

"I'm so sorry to hear that. Losing a mate must have been difficult for you. I feel for your mother and what I put her through." Anguish rolled off my father. "I missed so much. Just like I missed Evan's parents passing. Riley wasn't even born when they took me. She's such a delight, but why does she call your mother *Yiayia?*"

"Because Auntie wants grandchildren but doesn't think she'll get any." Evan chuckled. "Spencer took great care of us after my parents died, just like we tried to take care of him after Elaris passed. And look, we both have mates, a pack, and jobs we love."

My father nodded. "Your new company is quite impressive."

"Wait until you see all the amazing things we're doing in Special Projects," Grace told him.

"We're doing some good stuff, mostly because of Spencer's genius for finding cool shit," Wes added.

"We're okay, Baba." I looked at my pack. "You can stop worrying about me and enjoy your time with Mama. She's already booked your first trip?" I didn't want him to waste his time by feeling bad.

My father chuckled. "She has. I have to admit that I'm quite excited. I love my research and teaching, but I'd like to spend some time with her. You, too."

"We'll plan a trip for us, Baba. Promise." That would be nice.

"Nick? We should go, as should Spencer and Grace, if we're to meet my family on time," my mother called from the other side of the door.

Could I eat more food? No. Would I because I wanted to spend a little time with everyone? Yes.

"Thank you, Nick," Grace said. "I really appreciate you sharing everything with us."

"My pleasure." He stood and opened the door. "Coming, my love."

"Oh, Sonja's leaving. Let's go say goodbye to her." Evan glanced at his phone. "Bye, Uncle Nick, Auntie. See you soon." He hugged my parents and ran off with Grace as the rest of the pack left.

"Your pack is lovely but is there a chance we can have you to ourselves before we leave?" my mother asked.

I thought for a moment. "I could possibly get out of tonight's visit to the adventure park with *all* of Grace's siblings and have dinner with you instead."

My mother chuckled. "The older ones are boisterous. But those little ones are so sweet."

I went downstairs, trying to find some place they'd like with reservations available for tonight. Perhaps we could have something light, such as the fancy dumpling restaurant where everything came by on a conveyor belt.

Oh, there we were. The dumpling place had a later reservation. Perfect.

Still, all I could think of was that I'd finally know what happened to Elaris. I checked my email, quickly going over what the police in Boston, where the accident had happened, sent me.

I found Grace in the kitchen giving Zoie a hug.

"See you, soon," Zoie hugged her back.

"Let's go?" I offered her my arm and walked to my car, which we'd picked up this morning at the house, and dropped off my motorcycle.

"Dearest?" Grace pinned me against the car door, well the best she could, and pulled me down and kissed me. "I love you."

"I love you, too, my good doctor." I helped her in, and we drove away. "I sincerely regret that I must miss the festivities at the adventure park tonight. My parents would like to have dinner with me."

Grace played with the air conditioner vents. "Go, you should absolutely have dinner with them."

"Adriana named names," I said as I drove. "She hoped that doing so would lessen her own sentence. But whether it will remains to be seen. Between that and what Jett and I found, they did a little digging and got a confession from those involved with Elaris' car accident, before they even formally opened the case. It wasn't one person, it was a coordinated effort, and many people knew of it beyond who was directly involved."

"I'm here. I'll do whatever you need." She squeezed my knee.

"Thank you, Darling." I smiled, excited to start this new chapter of my life, with my pack, my sweet Grace, and my father.

Chapter Forty-Eight

Brennan

I zoomed past the members of the press crowded around my building as I entered the parking garage Tuesday morning. Nope. Not interested in talking to them.

As I entered the elevator, my phone buzzed again. Not interested in talking to my mother or her publicist either.

The doors opened into the lobby, and some people got on. A few people looked at me, one whispering to another, someone else checking their phone. Fortunately, everyone had the good sense to not say anything.

Oh, now Liam was calling. *Ignore. Fuck you.* Katie had also texted.

Katie

Alliance activated. I am out of fucks and ready to burn everything down.

Well then. There was also a text from Spencer's cousin.

Sorry your mom's a bitch. Not sorry for what I'm about to do. Offer stands.

Finally, I got to the floor my office was on. My assistant froze at her desk, fear wafting off her.

"I'm so sorry. Please believe me. I didn't upload it. I promise. Yes, I showed it to my brother, but I never thought that it would end up online. Please don't fire me," Shayla pleaded. "I didn't erase it in case you needed it."

Shayla was a beta and had been with me for a couple of years. I'd been wary of hiring her because she was fresh out of college and I wasn't sure she'd have the skills an executive assistant needed, but she'd been highly recommended.

And didn't disappoint.

"What? No. Why would I fire you? I know it's not your fault," I assured, just like I had yesterday when the video she'd recorded of my mother hitting me had first appeared on the internet.

I'd sort of hoped it would go away. Overnight it *exploded,* and this morning it continued to spread. I still wasn't mad at Shayla.

And I wouldn't be even if she *had* done it on purpose.

Relief crossed her face. "Thank you."

"Do you know how hard it is to find good assistants?" I told her. "Um, also... I don't want you to think that I'm getting rid of you, but I know you've been wanting more project management experience. I'd really like you to help Gregg with the project management for the non-renovation aspects of the opening of the estate project. Especially since we're holding our first event there in September."

While I'd still be involved, the time had come to put my teams in place.

Her face lit up. "You want me to help with the estate project?"

"Yes. I'm really impressed with how you took the initiative to get your project manager certification and take the exam. I've also heard good things about the work you've been doing with non-profits to gain experience. You're an ideal person to assist Gregg since I'll still want regular reports and will weigh in on things," I added.

"Thank you," she replied. "Um, you're wanted down in PR."

Of course I was. "They know where to find me."

With a sigh, I went into my office and logged in. My email and phone messages were flooded. Some were from people who actually cared about me, expressing concern. A few were business partners and colleagues asking for reassurance. Others were reporters, fake friends, nosey fucks, and people pestering me on behalf of my mother.

Delete.

Terrance popped his head in. "Do you have a minute?"

"For you, always." While I should deal with some of these emails, they could wait.

"Good." Terrance came in, closing the door and taking the chair in front of my desk. "I'm guessing you're not following all this with your mom closely."

"Fuck no." I didn't even have social media.

He sucked in a breath through his teeth. "So... it's gotten worse. While your mom is generally very careful and good at keeping up appearances, not everyone loves her, and she has slipped a few times. People are speaking up."

"I figured." I sighed. "She does throw her power around sometimes."

"Bren, one of them is someone from the rehab facility that your mom forced you into."

It was like being hit with a brick. "Fuck."

That was something few people knew. Most people just had heard that I was seriously hurt and took a while to recover, which was the truth. Even Caroline had dismissed it as me just needing some time to *heal and brood,* as she'd put it.

"Yeah, and that caused the ambulance driver to speak up about how we literally jail-broke you." Terrance's look went grim. "I'm going to have to make a statement before this spins out of control. I mean, it's all in our favor right now, but we want to keep it that way."

The last thing I ever expected was for all *that* to be in the media. Shit. I didn't like people in my business.

"You're also going to want to control the media–both for you personally, and the company. Right now, you're fine, but your brothers are being attacked big time, and so is the foundation," he added.

An email came through from Misty, the head of PR. *We really need to talk about what's going on and probably hold a press confer- ence.*

With a sigh, I replied. *Draft a statement and send it to me.*

I didn't want to hold a press conference, but I would if I had to. Maybe a statement would be enough.

"They're attacking the foundation?" I frowned.

"Yeah, they're calling for the resignation of your mom, Troy, and Liam from the foundation board. Right now, your dad is safe, but I wouldn't be surprised if he has to blame cutting the omega scholarships on them." Terrance rubbed his temples.

"Wow." The foundation had a backup plan for that exact sce- nario, but I wasn't sure my father would do it. "Is her company under fire?" It was privately held, but bad press could still affect so many things.

"Yep. Every project that is publicly held is taking a beating in the stock reports today. If I were a lesser man, I'd suggest buying up the

State Street project out of spite. But some shell company from the Mediterranean is gobbling things up while they're cheap."

My mind went back to Daphne's text.

"Morris Company has publicly traded projects?" I didn't know that. Not that I paid much attention to them anymore.

"A few. State Street is one of them," he replied.

I responded to Daphne, now getting what she was doing.

Me

> **Go ahead. Send over the papers when you're ready.**

"One of Spencer's business tycoon cousins wants to take over the State Street project and turn it into an artist colony. Pretty sure that's her," I remarked. "She was telling me about her project at Spencer's party. It sounds great. It's honestly not that different from what my mom wants to do, but instead of luxury apartments, it's artist lofts. The businesses are all local, not chains. The community workspace will have things like kilns and forges, and there's a place for plays and performances. Oh, and there are quarterly art festivals so you can see the artists' work. I agreed to sell her my building because she has a clear vision and an excellent track record."

"Yeah, I talked to her, too, and I love the sound of it. Hey, my family had a fantastic time at the party. That was the fanciest bouncy castle ever–and my kids loved being at the kids' table. When Grace's little sister comes to visit for camp, can we have a playdate?"

"That's a Grace question. But I think there's plans for Everydoll and Stuff-A-Stuffie," I replied, ignoring my phone as it rang.

He nodded. "My kids love those places."

My assistant called my desk phone, and I answered it. "Yes, Shayla?"

"Misty is here and needs to see you."

Of course she did.

"Send her in." I sighed and pinched the bridge of my nose between my thumb and forefinger.

The door opened. Misty, the alpha who headed my PR department, appraised us.

"Good, you're both here." She closed the door. "What the actual fuck? Your mom had you institutionalized, and Terrance and your sister broke you out?"

"Jett also helped." Shit. I should warn him. "Also, my dad fought my mother over it and lost." I felt the need to defend him right now.

"What happened?" She pulled over a chair.

I gave her the quick version. While the company had existed then, it wasn't the operation it was now. It was mostly a few of us doing too much. My being out of commission was part of what led to us actually getting proper staffing and offices, because Terrance needed help to keep the company from failing. Though he'd still overworked himself to keep everything going. Misty hadn't been there then.

"Fucking shit." She shook her head. "We *have* to get ahead of this. Especially since she and her company are doubling down. This could be terrible. At least you've already started distancing yourself from them. Changing your last name and them removing you from the foundation board speaks volumes. As does your sister leaving the company," she added.

"Katie's ready to rampage," I agreed.

"I sent you a statement, which I'd like to release five minutes ago. We'll probably need a press conference, too. Terrance, you'll need to say something as well."

"I already started drafting something. When I return to my office, I'll send it to you." Terrance nodded.

"Misty, I'd rather not do a press conference, but if it's needed, I will. While I won't trash my mother, I will speak the truth." I sighed again and opened the statement she sent me. "I'll make changes and get it back to you."

"Good. I'll set up the press conference." She stood and left.

I sighed. "Did you know that I fucking hate press conferences?"

"I know. I'll be there. Hey, maybe after the conference you can take off for the afternoon. Go for a ride or take your frustrations out on the piano or a punching bag," Terrance said.

"That sounds like a good idea." I sent Jett a quick text warning him.

"I should finish that statement. You know where I am if you need me. Um, can *I* trash her?" Terrance asked. He knew a lot of shit about my mom given how long we'd been friends.

"By all means."

Terrance left, and I made alterations to the statement and sent it back to Misty. Then I started replying to all the phone calls and emails that I had to and dealing with today's urgent business so that I could leave after the press conference.

My pack also kept checking on me. Including Riley, who wanted permission to implement the plan she'd come up with when this war first started.

Me

Let's hold that thought for a moment.

After all, my mother hadn't actually done anything other than state that it was all lies carefully crafted to slander her.

Riley

I'm ready when you are.

My phone rang as I sent out yet another reassuring email while trying to finish a spreadsheet.

"Your sister is here; can I send her in?" Shayla asked.

"Sure." I sent the email and started making a graph.

The door opened, and Katie stormed into my office in a cloud of angry spruce. "I'm going to fucking murder her."

"What did she do?" I paused to give my sister my full attention.

"Okay, first it was shitty that she hit you. I didn't know about that. Also, I made a statement about busting you out, because I'm a lawyer and all. But..." She paced. "Dad had the foundation make a statement that the Morris Foundation's views were not her personal views because donors and community partners are scared. This is a plan that we have in place. You know what she did? She fucking fired him."

"What? Can she do that?" Anger burst inside me. How dare she? Dad gave up so much of his own pursuits to support her business and the foundation. Granted he enjoyed it, but he would have rather been a professional rugby coach.

"No, she can't. Not according to the charter. Troy can be fired by only her, but Dad, he requires *all* of us to vote to be fired, and you know I'm not voting against Dad. He's the one who made the foundation powerful, even if Troy likes to take the credit," Katie replied as she continued to pace my office.

"Burn it down, Katie." I got on my phone, hands shaking from anger, as I texted Riley.

Me

Go ahead. Just don't do anything illegal and be careful.

"Oh, I will. She was aware he was making a statement and her publicist signed off on it. Will you speak out, too?" Katie asked.

"Yes. I have a press conference scheduled. Firing Dad is not okay. Okay, we'll probably need to implement Project Phoenix, which involves bringing in a new board that's mostly not family, changing the foundation's name, and clearing it of any problematic family members. That is, if Dad still wants to be in charge of everything. I'll send you the documents we created." I found them and emailed them to her.

My twin stopped mid-pace, hands on her pregnant belly. "You and Dad had a plan for all of that?"

"Well, yes. We always thought that there might be a time when we needed to distance the foundation from the company in order to continue to further the foundation's mission. But we never thought it would be because Mother melted down and fired Dad. We thought it would be more like some of her projects didn't align or Liam getting involved in a scandal," I replied. Picking my phone back up, I looked up my mother firing my dad to see if it was online–and the statement.

"Liam? It's Troy who has a fucking mistress." She grimaced.

"What?" I looked up in disbelief. His wife was a bitch, but she loved him–and they had kids.

"Yeah. I might just send her proof out of spite because I know she doesn't know. Spite being in that he's supporting Mom in all this. Probably because without Dad, *he's* in charge of the foundation."

I continued searching through social media. How fucking dare she?

"Yep. Don't worry, I have all the receipts." Her look went sly.

Katie had a ruthless side. Her dealing with the hospital that had been mean to Grace had shown me that ruthlessness wasn't always a bad thing when used to protect the people you loved.

I texted Dad.

Me

> **I love you. If you want the foundation, Katie and I will burn the world down. Already sent Katie the Project Phoenix documents.**

> **I've barricaded myself in my office and locked everyone out of everything. They want to play dirty? I can play dirty. I can't believe she'd do that. We had an agreement.**

Frowning, I looked at Katie. "Do our parents love each other? I mean, I know they did, once. But do they still?"

Her look went sad. "If they do, I think this may have killed it. A divorce will get nasty."

"Fuck. I'll protect Dad. When it comes down to it, he always took my side when I really needed him to." As much as the teasing and calling me *sport* angered me, I loved him.

Was I a terrible son if I admitted that I wasn't sure if I loved my mother? With another sigh, I replied to Dad.

> **Katie and I are on your side.**

> **Thank you.**

I looked at Katie, who was now straightening all my books. "Dad's preparing for war. He's fine with us burning shit down."

"Let's do this." Katie punched one hand with another.

I texted Wes to see what he could do to help, then looked back at her. "Let's. Because she's crossed her last line."

"That was incredible," Misty commended as the press conference finished, and I left the room, not wanting to talk to any other members of the press.

"Good, because I'm not doing that again." I felt nauseous.

Terrance joined me. "That was amazing. I can't believe your mom tried to fire your dad."

"Me neither." I headed to the elevator, Terrance with me.

"Go home, Bren," Terrance urged.

"I think I will." I looked at the family calendar. Grace was home this afternoon, but that was all right. I'd just let her know that I was in a bad mood and to steer clear so that I didn't accidentally hurt her feelings.

Going up to my office, I collected my shit and grabbed my helmet.

"I'm out for the rest of the day," I told Shayla, and went down to the elevator.

Yes. I'd go home, work my frustrations in the gym, then play the piano. By the time everyone got home, I'd be fit for human interaction.

I was almost at my bike when a small green motorcycle with a sidecar stopped in front of me.

Grace took off her helmet. "Get in the sidecar, we're going to buy some chickens."

"Um, what?" I just stood there blinking at her.

"I'm kidnapping you. Get in the sidecar." Her face went stern as she sent a text. "See, I even told Jett. I know today has been shitty. So, you're going to come with me, and we're going to feel better. Now, get in the sidecar."

There was something so fucking cute about her trying to order me around. Yeah, I'd been looking forward to some solitude, but the urge to make her happy was greater.

"Look, we don't have to talk. We can just exist together. Get in the sidecar? Please?" The pleading notes in her tone tugged at me.

"Will I fit?" Was I really going to squish myself into the sidecar to please her?

Yes, I was.

Putting on my helmet, I folded myself into the sidecar the best I could and fastened my belt. Huh. Yeah, this wasn't made for Alphas, but it wasn't that uncomfortable. Which meant the next time Wes made noises about not fitting, I could call him out on it.

Now, was this legal? I wasn't sure.

"Where are we going?" I asked as she took off.

"First is food, since it's past lunchtime."

"I could eat." That nauseous feeling I'd had earlier giving the press conference was passing.

We drove to an area I'd never been to that was a bit on the outskirts and stopped at some place called *Mom's Barbeque*. The place looked old, and cars crowded the parking lot.

"I really want some barbeque. I mean, we got a smoker as a mating gift, but I'll experiment with it over the weekend." She dragged us inside a very casual, but busy, place that smelled of roasting meat.

"Two?" the hostess asked, as she grabbed plastic menus and led us to a wooden table.

I looked over the menu. Okay, I could see what she was going for.

"This is supposed to be the best barbecue in the area," she said.

Someone came over to us to take our drink order.

"I'd like a whiskey smash, he'll have a bourbon, and two waters," she ordered. "We'll need a few moments to look over the menu."

The server looked at me, I nodded, then the server smiled at her. "Sure, Hun."

"I hope you don't mind that I ordered for you, I figured with the day you've had you might need it," she added, scent going a little anxious as she fiddled with the menu.

"It's okay, Grace." As promised, she'd been quiet on the drive over. It made me wonder if there was more to this kidnapping than just my having a shitty day.

Though either way, I was flattered that she'd do something like this for me.

The server brought our drinks and took our order. She was still quiet.

"I appreciate you kidnapping me. Does your boss know that you're on an adventure instead of working?" I asked.

"Yes. I was supposed to work from home this afternoon, anyway. The interns are on a field trip to the warehouse." She took a sip of her drink.

"Katie and I are getting violent. Also, I gave a press conference. Fuck. I hate them." My phone rang. Mother. Nope. I sent it to voicemail.

"I've never given one," she replied, taking a biscuit out of the red plastic basket and putting butter and honey on it.

"Ugh, they're a necessary evil." Without meaning to, I dove into what exactly had happened, not knowing if she actually knew specifics.

"I'm glad you're protecting your dad. I don't really know him, but we talked a little at the party and the science dinner, and he seems nice." She finished her biscuit just as they brought us food.

"He is. My dad annoys me sometimes, but when I asked him to stop doing something I didn't like, he actually did." I hadn't been called *sport* once since my request. If I'd known asking would make him stop, I would have done it years ago. I hadn't because it didn't work with my mother or brothers.

The server set an enormous plate of ribs in front of me, along with beans and creamed corn. Grace had a plate of meat chunks, mashed potatoes and gravy, and corn on the cob.

Grace took a bite of one of the meat chunks. "Ooh, yes."

Reaching for the squeezy tubes of sauce in the basket on the table, she tried the different sauces on her meat chunks. Her expressions as she thoughtfully tasted them were much more interesting than my own ribs.

"Do we have a winner?" I finally asked.

"We do. Try?" She stabbed a sauced-up meat chunk with her fork and offered it to me.

Leaning forward, I let her feed me. Smokey meat with a savory sweet sauce melted in my mouth. That was good.

"What am I eating?" I asked her, as I took a bite of my own ribs, which were absolutely delicious.

"Burnt ends. Beef. I've never mastered burnt ends. I'm pretty good at ribs though." She took a bite of potatoes. "Okay, these potatoes are not quite as good as the ones Spencer gets me from that fancy restaurant, but they're still pretty good."

"These ribs are incredible. Here." Cutting one off, I gave her one. "Spencer's ribs are delicious, but these are different."

"These are smoked, not grilled." She took a bite of corn.

I tried some sauces. "When you use the smoker, can you show me how to use it? Also, are you going to make a sauce with the peach bourbon?"

"Of course." She smiled, a little sauce on her nose.

I reached over and wiped it off, then tasted it. "Very good."

Grace laughed and made inroads into her food.

"Is everything going okay?" I finally asked, something tugging at me.

Her sigh said everything. "I mean, it's nothing compared to what you're going through."

"It's not a competition. Talk to me?" I ate another delicious rib.

"The lawyer that the pack lawyer found to help handle the whole thing with Adriana called me today." Grace poked at her mashed potatoes with her fork.

We'd wanted a lawyer who could practice in both states, fortunately, our pack lawyer was able to find someone who could handle both cases against Adriana.

"It's going to trial. There's a date and everything. But what I don't understand is that when I give a testimony, it'll be done in a lawyer's office, not on the stand. I'm confused." She nibbled on her corn.

"Some trials are like that, depending on the crime. It's to protect the victim from having to face the person who harmed them and having to recount everything with them there, unless they want to, of course. I'm guessing since you were a child when it happened, that's why they're offering you that. Do you want to testify in court? You can," I offered.

"Fuck no." Anxiety wafted off her. "In the trial for the Authority, it was awful as the defense picked me apart, belittled me, and tried to make me out as an unstable mastermind."

Oh. I hadn't known that.

"Come here." I held out my arms.

Grace slipped out of her chair and onto my lap.

I held her tight. "You don't have to face Adriana. You probably don't have to even attend the trial, just your lawyer."

"People don't have the right to face their accuser here?" She frowned.

"Alphas who commit certain crimes don't get that right unless you grant it to them. They just get your lawyer." I planted a kiss on the top of her head.

Grace thought for a moment. "Oh, I could see how that could be a great thing sometimes."

"Yeah, it is. Spencer will probably testify, but the stabbing case is separate," I told her. "They'll probably want witness testimonies, but yours can be filmed ahead of time."

She nodded slowly. "Good to know."

I looked at my phone. "My sister's wrath is wrathing today."

"We should send her a cake or whatever treat she's craving." Grace reached for her phone and texted someone, probably Rami.

I finished eating, holding Grace, who seemed mostly done.

A uniformed police officer walked in.

"Whoops, we've been caught," Grace giggled.

Jett came over to our table. My husband smirked at me holding her.

"I got a call about a possible kidnapping?" Jett looked us over.

A few people looked at us.

"Yes. I kidnapped this alpha and am making him hold me, eat barbecue, and go buy chickens," she told Jett solemnly.

"I see. And what's your ransom?" Jett asked her.

She shook her head. "No ransom. I'll give him back by dinner."

People chuckled as they realized what was going on.

"Did you really ride in the sidecar?" Jett laughed.

"Yeah. She asked." I held her tight. I wanted to make her happy. It had been hard at first to realize that it wasn't material items that delighted her, but things such as me sitting in the fucking sidecar and letting her take me some place.

My major fight against her was that she had to want something from us, such as money or expensive gifts. Like Caroline had.

Okay, Grace liked presents, but it was so different from my ex who demanded trendy handbags and expensive jewelry. When Spencer got her expensive shit, it was because either *he* wanted to give it to her, or she liked it and had no idea what it actually was.

Like that fucking doll he got her. She just wanted a doll to play tea party with at that tiny table she bought and didn't know that she fell in love with a collectible.

Mostly, Grace just craved love and acceptance.

I made the signal that meant *I'm fine* while shooting reassurance through the bond.

"Okay, I'm going to go to the bathroom. Then we can get some chickens." Standing, she gave Jett a kiss on the cheek and left.

"Are you okay, Dear?" Jett wrapped his arms around me.

"Today fucking sucked. But Grace is trying her best to make me feel better, and I... I..." I looked up at him. "I was going to go home and work out and play the piano and be grouchy, then she came. Instead of telling her *no,* I just did it, because making her happy was more important than sulking. Also, she said I didn't have to talk, and we didn't until I initiated it. I..."

"I know." Jett leaned in and kissed me. "You're hers. That alpha in you knows it, and has since I don't know, maybe the doll with the piano? Or perhaps earlier? I'm not sure."

Oh. Wait. What?

No. He wasn't wrong at all.

"I want her." All of her. I wanted more random adventures, concerts, and motorcycle rides. I wanted to fuck her. I wanted to love her every second of every day and need her like I needed oxygen.

Yes, I absolutely wanted to be Grace's mate, too.

"You have her." Jett held me tight. "It's been fucking adorable watching you court her without you realizing it."

"I have not..." Oh. "I guess I have."

Jett gave me another kiss. "You've already told her you love her. Go for it."

"I did?" Oh shit. I mean, despite telling myself that I'd never love her, I'd fallen for her, hard. I'd admitted it to Jett, but I hadn't realized that I'd told her.

"The night you brought the tiny ball of anxiety to bed. She proclaimed that we were now part of her husband collection." Jett smirked.

Yeah, I had no recollection of that. But I'd been exhausted. "She... she loves me back, right?"

What if she didn't?

"She does," he reassured. "She told you so."

"Oh, good." I hugged him tighter. "This isn't causing any trouble for you at work, is it? The ambulance driver coming forward?"

"No. Like half the station helped me plan that and most of them still work there. It's fine." He hugged me tightly.

"Do you want to get chickens with us, Jett? I don't want you to feel excluded." Grace returned and put an arm around both of us.

"I have to get back to work. But I'll see you both tonight." He kissed her, then me.

My heart caught in my throat as I faced her. I wanted to be with her. Not eventually. *Now.*

"Thank you." I kissed her long and deeply.

"For what? I just didn't want to eat alone." She gave me one of her cute little looks.

"Well, this was a lovely diversion. Are you done?" I asked.

"I am, shall we pay the bill and go get chickens?"

"Sounds good to me." Especially because I was so curious what *getting chickens* was code for.

Chapter Forty-Nine

Grace

We entered the feed store. I couldn't find a hardware store close to us that sold chickens, but this was just as good.

Taking Brennan's hand, we wandered around until we found the chicks, which were in big galvanized tubs with heat lamps. While sure, I could probably buy some really fancy chickens, I just wanted hardware store chickens.

"I didn't think we were actually getting chickens." Brennan peered at the tub.

"Yes. They put out the new chicks today." I looked at the cards on the tubs listing the different breeds. Some of the breeds were a little different here, but I'd done my research.

"Where are we going to put the chickens? Are we allowed to have chickens? Oh, they're so tiny," he gushed.

"I know, right? We can have six hens. Spencer got me a chicken coop. It's not here yet, but we'll need to keep them in a brooder for a bit, anyway." I got my phone out and showed Brennan the picture of my custom coop.

Brennan blinked. "It's a tiny version of our guest house."

"Since you thought coops weren't attractive, Spencer got one to match the house."

"Oh. That's very thoughtful. I'm not against chickens, I've just never had them. But if they make you happy, why not? So do we just... pick them?" He put his hands behind his back like he was afraid to touch them.

"We will. But you know, we should look at brooders first." Taking his hand, I pulled him along, grabbing a cart, and noting things I also might want to get.

I eyed all the cute seedlings. "Can I have a little garden?"

"That sounds nice. Chickens. Who will take care of them when we're gone?" Brennan asked me.

"A company called Chicken Tenders. They'll take care of Spencer's hedgehog, too. But we haven't gotten him yet." I studied small portable heated homes for the chicks to live in while they were too small for the main coop.

Brennan laughed. "That is an amazing idea. Chicken Tenders. Ha! Wait, Spencer's getting a hedgehog?"

"It's my present to him. Do you want a dog? You want a dog, right? You like big dogs who need lots of exercise, right?" Picking a brooder, I put it in the cart, Brennan helping me.

It came with bulbs, but we needed bedding and food.

"We could never have pets. Though for a bit Katie had fish that she won at the school carnival," he shared.

"Oh." I hugged him. "If you want a dog, we'll get you one for your birthday."

"Let's start with chickens and hedgehogs. I might want some bunnies," he replied.

Hmmm. Could the chicken coop place make us a matching bunny hutch? Jett mentioned bunnies, too. I could get them each a bunny.

I found the bedding and food and put it in the cart along with some other things, then headed back to the chickens.

"Um, Little Butterfly?" Brennan said softly as we watched the chicks.

"Yes, Bren?" Hmmm, did I want all six of the same breed, or two each of the three different breeds? I took some videos and sent them to Riley so that she could help choose.

"How are we going to get all this back on your motorcycle?" Brennan's arm slid around my waist.

My heart fell. "Oh. I was originally going to take my truck, but then I decided to bring you and thought my motorcycle would be more fun and forgot that even though I joke about it, it's probably not safe to bring chickens on a motorcycle. Well, maybe one in your jacket around the block so she can have a ride but not taking a whole box any distance."

"Can we come back tomorrow?"

"But the chicks were put out today. Tomorrow's chickens are the leftovers," I pleaded. We could wait until next week, but...

"Okay, how about if we see if we can pay for everything and ask Jett or Evan to bring them home?" he asked. "Um, where are we keeping them?"

"We can just keep them in the kitchen until they're big enough for the coop," I replied. "Though sometimes I'll probably put the brooder outside on the porch."

Brennan nodded. "Okay, we actually have hawks, but if the chickens are in their little house they should be okay. We might need a net or something if you have an area for them to play outside the coop."

"Oh. That's a good idea," I replied.

"Why don't you pick out the chickens, and I'll see if we can have them hold everything for pickup, okay?" Brennan gave me a kiss.

"Okay." While he left, I watched the chicks, noting which ones looked healthy and active and were eating, drinking, scratching, and joining in with the other chicks, but not too bossy.

An employee came over to me. "Would you like to get some chicks?"

"I would."

I asked some questions and then told her which ones I wanted as I carefully selected some from each group, until I had five, using some of Riley's suggestions.

"I'll let my alpha pick out the last one," I told her. My mouth shut. Why did I say that?

But he sort of was. Brennan was mine. Even if he wasn't ready, which I respected, I'd claimed him in my head.

"I get to pick?" Brennan beamed. "Oooh, what about that big one?"

"In my experience, the big bossy one ends up being a rooster, which we're not allowed to have." I put my arm around him, keeping him close. He heard that? Shit.

Brennan picked one, and she took them to the counter so we could pay.

Anxiousness shot through me. "I slipped and called you my alpha, I'm sorry."

"Grace, I *am* yours." Brennan kissed me. "I want to be yours."

He did? My heart danced.

"I want you to be mine, too." I kissed him back. "Now let's go pay for our chicken army."

"I meant what I said," Brennan said softly over the coms in our helmets as we drove back to the house. "I was so afraid when you arrived here. The last time that someone came into our life, they tried to ruin it. I was so convinced that you would do the same that I refused to see there was a chance that you wouldn't. Um, I'm sorry for the damage I caused because I was blinded by the past. I don't think I ever properly groveled for that night when you got sick because of me."

"You don't need to grovel, Bren," I soothed. "I really don't understand why it's a big deal. If anything, I feel bad undoing all of Evan's hard work."

"Sometimes I forget that you're not from here. Also, Wes and I are used to being more hands-off than a lot of alphas because that's what Evan needs. We're having to learn how to take care of you the way *you* need. I'm glad we have Spencer and Jett to help us, and Evan, of course," he added.

"Evan's very good about knowing what I need before I do," I replied.

Brennan was quiet for a moment, and I let him compose his thoughts. It felt like he needed to say things, so I'd let him.

"One thing that my mother said when you first arrived was that yes, you wanted something from us, but that didn't mean what you wanted was a threat to us. It really didn't take long to realize that you didn't want our money. But what you wanted from us was far more terrifying. You wanted our love and acceptance. Evan once said that opening up your heart means opening yourself up to the possibility of heartbreak..." His voice grew ragged.

The stoplight changed to red, and I came to a stop. I reached over and squeezed his hand.

"Bren, I'm not going to break your heart. Also, you're allowed to be wary of bringing strangers into your pack. After all, I was hiding something." It meant a lot that he was saying all this, even if I already understood it on some level. The light turned green, and we started moving again.

He chuckled. "Yeah, that was a lot. For a moment I was so mad. That night Wes and Spencer told us where you were from, I ranted to Jett. And you know what Jett did?"

"What?" I didn't know much about what happened on their end after I was taken other than they went to the cabin and Evan had his heat.

"He held me tight and said, *If she'd actually come to us and told us that, would you have believed her, especially after everything that's been between you so far?* It made me realize that it was unfair of me to expect you to confide in me something so private when I'd been shitty to you. After that, I was more confused than anything. Scientific theories are not my area of expertise," he confessed.

"I'm glad that Jett stood up for me. He's such a calm and supportive presence. I enjoy doing things with him, like going to the boxing gym and watching movies with him and Evan," I replied as I turned the corner so we could enter our subdivision.

"Jett's my rock. He has such a big, fucking crush on you."

I couldn't help but smile. "Yeah, I like him too. I understand how you fell for him."

"He's the one who told me that I've been courting you without realizing it. I hope it's not unwelcome. I want to be with you, Grace. Obviously, I don't want to overwhelm you, but at some point, I... I would very much like to bond with you, Little Butterfly. You very much belong not just in my pack, but with me."

He wanted to bond with me? Awww. His words made me want to explode with happiness. Not just because they were heartfelt but because of how far he'd come.

"I would like to be with you, too, Bren." We were nearly home, and the house should be empty. Maybe we could *be together* a little bit? I'd never been with him alone.

"You still confuse the fuck out of me. But a lot of that is me figuring out how you need to be loved and cared for, given it's different from what I'm used to. *You're* different from what I'm used to, though it's not a bad thing. No, it's a good thing. I never realized that I needed to be loved the way you love me. I never thought I'd want to be cared for the way you care for me. Grace, I need you in a way I never considered that I'd need anyone."

His heartfelt words melted my core. Yeah, I was dragging him into my room and kissing the shit out of him.

"You saying that means everything, Bren. I'm proud of you. I love you too, and I love that you let me love you my way and kidnap you to buy chickens and call you a good boy. Playing the piano with you is fun, and we should go to more concerts." It just seemed to me that Brennan needed to be taken care of a little, too.

"Don't feel like you need to wait. I'm ready whenever you are." I may have added to my heat plan that I'd be *just* fine if he bonded me.

The house appeared. Finally. I pressed the button to open the garage door.

"I should probably talk it over with everyone as a courtesy, but I'm sure no one will have a problem with it."

"Yeah, I guess we should, considering communication is key and all that." I pulled into the garage, which was pretty empty, considering everyone was still at work. Though my pink truck sat in the driveway.

"Also, I don't need a mating party or to be part of your wedding or anything," he added. "You know me and big social events."

Yep. Like after his dad left the party, he'd avoided people by using guarding Spencer's motorcycle as a reason to be alone.

I parked, took off my helmet, and put it away. Brennan did the same. Grabbing his tie, I pulled him down and kissed him, hard.

Wrapping my arms around him, I rubbed against him, letting him know that I loved and wanted him.

"Also, I accept. You're my husband now, too. I want all the husbands. Jett as well, at some point. Now," I kissed him again. "Let's go to my room."

Yep. All five of them were mine.

"Your room?" He picked me up and threw me over his shoulder.

"Yes. My room, my rules. Also, the only person who has ever dick fucked me in it is Jett. I think my room needs more dick fucking." I laughed as he took off his shoes and mine.

"Well, since it's not dinner yet, I'm still technically kidnapped, so okay." He went up the back stairs, with me still over his shoulder.

We went up to my room, and he sat me gently on the bed.

"Thank you." I kissed him, then took two socks out of my drawer to prevent interruptions. One went on the outside door-knob of my room, and the other went on the doorknob in Evan's bathroom. I closed both of them. *Do not disturb.*

Brennan was all mine. I turned around and took off the T-shirt dress and leggings I'd been wearing this afternoon. Also, I moved Mr. Hippo off the bed and put him on the dresser.

"Would you like to take my clothes off?" Brennan asked.

"Yes." Going over to him, I met his eyes as I took off his jacket, trying to show him the same care that he showed me. Brennan had a very tender heart, more so than I think anyone other than Jett realized—even Brennan himself. Jett did an expert job of taking care of Brennan, and I'd like to do the same.

After all, mates took care of each other. Brennan needed to be cared for differently than my other mates.

Well, at least by me.

Carefully, I put his jacket on the back of my chair. Then I took off his tie. Biting my lower lip, I undid the buttons of his shirt one by one. With each button, my want and need for him grew.

My room filled with his pine scent and his desire, but he sat there patiently, allowing me to undress him.

The tie and shirt went with his jacket.

Hmmm. Should I play *tease the alpha* a little? Something about Brennan made me want to be playful with him.

Getting down on my knees, I unzipped his pants, making sure I kept brushing against him.

A little growl ripped from his throat. "My patience only goes so far, Grace. Keep doing that, and you're going to get pinned to the bed."

I laughed as I tried to tug his pants off. Putting his pants on the chair, I dove at him, knocking him backwards onto my daybed. I was still in my bra and panties, and he was in briefs and an undershirt.

My nose touched his. "Pinned you."

"Oh, you are not ready for this game, Little Butterfly." Looping his fingers through mine, he flipped me over, holding my hands over my head without pinning my wrists.

I grinned. "Maybe I want to be under you."

"Mmmm, I want you under me." His mouth attacked mine, and my legs wrapped around his waist.

Yes, please.

"I'll be a good girl for you, I'm just having a little fun." I kissed him back.

"What exactly are your expectations, my small captor?" His eyes met mine as he kept me there on my back under him, my hands still above my head.

For a moment I considered this seriously. What do I want from him?

"I like how you're gentle and considerate with me. I mean, no one in this house isn't. But it's different. I can't explain." I frowned, the words just not coming. "Um, I've never been with just you alone. I suppose I'd like some dick, along with some orgasms, and a knot, if you please, my captive alpha."

"I can do that," he agreed. "This is your room, but I do like to be in charge, Little Butterfly. Is that okay? Safe words still apply."

Brennan liked to be in charge? So surprised. *Not.*

"I'm okay with that," I replied.

"Good. Also, talk to me. You are tiny compared to Jett and Evan, and I don't want to harm you by accident. Are there any limits we haven't previously discussed that I should know?"

"With me? I don't think so. What about you? Do you like being tickled? What about raspberries on your belly?" I wanted to know more about *him.*

"Oh." His head cocked. "I don't like being tickled. I don't know what the other is?"

Wriggling out of his grasp, I pushed him over, pulled up his undershirt and blew on his belly. I looked up at him.

He thought for a moment. "I have no idea how I feel about that. I don't like my feet touched unless I'm getting a foot massage. Well, when you hook your foot around mine at night, that's okay."

"When did I do that?" I looked up at him, laying over his chest, trapping him.

"The night you were a tiny ball of anxiety. At some point you curled into Jett, but your foot reached out, like it was searching for me, and then caught mine. I like it. You did it once or twice in the nest during Evan's heat, too." His smile went bashful.

Awww.

"I like Jett, as well," I said softly. "I enjoy being with the two of you, and the three of you. But I like being with everyone individually, too."

Brennan kissed my forehead. "That's not a problem. Speak up if you're not getting enough of someone, okay?"

"Same. I don't want anyone to feel neglected." I ran my fingers through his hair.

"Oh, and while I know you playing with my piercings makes you feel relaxed and sleepy, it makes me want to fuck you." His voice grew low and growly, which did things to me.

"Maybe I like being fucked to sleep." I laughed and kissed his nose.

"Um, thank you for the message in the bear. I just found it this morning, when I was making the bed. Though Jett found it a while ago and was waiting for me to discover it."

I stroked his hair. "Evan once said he got different things from everyone in the pack. And I do, too. I'd like to think I give everyone something different, something they need and don't get from anyone else, as well."

A smile played on his lips. "Right now, I need to get you naked."

Reaching around me, he expertly unhooked my bra. Making eye contact, he moved me and took off my panties. He put both of them on the chair. For a moment he just stood there, looking at me like I was an ice cream sundae.

"Just look at you." Hunger flashed in his eyes as he pounced on me and started covering every inch of me with kisses.

I giggled as his lips explored my body, given some places *tickled.* But I didn't mind. Not one bit.

Brennan kissed the inside of my thigh, then his tongue lightly caressed my clit, and I sighed.

"Someone likes their pussy eaten first, right?" he murmured as he spread my thighs wide.

"I do like my oven preheated, thanks." I tangled my fingers in his dark hair as he went down on me, in that very deliberate way he did everything with...

...oh. I gasped as two fingers entered me as he continued to explore my pussy with his face. His fingers curved, and an orgasm shook me.

"Good boy," I sighed, as he slid another finger inside me.

"Come for me again, Little Butterfly, so I can fuck you, knot you, and let you know how happy I am that you're here with us," Brennan murmured as his tongue flicked my clit.

"Yes, Alpha." I wrapped my legs around him to keep him close.

Both his tongue and fingers picked up the pace. I gripped his hair tight. A moan ripped from my throat as another orgasm thundered through me.

He looked up at me and smirked, his face glistening with my juices. "Good girl. Would you like my cock now? Or do you need another first?"

Decisions, decisions.

"Please, fuck me, Alpha." Yes, I wanted that beautiful, pierced cock to slowly slip inside me.

"Mmmm, so sweet." Brennan straddled me and kissed me, letting me taste myself on him.

I could feel his hard cock pressing into my stomach as he leaned forward and kissed me again.

But he didn't enter me, no, he took his time, kissing my breasts, my neck, my lips, until I wanted to take that cock and stuff it in me. *Now I know why he asked if I wanted another orgasm.*

"You are so patient. I love that you're such a good listener," he murmured in my ear as one hand reached down to play with my pussy.

"Yes," I breathed as he continued to touch me, molten heat pooling between my thighs.

Withdrawing his hand, he grabbed his pierced dick, knot fully inflated, and slowly worked it inside me. As he entered me, inch by maddening inch, his lips continued to conquer my upper half.

Languidly he started to thrust as we continued to make out, my hands in his hair as his fingers found my clit.

"Bren," I gasped as he sucked on my neck. What would it feel like when he bonded with me one day?

His body rocked mine, slowly, maddening as another orgasm crested, then another, until I was gasping underneath him, wet and wanting his knot. His pace got faster and faster, the kisses more fervent until I couldn't take it anymore.

"Please, please knot me," I begged, pleasure so overwhelming part of me wanted to rip his fingers away from my clit, the other part of me wanted to drown in it.

I needed all of him. Now.

Chapter Fifty

Brennan

Her pleas were sweet music to my ears. While I enjoyed exploring her body, I wanted to knot her, fill her, and make her mine, now that I'd finally realized that she really, truly belonged with all of us.

I continued to suck and bite down on her neck as I thrust inside her over and over.

"You're so ready for me, aren't you? My needy, greedy, little butterfly needs a knot, doesn't she?" I murmured, as I sucked on her neck again.

Would she let me mark her here on her neck opposite Spencer's? That's exactly where I wanted to bite her—right where everyone could see.

"Alpha, please," she begged.

Her pussy gushed around me, as that scent she made sometimes, the one that was almost like omega perfume, clouded the air. What did Evan call it? Oh. *Eau d'fuck me alpha.*

And fuck her I would.

My lips crashed into hers. "I'll knot my good little butterfly."

Arching my hips, I thrust, pushing my knot into her, filling her.

"Bren." She gasped.

"That's it, you take me so well," I praised. "So good."

"Good boy," she whispered.

Fucking shit, I liked being called that while I was knot deep inside her. Even though I was locked inside her, I didn't stop, needing to coax one more orgasm out of her. Yes, I wanted my little butterfly to scream my name and beg again.

I rocked against her in a way I knew would feel good. My fingers continued to rub her clit as I nipped at her neck.

"Yes, please, don't stop, please," she begged.

I kept nipping at her neck, so everyone would know she was mine. My teeth ached to bite her. It would be so easy... no one would mind...

"Bren," she shrieked, coming in my arms, bringing me back to reality.

No, no bites today. My lips sealed over hers, as I let her know how much I loved that I could make her shatter like that.

I laid my head on her bare breasts. "You are perfect for us."

"You're all perfect for *me*." She stroked my hair and planted a kiss on my temple.

"Are you okay? It wasn't too rough?" That was a big fear of mine.

She shook her head. "No. It was just what I needed."

Me too. I hadn't thought I needed a little gentleness in bed, but I guess I did.

"Good." My fingers trailed her throat. "I marked you up good. You might need to wear a high-necked blouse to work tomorrow. But don't worry, I didn't bite you."

"I'd be fine if you did. You and Jett can bite me and mark me up. I'm all yours." Those big blue-grey eyes gazed up at me, full of love and devotion as her sweet, peachy scent surrounded me.

Leaning over, I kissed her collarbone.

I looked around her room, which was immaculate, other than a water bottle and her e-book reader on the window seat with some blankets and pillows. Mr. Hippo sat on the dresser, watching us. It wasn't on purpose; I was sure, but still a little creepy. At least he wasn't in bed with us.

She peered at me. "What are you looking at?"

"Mr. Hippo is watching," I replied.

Grace giggled. "Always watching."

She snuggled into me and dozed off, my knot inside her.

Finally, it deflated enough for me to slip out of her. Rolling off her and out of bed, I went into the bathroom, hoping no one minded. I used the bathroom and filled up her water bottle. Why was there a sock on the doorknob? But I'd leave it there.

I noticed the full-ass kettle setup they had on a shelf in the bathroom, complete with a brass teacup holder and basket of tea and instant hot drinks.

Yes, I'd make her some tea. I filled the kettle and put it on.

Everything was probably from that omega home store they spent a small fortune at recently. *Spoiled.* She and Evan were so spoiled.

Both of them deserved it. I loved that Evan was letting us spoil him more, something he'd pulled back on after Caroline.

And Grace? Yeah, with everything Rosalind put her through, all the neglect she suffered, she should have all the attention, blankets, stuffies, and love that she needed and wanted. It absolutely was a good thing that Rosalind was dead or there'd be some serious reckoning.

There didn't seem to be any massage oil in the bathroom, and I didn't want to go into Evan's room without his permission. Setting the water bottle on the nightstand, I went down to my room while the water boiled in the kettle.

While we had a variety of oils, I wasn't sure there was anything that she'd like. I didn't have peach or vanilla which was what Evan always got for her scent-wise. I grabbed the lavender since it was relaxing, and one that was fresh and crisp, and went back up the stairs.

"Bren, where did you go?" Panic flowed through her voice.

I burst through her door. "Grace, I'm right here. I went to get something. Hey, I'm right here."

She looked so small and worried on the very pink bed.

Kissing her, I put the oils on the nightstand. "I used the kettle in the bathroom. Have some water, and I'll get your drink, okay?"

"Okay." Looking anxious, she grabbed the bottle.

"I'll be right back. Promise." I kissed her again and went back into the bathroom.

Which one? I looked at all the teas and packets. Hot chocolate? Tea latte? Oh. This one. Opening the packet of instant apple cider, I inhaled the scent that immediately brought back memories of skiing with my dad and Katie as a child.

After adding water and mixing it, I carefully brought the cup back into her room. I frowned at the nightstand. There wasn't a coaster. Well, hopefully it wouldn't ruin the finish.

"I made that for you, careful, it's hot." I got back on the bed with her.

"Oh, apple cider?" She took a sip. "It tastes like paper packets of happiness."

Paper packets of happiness? I loved that.

I put an arm around her. "Precisely. I'm not the biggest fan of hot chocolate, so I always got apple cider. Sometimes it was real apple cider, but usually it was this."

"It's perfect." She took another sip.

"Could I interest you in a foot massage?" I held out the oils for her to sniff.

"Lavender is my favorite." Grace smiled over her cup.

I put the other back on the nightstand. "Noted."

Scooting down to the end of the bed, I took one of her feet. I put some oil in my hands and started massaging her feet.

"Mmmm." Sighing, she took another sip. "You learned foot massage at alpha camp?"

"I did. We learned about all the pressure points that feet have. Which made for tons of jokes as we practiced on each other, because we learned about pressure points in our martial arts classes, too. The instructors are mates." I worked her little foot over, watching her expression and body language as I tried to get all the right spots.

She giggled. "Sounds fun. Did you ever go to other camps?"

"I went to music camp a time or two—and rugby camp. Did you ever go to summer camp? The fun sort?" I worked my way up her foot.

"Cheer camp was always a good time. Exhausting, but great. Sometimes I went to church camps, which were varying degrees of fun. I would have loved to go to music camp—or math camp. I got a scholarship once but wasn't allowed to go." She sighed.

I massaged her toes. "Maybe they make an adult math camp? They have adult summer camps, where you can bring your pack and canoe and do ropes courses and arts and crafts and roast marshmallows."

"I love that."

"Are you doing okay? Settling into everything?" I switched over to the other foot.

"Yeah. Work can be a lot sometimes because your science is more advanced and the terms are different. For example, have you ever given thought to how many things are named after people? While we have many of the same concepts, we often, but not always, have different people that they're named after," she said.

"Oh." I pondered that for a moment as I lavished her other foot with attention. That was something I'd never considered. "We're here. You're not alone. We take care of each other."

"I know." She smiled at me.

That smile was everything.

Chapter Fifty-One

Jett

I took the cardboard container of baby chickens out of my convertible. Yeah, that wasn't a sentence that I ever thought I'd say. Going inside, I put it on the kitchen table, then got everything else Grace bought at the feed store.

The little chicks made little *cheep cheep* noises. It felt mean to keep them in the box. Also, Brennan was occupied, probably with Grace.

I mean, as he should be. His realization today that he really wanted to be with her *now*, not *someday*, was big.

Not to mention, I'd stayed at the restaurant long enough to see him in the sidecar and took some pictures. His leaving work to go on an adventure with her in the sidecar was the epitome of an alpha wanting to make someone they loved happy... and told me everything that I needed to know.

Getting an old end table out of the basement, I made space in the kitchen for it. Following the directions from the guy at the feed store, I got the little chicken TV ready. Okay, it was called something else, but that little see-through temporary home for them was going to be a chicken TV for every cat and hawk in the neighborhood.

By the time the baby chicks were settled in their little house, with food, bedding, water, and the lamp, I could feel that Grace and Brennan had finished. I cleaned up and put the rest of the food and bedding on the bottom shelf of the small table. Yeah. That looked nice. Especially with the two omega lilies we now had.

I liked the idea that we were adding pets. Also, I'd been serious about the bunny army. Brennan liked bunnies, too.

The door opened from the garage, and Evan came in.

"Um, we have tiny chickens?" Evan took off his shoes.

"Grace kidnapped Brennan, and they got chickens." I knew Brennan would be fine with her. I'd only checked on them today because I wanted to make sure that *she* was okay, and his temper wasn't getting the best of him.

Okay, that and Cam thought it was hysterical and said if I didn't go that she was going to find them and pull them over for funsies because she wanted to see Brennan in a sidecar.

It was also sweet that Grace had let me know she was absconding with him. My one regret was not ordering some food at that restaurant because it smelled amazing.

Evan put an arm around me. "Grace texted me that she was going to take him to lunch. I wasn't sure he'd go with her."

"He was taking the afternoon off anyway because of the press conference. Also, he admitted to me that he really likes her and wants to mate with her." I kissed Evan.

"Finally. Mmmm. I want to watch that." He grinned. "You're next?"

"I'm already hers. I don't need anything." Okay, more dates. I should probably start advocating for more alone time with her.

Evan's head tilted. "Those chickens are tiny and fuzzy."

"That's why they're in the chicken TV. I think they need feathers before they go into the coop. Which we don't have yet. Hey, should we go find Bren and Grace? She told me that she was only kidnapping him until dinnertime." I got contentment through the bond with my husband. It was probably a good time to find them.

"Wait, kidnapping?" Evan laughed.

I told him about it as we went up the stairs. They weren't in our room. He went to her room? Yeah, Brennan's inner-alpha was over-the-moon in love with her.

"What are we doing for dinner?" I asked.

"Riley's going to Hiro's. Spencer and Wes have work. I'd planned on trying to make Brennan's day better," Evan said.

"You still could." Maybe I could take Grace out, or at least we could go pick something up for everyone.

"Why is there a sock on the doorknob?" My eyebrows rose.

"I don't know. Let's go through my room." Evan took my hand, and we went into the bathroom.

The closed door between their rooms also had a sock on it. I didn't understand the socks.

I knocked on the door and opened it, taking off the sock. "Kidnapping's over."

Brennan and Grace were cuddled together on her little daybed. There was a water bottle, a teacup, and some massage oil on the nightstand. I could smell the lavender oil mixed in with the scents of them and their lovemaking. Her neck and shoulders were covered in love bites and hickeys.

My husband took up most of the bed which wasn't meant for alpha sleepovers. He looked so fucking cute wrapped up in the pink sheets.

Grace gave me a look. "Um, there's a *sock* on the door."

"I know." I held it up. "Why?"

"Oooh, there's a boy in your room," Evan teased.

"Well, yeah, that's what the sock means, *Do not disturb, I'm entertaining.* Is that not what you do in the dorms here?" She made no move to get up from her Brennan pillow.

"Oh, that's what that means. We just used the underwear of the person we were fucking," Brennan replied.

Evan thought for a moment. "In the military we put a condom on the doorknob, or a rubber band."

I looked at everyone in horror. "What? Why didn't your dorms use the light system? We literally had lights by each door, and there was a panel inside where you could change the colors to indicate if you were at home, asleep, in class, studying, *busy...*"

Okay, I'd seen the underwear on the doorknob a few times when we'd gone to parties at Rock State. But I thought that was just something stolen from the movies and they were being funny. People really did that?

And a *condom?* I mean, the red light could theoretically mean a lot more than, *Don't come in, we're fucking,* but there was no doubt what a condom on the doorknob meant.

"Yeah, you went to the nerd university." Evan laughed, going all the way in.

"The light system is a good idea. You can come in," Grace added.

I came over to the bed. "I installed your chicken TV. The cats are going to sit in the window and watch them like they're the new hit show."

Grace laughed. "I love it."

"It's just us four for dinner, what should we do?" Evan waggled his eyebrows and eyed them suggestively.

"It's Tuesday." Grace looked at me. "Will you take me to Cam's class, and then we can get noodles?"

I felt a little pout through the bond, because obviously Evan was suggesting a sex party for dinner. But I liked the idea that she'd rather the two of us do something together.

"Of course, Peaches. Though you don't need me to take you. You have a membership and a car. But…" I recalled my earlier thought about wanting to spend more time with her. "If you'd like to, maybe we can make it a regular thing that we do together? I'd really like that." Reaching out, I stroked her hair with my hands.

She beamed. "You and noodles every week? Amazing."

"Um, can we get noodles too?" Evan asked.

Grace thought for a moment. "Sometimes. But only if it's okay with Jett."

"Yeah. I mean, you wanted to spend a little time with Brennan anyway, so you can just meet us at the noodle shop tonight after you're finished?" I suggested.

"You want some time with me, Love?" Brennan held out his hand.

"I was going to come home and make you feel better. Peaches beat me to it." Evan grinned.

"You can still make him feel better." Grace laughed.

I looked at the clock on the nightstand. "If we're going, we should get dressed."

"Okay." Grace kissed Brennan and rolled out of bed.

I kissed him, too, then went to our room to change and get my stuff.

A moment later, Brennan came in, smelling of sex and peaches, still completely naked, clothes in his arms. Putting his clothes down, he hugged me to him.

"Hi, Dear." He kissed me.

"How was your day, Honey?" I asked.

"Ugh." With a sigh he filled me in.

Outrage filled me. The Queen Mum did what?

"I'm sorry that happened. Did you have fun being kidnapped? Do I need to look you over and make sure that Grace treated you well?" I teased as I pulled on sweatpants.

"She was a very good captor. We had a great time. Thanks for getting the chickens. I... I'd like to bond with her soon at some point. Are you okay with that?" he asked.

I pulled on a t-shirt. "I told you I am. I'm surprised that you didn't do it this afternoon. You already told me at the restaurant."

Brennan gave me a look of horror. "And not talk to you about it properly first?"

"Go right ahead." I sat on the bed so that I could put on my socks.

"Would you like to be there? I have no issues with that." He sat down on the bed with me.

Much of everything with Evan had been together because it was really important to Brennan that I felt included in the process.

Which came in handy when I needed to take over planning courting gifts and dates when Brennan had problems with being subtle and figuring out what *really* delighted Evan because Caroline had loved everything with a high price tag that looked good on her socials.

Fortunately, he quickly figured out how to be more observant.

Leaning over, I kissed him. "If it works for the moment, I'd love that. But don't not bite her in the perfect moment just because I'm not there. I think Evan wants to watch."

"Of course he does." Brennan smirked.

"As for tonight... I get my first weekly date with Grace."

"You must really like her to agree to take Cam's class weekly," he teased.

"You got in her sidecar. We're all hers." I smirked.

"Well, yeah." Evan came in.

I tugged him to me and kissed him. "Don't be mad that she wanted to spend time with me, Baby."

"Mmmm, only if Brennan makes it all better." Giving his alpha a cheeky grin, he kissed him.

"Always." Brennan wrapped his arms around Evan. "Are you okay if I court her a little and bond with her at some point?"

"Um, yeah. I want to watch. So... I meant that about wanting to make you feel better."

"Yeah, warn Grace, *please,*" I told him. Tying Evan to the bed in the playroom always made Brennan feel better.

Brennan's look went serious. "Of course."

"Can we still join you for noodles? If we're done in time?" Evan gave us a sly look.

"I don't have a problem with it." I got my stuff and headed downstairs. Brennan, wearing only shorts, followed me.

"Is that a cat in the window?" Brennan asked, gazing at the window that looked out onto the patio.

I turned but didn't see one. Brennan probably startled him.

"That's going to be entertainment for the neighborhood cats," I replied.

Grace stood in the kitchen with her things, holding a water bottle, watching the chickens. She wore leggings and a T-shirt and was eating an apple.

"Thanks for setting them up." She gave me a kiss.

I smirked as I realized she was wearing one of *my* shirts.

"Grace, Evan and I might be a bit much for you while you're in class, so you want to keep things locked down, okay?" Brennan stroked her face. "Jett will hug you tight if you need him to. He gives great hugs."

"Thanks." She buried her face in his bare chest.

"And then we're getting noodles." Evan joined us and picked her up and spun her around. "Is that Jett's shirt?"

Grace gave him a look. "Laundry tax. If I do your laundry, I might steal your clothes."

"I think you do laundry to steal clothes." Evan gave her a kiss. "Are you going to ride with Jett to class? Because if you are, maybe you can ride back with *me*. I feel like I don't get enough of you on my motorcycle with me."

"Well, I was thinking about letting Jett have a turn in the sidecar, but okay." Grace finished her apple and tossed the core in the food scrap bin.

He turned to me and gave me a kiss. "Have fun."

"We will."

Grace and I put on our shoes and went into the garage. Grabbing our helmets, we went over to my motorcycle.

"This is okay?" I asked.

"Absolutely."

We put on our helmets and drove to my boxing gym.

"I hope you don't mind that I wanted to go to class with you," she said over the coms in our helmets.

"Honestly, I adore that you'd rather do something with me than have a sex party," I shared.

She snorted. "That was an option? Both Spencer and Riley really want me to play tennis doubles with them, and during my tennis lessons I realized that I need more cardio in my life."

"Extra cardio is seldom a bad thing. Yeah, Evan was sort of silently suggesting that for dinner. But he's with Bren, it's fine. And, well, I want to spend more time with you," I admitted.

"Me, too. I don't want you to feel left out just because you don't literally carry me off when you want my attention. If you don't actually want to take the class, we can just work out. All I want is to spend some time with only you," she said.

That meant everything. "Same. Though I can carry you off if you want me to."

She giggled. "I'm fine with it."

"I'm glad Bren finally realized that he's courting you. It's been really fun watching you two like you're at a middle school dance," I laughed.

Marti grinned at us from the desk when we went inside. "Cam's here. So, are *you* taking her class?"

"We are. I love Cam's class." Grace beamed at her as we signed in.

And I loved her.

"I still think we should train her for Omega League. Maybe weapons division? They're always needing enough omegas for the competitions to count," Marti told her.

"Weapons? Like swords?" Grace perked.

"There's a few weapons to choose from; you should watch some videos," she suggested to Grace.

"That sounds fun."

Huh. Grace in weapons division. Though her competing in Omega League would be nice. They usually were part of the same competitions as my league. She could come with me.

When we came out of the locker room, we found people already getting ready. Cam included.

"Hi, Cam!" Grace waved.

Cam waved back. "Grace, did you kidnap Jett this time? Please tell me that he rode in the sidecar?"

"No, we just took his motorcycle." Grace stretched.

I enjoyed her arms being around me.

Class started, and it was obvious that Grace was having fun. I felt Bren and Evan and kept looking over at Grace to make sure she was okay.

We took a quick water break. I wrapped her in my arms. "Are you doing okay?"

"I'm okay, thank you." She leaned her head on me.

We finished class. Afterwards, she laid down like a starfish. "Excellent class, I'm beat."

I stretched and checked my phone.

Brennan

Running late, but we'll be there.

"Want to work on a few things? Bren and Evan are running late." I helped her up off the floor.

"Okay." She shrugged.

We went through a few things in the main gym. I checked their location, and they still hadn't left.

"Can we get the fruit candy on sticks while we're waiting?" she asked.

"Sure."

I let them know, and we left the gym and took off for the outdoor market. I parked by the noodle place, and we walked over to the vendor and bought them. Checking my phone, I saw they were almost here. I got one for Evan since he liked them, too. Brennan didn't like the candy coating, so I got him a plain one.

Tucking Grace under my arm, we walked toward the noodle shop. Yeah, this was nice, and I was happy we'd get to do this every week.

Chapter Fifty-Two

Evan

"Hey, I love you, and it'll be okay," I assured Brennan, again, as we parked my motorcycle, which he'd driven, and went to find Jett and Grace.

"I know. I just don't want to deal with that. You know, I don't care if people like me, but I don't like my character being trashed." With a sigh, he checked his phone and put an arm around my waist.

"Who does? But hey, your publicist is on it," I assured as I glanced at my phone. "They're this way."

Brennan and I had a great time together. But then he checked his phone, which was full of bullshit that he had to deal with. I wished that there was more I could do other than hold him and tell him that it would be okay.

The market was lit up with lights, the evening air pleasant, as people shopped and got things to eat. Delicious smells made my belly grumble. *Soon.*

Jett had Grace tucked under his arm as she ate candied fruit on a stick.

I felt Brennan's reaction through the bond as her lips wrapped around a strawberry.

"Oh, you look so fucking sexy eating that." I bounded over and stole a candy-and-strawberry kiss. I turned to Jett. "Hi." I kissed him too.

"Hi. Hey, Baby, I got one for you." Jett gave me a fruit stick that was like Grace's. "I got you a plain one, Honey." He handed Brennan one.

"Oooh. Thank you." I swirled my tongue around it, catching Grace's eyes.

"Thanks, Dear." Brennan kissed him.

Grace mimicked my gesture. Brennan growled and put his arms around both of us.

"Wes and Spencer are missing out," I laughed. I took a selfie of me and Grace and dropped it in the group chat, making sure the picture wasn't inappropriate, since Riley was in it.

Me

> **We're going to get noodles. Don't you want to join us?**

Suddenly, I wanted us all together.

Riley

> **I'm busy, you fuckers. Thanks, tho.**

Wes

> **Oh, that sounds good. Spencer and I are just finishing up.**

Thank you for the invitation. We'll be there soon.

Wes and Spencer were coming? Amazing. I didn't know why they had to work late tonight. Maybe it had to do with Elaris' case being re-opened? Who knew?

We'll save you a spot. Here's the address.

I wasn't sure if they'd ever been to the noodle shop, so I dropped the address in the chat along with a few suggested places to park, since car parking wasn't plentiful.

As we walked, we finished our fruit and threw away the sticks.

"Grace!" One of the young servers waved as she greeted us in Mandarin. I think she was the daughter of the owner. "How many, four?"

"Six," I replied. "The other two are coming."

"They are?" Grace beamed. "How fun."

The server showed us to a table, and we ordered beers. She and Grace excitedly talked to each other, mostly in Mandarin, with some English sprinkled in. The server left to help someone else, and the four of us looked at the menus. I had no idea what they were saying.

Jett nodded. "You're really improving."

"I've been using those programs from Brennan," she replied.

Someone brought our beers.

"I'm sorry we were late." Brennan sighed. "Caroline had a press conference mentioning how horrible I am and how she supports my mother."

Jett nearly spit out his beer. "Fuck that shit. Seriously?"

"Yeah. But don't worry, we shut that down, since you know, there was legal action against her for what she did to the company, and the restraining order. It's just not what I need." He put his head in his hands.

I put my arm around him.

"Fucking bitch," Grace muttered.

Yep. She should have stayed out of it.

"It'll be okay, Honey. Is your dad still barricaded in the foundation office? Do we need to bring him noodles?" Jett offered.

"Maybe? Given that I now own the building, I might have banned people from said establishment. He's still barricaded in there trying to go through the emergency procedures in the foundation charter to take over the foundation completely," he said, taking a sip of beer.

"Does our foundation have that?" I asked.

"Yes. It also has what happens to the foundation if the pack dissolves and all sorts of contingencies," Brennan replied.

Grace paused. "That's basically a pack divorce, right?"

"Yes, and it can be very messy, especially if people have to un-bond," I told her. "We see it sometimes at the Center."

"That sounds awful." Grace looked stricken.

I kissed her. "Usually, it's for the best. Sometimes, packs just don't work out. Also, people change, and not always for the better."

Honestly, if that mom in Grace's bio-dad's pack got convicted of trafficking Grace, I would see her dad wanting to do just that–or at least cut her out of the pack.

"Anything else going on with everything with your mom, Bren?" Jett asked, putting down the menu.

I think I'd just get my usual.

"Well, she's pissed as fuck because both Katie and I publicly sided with Dad, and Katie's helping him with gaining control. I'm not a voting member anymore, so there's not much I can do," he told us. "Oh, and Troy's wife has been blowing up my phone wanting to know if I knew about Troy's affair. Which I didn't until Katie told me this morning. I don't really care for her, but I offered to get her and the kids a hotel."

"Oh, that's nice. Wait, Troy is having an *affair?*" Jett blinked.

"Yeah. Katie found out about it and told her," Brennan added.

"As she should." Grace took another sip of beer. She looked at the door. "They're here."

A moment later, Spencer and Wes walked in, still dressed for work.

Grace got up and wrapped her arms around Wes, kissing him, then she did the same for Spencer. People were watching.

The server grinned and said something to her.

Grace laughed and replied as she took Wes and Spencer's hands and led them to the table.

"Brennan, I'm so sorry that things have escalated. Rest assured, me and my company are behind you," Spencer told Brennan.

"Thank you, Spencer," Brennan replied.

"Oh, I took care of Caroline. Bitch." Wes took a sip of Grace's beer.

The server came over and took their drink orders. Wes and Spencer looked at the menus.

"What did you do?" Brennan asked.

"Something like what you told Riley she could do to your mom, only with the company she now works for. You told Riley she could do that, right? One reason I stayed late was that she wanted my help with stuff. Though eventually she went with Hiro." Wes frowned over the menu. "I have no idea what to get."

"I did. Will I regret it? I'm not sure. Wait, you have a backdoor into the server for Caroline's company?" Brennan asked.

"Yes. Her pack's company, too. I also have all sorts of shit on them. I've been compiling a *fuck you* file. I don't have one for your mom. But oh, that virus Riley built was beautiful. We did a few things to make it harder to figure out who made it and where it came from, since you know, laws and shit," Wes said quietly.

"Um, *what?*" I glared at my packmates.

"Oh, you should have seen it. Riley is a fucking genius," Wes praised.

Brennan frowned at me. "You knew of this plan. She came up with it a while ago."

I sort of thought it was a joke.

"We did everything through me, so I'll take the fall if anything happens," Wes assured.

Yeah, I didn't like that plan either.

"It will be fine." Spencer looked over the menu.

Probably.

Brennan squeezed my hand. "I'm sorry. I probably shouldn't have done that. But they went after my dad, and I told her not to do anything illegal."

"I know. I like your dad." I squeezed his hand back.

Wes frowned. "I didn't know about the *not illegal* part. Because that plan isn't really legal. What if it's only a little illegal?"

The server came back, and we placed our orders.

I got a picture of Riley at a very fancy sushi restaurant with Hiro. She was dressed nicely, as was he.

"Um, is my sister on a date with Hiro?" I looked at Grace.

Grace thought for a moment. "Maybe? Those two like each other a lot. It's not a problem at work, but it's obvious."

"Hiro, not Marcos?" Jett asked. "Is her dating the son of a councilman better or worse than a police sergeant?"

"I don't know," Brennan replied.

"How's Rose?" Grace asked. "She gave me the prettiest bracelet on Saturday."

"She's doing great with her summer classes and looking forward to seeing her dad," I said.

We talked more as we waited for our food, sharing about our day.

"I really want to see Brennan in the sidecar," Wes laughed.

Same.

"I'm glad Riley's doing well at the internship," I added.

"Tru is very excited. She wants to go to the adventure park again," Grace told us.

"If we have time, I'm all for that," I replied. The couple of hours we spent there for dinner, fireworks, and a couple of rides had been a good time.

"Terrance wants to have a playdate for his kids with her. Maybe at Everydoll or Stuff-A-Stuffie?" Brennan added.

Grace nodded. "I love it."

The server brought everyone's noodles along with some tea.

I took a bite and moaned. "Perfect."

"How's everything with Elaris' case? Let me know if I can help." Jett put chili sauce on his noodles.

"Thank you. They don't need anything from me. It's going to trial. There are several people directly involved. The organization might face charges as well, since they sanctioned it." Spencer picked up his chopsticks.

"When's your mom and dad heading back?" Grace, too, added chili sauce to her food.

Spencer took a sip of his tea. "They'll be here for longer than they thought. Given my father was declared deceased, even though there was no body, they now have to have him un-deceased before returning to Greece. My grandfather is helping them. They're planning on seeing some other friends here, but he wants to spend the day with me at the office tomorrow."

Grace beamed. "Send him over and I will show him everything."

His look went fond. "He's very excited about your projects."

Grace looked at her phone and laughed. "Verity crashed a party today in Paris at Supressa. She looks *stunning.*"

She passed around her phone, showing us selfies of her sister and a photo of her on a runway.

Spencer turned to Brennan. "Oh, I might be buying shares in companies."

"State Street? Your cousin warned me." Brennan took a small bite of his noodles.

"No, the science complex they're building over by the SpacePlex. At some point we'll probably have to relocate Special Projects," Spencer clarified.

"Oh. I didn't even know they had that," Brennan replied. "I was considering moving my company to my building once enough leases are up to give me the space. Since I don't own the building we're in, and now I have one that's not too far away, it makes sense. No, I'm not going to evict the foundation. Especially if my father succeeds."

"What exactly is he going to do?" I was so confused.

"Change it from a family foundation to a full foundation, which includes bringing on non-family board members and changing the name. There would be a program refocus, too."

This was nice, but I missed Riley being here with us.

Me

> **Are you okay? Let us know when you need to be picked up.**

Riley

I'm fine.

I got more pictures of fancy sushi.

A sigh escaped my lips.

Brennan shot me a look. "Is everything okay?"

"Our pack has a teenager." Dating. My sister was dating and probably going into full-on teenager mode where she just wanted to be with her friends.

"Yeah, kids do that," Grace replied.

Brennan and Spencer started talking about our foundation. Grace crawled into my lap and snuggled into me. She smelled of sex, Brennan, Jett, and sweat.

"Are you tired, my good doctor?" Spencer looked at her with concern.

She nodded. I stroked her hair as I finished eating.

Yeah, Spencer could tuck her into bed with him. I think I'd spend the night with Wes. But first, I was going to take my peaches home on my motorcycle.

Chapter Fifty-Three

Wes

Happiness coated me as I went up to the floor of Compass BioTek where the executive conference rooms were. It was on the same floor as Spencer's office.

Spencer and his dad stood in the hall, speaking softly in Greek. Nick had spent the past couple of days at Compass BioTek, mostly asking Special Projects all the questions and hanging out with Grace.

"Your company is amazing. Perhaps I should convince your mother to move here so that I can work for you," Nick added in English.

"I'd hire you in a moment, Baba, but you know Mama wants to travel the world with you. Enjoy your trip and I'll see you soon." Spencer hugged his father.

"I can't wait." He hugged him back and turned to me. "Goodbye, Wes."

I waved, and Nick left. I looked at Spencer. "Is it just us so far?"

"Grace is with Katie in one of the small conference rooms. The hospital has offered her a generous settlement, and Katie thinks she should take it." Spencer looked a little nervous.

I nodded. "Sounds good to me. I mean, it's her decision, and considering how feral Katie has been about this, if she thinks it's good, why not? Then Grace can buy ice cream for our scholarship kids."

"Absolutely." Spencer nodded.

"Your dad is heading off with your mom?" I asked.

"Yes. They're going to visit some friends. My grandfather is calling in all the favors, and my father should have everything in order soon so that they can head back to Greece," Spencer told me.

Riley came down the hall, holding an ice cream cone. "Fuck of the morning, to you."

"Hi Riley, will you be okay waiting in my office until we're ready for you?" Spencer asked her.

Her eyes rolled. "Yes. I don't need to hear any arguments over whose room she sleeps in on what nights."

Spencer put an arm around her. "Noted. We want to make sure you feel heard."

"Thanks, you sap. Do you still have all the cool shit in your office?" she added.

"Only a few things that we're going to keep but haven't brought to the house yet. Everything else has been donated," Spencer told her.

Right, all the mating gifts they got from random people. Grace had been handwriting thank-you notes to people Mrs. K said were important.

Riley went off to Spencer's office.

"It'll be fine. This is just a formality." Spencer squeezed my shoulder.

While in some ways this was a formality, it was an important one. I remember when we did this for Evan back when we were forming the pack.

And now... now we were doing this for Grace. Once this was done, we'd submit the paperwork, and after it was accepted, Grace would officially be part of the pack.

Fuck. Grace was joining the pack. As she should be. My shoulders wiggled in happiness.

Brennan came up along with our pack lawyer, named Alison. She was an alpha who was about Spencer's age, and an absolute shark of a lawyer. Brennan had known her for years and respected her.

Alison looked around. "Who are we waiting for?"

"Not me. I'm here." Evan came over with Mrs. Beekman and Carly. Evan was dressed nicely. Mrs. Beekman wore pants and a blouse as usual. Carly had on her Omega Center polo.

Why was Carly here?

Brennan looked at his phone. "Jett is parking."

"Riley's in my office eating ice cream," Spencer said. "Hello, Mrs. Beekman, you look well. Hi, Carly."

Carly smiled. "Hi, Spencer. Hi everyone."

"Boys." Mrs. Beekman looked around. "Where's Grace?"

"With Katie in the small conference room. Let's see if they're ready for you?" Spencer led her down the hall.

"Katie's here?" Brennan's eyebrows rose.

"Grace has the right to her own lawyer. Katie volunteered," Evan told him. "I don't need a lawyer, but Mrs. Beekman said she'd feel better if I had Carly."

"This is always such an exciting part." Carly practically bounced with excitement.

"I'm pretty excited," I admitted.

Jett ran down the hall, also dressed nicely. "Sorry, it was a day."

"It's okay, Dear." Brennan hugged Jett to him. "We're all here."

Alison turned to Evan. "Do you need to consult with your advocate before we start?"

"No, I'm ready to start when you are," Evan replied.

Spencer came back out. "They only need a few minutes."

"Bren, I saw the announcement your dad made about the new foundation. I love the omega scholar-athlete program they're adding in addition to all the youth sports. I'm so happy he could take care of everything so quickly," I said.

Things were not going well for the Queen Mum. Not only was her company and reputation in ruins, but Brennan's dad had successfully taken over the family foundation, booted her, Troy, and Liam, and was making it into something new and amazing.

"Me, too. The new program aligns really well with the foundation's mission and fills a need. I'm proud of him," Brennan replied. Both he and Katie would be on the board along with some of Brennan's dad's contacts and former rugby teammates.

The past couple of days had been hard on Brennan, but hopefully everything would die down and go back to normal soon.

Brennan got close to me and Spencer. "I got a weird phone message from the Bureau of Investigation about them wanting to talk to Grace. Did you get any?"

"No. But Grace and Creed were upset because something happened at the university where the professor's teaching summer school. They didn't get many details other than that everyone was okay and there was a gun. They got worried," I explained.

"What?" Brennan frowned. "Someone brought a gun to a university? Who does that? That's awful. I'm so glad that everyone is okay."

Mrs. Beekman came out and nodded to Brennan. "We're ready when you are."

"Let's get started then." Spencer led us to the big, fancy executive conference room. It had very nice leather chairs and a big, shiny table. Someone, probably Riley, had written *Grace is the best* on the whiteboard in green marker.

This room also made me nervous. It wasn't where we held staff meetings, this was where important shit happened.

Of course, this could be classified as *important shit.*

Grace, Katie, and Mrs. Beekman sat on one side of the table. My peaches wore a really pretty green floral dress. Evan and Carly sat on the same side but a couple of seats down. We all sat on the other side. Brennan was next to Alison. Jett was next to Brennan, then me, then Spencer. No one sat at the ends.

This was so the omega could see that they were equal to the pack that wanted them. They could have their own lawyer and an advocate. It wasn't uncommon for a parent or older alpha sibling to be part of it as well.

Evan had said that he would sit on the other side but separate because he, as the existing omega in the pack, got a say. Not just as tradition, we'd literally had it written into our charter after Caroline.

"Are we ready to begin?" Katie asked Alison.

Alison looked at Brennan. He was head alpha, so this was his meeting to preside over.

"We are." Brennan shifted nervously in his seat.

"The Thanukos Pack would like to formally bring Dr. Grace Thanukos into the pack," Alison stated. "Has the latest version been reviewed?"

"It has and meets all legal standards." Katie nodded.

"It's been reviewed by both Dr. Thanukos and myself. It meets all Center standards," Mrs. Beekman stated. "The pack has found our changes to be acceptable?"

There were some minor wording changes Mrs. Beekman had asked for, mostly in clarifying that Grace had full control over her career.

Alison replied and focused on Grace. "Yes, the pack has. The asset is acceptable?"

"Yes, I accept the beach estate on my own island." Grace laughed, her face lighting up.

"It is acceptable," Mrs. Beekman replied.

"Has everything else been deemed suitable?" Alison inquired.

"The home has passed inspection, as have they." The look Mrs. Beekman gave us clearly indicated that we should feel fortunate that she deemed us worthy.

I know I did.

"Are there any non-negotiables or requests to be added?" Alison added.

Sometimes there were multiple meetings like this, especially if an omega had specific requests that needed to be addressed.

Evan had one client who was raising a younger sister, so she needed to make sure the sister was provided for if anything happened to her. Another client had horses and wanted a certain type of stable for them.

Grace smirked, and I wondered what she was asking for.

"Ice cream?" I whispered to Spencer. It was all I could think of.

"Grace's one non-negotiable is that there always be chocolate chip cookie dough ice cream in the freezer." Mrs. Beekman tried not to laugh.

"Called it," I murmured.

Alison looked at Brennan.

"Yes, we find that acceptable. We can make sure there are back-ups in the garage freezer," Brennan assured, as the rest of us chuckled.

"I find that acceptable," Grace replied, still smirking.

"Noted." Alison nodded.

We went over some more things. Grace glanced at her phone and frowned. Finally, Alison looked over at Evan.

"Have you read the agreement and find it acceptable?" Alison inquired.

"We have, and the Center finds it acceptable." Carly glanced at Evan, who nodded.

"Do you have anything to add, rebut, request, or reject, as is your right set forth in the charter?" Alison asked Evan.

"No. I'm really glad that Grace is joining our pack. I have no desire to veto, I have nothing to add, and there are no terms I want to reject or rebut," Evan said.

Good. But then he'd been in love with her from the moment he brought her home.

"Is there anything else to add or anything anyone would like to address before we bring in the child?" Alison surveyed the table.

Spencer got on his phone, probably texting Riley that it was time to come in.

Katie looked at Mrs. Beekman and Grace, who shook their heads.

"No, we find everything acceptable and are ready to proceed," Katie replied.

Carly looked at Evan, who nodded. "We're ready to proceed as well."

"I'd like to say something." I focused on Grace, because this was just for her. "Grace, I'm so happy that we're finally together, just like we used to talk about. I'll love you until the end of the universe."

After everything Grace and I had been through, we were literally sitting across the table finishing the negotiations for her to be part of her pack. While it wasn't something I'd really talked to her about, because she didn't know what packs were and I wasn't part of one, if we ever actually got to be together in real life, I knew it could happen.

Here we were.

"I'll love you until the end of the universe, too." Grace sniffed and made a heart with her hands.

Carly put her hand over her heart in an *aww, so cute* gesture.

"I'm happy you're here, my good doctor," Spencer whispered.

"Me, too," Jett told her.

Brennan met her gaze. "Yes."

"Um, yeah, my mate is sexy and amazing." Evan smirked.

"I'm really happy to be joining the pack." Grace beamed and did a happy little dance in her chair.

There was a knock on the door.

"Enter," Alison called.

The door flew open. Riley strode in, followed by her friend Kilroy. He was a young alpha and a huge boy with red hair and green eyes.

"Why hello lawyers, Center people, doofuses, saps, fuckers, and Grace. I'm Riley, the best pack member, and this is my counsel, Kilroy." Riley plopped down in the seat at the head of the table.

"Riley, when I said you could have a lawyer if you wanted, I meant an actual lawyer," Brennan chuckled.

"Kilroy's dad is The Lawyer, so he's practically one." Riley shrugged.

One of Kilroy's dads was part of the Extreme Fighting Entertainment Network and was called *The Lawyer* because when you fought him, you got served. I'm pretty sure Kilroy and Riley met in detention.

Alison tried hard to keep her composure. "Welcome, Riley, Counsel. Have you read what you were given?"

"We have," Kilroy nodded. "Hiro had to explain a bunch of shit, I mean, items, to us, but we've reviewed it, and my client finds it acceptable. Personally, I think this is cool as fuck."

"Excellent, do you have anything to add, rebut, request, or reject?" Alison asked her.

"I mean, I'd like them to not be possessive assholes or saps, especially in public, but that's not going to happen," Riley replied. "So, no, I don't."

"My client is good," Kilroy agreed

"Is there anything you'd like to say? This is your chance to be heard," Alison added.

"I'm glad Grace is here," Riley said. "No seriously, I feel like we're more of a family now. We were a family. But now we're more of a family, if that makes any sense?"

Yeah, it did. We were truly a family now.

"Thanks, Ri." Grace smiled at her.

"Great. Is there anything else to add or discuss?" Alison added.

Brennan shook his head. "Everything has been addressed to my expectations. Everyone?"

He looked at all of us.

"We're good," I assured.

"I believe everything has been addressed to my client's satisfaction?" Katie looked at Grace and Mrs. Beekman.

"Yes." Grace beamed and blew me a kiss.

"Us as well," Carly replied.

"All good here," Riley told us.

"Excellent. I'll make the changes and send the document for you to submit," Alison informed Katie. "I think we're done here. Welcome to the Thanukos pack, Dr. Thanukos."

Everyone stood, and we left the conference room.

"Thanks, Kilroy." Riley gave him a hug.

"Anytime. And good timing. My dad's downstairs. Smell you later. Congrats, Dr. Grace. Please bring those crackly cookies to the next book club so I can sneak in and eat them." Kilroy waved and left.

"Um, what was that?" Brennan asked Riley.

"One of his dads had a meeting next door, so he came to hang out with me. We tried to be profesh." Riley gazed up at him.

Katie hugged Grace. "Welcome to the family. Oh, and thanks for the cake. That bakery is my favorite. Baby and I loved it."

"You're welcome," Grace replied.

Brennan hugged his sister. "Thanks, Katie."

"You're ours now. We aren't letting you go." Riley wrapped her arms around Grace.

Grace hugged her back. "Sounds good to me."

Mrs. Beekman gave us a hard look. "Please behave, boys."

"Of course, Mrs. Beekman. We've been taking your advice and staying close," Spencer told her.

"I'll be in touch, thank you and congrats," Alison announced.

"Bye, Evan. Congrats, Grace." Carly waved and left with Mrs. Beekman, Alison, and Katie.

"You're ours for now and always." I picked up Grace and held her tight. My peaches. My mate. My love from across the universe. Mine.

"Are we going to eat someplace nice now? I'm hungry, so feed me," Riley said.

"We are," Spencer replied. "Shall we?"

Still holding Grace, I walked toward the elevator. "Sounds good to me."

Chapter Fifty-Four

Spencer

We pulled up to the valet in front of Zano, a very elegant restaurant. The valet opened my car door. I got out and went around to help Grace out. Wes and Riley were also in my car. Jett and Evan pulled up behind us in his sports car, Brennan arriving on his motorcycle.

"Fancy," Riley breathed as we walked up to the doors.

"We have a lot to celebrate." I put an arm around her. So much. Everything was finally coming together. We were coming together.

The seven of us entered the restaurant. It differed greatly from Supressa. Here, the ambience was understated and relaxed, meant to complement the food, not immerse you, yet impressive all the same. This was the type of restaurant that made wishes come true, where every night was memorable.

A woman in a suit greeted us. "Welcome to Zano. We're excited for you to dine with us tonight. Could I please have your name?"

"Reservations for the Thanukos pack," I stated.

"Welcome. The chef told us that it's a special day for you, congratulations," she replied, having a server take us to a comfortable, low-lit booth in the corner.

Brennan, Jett, Evan, and Riley sat on one side. Wes, Grace, and I on the other.

"How did you get reservations here?" Brennan asked as we looked at the cards listing the set menu.

"The chef is part of my club. We were talking yesterday, and then she called me this morning and told me that there was a cancellation and asked if we wanted it." I'd been planning on taking us to one of the usual places, but I wasn't about to turn this down.

"Oh, you went to the club yesterday. We... we're not banned, right? Because of the fireworks?" Grace's scent went worried.

"Don't worry, I smoothed everything over," I assured. "They were more concerned about the bouncy castle almost going into the lake than about the fireworks." Everything was okay, not to mention that all our vendors had been tipped generously, especially the wedding planner, the string quartet, and the bouncy castle provider.

"Good, because we need to get better at tennis so we can play Kilroy and his mom, and why are there hardly any choices on this menu?" Riley frowned as she flipped the card over.

"It's a set seasonal tasting menu. Though they accommodate dietary restrictions and food allergies," I explained. "The beverages complement the courses."

Grace looked around. "This is beautiful. Is this the place you mentioned as an option for our party?"

"Indeed. They're only open for dinner, so they're often available for rentals during the daytime." Really, I'd been considering this place for simplicity's sake, given my injuries. It was understated and convenient.

Our party had been far more tailored to us. Many people who attended kept telling me how much fun they had.

"Welcome to Zano. Congratulations and thank you for celebrating with us. Here is some complimentary champagne and sparkling apple juice." A server appeared with champagne flutes on a tray and handed them out. He explained the menu and took orders.

Grace squeezed my hand. "This is wonderful. Thank you."

"It is a special day. You're part of the pack now." I kissed her. Officially, it would probably take a week before the forms were processed, and it populated in her file, but that was simply a technicality.

"We have something for you." Brennan nervously took a small box out of his pocket and handed it to her.

"Always with the presents." Grace smiled and took it from him. She opened it and sucked in a breath. "I get one?"

"Of course you do." Wes took the pack ring out of the box and slipped it onto her pinky.

"Now we all match," Riley said. "So, when do we get those tattoos?"

"We were thinking of waiting until you turned sixteen, then we could all go together," Jett replied. "There's a great tattoo artist who goes to my gym who would be perfect."

Riley thought for a moment. "I approve of that idea."

"Tonight's amuse-bouche is a mascarpone and grilled peach crostini with local honey and crispy pancetta." The server set the delicate, colorful appetizer in front of us.

The sommelier poured the wine that matched, explaining the choice to us. Someone brought Riley a non-alcoholic beverage that also paired with the dish.

Riley took a photo of her plate. "It's so pretty."

I took a bite, savoring the flavors, then had a sip of wine. Ah, that pairing made sense.

"Um, I have a present," Riley said to Grace as they cleared our plates.

"You do? Thank you." Grace put a hand to her heart.

"I don't have a lot of memories of my parents. Mostly they're memories of pictures I've been shown and stories I've been told so that I don't forget them. But one of the earliest memories I do have is of my mom's charm bracelet that she always wore. It would jingle and sparkle as she'd pick me up." Riley bit her lower lip, and her brother gave her a squeeze.

I recalled that charm bracelet well. My mother had gotten her several charms for it over the years.

"She got it for her excellent eighteen and the charms she put on it over the years represented things—like there are charms for me and my siblings, graduation, and when she married my dad. But there's also ones from travels and things people got her and stuff. Anyway, Sonja has it. When I was there for spring break, she gave me my charm from when I was born and said I could pick some charms, and to think about what I wanted." She removed something from her mini backpack.

Evan nodded, probably remembering when Sonja gave him his charm back when he and Wes mated.

"Um, so I don't actually know the story behind this charm. Sonja didn't either. But I asked her if she could bring it when she came to the party because it reminds me of you, and I wanted to give you one. Hiro helped me get a bracelet for it. Um, welcome to the family. You're stuck with us." Giving Grace a bashful look, Riley handed Grace a small box across the table.

Grace opened the box, and tears pricked her eyes. "Thank you so much for trusting me with something of your mom's. It means everything."

Inside was a little pink cupcake charm on a gold bracelet.

"I don't know the story of that one," I admitted. "It wasn't one my mother bought."

"Oh, your mom bought some for my mom? You should tell Sonja. She likes to hear all the stories," Riley said.

"Can I see?" Evan held out his hand. Grace passed it over. Evan started to laugh. "I know this story."

"You do?" Riley perked. "I picked it because one of the first things Grace and I did together was make cupcakes."

"Anniversaries have themes, and couples often give each other little gifts based on the theme. Mom was the one who usually told our dad that year's theme. One year, he misunderstood and thought it was the 'cupcake' anniversary, so he got her this and a box of the most beautiful cupcakes from the fanciest bakery in Rock Springs. They were works of art with edible flowers on them," Evan shared. "She loved it, and her friend group adopted the cupcake anniversary instead of whatever it was supposed to be, and they'd try to outdo each other with the fanciest cupcakes."

Riley put a hand to her heart. "Awww. That is so stinking cute."

"Mom would have loved you, Grace." Evan handed it back to her. "Riley, that was so thoughtful."

"The bracelet you and Hiro chose to put it on is nice, too, thank you," Grace praised.

"Allow me?" I fastened the bracelet around her wrist.

Jett turned to Brennan. "Now I want a cupcake anniversary."

The server came back with the next course. "Chilled watermelon soup with lime crema."

The sommelier brought us a new wine, and Riley got a different drink.

"Such a pretty color." Riley took another picture of her pink soup, swirled with light green cream.

Wes wiggled nervously. "Um, here."

Taking a large envelope out of his suit jacket, he handed it to Grace.

She sucked in a breath as she opened in and withdrew a piece of paper. "You re-did it?"

"Yeah. I thought you might like a grown-up version. Now you have choices when you get the dress made." His look went bashful.

"I wanna see?" Riley took the paper. On it was a sketch of Grace in a gold wedding dress with roses on it.

Grace kissed him. "I love it. Hiro's mom sent me her dressmaking contacts, and one of them even emailed me back so far. I love both sketches so much."

We were brought the next course–seared scallops with radish, grapefruit, fresh herbs, and edible flowers.

"Every course is just so beautiful," Grace commented.

"It really is," Brennan agreed.

Grace's phone rang, and she frowned at it. "I've been getting weird calls. I haven't answered them, but I think it's the Bureau of Investigation. Ugh, I wish they'd just leave me alone."

Brennan frowned. "I got a call from the Bureau of Investigation, too. Do you think it has to do with the professor? He's okay, isn't he?"

"The professor won't answer me, but from what Creed and I could find out, he's okay." Grace's brow furrowed.

"At least he's all right." I squeezed her hand.

"Yeah. I'm glad it's okay. That call is probably just the same old same old," Wes said. "The Bureau wants whatever was in the vault. Did we ever learn what she stole?"

"No." Brennan shook his head.

Riley gave us a sly look. "Want me to find out?"

"No thank you." Brennan shook his head. "But I appreciate what you and Wes did to help with my mother."

Their virus had incapacitated the company system and would take some time for them to come back from it.

"I haven't heard from her or my brothers at all today. I think they're finally going to leave me alone. Caroline, too. All I want is to be left alone with my pack," Brennan said.

"The next course is wagyu sashimi on a bed of mashed potatoes." The server brought on the next course, as the sommelier poured the wine.

"To our pack and our new life and everything getting back to normal." Wes raised his glass.

"To us." Brennan raised his glass, as did we all.

Yes, it would be nice to finally settle back into a routine. I was also happy that all the drama we'd had was wrapping up. Just like I was relieved that I was getting justice for Elaris–and I had my father back.

"Oh, these mashed potatoes." Grace made a happy noise as she took another bite.

That's exactly what I wanted to hear.

Grace's phone rang. "It's Hale."

"Take it," I urged, knowing she was worried about the professor.

"Hale? Is he okay?" she asked.

I pulled her to me, and Wes took her hand.

"Me? Why would Pippa blame me? Never mind. Everything's always going to be my fault, isn't it?" She sighed. "What... they what? Do you know who or why?"

All of our attention focused on her. What was going on?

"Okay. Maybe that's why the Bureau of Investigation has been calling. Thank you for telling me. I appreciate it." Grace ended the call and looked up at us, her peach scent taking on the burnt sugar tang of fear.

"What happened?" Brennan demanded.

"The professor was held up because someone was looking for me. Who would look for me?" Her hands shook. "Now Pippa hates me more than she already does. First, I wrecked her family, and now I put her omega in danger."

"Hey, I've got you." Wes squeezed her.

"It's okay, Grace. You're safe. I'll call in some favors and figure out who it is," Jett assured. "Honestly, it's probably someone looking for Rosalind and thinking you might know where she is. Especially if she ran off with the treasure or whatever."

"That makes sense, given the professor has been telling people about you," I added.

Frowning, she called someone. "Um, this is Grace, you keep calling? Call me back."

Jett was busy texting. "Yeah, it's probably someone looking for Rosalind, and they wanted to warn you."

"True." Grace still smelled scared, and I kissed the top of her head.

"Let me at them. We've got you," Riley stated.

"Yeah. Do you want to go home?" Evan asked.

Grace considered this for a moment. "Why don't we finish this lovely meal? You're right. Someone's looking for Rosalind and thinks I know where she is. The joke's on them, because she's dead, and I have no idea what the treasure is, let alone where it is."

"As you wish. Let's enjoy this night together," I replied.

We finished our delightful course, and the server brought another. "Micro-greens with raspberry vinaigrette, goat cheese, and roasted almonds."

Still, chills went through my body at the idea of someone looking for her. But, really, Jett was correct. Someone wanted Rosalind.

After all, that was the only reasonable explanation. Because who'd be searching for Grace?

Chapter Fifty-Five

Grace

"I love cheese," Riley commented, as she helped herself to some off Evan's plate.

We were now on the cheese course, where we each got a tiny wooden board filled with tiny cheeses along with some fruit, nuts, and honey.

"I don't remember what present course we're on, but here's mine." Jett handed me a small red box with gold ribbons.

"Thank you. Present course?" I took the box. So many presents. I felt spoiled.

"I feel like we should be giving you a present with each course? But we got distracted," he admitted.

It had been scary enough to discover there was an active shooter at Briar. Creed had been beside himself because that just wasn't something that happened here.

While the professor was okay, the idea that someone was looking for me, so they went for *him,* made guilt churn in my belly.

I opened the box, revealing a pendant–a peach carved out of jade.

"Jett, it's beautiful. Thank you," I breathed, wishing I could lean in for a kiss. *Later.*

Brennan looked bashful. "I suppose I'll give you yours as well?"

Did they all have something for me? He handed me a small blue box.

"Is that from Stephanie's?" Riley's eyebrows rose as she stole more of Evan's cheese.

"Yes. They do nice engraving," Brennan replied.

Riley and I had browsed all the beautiful things there, and she'd told me that she really wanted a tiara from there for her excellent eighteenth.

Taking off the lid of the blue box, I saw a gold bracelet with music notes engraved. Knowing Brennan, I studied the notes for a moment, humming them.

Oh? I hummed them again. *Oh.*

"Are these the opening bars of the third movement of Kirkorov's 4th?" It was pretty much my favorite piece here, though I loved Volkov.

Brennan beamed. "It is."

"Thank you." Yet another thoughtful present.

Spencer helped me put the necklace on while Wes slid the bracelet on my wrist.

"I might as well give you yours." Evan handed me a little tissue-wrapped packet, as the server cleared the plates.

Undoing the tissue, I found an incredibly detailed bracelet of seed beads made into mauve and peach flowers and green vines, with letters spelling out *peaches.*

"Did Rose make this? It's so pretty." It probably took her a ton of time, too. I held it out so that Wes could put it on my wrist, too.

"She did," Evan replied.

The server brought dessert. "A trio of mini desserts—a tropical fruit pavlova, strawberry chocolate mousse cake, and a fig tart."

The sommelier brought our last course of drinks.

"These dishes are all so fucking cute. We should have shit like this when we play doll tea party." Riley took another photo.

"That sounds lovely. Taste." Spencer held the tiny tart up to my mouth.

The delicate combination of tastes exploded across my tongue. We finished our desserts.

"I have the last gift," Spencer finally said, handing me an envelope.

I opened it. Inside was a picture of a peach and white swirled soft serve cone.

"Princess Peaches, a delicate combination of fresh summer peaches with bourbon vanilla?" I read off the description next to the photo.

"Spencer, did you just name an ice cream flavor after her?" Wes gave him a look.

"I did. Thank you for the idea—and the flavor name. It will be a new, permanent flavor in the cafeteria. Don't worry, we'll still have the same number of rotating flavors," Spencer added to Riley.

My heart burst. "That is amazing. Thank you."

Spencer's lips met mine. "I know all you want is love and ice cream. Now you have both."

I didn't miss how he smirked at Wes, who rolled his eyes.

"You didn't all have to give me presents. Thank you so much, I feel so loved," I told them.

Wes focused on me. "As you should. Every single fucking day. Because you're our peaches and we love you with all our hearts."

The server brought us some candy and the bill.

"Should we go home?" Brennan stood and helped Evan up.

"Dibs on Peaches tonight." Evan reached over and tagged me.

"That's not how it works." Wes made a face.

I thought for a moment. "Why choose? Can't I just have you all?"

"Um, children present," Riley snorted as we went out front to wait for the valet to bring our vehicles.

Spencer draped an arm over my shoulders. "Did you like it, Darling?"

"I loved it." I pulled him down for a kiss.

"Grace, there you are. I've been looking everywhere for you." A man rushed over to me.

"Who are you?" Spencer snarled, pulling me close, with Wes at my side.

"What are you doing here, Abel?" The air whooshed out of me. What the actual fuck?

Abel was the middle of my three brothers I'd been raised with and four years younger than me. I hadn't seen him since the day he and Solomon had come to my university, stolen my truck, and trashed all my things, after I'd defied Rosalind and left for my new PhD program.

Puzzlement flashed in his blue-grey eyes. My eyes. Rosalind's eyes.

"You shouldn't be here. If they catch you, it won't be a good thing." I had no idea if Abel inherited Rosalind's designation. While I didn't really like him, I didn't want the Office of Designation Management to get a hold of him either.

"Catch me? What are you talking about? We've been looking for you. You're hard to find." His voice was so sincere that one could almost believe him.

If not for two minor details. We'd grown up on another world, and he smelled of neutrons.

I could feel all the confusion through the bonds with my guys.

"You were just as awful to her as Solomon. There's a reason why she went no contact with you. Now get the fuck out of here," Wes snapped, taking a step forward, look menacing.

Wes knew all about my brothers. Abel idolized our brother Solomon and did everything he told him to, including terrorizing me.

"She's our sister. You need to come with me." Abel grabbed my wrist.

Spencer punched him in the face. "Don't touch my mate. She told you to leave. The authorities have been called."

People were watching, and a few were on their phones.

"Hey, that's assault." Abel put his hand to his face.

Hmmm... here that depended on a lot of things. In this case, probably not.

"I'm not your sister," I retorted. "Rosalind is my aunt, not my mother, and Dad, sadly, is not my bio-dad. How did you even get here?"

Horror struck me. Was he the one who'd confronted the professor?

"What? Of course you're our sister." Confusion crossed Abel's face.

"This is taking too fucking long." Solomon strode over. He was a large, broad guy who favored his dad, with his dark hair and eyes.

"Solomon, leave," I growled. Fuck. Of course, Solomon would be here, too. Holding up the professor seemed more his style. Shit.

The valet pulled up in Jett's car.

"Get out of the car," Solomon yelled at the valet. "Grace, get in."

"No. Why do you even want me?" *Two* of my brothers were here? What?

Sirens echoed in the distance.

"I don't. Get in the car, Grace." Solomon laughed and brought out a strange gun.

"Stop, police." Jett charged, gun out.

Before I could blink, my brother fired at Jett, Brennan, Wes, and Spencer in rapid succession. All four of them slumped to the ground. Evan literally held Riley back.

"No, let me at them," Riley yelled.

"Solomon, no." I charged at my brother, anger flaring inside of me. How dare he?

He shot at me with his weird gun.

Pain seared me as I froze. Literally I froze. It wasn't bullets; it was some sort of stun gun. Oh. The guys were okay, just frozen. I could see Evan on the phone, literally trapping Riley between the restaurant and the wall. People were filming us, and the sirens grew louder.

Solomon kicked me. "You fucking ruin everything."

Two years younger than me, Solomon had looked down on me from a fairly young age, catching on to all the ways my mother degraded me even before the bad things started. He'd even mess up my room when I was out. I got punished, he got ice cream.

"You fucked up Mom's shit, and she's pissed as hell. So here I am, once again, cleaning up your messes," he sneered.

I wanted to answer. But I couldn't. Whatever he'd shot me with wouldn't let me say anything.

My heart skipped a beat. Rosalind *was* dead, wasn't she? Solomon was the one who told me she was dead. Dad went to her funeral.

"She said Mom and Dad aren't her parents." Abel squirmed. "That guy we saw today looks a lot like her."

Shit. They'd gone to the professor to find me. But how did they know to go to him? Why were they here? How were they here?

Even if Rosalind was alive, how would she know that I'd contacted my bio-dad?

"She's a liar. We know this." Picking me up like I was a sack of feed, Solomon threw me into the car and climbed into the front seat.

"Which guy did she dream of?" Abel asked.

"Come on, Abel," he yelled.

He hopped into the car, and they drove off with me.

Rosalind was alive and once again, mad at me for something.

Fuck.

Chapter Fifty–Six

Evan

"Can you also send an ambulance? Five people have been shot, one of whom was taken with the two suspects," I told the dispatcher that Jett had called. He'd handed me his phone when he'd gone to confront that guy, who I guessed was one of Grace's brothers from her world.

Who'd fucking shot them. All of them. Then took my mate.

The audacity!

Riley squirmed out of my grasp and ran to my four packmates on the ground. A couple of bystanders joined her.

The thing was, I got no pain from their bonds, only confusion. I gave the dispatcher the license plate number as I went over to them.

"There's no blood," one bystander said. "Were they stunned? The guys didn't look military."

"The stun guns were probably stolen. You know those fucking fundies," I replied. "Grace didn't mate with who they wanted." Yeah, that would work, and her brothers sort of had that fundie militia look to them. The military had guns sort of like this, but civilians didn't.

Though these didn't look like the ones we'd at all.

I crouched down and looked them over, while still on the phone with the dispatcher, the sirens growing. No wounds.

"What the fuck did they do to them?" Riley sobbed. "How did her brothers even get here?"

"They're stunned. I don't know how they got here. Grab Brennan's phone. We need to call the Bureau of Investigation." Given Grace's brothers had been the shooters at the university.

Also, I hadn't missed what they said about Rosalind.

You okay? I reached out to Brennan with the bond code he'd developed.

Go.

Go?

A valet pulled up with Brennan's motorcycle. Police sirens came closer.

Go. It came again, this time from both Brennan and Jett.

"Tell the police what happened. I'm going after Grace." I handed Riley Jett's phone and grabbed Jett's gun.

"What the fuck? You're not a superhero." Fear leaked through her voice.

"No, just ex-military. I'll be back. Promise," I told her, getting approval from the bonds of all three of my mates. Especially Wes, who knew exactly what I'd done for the military before getting desk duty. I didn't know what Spencer thought, but surely, he'd approve.

Without waiting, I got on Brennan's motorcycle. I pulled up the location tracker on my phone, used it to track Grace's phone, and hooked it up to the comm system in Brennan's helmet.

"Love you," I called as I took off toward Jett's car.

The guys should hopefully be okay. The stun would wear off. But Grace... she needed our help *now*. There wasn't time to wait for the police or the guys. I couldn't let her brothers take her to Rosalind–or another world.

Following the navigation, I sped after Jett's convertible. While I'd never been part of some elite strike team back in the military, because of my size, I had been on a retrieval team. We did a lot of breaking down doors, busting heads, and speeding after people, on jobs where they didn't need anyone fancy, just a bunch of large people with guns.

Usually, we'd have someone helping us–changing stoplights, unlocking doors, and blurring cameras. It was how Wes and I met. Well, sort of. I knew his voice long before I ever saw him.

When I saw him, I knew I wanted to be his. He'd also been fucking pissed at me. While he hadn't been part of my most recent op, the team I was on had sort of fucked up his.

But he forgave me. Oh, did he ever forgive me.

Jett's convertible came into view, the top still down. I got closer, hoping they'd think I was just a guy on a motorcycle.

Yeah, those assholes paid me no mind. They weren't even really speeding. Did they not think that they'd suffer any repercussions?

Mmmm, between their potential to be sigmas and whatever their mom told them, probably not.

Grace was in the back seat, just there, like a sack of potatoes, not even belted.

I drove up beside them, hoping that Brennan–and my body– would forgive me for what I was about to do. I leapt off the moving motorcycle into the back seat of the car. *Ow.*

"What the fuck, man?" one of them yelled.

Without waiting, I grabbed Grace, opened the door, and jumped out, rolling to help shield the both of us from the impact. Taking Jett's gun, I shot at the tire. Missed. Fuck. I should spend more time at the range with Jett. I shot again, and one tire blew, and the car careened. That was what I was talking about. I shot out another.

"Take that, assholes. Wow, I've still got it." I looked at poor, frozen Grace, getting surprise and gratitude. "I wasn't always a social worker. One day I should tell you about working with Wes back in the Army. Yeah, maybe it was dumb of me, but didn't you once say about why not save someone you love if you're capable?"

Pain coursed through me. I wasn't in my twenties anymore–and slightly out of shape. But shit, it felt good to do that. Finally, a situation that I could handle.

Police cars surrounded us. "Hands up."

I put the gun on the ground and my hands up, holding Grace. One brother leapt out of the car and started running. An officer ran after him and tackled him to the ground.

Panic came through my bond with Grace.

"You're safe," I assured her. Then I got it. "Oh, they might be like your mom. They're also not in the system. Shit. But we couldn't let them take you."

Hopefully, they'd be betas or something, given her dad was just some regular dude.

"What the fuck was that? I'm guessing you're Evan? Your sister is not pleased you ran off to be a hero," an officer said.

"My sister thinks that I sat on my ass at a desk when I was in the Army," I explained as the two of them were taken away.

"I'll tell you exactly where my mom is." Abel rattled off an address.

"Abel, shut up," Solomon said as they got put in the back of the police car.

"Army?" The officer's nostrils flared. "Pink team?"

No fucking clue what that was. "I wasn't always an omega. Are the others okay?"

They felt okay. Annoyed. Worried. But not hurt. My clothes were ruined, but aside from a few scrapes, I was okay.

"They're being taken to the hospital. Hopefully, the stun will wear off soon." He looked at Grace. "Is she stunned, too?"

"Yep. And she's small, so it might take longer to wear off." I looked at the gun. "That's my mate's service weapon. Jett's an officer at Midtown."

"I'll take it and give it back to him," the officer said.

An ambulance pulled up. I picked up Grace, who was silently sobbing.

"I'm sorry, Peaches. We couldn't let them take you. I'm so sorry." I held her hand as we got her in the ambulance.

Oooh, I was going to feel it tomorrow. But saving her was worth it. I'd just take some pain reliever and a long hot bath. Preferably with her in it.

Her phone was ringing. I answered it, thinking it was the Bureau of Investigation.

"This isn't over, you little bitch," a female voice shrieked. The call ended.

Fuck.

We got to the hospital and took her to the others.

"What was that?" Riley flew at me, hitting my chest with her fists. Then she looked up at me. "Someone caught it on their phone. That was some fucking action movie shit there. I'm not sure Marcos' dad could do better. Where did you learn to do that?"

"The military. Before I awakened as an omega, I did cool shit. Sometimes I even jumped out of helicopters," I answered.

"But nothing can happen to you." She sobbed into my chest.

I wrapped my arms around her. "We couldn't let Grace get taken... elsewhere."

Though that phone call meant Rosalind was here. Why? While I could see her risking her kids to do her dirty work, would she risk everything to come here? How had she even gotten Grace's number? No, that was easy enough. Still...

"Hey," Brennan croaked. "Can't move, but I can talk."

"I rescued her because I'm a fucking badass." I went over to my alpha and kissed him.

Someone had tucked Grace in with Spencer. Jett was with Brennan. I gave him a kiss, too. Then went over to Wes. "Yes, you get one, too."

The officer I'd talked to previously, appeared. "Um, hi. I have questions. So many questions. Those guys aren't in the system. They're fundies?"

Shit. "I think they might actually be equalists," Wes struggled to say.

Right. That was some place in Grace's backstory. Maybe. I could feel Grace sobbing through the bond. Going over to her, I stroked her hair.

A bunch of people in dark suits swarmed in.

"You can go now," one of them said to the officer. "This investigation is ours now."

Chapter Fifty-Seven

Grace

"Get in there." Some nameless agent from the Bureau of Investigation shoved me in a holding cell.

"I want my advocate, a lawyer, and my mates," I yelled as they locked the door and walked off.

Ugh. I still felt horrid from the effects of being *stunned* by Solomon. While I was happy that my guys and I weren't shot with bullets, it wasn't very comfortable.

It hadn't even worn off yet when we were transferred from the hospital to their local offices. Immediately, we'd been separated and questioned.

And just like last time I'd spoken to the Bureau, they didn't like my answers.

Now, here I was. I was pretty sure that they thought I was part of all this. Not that they—or me, for that matter—understood what this even was.

"Hey, are you okay, Grace?" a male voice whispered.

Great. They put me in with Abel.

"I want my mates." I sat down on the bench, feeling a little hopeless.

The two of us were alone in the small cell. Abel was cuffed to a ring in the wall. My brothers were here, in a world that was only half theirs–and Evan had spectacularly rescued me from him.

Yeah, I needed more stories about his and Wes' Army days.

He frowned at me. "You'll get us out of trouble, right? It wasn't supposed to be like this. You were supposed to come with us."

"You thought I'd just go with you?" I gave him an incredulous look.

"Well, yeah. You're our sister. Mom only wants to talk to you. We'll bring you right back." His baffled look made me think that he *actually* believed that I'd simply go with him.

They'd bring me right back? Mmm hmmm. *Sure.*

"You held someone up at gunpoint to find me." I scowled, angry they'd have the audacity to do that.

"That was Sol. I tried to ask the guy, and he wouldn't tell me. Mom's going to be pissed." He looked away.

His scent didn't get salty, and honestly, he just sort of smelled like body spray. Maybe he didn't inherit Rosalind's genetics and was like Dad.

Yet, there he went again with the *Mom* stuff. I'd hoped I'd misheard.

"Rosalind's not dead?" Of course she wasn't dead. I curled into a ball. Spencer sent me love. Evan was worried. Wes was pissed.

"Mom? I didn't know she wasn't dead until yesterday. It absolutely shocked me. But Sol's known the whole time. Um, I thought you were dead, too. We all did. Well, maybe not Mom? Though she knows you're not dead now," he blabbed.

Ugh, I'd forgotten how much he talked.

"You thought I was *dead*?" I shot him a look. Not missing. *Dead?*

He nodded. "Well, yeah. Your work caught on fire, and a bunch of people died, including you."

Oh. Well, I guess if the Temporal Authority exploded the super collider at Spencer's dad's work, that they might *burn down* mine.

It hit me. No one looked for me. Because they thought that I was dead.

"Dad was really sad. He got all your stuff from your apartment. I think he gave your insurance money to your college for the cheer squad and bought the church a piano. It has a little brass plate on it with your name. It's not at Mom's church, but the new church Dad joined after the divorce." His face scrunched.

Someone mourned me. Missed me. The fact that he'd done those things with the insurance money was sweet.

"Sol was really weird about it though. I guess it's because the company you work for does so much for the military? I don't know." His brow furrowed. "Do I tell Dad when I go home that you're not dead?"

"Considering I'm not going back, probably not," I said softly. "The last thing I ever want to do is hurt Dad. Though if you talk to Levi, you can tell him I have lots of boyfriends who are also boyfriends."

No one talked to Levi. He left after high school graduation while I was getting my PhD and told us all to fuck off. Even me, because he truly thought the divorce was my fault.

Why Rosalind had been against him being gay when she came from this world was beyond me.

"You actually used math to get to another world. That's amazing. That's how you didn't die in the fire at your work, right? You escaped to this world?" Abel asked.

"Abel, how is Rosalind not dead? How the fuck did you get here? And why does she want to talk to me?" I snapped. I really didn't want to do this.

What I wanted was answers. Well, that, ice cream, and my guys.

"Wow, such language. Um, how is she not your mom and Dad not your dad?" he pressed.

"She's my aunt. My mom is her twin. My bio-dad is from here. Um, do you know it could be dangerous for you here?" I asked.

"I think I'm okay. That's why they brought me in. Solomon wasn't supposed to come, but you know him." Abel shrugged. "Mom got mad, but he's a control freak. Did she really expect him not to want to help me?"

"Answer my question," I prodded. Yeah, I could see Solomon being a sigma.

"Geez, you don't have to be mean," he pouted. "Um, okay. So, I don't know a lot. I was really just brought in to get you. Um, yeah, Mom came to our world from this one to help people. But something happened, and she needed to leave, so we thought she was dead. Then Solomon said we needed to get you, because now people were after Mom, and you needed to tell them it wasn't her," Abel replied.

"Rosalind wanted to help people?" I blinked. Altruistic Rosalind always had a motive.

"Um..." Abel's brows furrowed. "She had instructions from here that she took. Those refugees we used to help at Church? They were from other worlds. Some stayed, some went elsewhere."

"Did they pay her or something?" What was even happening here? Rosalind helping otherworldly refugees? Though I remember the church adopting people who'd come seeking asylum.

"It's her side hustle. Solomon's been helping her," he told me, nonchalant like she sold essential oils or something.

"Instructions?" Was Abel trying to tell me that what she stole from a federal vault were instructions for parallel world travel?

"Um…" He frowned. "She thought it was stupid that people didn't want to help those like her. So, she stole the information, and came to our world, which was neutral, and helped other people establish a network of neutral worlds to get around the gate-keeping assholes."

My belly sank. Shit.

Rosalind was casually running a smuggling ring among worlds that didn't have designations. At least that's what I guessed *neutral* meant.

It also didn't sound like she was working alone.

This felt well-planned. How did information like this get into a federal vault in the first place?

No. I knew how. People were curious. Someone discovered something, something happened, someone got freaked out and locked it up. Scientists had friends, so someone probably knew where it was and didn't have the same scruples and hired some thieves to get it for them.

Yeah, I hadn't sometimes laid awake at night considering the actual ramifications and implications of reliable travel between worlds.

I sucked in a breath. If she had had access to some sort of technology to smuggle people, that meant she might have been able to send me to Wes.

Fuck.

Fuck. Fuck. Fuck.

She didn't have to get rid of my omega so that I wasn't a biological problem. Rosalind didn't need to tell me that my soulmate was imaginary. She didn't have a genuine reason to keep me away from my theories.

All she had to do was send me back to this world. She could have sent me to her mom or fucked some shit up by sending me to the professor, or even just dropped me off at some Omega Center and told me that they'd help me find Wes.

So much anger and hatred coursed through me. They better keep me from her, or I might end up in jail.

Tears ran down my face.

"Hey. Don't cry. She was helping people. Mom's not mad at you, she just needs you to clear some things up," he remarked.

"Not mad at me? She's always mad at me. Is she here? Why would she come here if she could get in a lot of trouble?" That seemed risky.

"She's at Grandma's. I really like Grandma, she's nice. She says she hasn't met you, yet, though," he added.

It hit me. Her mom knew I'd been in contact with the professor. If Rosalind couldn't find me because my last name here had been changed to Thanukos, which Mrs. Silvers might not know, she must have sent my brothers to find out where I was...

"But what can I do?" I pushed. How did I even factor in with all of this?

"Something about the people who govern parallel world travel." He frowned.

Great. What could I do that could help her that would be worth risking everything?

Unless...

Had I unwittingly caused the Authority to come after her? Did she need me to be a character witness or convince them that she wasn't doing anything wrong?

I laughed bitterly. Like I had that sort of power. Still, it must have made her desperate.

"Everything is going to be okay, right?" he asked. "I have a job and a girlfriend at home. Um. I didn't think we were going to hold someone up at gunpoint or kidnap you or anything. I thought we were just going to talk to you and go home. We weren't even going to bring you back. That's why Mom met us here."

Odds were, she wanted to take me elsewhere–and didn't trust them to do it, which was why she took the risk of coming here.

"One of the people you were with is the guy you dreamt of, right? I never believed you, that he was real or other worlds were real. But they are, so… sorry?" Abel made his *I'm an innocent angel* face.

Could he just shut up? Was this my punishment? Death by Abel talking?

"He was there. I like this world, Abel. It's *my* world. I'm happy here. The world we grew up on might be neutral for Rosalind, but it's not good for people like me," I replied.

The door opened.

"Hey, I have to piss," Abel yelled.

Someone came in with Solomon and cuffed him to another ring on an opposite wall.

Solomon scowled from his spot on the bench. "Why am I cuffed, and she's not?"

"She's under omega law." The agent shrugged and left.

His head cocked. "You're an omega? How is that possible? Mom and Dad aren't omegas."

So, Solomon knew what omegas were.

"*My* bio-dad, the one you held up at gunpoint, is an omega. Me? Rosalind literally had my omega killed at wilderness camp," I countered.

Abel frowned. "I don't know what that means."

"You and Rosalind are running an interdimensional smuggling ring?" I prodded, wanting answers.

"What? No. That would break the law. We just help people sometimes." Solomon shrugged.

"For a fee?"

His eyes rolled. "She's allowed to have her own money."

"What do you need me to do?" I asked curiously.

"Look, we make most of our money off things that technically aren't illegal. Sure, sometimes we help people. But, all you need to do is tell them we're not doing anything wrong," Solomon answered.

Sure.

"You do know that the Temporal Authority puts people in prison for *helping*. The world we grew up in is Class IV." Yeah, I still didn't know why they thought I could help.

"Prison?" Abel looked worried.

"We won't go to prison." Solomon shook his head.

"I'm supposed to help my aunt, who stole me and hurt me so badly that it changed me genetically, and the two of you who were awful to me because..." The logic wasn't logicing.

"We're family," Abel said. "Look, sorry I was a shitty brother. No, really. In college, I realized that I was an enormous dick. I just was afraid to apologize to you, though Dad said I should. It's just a lot easier to be a dick when I'm around Sol and Mom."

Solomon shot him a look.

"Well, it is," Abel replied.

"Because of you, Mom's in trouble, so it's your responsibility to fix it." Solomon stared at me.

"What did I do? Rosalind 'died' before I even graduated." I put *died* in finger quotes.

"She left because we made some poor business decisions, and she went to help someone elsewhere while I handled things here. Then, just as she was ready to come back, people started inquiring after her and asking questions that could topple the whole thing," he told me.

I snorted. "I'm not helping you."

"You owe me," he scoffed.

"For what? What did I ever do to you, Sol? I was a good big sister. I never told on you, I didn't hurt you, I wasn't mean to you." All those things would get me into more trouble, anyway.

"What did you do to me? You were a freak, and no one wanted to be friends with me because of you. Also, I had to pick up the slack after you left," he snarled.

"Pick up the slack? You moved away and played football for your dream college." I snorted. "Freak? Honestly, I was pretty popular until after wilderness camp." Mostly because I was a cheerleader.

"Look, I fucking hate you. So just clear Mom and we'll let you go back to your weird life here," Solomon threatened.

"Or what? You're going to kidnap me and make me go back to a world where I'm dead? Also, do you understand that the Temporal Authority isn't anyone to mess with? Not to mention that Rosalind is *wanted* by two different federal agencies here. Her coming here is dumb. But it means she doesn't actually trust you enough to do it yourselves, so she has to risk her own life. And look, you blew it. Dumb and Dumber couldn't even kidnap me properly. Rosalind must be so proud," I retorted, angry, annoyed, and just done with all of this.

"Ow, Grace. That hurt. I know I was a dick when we were kids, but I try to be better. Hannah and I are going to move away, eventually. She makes me a nicer person. You'd like her," Abel stated.

"That doesn't fix everything you two did to me. Also, it's not her job to make you not be an asshole." I rubbed my forehead.

"Dr. Thanukos? We need to question you again," a female voice said as the door opened.

"Do I have a choice?" I got up and went to the door.

"Hey can I be uncuffed? I have to piss," Abel shouted.

They let me out, and I came face to face with the Bureau agent from the hospital. The one that out of frustration I told that I grew up somewhere else.

"You were telling the truth." She studied me. "Somehow you got to another world."

"Did you throw me in there to get them to talk?" I disliked being used like that. "What was in the vault?"

"Dr. Kepler's research on parallel worlds. Initially, no one thought anything of it. But at some point someone realized what it actually was and got very upset, because it was locked away for a reason," she replied as she led me down a hall.

Wait, I'd come across some of Dr. Kepler's research in my work for Spencer. She'd been a renowned quantum physicist.

"I don't know where to go from here. I have two people who aren't in the system. The mother and the grandmother aren't talking," she added.

I sucked in a breath. Rosalind was in custody. So was Mrs. Silvers. I realized I had no idea where Mrs. Silvers lived, where Thora had grown up.

"Though," the agent continued, "Rosalind is in the system. We can circumvent The Office of Designation Management until we get an answer from her. But of course, that really doesn't help, because they know that once they talk, we'll turn them over."

I wasn't sure I wanted her to die.

"Can I go home?" This made my head hurt. My heart hurt.

"Right now? No. This is a nightmare. But I can take you to one of your mates. Would you like that?" she asked.

That was better than nothing. "Yes, I'd like that very much."

Chapter Fifty-Eight

Wes

"Can I see Grace, please? Does she know Rosalind isn't dead?" I pleaded with the agent from the Bureau of Investigation when he came back into the room.

That was going to be a shock to her. It was a shock to me. But why should Rosalind be dead? It made sense with what I knew about her. She probably faked her death and let her sons do her dirty work.

"That's not my call." The agent handed me a cup of coffee.

I was in a small fishbowl of a conference room, not a mirrored interrogation room. I kept looking out the glass windows to see if Grace walked by. Sadness, anger, and annoyance kept shooting through my bond with her.

"Thanks. Can I see Rosalind, then?" I took a sip. It was late, and fatigue pressed down on me. Worry for Grace made my stomach hurt. Also, I wasn't sure where everyone else was.

The agent's look went skeptical. "Why?"

"She's not dead, so I'd really like to punch her." Okay, I wanted to do more than that. "Do you know what she did to my mate?"

I then proceeded to trauma-dump everything that Rosalind ever did to Grace, and to some extent, me, leaving out the entire parallel world thing.

The alpha agent sucked in a breath. "She hurt your mate so badly that even with a mate bond you thought she was dead?"

"Yeah, and Grace is now a gamma because of her. I know the law will take care of it, but do you blame me for wanting a piece of her?" I asked.

"That is fucking awful. If someone did that to my mate and I realized that she wasn't dead, I'd want my revenge, too," he agreed. "I don't know about punching her, but I think they're going to let your pack be together soon."

"Fair. I'd like to be with them, especially Grace, Evan, and Riley." Movement caught my eye, and my head whipped toward the glass.

Two agents dragged a cuffed woman down the hall. Grey streaked her dark blonde hair.

"I'm not the person you're looking for. I'm Thora Silvers, and I'm innocent. It was my sister, Rosalind, who did all those awful things, and she's dead. You executed her instead of me, which is fair because she robbed the vault, not me. Now please, let me see my sons," she begged.

While her words seemed the epitome of innocence, the hard look in her blue-grey eyes said otherwise.

Given I wasn't cuffed to the table, I stood and flew out of the unlocked door.

"What about your daughter, Rosalind? Oh wait, you don't have one, just your niece that you brutalized until she became a gamma. The niece you hurt so badly that she forgot her mate." My fist contacted her face.

Oh, that felt good.

"How dare you pretend to be Thora? How dare you come back for Grace? She owes you nothing. Not to mention she did *nothing* to you." I punched her again.

All the guards just stood there, though the one that was holding her looked to my guard.

The agent shrugged. "Making someone forget their mate and think they were a dream is shitty. Not to mention, you have to hurt an omega pretty badly to make them a gamma."

"Fuck, she did that, too? Fucking variant scum," one of them spat.

"You didn't have to hurt her. You didn't have to make her forget me." I punched her again.

"What was I supposed to do? There aren't any omegas where we were, and sending her back would ruin everything," Rosalind sneered.

"Really?" Grace barreled over and punched her *in the tits.* "You stole me and took me away to make it harder to find you."

"I didn't steal you, I bought you," she scoffed. "And yes, it was easier to convince the scientists to send me elsewhere as a single mom. Given I was wanted because I stole something for them, it was only right for them to use their technology to get me to safety, especially since they were already planning on sending themselves to other worlds. You brought this upon yourself, you know. From the moment you started nesting in the laundry, I knew you were going to be a fucking problem. Why did you have to be an omega instead of taking after your mom and me?"

"Why did you have to hurt me? You could have sent me back." Grace started to cry, and I wrapped my arms around her.

"Send you back here?" She cackled. "We were helping people escape; sending you here would have made people notice us. Not to mention you don't deserve to be with your mate."

Several people growled.

"Why wouldn't I deserve Wes?" Grace sobbed.

"You're too much like her. I was supposed to be the favorite. I'm the rose, she's the thorns. But *no,* everyone always loved Thora, who was nice and played the piano. It was always, *Ros, why can't you be like your sister?* It should have been them asking her why she couldn't be like me. I'm smarter, I'm better. She wouldn't even take the blame for me. Here, I thought we were sisters," she scoffed.

Wow.

Rosalind focused on Grace. "And you, everyone always just loved you. Mostly because of your name. If I hadn't slipped and called you *Grace* instead of *Cassidy,* it could have been different. Fucking religious hicks. I mean, sure you got me a good husband and a nice life. But then you ruined it, just like she ruined everything."

With a shriek, Rosalind lunged for Grace. The guards held her back but didn't take her away. No, people gathered like they were watching a serial drama.

"Me? I ruined your life? He divorced you because you disowned me for studying *math,*" Grace snapped.

"Maybe I was trying to save you. You have no idea what alphas are like, what pitiful lives omegas lead here," she added.

Grace laughed. "My life is just fine, no thanks to you. You're not even fazed that I'm here with Wes."

"Him? *That's* the alpha soulmate you dreamt of? Wow. Even your soulmate is pitiful. Though your mom picked a sorry-ass mate, too." Rosalind gave me a distasteful look.

"I love Grace more than you ever did." Letting go, I punched Rosalind again and blood trickled down her face.

"It's all thanks to me." She spit blood. "If I had known you were working for Rydor, I never would have sold them the equipment. That's how you got here, wasn't it? You used the equipment and somehow made friends with the Temporal Authority? I bet you turned them in, too, didn't you?"

Grace sucked in a breath. "Professor Jaffey got the equipment from you?"

"I should have let the camp kill you," she spat.

Grace looked Rosalind in the eyes. "You didn't want to talk to me, did you?"

"Oh, I did." Her eyes gleamed with hatred and malice.

"But you weren't going to let me come back." Grace's quiet words cut through the hall.

And my heart.

What?

"Why would I? You destroy everything. Even in another world, you still ruin things for me," she spat. "Why should you be allowed to be happy?"

"Everyone deserves to be happy," I fired back. What a miserable woman she was.

An agent who looked vaguely familiar rubbed her forehead. "This is above my paygrade. Get her out of here, and I need the recordings of all of this."

I pulled Grace to me. She cried into my shirt.

"Why did you make me play the piano if you hated Thora for playing the piano?" Grace looked over and hiccupped.

"I wanted to see if you were as good as her. You're not," she scoffed as they dragged her away.

Just... wow.

"Hey, it's okay. You're here with me, and safe. And you got to punch her in the tits. I'm proud of you for doing that," I soothed. It had been amazing to see her do that.

"I did, didn't I? It felt good. Also, my brothers are idiots." She pressed her face back into me.

"You don't ruin everything," I whispered. "You are my perfect princess peaches, and I'll love you to the end of the universe. I don't understand why she'd risk everything to come after you like that."

"I do." Her voice was a whisper. "First, she's used to getting her way. Second, she's fueled by the one emotion even stronger than love–hate."

That seemed stupid, to come to a world that wants to execute you just because you hated someone so much that you couldn't stand the idea of them being happy.

I hugged Grace tighter, sending all my love through the bond, trying to heal her with my soul.

"Hey, who are you and why are you here?" an agent demanded as a bunch of people approached us.

"This is now our investigation," someone stated. "The building is locked down. You all need to report to the main conference room."

They all smelled weird and looked like Agent Weigmier.

Oh shit. The fucking Temporal Authority was here.

Chapter Fifty-Nine

Grace

"You're not taking me away." I held onto Wes. "My pack and I are innocent. I thought she was dead. I had no part in this."

"Are you Dr. Grace Ellington?" a female voice inquired. "I'm Jira. You're going to be okay. Just come with me."

My arms tightened around Wes. "He comes with me."

"Oh, is this Fade? Hello, Fade." Jira's dark hair was in a pixie cut. She wore a dress, not a uniform or a suit like Agent Weigmier.

"I'd like to stay with her." Wes didn't let go of me.

"Dr. Ellington, your family isn't under investigation. In fact, you have helped us solve several questions that we've been asking since the incident you were involved with back on world 1218," an agent said.

I couldn't remember her name, but I recalled her vaguely from my time at the Authority.

"Go with Jira," the agent said. "It will be okay."

"I'm with the Precious Population Protection Protocol unit. I work a lot with Alister. Don't worry, I won't hurt you." Jira gave me a soft smile.

Alister? Who the fuck was Alister?

"It's the cat, right? The cat's name is Alister?" It's all I could think of.

Jira blinked. "What cat? I was speaking of Agent Weigmier."

"His first name is Alister?" Wes chuckled.

Agent Weigmier had a first name?

"Please?" Jira pleaded.

I noticed she had a tote bag and wasn't dressed like the others. Wait, there was one other person not in a uniform or a suit, who also had a tote bag. She spoke to a sharp-featured, uniformed woman with blue eyes, black hair in a bun, and vampirically pale skin. Huh. I didn't remember people like that from my time at the Authority. Though the woman with a bun reminded me a little bit of Gloria in processing.

"Will I be returned to Wes?" I prodded. It was probably better to cooperate than resist.

"Yes, I just need to talk to you about some things."

"As long as it's here and not back at your station. Love, you, Wes." I gave Wes a kiss and followed Jira.

She led me to a room that could be where they questioned children. It was comfortable, with a couch and chair, along with toys and some child-sized furniture.

"Hi. Are you okay?" Jira got out a little tablet that reminded me of the one Agent Weigmier had.

"I'd like to go home." I plopped down on the couch.

She took a chair. "I'm sure this evening has been taxing. We'll get through this as speedily as we can. I don't think we'll need to go to the station. Now, do you wish to stay with your family, or would you like to be taken elsewhere?"

"I'd like to stay with them," I replied.

Jira tapped on her tablet. "Do they treat you well? Do you have access to your world's currency or a job to earn your own? Are your needs being met?"

Her questions reminded me of Mrs. Beekman's.

"Yes, yes, and yes."

She asked me a few other questions, then got her tote. "Would you like some snacks?"

Jira took some strange snacks out of her bag and put them on the table. I stared at them.

"Also, I have some comfort items. Would you like a blanket, plushie, or some socks?" she offered, adding more items.

Was Jira a social worker?

"Jira, what do you do for the Authority?" I picked up a box that was filled with the same star candy I'd gotten last time.

"I'm a wellbeing assessor," she replied, with a smile. "Given the delicate nature of your status and designation, I've been sent to make sure that you are comfortable, treated appropriately, and that the proper amount of discretion is used."

Yep. She was an inter-dimensional advocate. One Agent Weigmier sent to make sure all the work he did to erase my footprint and keep me with my family wasn't undone.

"Oh, Agent Weigmier has a message for you. I hope that you know what it means because I don't," she laughed. "Um, he said to let you know that if Eugene is sleeping in your office, to please give him back to one of us."

Jira gave me an expectant look.

Who the fuck was Eugene?

I thought for a moment. Oh. The cat. I made a joke about the cat being a shifter named Eugene who'd snuck into Agent Weigmier's office for a nap.

"No, Eugene isn't in my office. But if I see him, I'll tell him to return to duty," I replied as I ate some candy. No, I didn't steal the cat. I'd already told him that.

"I'll let him know." She tapped on her tablet. "You can sleep a little if you like."

"I'd like to see my mates," I stated.

Jira nodded. "We need to talk to everyone, neutralize the situation, and get the rest of the answers we need. Also, another wellbeing assessor is here, given you have an omega and child in your family."

Well, that was nice. I didn't get that sort of treatment when I was being held by the Authority, even after I turned witness.

Taking one of the offered blankets, I curled up on the couch. But I couldn't sleep. Fuck. Rosalind wasn't dead. I'd punched her in the tits. Which felt *good*.

Still, Rosalind wasn't dead.

I reached out through the bonds to make sure everyone was okay and got reassurance and love in response.

It all came down to jealousy, didn't it? Rosalind had been jealous of my bio-mom, and I reminded her too much of her. Also, I had the audacity to be an omega.

And the potential to upend all her plans.

Fuck-a-duck, this was a mess.

Finally, the door opened.

"Dr. Ellington. I'm Agent Cora. I'm not sure if you recall me." The agent, who seemed familiar, walked in, closing the door behind her. Pulling over a chair, she joined us.

"A little?" What was I even supposed to say? I had no idea if I was supposed to admit that I remembered everything. Though clearly, Agent Weigmier and Jira knew.

"One thing that concerned us about the events that happened on world 1218, was that we didn't know where your colleagues got the technology. They admitted that they didn't invent the devices after it was proved that you didn't create them with your research. All that your colleagues told us was that they bought it off someone but didn't actually know how to get in touch with the sellers. Which was concerning because this has been happening for a few decades across several worlds. So many things point to world 1218 playing a role in these events. But it's puzzling because it's Class IV. Not to mention most of the worlds involved are Class IV or V and Type H. Thanks to you, we've figured it out," she explained.

"Me?" Sitting up, I looked through the snacks on the table.

"We've had someone undercover in this world for a bit, because people here keep taking part in smuggling rings and because of Dr. Kepler's discovery. When our undercover agent realized what was in the vault, and that the person who stole it escaped to another world, during a part of the smuggling ring on this world that was especially problematic, along with several scientists, things came together," she said.

Oh. Well, that fit with what the agent from the Bureau told me.

"So, Dr. Kepler discovered other worlds, but did so more concretely than Dr. Thanukos and Dr. Katsopolis, and whoever else in Europe discovered stuff?" I ate the weird little cookies in a pink bag.

"Yes. She was actually working with a team from our Outreach department. But one day, some events here made her realize that your world wasn't ready, so she locked her research in a vault and left it behind. Dr. Kepler didn't destroy it, hoping one day your world would be able to handle it," Agent Cora told me. "We didn't know the data had been stolen."

"Okay. So, my aunt stole it, and what?" I blinked. Though she said that she'd been hired by the scientists, then asked her to take us with them.

"Within the omega-smuggling ring, was another smuggling ring that was less altruistic. As far as we can tell, Rosalind Ellington and her brother were hired to steal the information from the vault. After realizing its value, and the death of her family members, she used the information as a bargaining tool for safe passage for you and her. She became a very active part of an information, people, and equipment smuggling ring across a number of Class IV and Class V worlds. They were quite clever, working hard to circumvent our laws, and mostly moving among mostly Type H worlds that weren't monitored by the Authority," she explained.

"Oh." Now Rosalind's comment about people noticing if I was brought here made sense. This world was being monitored.

So did Solomon's comment about Rosalind making a bad business decision and needing to help elsewhere. She sold stuff to the wrong person and needed to escape the heat. However, she only removed herself and not Solomon. So telling.

Just like her sending Abel to get me.

I looked at Agent Cora. "Rosalind and her friends were selling the information, and sometimes the equipment, to move through worlds. Which isn't technically illegal?"

"Yes. It's the act of moving between worlds and not sharing the information or technology that's illegal because we never thought we'd need to make it illegal for Class IV and Class V worlds to do so, given that these worlds aren't even aware of these things. Obviously, we need to fix that. We can't be having worlds have free access to world numbers, coordinates, schematics, and such without fully understanding what they're doing," she replied.

"Okay, that makes sense." Though I'm sure some moving of worlds happened, otherwise how would the information be disseminated?

It was also so silly that Rosalind didn't know I worked for Rydor Corp. After all, Dad knew where I worked. That was probably why my brother got 'weird' after I 'died'–he realized how and why.

"Please don't kill us or stabby-stab us or blow things up. My family, and I, are innocent," I pleaded, needing to protect my family.

Jira nodded. "You won't be harmed."

"The good agents of this world will forget the things that we need them to, but there is no need to level the building. Probably just erase some files. Your immediate family in this world will not be harmed. The men who say they're your brothers, Rosalind Silvers Ellington, and her mother, are another matter," Agent Cora said.

I sighed. "Can you just erase Abel's memory and send him home to his girlfriend? He's an idiot, but he also didn't know about this until yesterday. They told him about it because I'm guessing he's not illegal in this world."

Agent Cora looked at her little tablet. "Abel, and not Solomon?"

"As far as I know, Solomon was working with Rosalind and fully aware of what was happening. Abel does what Solomon and Rosalind tell him and honestly thought they were just going to talk to me." I rubbed my forehead. "That doesn't deserve prison. Though if you can make him nicer, that wouldn't hurt."

"Noted." She tapped on her tablet

"Maybe do the same to Mrs. Silvers? I don't know what her role is in this."

She nodded. "I see."

"Um, are you going to try Solomon and Rosalind?" I was curious about how all this worked. Also, Rosalind would absolutely turn witness for a lesser sentence.

"Yes. They will most likely be found guilty. If they are found innocent, a request has been made for Rosalind to be remanded to this world to be tried for her crimes. We are unsure about Solomon. If found innocent, his memories will probably be erased and he'll be returned to his world of residence," she told me.

"Sounds good to me." Even though I'd once grumbled to Agent Weigmier about remanding Rosalind here for her crimes, I'd rather she rot in inter-dimensional prison.

She asked me a few more questions. Jira disappeared and returned with a sandwich and some coffee for me. I ate it while Agent Cora finished up.

"We should be able to give you back to your mates soon," Agent Cora said. "Thank you for cooperating."

"Of course." This felt too easy, but wasn't I due for easy?

Food finished, it was once again just me and Jira.

The full weight of everything hit me. Curling up on the ccuch, I began to cry.

Chapter Sixty

Jett

I was exhausted. I'd been with Evan and Riley until there'd clearly been an agency change. One that I was pretty sure was the Temporal Police. It was either them or the Agents in Glasses.

They'd separated me from Evan and Riley and asked me a bunch of questions. Quickly the agents realized that I wasn't very interesting and left me alone. Now, I was in a small room with a recliner, a refrigerator, a magazine and book rack, and a tea and snack station.

Yeah, I was pretty sure they were holding me in the lactation room. The Bureau only had a very small set of offices here. Once in a while my work brought me here.

But, there was reading material and snacks. Evan seemed fine through the bond, though Brennan was agitated.

I looked through the packages of healthy snacks. A lactation cookie wasn't going to hurt me, right?

Helping myself to two cookies and a cup of tea, I went back to the recliner wishing that I had my phone. But I didn't, so I picked up the romance novel I'd started.

I could see why Grace liked romance novels. Also, it helped me keep my mind off the fact that we were being investigated by otherworldly police–and that I was separated from my pack.

What would our fate be? Hopefully, we'd just be let go.

The person I worried about most was Grace. Her brothers had somehow gotten here. Her mom might be alive.

Those brothers of hers had also shot me with some sort of freeze beam, though I was fine now. A little mad at myself that I'd gotten shot. But fine.

I was proud of Evan going off after Grace like that. I'd hate to think of what might have happened to her if he hadn't.

Did he have to shoot out my tires? But whatever. Hopefully, the damage to my car and Brennan's motorcycle was minimal.

At least Evan and Grace were okay. Riley had shown me the video someone had taken. While I knew Evan had been in the military, I didn't realize he'd done cool shit like that. He and Wes didn't talk about their time in the Army much beyond their relationship and Evan's desk job.

Finally, the door opened.

"Hello." The pale woman with the dark bun who stood there in front of me was probably not human.

"Hi." I waved.

"The head of your family has requested you. You are a snack, yes?" she asked.

I had no idea what she was asking. Did she want to know if I'd had a snack? Needed a snack? Was she telling me that I was sexy?

"Um, yes?" What else did I say? I grabbed the book and stuffed some snacks in my pocket in case Brennan didn't have any.

"Good. Please come." The unnamed agent led me out of the room and down the hall.

She led me to a door and unlocked it. The room had a couple of couches and a small conference table.

"Here is your snack." She pushed me into the room and left.

"Jett." Brennan hugged me tightly.

"Hi, Honey. You asked for me?" I kissed him, happy to be with him, finally. I hadn't seen him since the hospital.

His look went sheepish. "I asked for something to eat. The mini fridge has water and soda but no food."

"Got it. She's a vampire, and because I'm a beta, she thinks I'm your dinner. I'm pretty sure I've seen that movie." I grinned. "Oh, maybe she wasn't a vampire? But I would think vampires would look like her. She's not human, I'm sure." That was what just happened, right?

Brennan thought for a moment. "I agree with that. Grace said there are lots of different people out there."

"Good thing I have actual snacks." I took them out of my pocket.

"Thank you. How did you get them?" He held one up to read the label.

"I was in the lactation room. It could be worse." I plopped down on the couch. "What is going on? Have they told you anything?"

"They've told me a lot, and this is wild. I'm worried about Grace." His brows furrowed as he ate a package of dried fruit.

With a sigh, he sat on the couch with me. He filled me in on how Rosalind was very much alive and part of a group of people across multiple worlds that were selling information and equipment to anyone who wanted it.

"That was what they stole from the vault? Inter-dimensional information?" I asked.

"Yes."

"Shit. What are they going to do with Grace's brothers and Rosalind? Us?" I went to the mini fridge and got some water.

"I think we'll be okay." His look went pensive. "Her brothers and Rosalind? I'm guessing the same thing will happen to them that happened to Nick."

"Do you think we can punch Rosalind?" My fists thirsted for justice.

Brennan laughed. "Wes and Grace already did. Apparently, Grace got her right in the tits."

Pride welled up inside me. "That's my Babydoll."

As he ate the rest of the snacks, Brennan told me everything he knew.

Finally, the door opened.

"Here's some sustenance for the snack. Can we bring you the precious? She needs her leader." Vampire lady came in and put three sandwiches and a cup of what could be coffee on the table.

"Thank you. Yes, you can bring Grace here. What of the others? Can you bring them here, as well?" Brennan asked.

The precious? But she was. I grabbed a sandwich and started eating.

"The big precious and the child are with the wellbeing assessor. Your child is quite rare. She would make a good agent," vampire lady added. "One of your brothers is being moved to be with them. The older one is with Agent Cora."

Okay, Wes was with Evan and Riley. Spencer was being questioned still. Precious must mean omega?

"Riley is pretty special. We'd like to be all together as soon as possible," he remarked.

"Understandable. Your people are well." With a nod, she left.

I tossed Brennan one of the sandwiches and took a sip of coffee. "Want some?"

"Sure." Brennan took a sip.

I eyed the other sandwich. No. We'd wait and see if Grace was hungry.

A few moments later, the door opened. There stood a woman in a dress with a tote bag. Grace was with her.

"Here you go. You'll be safe with them," she assured Grace. "Have some snacks." She put a handful of snacks on the conference table, along with a blanket.

"Thank you, Jira." Grace ran right into my arms. "Jett."

"I've got you, Babydoll." I held her tight.

"If you need anything, just ask for me. I'll remain here until you're returned home." Jira left, closing the door behind her.

"Hey, I have you," I whispered to her as she whimpered. "You're with Bren and me, and we have you."

Brennan put the coffee on the table. "You're okay. Do you want some food?"

Grace shook her head and went to him. "I had some already."

Taking the last sandwich, I tore it in half and gave part of it to Brennan. I stuffed the other into my mouth.

"Are you sure?" Brennan asked, pulling her onto the couch.

"I'm fine." She curled into his lap as he ate the rest of the sandwich.

No, she wasn't fine. I could smell how out of sorts she was.

Grabbing the blanket, snacks, and coffee, I joined them on the couch. I put the blanket over her and set the coffee and snacks on the little end table.

She sniffed and settled into us, quickly falling asleep. We finished the snacks, coffee, and the rest of the waters from the fridge.

"Grace doesn't smell good. I'm afraid she's going to spiral." Brennan stroked her hair.

A whine escaped her throat.

"What do you need, Babydoll?" I asked her. No, we didn't need her spiraling.

"I want to go home and be knotted," she whispered. Her scent had grown very sweet as she slept.

"You're burning up, Little Butterfly," Brennan said softly.

"Can we be all together? I want to be all together." Her hand went down Brennan's pants.

"We can make a big cuddle pile in the sunken living room if you just want to sleep," I said. "If you want more than sleeping, I'm not sure, other than maybe going to the nest in the basement? That has an enormous bed."

Brennan sucked in a breath. Yeah, she had her hand around his cock, didn't she?

"I want to be fucked by everyone, a lot. Then I want crepes." It looked like she was trying to get Brennan's pants off.

"That sounds like a good plan. Do you need something now to feel better?" Grabbing the blanket, Brennan tried to put it between him and the couch.

Grace needed to be fucked. I could smell it.

I helped him get his pants off, her panties off, and put the blanket on the couch.

"There you go, let me fuck you so that you feel better," Brennan told her, as he lowered her onto him. "When we go home, you can be fucked by anyone you want, as much as you'd like. Spencer will absolutely make crepes for breakfast."

"Yes, please," she moaned, as she moved up and down on him.

Sweetness continued to fill the room, almost cloying. Brennan's eyes got a little glassy, his pheromones on full blast.

The door opened. Shit.

"Here is your brother. Oh, you're just in time." The vampire agent pushed Spencer in.

Spencer looked bewildered as the door closed behind us. I wasn't sure Grace and Brennan even noticed.

"She's not okay," I murmured. Fuck. Had Spencer ever seen someone else having sex with Grace?

"No, she's not. I'd rather have that than a spiral, given what's happened tonight. We'll just need to make sure that if it takes a turn for the worse, we get her to the hospital immediately."

Grace sighed and closed her eyes as she and Brennan clearly finished.

"What are you talking about?" I frowned at Spencer.

Spencer's expression grew tense as his nostrils flared. "I think she might be going into heat."

Chapter Sixty-One

Spencer

It took every ounce of control to not pounce on Grace–or growl at Brennan–as my alpha instincts threatened to take over. Her scent made my mouth water, as my cock strained against my pants. My hands fisted so that I wouldn't rip her away from him and fuck her on the conference table.

Mine.

I pushed those thoughts away. Obviously, if she needed Brennan, then she should have him. *Her* needs were the priority, not mine.

After all, Grace's fragile world had been shattered–by selfishness, narcissism, and unbridled hatred.

Agent Cora had told me everything, and my heart broke for my good doctor.

All of this was probably driving Grace to seek comfort. As I told Jett, I'd much rather her go into heat than spiral.

The doctor had said that due to the reset, if her body ever went into heat that it could come at any time without warning. Powerful emotions were known to bring on a heat.

At the same time, deep concern tugged at my heart. The reset didn't guarantee that she'd have a healthy heat. Could her body even take it?

My good doctor just couldn't catch a break.

"Are you okay, Spence?" Jett inquired.

"We need to get her home." I remembered how small she'd looked in the hospital bed. How they'd given her countless medicines over and over to help repair everything that had been done to her.

Jett nodded. "I think she's okay for now. I don't smell anything like I smelt that night."

"Good. We still have to be careful with her. Also, we need to care for her heart and soul. I'd promised her that we would." It would be difficult to do that here.

"We will, Spence. How do you propose that we get out of here?" Jett glanced over at the door.

The more comfortable she was, the easier it would be for her to have a full and proper heat. Not to mention, no one should have their first heat in a conference room at the Bureau of Investigation.

"Spencer." Brennan looked over at me, surprised.

"I'm going to see if they'll let us leave." I'd try reason first.

Jett's eyebrows rose. "Do you think they will?"

"We won't know unless we try." I knocked on the door.

A woman in a dress answered. "Is everything all right?"

"No. We need to take Grace home. She is so upset that it is making her unwell," I explained.

"Oh." Her look grew concerned. "Earlier, she cried so much that she threw up, so I brought her here. It's not enough? I think we can bring everyone else here."

Mmmm, no, given Riley was with us. Riley. We needed to take her somewhere else. Due to the late hour, all I could think of was the sister pack.

"I think it would be best to let us go. Or at least let myself, Brennan, or Wes leave with her. She needs to be at home. Grace can be... delicate and she needs an alpha." I wasn't sure if telling anyone that Grace was in heat would mean anything. Certainly, I didn't want to explain specifics about her health to strangers.

"Many like her are. Let me check and see where things are," she replied.

"Could we have our phones back, please? Or could I at least have mine?" We needed to be prepared.

"I will." She closed the door.

"Well, that was reasonable," Jett muttered.

I got the feeling that if you weren't breaking their laws, they could be quite cordial.

"Spence?" Grace's hand reached out, searching for me.

"Darling?" Taking her hand, I kissed it. "You're not feeling well?"

"My heart hurts." She started to cry.

Leaning in, I kissed her temple, Brennan still right there under her. Not that I had an issue with it, I just wasn't used to it. But they were my packmates, my family. Given she'd made no secret of wanting all of us, it was time to adjust.

"Someone is checking to see if we can leave." I smoothed her hair. Her forehead burned, and her scent was still cloyingly sweet, but not sickly.

"I want to go home." Tears pricked her eyes. "Rosalind hates me so much that she risked her own life because she didn't want me to be happy."

"Fuck Rosalind," Brennan told her. He was naked from the waist down, and possibly still knotted to her.

"Don't let her live for free in your head, she's not worth it." Jett knelt by the couch.

"That's good advice," I agreed.

The door opened, and that same woman handed me a bag with phones and purses. "I can give you your communication devices. They'd very much like to keep everyone until we can corroborate stories."

"I'm unsure that Grace will be okay for that long," I replied. If this relied on Rosalind talking, we'd be here for too long.

"Noted. I'll do what I can." She closed the door.

Jett looked up at me from his spot on the floor. "Um, a weird space agency literally took over the Bureau of Investigation's building. People *will* notice as they show up for work in a few hours."

"If they're giving us our phones, they either have no idea what we can do with them here, or they're about ready to let us go and not erase our memories." Brennan put his pants back on.

"Not erasing my memories would be nice," Jett agreed.

"Call out of work for tomorrow, and probably Monday as well." I took out my phone, put the bag on the conference table, and sat on the other couch.

Grace got off the couch and climbed into my lap. "Can I have tomorrow off? I'm tired and want knots and crepes."

"Anything you wish." I kissed the top of her head, as I went into the program on my phone and marked Grace, Wes, Riley, and me off. At least today was Friday, and we'd have the weekend. Though who knew how long it would last? I also marked us off for Monday.

Grace curled in my lap and went to sleep, smelling of sex, Brennan, and very ripe peaches.

"We'll need someone to watch Riley and the chickens," I said as I rescheduled my meetings.

Brennan grabbed his phone and looked at me. "Don't the Chicken Tender people come and get them? Like dog boarding, only with chickens?"

"Usually, they come to your house twice a day. Given the chicks are not in the coop yet, it's best to ask the sister pack to take them." I added a few basics to my online grocery cart for immediate express delivery. We'd worry about the post-heat feast later.

"Why are we doing this?" Brennan was on his phone.

"Spencer thinks that she's going to go into heat." Jett grabbed his phone and sat with Brennan.

Grace looked up at me. "Do you really? What if I get sick?"

"That's why we need to get you out of here. We'll tend to you at home, and if you get sick, we'll take you to the Center, just like we talked about back in the hospital." I stroked her hair. "No matter what happens, we'll take care of your heart and soul."

"I just want dicks and crepes," she mumbled, pressing her face into me. "You smell good enough to lick."

I gave Brennan a look as if to say, *See?*

"Understood." He got back on his phone.

"Dicks and crepes? That can be arranged," I soothed.

"How do we get home? My bike and Jett's car have been towed to the repair shop. Is yours still at the restaurant?" Brennan asked.

"It's here. We might need to hire a car for the others." We had little time. I could feel the tension building inside her through the bond, like a wire ready to break at any moment.

The moment it did, my cordiality and patience with the Temporal Authority were done. While I was grateful that they hadn't taken us to another world for questioning, we were on a tight schedule.

A pitiful whine ripped through the room, and her scent exploded into a cloud of need, arousal, and desire. *Fuck.*

The urge to fuck her over the table returned.

"Shit." Brennan sat up, expression tight.

I put my phone in my pocket and stood with her in my arms. "Jett, grab the bag of phones. Her purse is in there, right?"

"Yeah. Hers and Riley's." Jett got up and grabbed it. "I'd like to get my gun back. They took it when we were brought here."

I rapped on the door. The same woman opened it.

She frowned at me. "Is she still ill?"

"Yes." I pushed the door open, clutching Grace, and strode out. "We have to get her home." I kept moving, not looking to see if Brennan and Jett followed.

All of my instincts screamed at me to get her home and keep her safe.

"You can't leave yet." Agent Cora tried to block me in the hall. A couple of large, armed guys who smelled like dogs were with her.

"Agent Cora, she needs to get home before she becomes serious-ly ill. Get us the others," I demanded, voice hard, as I slipped past her and kept moving. I didn't use my bark because I wasn't sure if it would work on them.

Did I know how to get out of here? Not really.

"He's right," Brennan added from behind me. "You can send someone in a few days to follow up. We need Wes, Evan, and Riley, now."

"Um, Agent Cora, I think you need to let them take her. Or this could be bad," one of the big guys said.

Her scent filled my nostrils as every part of me ached to get her under me and sink my knot into her over and over again.

Grace whined again. "Alpha."

"I see. Please try not to leave your residence," Agent Cora called.

"We might need to go to the hospital," Brennan called back. "Jett, you get Evan, Wes, and Riley, and meet us at home. Lexi will get Riley and the chickens. I'm going with Spencer."

Their offices were on the second floor of a government building, and I took the stairs. Footsteps followed me.

"Shit, you're fast," Brennan panted.

"Spencer, will you take me home and knot me?" Grace whined, trying to get her hands down my pants as I carried her down to the parking garage.

"Oh, I will, Darling." I found my phone and activated the alert so I could find my car.

"Can Brennan watch?" She squeezed my dick.

I gasped, looking for flashing lights. There. "That's up to Brennan."

"Whatever you want, Grace," Brennan assured, trying to keep stride with me.

Using my phone to unlock it, I found my key fob in the glove box.

"Grace, sit in the back with Brennan, okay?" I put her in the back and buckled her. Brennan climbed in. I didn't wait for him to put on his seatbelt before I sped out of the garage.

"Mmmm, where's my fidget toy?" Grace murmured, leaning over to kiss him.

Her peachy scent suffocated me, and I rolled down all the windows, trying to concentrate on the road and not on the fact that her hand was down Brennan's pants, his pine scent thick with arousal.

"Jett's getting Wes, Evan, and Riley." Brennan glanced at his phone.

"Good boy," she whispered, eyes closing. "I wanna be the filling in a Brennan and Spencer sandwich."

"Whatever you wish, Darling," I said. "Brennan, if you need to have her in the car, please go ahead."

"How did you get your car here?" Brennan gasped. "Gentle, Little Butterfly."

"Sorry." Grace giggled.

"The valet from the restaurant brought it to the hospital. One of the police officers kindly brought it to the Bureau for me. I should send them gift baskets."

"I don't feel good," Grace whined.

"We'll be home soon," I soothed. Given it was the wee hours, there weren't many cars, so I challenged the speed limit.

"What do you need, do you need my cock?" Brennan unbuckled her and got her down on the floor so he could feed her his dick.

Even with the windows open, our scents and pheromones were suffocating.

We pulled into the garage. I noticed the groceries by the front door, and I texted the group chat to bring them inside.

"Oh, that's so good, Little Butterfly," Brennan praised. "Let's get you inside." He scooped her up and went inside. "Downstairs?"

"Yes." The nest she and Evan had been fixing up would be the best place.

"I want dicks," Grace sang. "Dick, dicks, dicks, dicks, dicks."

We went downstairs into the nest in the basement, which I'd never been in before, though I knew Wes and Evan had done a bunch of work on it. I turned on the lights. A giant bed, with pink and green brocade bedding, lots of pillows, and things clearly stolen from all of us, sat in the center. The walls were mauve. Art hung on the walls, and the couch and chair covers matched the walls. A pretty little chaise was there as well.

Oh, I could see fucking her on that.

Brennan tossed Grace onto the bed and began kissing her. I texted the group chat and took off my clothes, putting them on the chair.

I held out my hands as Brennan tossed me his and Grace's clothes, and I added them to the pile. My phone went onto the nightstand. Looking around, I adjusted the mood lighting. Yes, everything seemed like it would be nice and comfortable.

Another whine cut through the room. "Please, Daddy, I want my knots now. I've been so good."

"Oh, yes, you have, Baby Girl." I joined them on the bed and kissed her. She kissed me hungry, pawing at my body. "Tell me what you want."

"Sandwich." She gave both of us a challenging look, as if daring us to say *no.*

As if I could say *no* to her.

"Sandwich? We both have a hole with you in the middle?" I clarified, wanting to make sure I understood her.

"Yes, please." She nodded.

"We can do that." Whatever made her happy.

"Is there lube in here or do I need to run upstairs?" Brennan, bare-ass naked, rolled over and opened the nightstand. That was an impressive number of piercings he had there.

He pulled out a bottle of lube and a tub of wipes. "Look at that. She and Evan must have stocked it as part of their planning."

Grace pushed me down on the bed and kissed me, straddling me. Her eyes gleamed hungry as she eyed my body as if it were a giant hot fudge sundae.

"Is this how you want me, Darling?" I accepted her greedy kisses as our three scents combined. Oh, how I yearned to bury myself inside her. *Soon.* For now, I'd let her set the pace.

Straddling me, she slid down onto my cock. Bliss coated her face. "Oh, yes."

"That does feel wonderful, Darling," I moaned, as she seated herself fully on me.

Grace moved up and down, undulating her hips. Eyes half-lidded, her sweet scent suffocated me, as she started singing about dicks again. Brennan had the lube and was working her ass.

"You good, Spence?" Brennan said softly.

"I'm okay." My hands went to her hips to guide her up and down. "You?"

"I..." His eyes went glassy. "I don't know if I can stay in control."

"Why would you need to? All that matters is making sure she gets what she needs." I kissed my baby girl mid-chorus. "What a lovely song, Darling."

Ever since she'd asked me about joining in on her heat, I'd done my research. Weren't you supposed to surrender? After all, our inner-alphas wouldn't let us hurt her or leave her wanting.

"Okay. I love you, Little Butterfly, if I'm too much, I'm sorry." Brennan worked his fingers in her ass.

"You won't. You're my good boy." Tilting her head back, she batted her eyelashes at him as she continued to bounce on my cock. Grace felt so good riding me.

"Brennan, you know what she needs," I reassured him. Grace's want shot through me, and I quickened the pace.

She whined again. "Bren, I want you inside me."

"Of course." Brennan kissed her. Grabbing the wipes, he cleaned off his hands and lubed up his cock.

"You feel extraordinary," Brennan gasped as he entered her.

My mouth tackled hers as we fucked our sweet girl. The two of us got into a rhythm, as he fucked her ass while she continued to ride me. Passion and desire consumed me as she orgasmed.

"Knot me, please?" she keened.

"Whatever your heart needs." My mouth crashed against hers. Grabbing her hips tight, my hands pushed her down onto my knot. I gasped. While knotting her was always wonderful, this was sublime. My forehead tipped to hers as I flooded her, and my love for her, my need to satisfy her, consumed me.

Mine.

"Come for me so I can knot you, too. Does my little butterfly need two cocks in her at once," Brennan growled, his hand reaching around to rub her clit.

"Alpha." Her head tilted back as another orgasm took her. Her pussy spasmed, squeezing my cock in a way that made me gasp.

"Good girl," Brennan praised as he slammed his pierced cock into her ass.

"Yes," she moaned. Slumping forward, laying her head on my chest.

"You took him so well, Darling." I kissed her. "Are you okay?"

"I liked that. I will want more," she warned.

"Fine with me." Brennan lay half on top of her.

"Whatever you wish." I threw the blanket over the three of us, as I kissed her again. Brennan stroked her hair.

A phone rang in the background, but none of it mattered. All that was important was the woman on top of me.

Chapter Sixty-Two

Brennan

My hands clamped down on the hips of the delightful woman underneath me. On her knees, she sucked Spencer's cock hungrily. Spencer's hands tangled in her hair, as he gasped. Oh, she looked so pretty on her knees, mouth full, as we pleased and satisfied her.

Every gasp, every sweet whimper, filled my heart full. My balls smacked her ass as I had her from behind.

Peaches, leather, and pine cocooned us. Someone might be knocking on the door, but I ignored it. A phone rang, but whatever. I reached around her to toy with her clit, so she'd make more cute little noises.

Yes, I needed to focus on ensuring that my little butterfly had enough knots. Oh, I felt so fucking good making her come, giving her knots, hearing her plead for us.

She felt so fucking good. So wet, so slick, so fucking responsive.

Grace gasped, my other hand toyed with her nipple, rolling and plucking at it. *Mine.* She was mine. Mine to fuck. Mine to knot. Mine to satisfy.

I trailed kisses up her spine as I continued to pound her. She made another happy noise as I sucked on her neck.

"More," she gasped, mouth full of cock like the good girl she was.

"As you wish." I continued to suck on her neck, nipping and biting on the beautiful blank space that begged for me to bite her. My teeth ached to mark her.

An orgasm shot through her, and her wet pussy squeezed me in all the right ways. I nipped her shoulder to let her know how much I loved it when she did that.

"I'm going to cum, Baby Girl. Suck it all down for Daddy," Spencer instructed, his hand holding her chin, the other in her hair.

His scent flared and he sighed. "That's my good baby girl."

"You swallowed him down so well," I praised.

"More," she gasped as his cock left her mouth.

Kissing her, Spencer grabbed the lube and came over to me.

I growled a little at this intrusion. *Mine.*

Spencer rolled his eyes and patted my hip. "Make room."

He lubed up his cock, his knot re-inflating. I went back to fucking my girl, making sure that my lips paid attention to her neck and shoulder.

"Bren, I... I want you..." She moaned as I nipped at the juncture of her neck and shoulder.

"You have me," I promised, giving her another nip.

Spencer slid into her ass. "Better?"

"I feel so full. I love my alphas," she sighed as we fucked her, side-by-side.

"And we love you," Spencer assured.

"I love you so fucking much." Yes, I should let her know how much I loved her.

My fingers kept toying with her clit. My bites grew harder and harder and my pace became faster and faster. My love for her, my yearning, my need to be joined with her forever consumed me. There were noises coming from somewhere, but I ignored them because they weren't her.

"More," she gasped. "Harder. I... I need..."

"Do you need our knots?" Spencer asked.

Oh, yes, she did. But she needed more than that.

"Please, Alphas, knot me," she moaned.

I thrust my knot deep inside her, as she orgasmed again. Yes, that was what my little butterfly needed, more knots, repeatedly. Fortunately, I was happy to oblige. Oh, it felt so good to be lodged inside her. Spencer knotted her as well, murmuring sweet things to her.

"Brennan, I need..." Grace didn't have to finish her whine. I knew exactly what to do.

My teeth clamped down on her as I gave in, sinking my teeth deep into her flesh. The bond sizzled inside me like a fuse, then exploded in my heart like fireworks as I flooded the bond with love, so that she'd know without words how I felt about her. *Mine.*

"Bren..." she gasped.

Grace laid down flat, the two of us on top of her, trapping her to the bed, still knotted to her.

Oh, this was the best feeling, her stuck between me and the bed, unable to move between my knot and my body. Satisfaction shot through our bond. *She liked it.*

Languidly, I licked the bond mark. "Are you all right, Little Butterfly?"

"The best. I want to bite you back next. I want you both in my pussy at the same time." Grace made a happy noise.

That seemed probable.

"You marked her," Spencer whispered to me as the three of us laid together in the comfortable, large bed.

I looked over at him in the low light. Um, yes, I had. She was mine.

"I know that you'll take excellent care of her," he assured.

Of course I would. Because I was her good boy and I was made to fuck her.

Chapter Sixty-Three

Grace

Love coursed through my bond with Brennan. Brennan had marked me, bonding with me. *Finally.* Spencer gazed at me adoringly. Mmmm, having those two together was nice.

Both of them purred for me and told me that I was a good girl. I didn't feel trapped with their large and sweaty alpha bodies pinning me to the bed. No, I felt secure. Taken care of. Treasured. Everything felt pleasantly hazy.

Something seemed to be missing. But what? Something shot through me, and I whined, as the need to be knotted again consumed me.

"Does someone need to be knotted again?" Brennan's voice was a low rumble.

"Yes." My eyes met his. "I need both of you in me at the same time. And I want to bite you."

Brennan's eyes gleamed. "Bite me as I fuck you."

"Both of us at once? Oh, my good doctor, that would be my pleasure. Let me clean you up," Spencer breathed, easing out of me.

Brennan slipped out of me and lazily had me sit up and sip some water as Spencer cleaned us all up.

But I wasn't feeling lazy. I pouted at them. "Knots. Knots knots knots knots, knots knots knots knots, knots knots knots knots, knoooooots, knot knot," I sang loudly.

"Yes, Darling." Passion in his eyes, Spencer kissed me.

"Wait. I forgot to preheat the oven." Pushing me down on the bed, Brennan threw open my legs and buried his face between my thighs.

"Oh, yes." My body bucked as he hit just the right spot with his tongue. His fingers entered me.

"Preheat the oven? Oh, how clever." Spencer chuckled as his lips seized my breast.

Pleasure coursed over me as I orgasmed. Both of them kept going, lavishing me with attention. *Mmmm, preheat my oven, alphas.*

Yes, both these impressively cute guys were mine.

"You taste so good. Sweet and tasty," Brennan mumbled. "Spencer, taste."

Spencer joined him and both of them licked me together. *Stooop.* No. Don't stop. Wave after wave of delight washed over me as both of them moved me closer to my peak. I came again.

"Good boy," I sighed. "Good Daddy."

Brennan's head popped up, chin glistening. "Ding. Oven's ready. I can knot you now."

"Please." I giggled. "I need both of you in me now."

"You need me? I love that." Spencer breathed.

There were more weird sounds coming from some place.

"Yes, at the same time. I need knots." I started singing again, this time to the tune of Volkov, to drown out the noise coming from someplace.

Spencer pushed one of my legs into the air, then thrust into me. Brennan did the same. I kept singing, even as they started to trust. As good as it felt, this wasn't a knot, and I didn't want them to forget my request.

"Oh, this feels so nice," I sighed, legs in the air, both of them side by side, pumping in and out of me.

"You feel good," Spencer growled, kissing me.

"The best." Brennan kissed me again.

A hand brushed my clit, and I groaned, orgasming again. So many sensations bombarded me as I lost myself to it, keeping up my tune.

"I'm going to knot you now," Brennan finally groaned, kissing me deeply.

"Yes, let's knot her," Spencer agreed.

Finally.

As they pushed into me, Brennan kissed me again, then his eyes focused on mine, face still close to me. The sensation of two knots snapping into me at once made me squeal with delight. Song no longer needed, I bit Brennan's shoulder, bonding him back.

"Mine." I gazed at him.

"Yes," Brennan agreed.

Happiness flowed through me. *Good boy.* That good boy was mine.

Chapter Sixty-Four

Evan

"Grace isn't okay," I informed Wes, as Riley used me as a pillow. We were in a room at the Bureau that was probably used to hold omegas, with some fluffy couches and soft lighting. Wrappers from snacks and sandwiches, as well as empty cups, littered the low table.

Pimm, our *wellbeing assessor,* sat in a chair nearby on her tablet. She was basically the inter-dimensional Blanket Brigade, and we'd had a great conversation about it before Riley got too tired and wanted to sleep.

Riley and I had been kept together this entire time, which was nice, but I was glad Wes was now with us.

I wished all of us were together. Though from what I'd felt a little bit ago, it seemed like Grace was with Brennan and being *taken care of.* Yes, I'd like some of that when we got out of here.

Wes rubbed his chest and frowned. "Well, yeah, Rosalind isn't dead."

"At least you got to punch her," I replied.

"And you saved her, thank you." He kissed me.

"She's my mate. Though I think I'm going to need a really long, hot bath with her tomorrow. I'm not as young as I used to be," I chuckled.

"Anything for you." Wes cupped my face with his hand. "It was scary seeing her taken, but when I saw you go after her, I knew she'd be okay."

That feeling that something was wrong with Grace continued to dig under my skin. What was it? Was she spiraling? It would be pretty easy for her to spiral with all of this.

"She's sick, I think." Wes' brows knit together.

I reached out through the bond. Brennan was frantic, Jett was determined, and she was...

Fuck.

"Pimm, I think Grace might need, um, medical attention," I finally hissed. "Can you check on her?"

Pimm got up and went to the door and spoke to someone. She came back to us.

"Grace has left with two of your family. The other is waiting for you. Agent Cora is just finalizing everything, and then you all can go home," she said.

"Good." Shit. I didn't have my phone. If Grace was going into heat, we were going to need someone to take care of Riley.

"Grace left without us?" Wes frowned.

"I'm pretty sure that she's going into heat. I'm guessing they let her go home with Brennan and Jett." At least they let her leave.

"Oh. We're going to need to be so fucking careful," Wes breathed.

We sat there and waited, as any doubt I might have had of her going into heat left.

"Fuck." Wes squirmed.

Yeah, I felt that, too.

Finally, the door opened, and Agent Cora walked in. "Everything has been settled. You're free to go. Please don't go far. We might have more questions."

Riley sat up. "We can leave? Fuck-a-doodle."

My sister gathered up the things Pimm had given her, which included a plushie, a blanket, and star-shaped candies. Not only had they let her stay with me because she was a minor, thetas were also considered precious—and apparently quite valuable to the Authority.

Jett came in and tossed everyone their phones. "Come on, Lexi is waiting."

"Thanks for the snacks, Pimm." Riley waved.

"You're welcome. If you reconsider, let me know," she replied.

"Thank you, Pimm." Yeah, I was pretty sure my sister didn't want to leave this world to go to the Authority Academy, but it was a nice offer considering Pimm would have to petition on Riley's behalf because our world was Class IV.

"Lexi?" Wes asked, as we left the room.

"Yeah, Brennan and Spencer took his car. Um, Riley, we think Grace is going into heat. So, once we get home, we need you to pack and go with Lexi and the chicks. I think Spence has called you out of work for tomorrow and Monday, but you can go if you want. Sorry, we weren't expecting it." Jett led us down the hall.

Riley whistled. "Poon patrol time. Got it. Don't want to be around for that."

"Yeah, not sure you're using *poon patrol* right," Jett chuckled.

"You'll be okay?" I asked.

She rolled her eyes. "I can amuse myself. Text me when it's over. Considering work is in a couple of hours, I will probably sleep. But I'll go on Monday. We're supposed to code shit with Blaise. As for the weekend, I have plans with Hiro, Marcos, and Kilroy."

Lexi was waiting for us at the curb in a brand new SUV.

"Wow. Baby-mobile?" Wes asked as we got in.

"I mean, we know you can't fit three car seats in a sports car," Jett added.

"Yes." Lexi yawned. "Shit, I must love you fuckers."

"Same." Riley ate some candy.

"Do I even want to know why you're at the Bureau of Investigation in the middle of the night? Though I saw the video of Evan's epic motorcycle chase." Lexi took a sip of coffee as we drove away.

"Grace's brothers and her mom showed up, chaos ensued," Wes replied.

Jett blinked. "Does Lexi know about, *you know*?"

"Did I never mention that? I mean, she's literally a detective because she discovered that she had a knack for it while helping me try to find Grace." Wes pulled me close.

I got a jolt of pleasure through the bond. Grace and Brennan were fucking. Mmmm. Yeah, I absolutely wanted some of that.

Getting on my phone, I canceled my appointments and let Claire know I'd be out for a few days. Monday? Spencer thought we'd be done by Monday?

We got home. I brought in the groceries Spencer had ordered, Jett took Grace's things upstairs and then got the chicken stuff for Lexi. Riley packed her things.

Already, I could smell them downstairs. I itched to join them, but I needed to see Riley off.

Lexi got some juice out of the fridge and poured herself a glass.

Wes was on his phone. He frowned. "They're not answering."

"I'm pretty sure that's not how heats work." Lexi chuckled as she finished the juice.

"It's Brennan and Spencer. Those are the world's most in-control alphas. I'm surprised Spencer hasn't come up." Wes got a basket out of the pantry. "We should bring snacks, right? Usually Spencer packs the snacks."

"Yes, water, sports drinks, snacks." Jett held up the box of chicks. "I'll put this in your car."

"Oh, they're babies," Lexi cooed. "When did you get chicks?"

"Brennan and Grace just got them." I put some things in the basket. Gummy bears. Protein bars. Meat sticks. Chips. Cookies. Water bottles. Vitamin waters. Sports drinks. Yeah, that should work.

Wes grabbed the basket. "I'm going to take these down. Bye, Lexi. Thanks."

"Anytime." Lexi put her glass in the sink.

"Okay, see you down there," I replied as he disappeared down the stairs with the basket.

"Ready." Riley came into the kitchen. "Love you, you doofus."

"Love you, too, Ri." I hugged Riley. "Thank you, Lexi."

Jett went out to the car with the chickens. I went upstairs, put on something more comfortable than my torn clothes, gathered a few things, and went down to the kitchen.

Shit, they were having a good time, and I squirmed. *Soon.* I'd be with them soon.

In the kitchen, Wes held a drill, and Jett had some lock-picking tools.

"What's wrong?" Those weren't my preferred heat accessories.

"They locked us out. We can't find the key." Wes frowned, hurt coming through the bond. "I called and knocked and everything."

"There's no key, remember. They locked us out? Oh, that's weird. Maybe they wanted her to feel safe and forgot we needed a new lock? Let's go pick some locks." Yeah, had been next on the to-do list. I followed them down the stairs to the basement and was hit with a wall of their scent and felt something well up inside me.

"She smells okay, right? Not sick?" Wes seemed a little nervous.

"Grace smells fantastic," I agreed. Mmmm, I needed some of that. Yes, I needed to make a whole lot of Grace sandwiches. I'd make her heat so good.

Jett paused. "Brennan doesn't feel okay."

"What? He feels like he's having a great time," I replied, as we headed toward the nest. I was a little curious about Brennan and Spencer being with her. Sure, they were both alphas, which made sense, but it's not like they were used to working together.

"Too great." Jett's look grew concerned.

Too great? How could he be having too much fun fucking Grace? Such a thing didn't exist.

I sniffed the air again, trying to get the undercurrents. Oh? "Brennan? In rut?"

Huh. I could count the times he'd been in rut on one hand. Even when he let go during a heat, he rarely went into rut.

Something blazed through me, like sweet fire, lighting up my soul.

"Did he just bond her?" Wes rubbed his chest, running toward the nest.

"We'll get to her. She's okay with them," Jett soothed as we got to the door. He banged on it. "Bren, it's us, let us in."

There was no answer.

Jett got out the lock picks. The urge to push Wes up against the wall and make out with him consumed me. The scents, the pheromones, the feelings, it was so much. A little whine slipped from my lips as the urge to fuck and be fucked consumed me.

"I know. I feel it too. It's not Brennan bonding with her. It's that my mate is in heat and I need to be there." Wes brought me to his chest and held me tight.

It was a completely understandable feeling. I wanted to be with her too, and I wasn't an alpha.

"This was why I thought we should install an electronic lock down here that we can open with our phones. But no, since we hardly use it, no one thought we needed one," Jett sighed, as he struggled with the lock picks.

"Should I just kick it down?" I asked. "I'm feeling pretty capable after tonight."

"If I drill the pins out, we can at least close it. I'm worried if we break the door that she might not feel safe and it will interrupt her heat and she'll get sick," Wes replied.

"True." I sucked in a breath as it felt like they started again. But then knots could deflate faster during heats, especially when female omegas were involved.

"Should I get out the drill? I'm pretty sure we have the right bits." Wes started kissing me.

Yes, please.

"Wait... come on, be a good lock for me," Jett muttered.

There was noise coming from the room. And not just sex noises.

"Grace keeps singing about dicks to the tune of Volkov." Jett chuckled. "Okay, almost there... Yes, talk to me."

Jett opened the door and...

"Oh, fuck." Need swept through me hard enough to make my knees buckle.

The scent of alpha rut and omega heat made me whine. Grace was on her back, legs in the air. It looked like both Spencer and Brennan were fucking her at the same time.

Jett put away his lock picks. "Close the door and turn on the air filter."

But all I could do was stare at her. Brennan kissed her. She stopped singing, her mouth on his shoulder. More sweet fire rushed through my soul.

She bonded him back.

A door clicked and a fan whirred.

He placed a couple of water bottles and snacks on the table and then went into the anteroom to load up the mini-fridge.

I put the things I'd brought now on the couch. As I got out a pack of tablets, I whined.

The two of them cuddled her tight. Their purrs filled the room. Awww, Brennan and Spencer looked so cute snuggled up to her.

Grace giggled and kissed them as they talked softly. She looked up and noticed us. A big smile crossed her face. She made grabby hands. "There you are! More dick, please."

Spencer shot Wes an annoyed look.

Brennan scowled at Wes as well. But his look grew soft as his gaze fell to me. "Hi, Love."

"Evan has been so good, you should suck his cock as a reward, Peaches." Wes shoved me to her as she started singing about dicks again.

Sounds good to me. Take my cock, Peaches.

"Here, everyone needs one." I popped one of tablets in my mouth and took one to give Grace. We didn't need any post-heat UTIs. I passed the package to Wes.

Taking off my clothes as I went over to the bed, I realized Brennan and Spencer had been fucking her pussy *together* and now were locked inside her.

"Want my dick? You look so pretty being knotted by your alphas. Take this first." Kneeling on the bed, I put the dissolving tablet in her mouth.

She took it without question.

"That's my peaches." I fed her my cock, tangling my hands in her hair. She was warm, flushed, and smelled of *eau d'fuck me alpha* and a little extra. Yeah, our peaches was in heat.

"I want my Boo-Bear, too," she whined, my cock still in her mouth.

"Of course you do. You'll get him," I soothed.

"I'm right here." A naked Wes climbed onto the bed with her. She beamed at me. Brennan growled a little.

"I'm not taking her from you, I just want to share." Wes put his hands up in surrender.

Jett's arms wrapped around my waist, his cock poking against my ass. "Do you need me, Baby?"

I leaned back and kissed him. "Always."

Chapter Sixty-Five

Wes

"That's it, you're taking me so good," I praised Grace as she rode me, a look of sheer delight on her face. Her peach scent surrounded me, her face flushed, skin warm to the touch.

"More," she begged, as she moved up and down on top of me. "I want everyone all at once."

Everyone?

"Can you handle three dicks in your pussy? Three knots sound insane in all the right ways," Evan breathed from the chaise, having been just fucked by Brennan.

While Brennan didn't seem to be in rut anymore, he still was pretty far gone. Honestly, it was nice to see him just tending to their needs without being heat cruise director.

Spencer was absolutely not in rut anymore and was napping on the couch. Grace's heat had been pretty intense for a while, but things seemed to be slowing down. Though the next round was probably coming.

"Yeah, Wes, Bren, and Evan in your pussy, Spencer in your ass, and I'll take your mouth." Jett crawled on the bed and started playing with her ass.

"Yes! More knots, I need more." Grace gave us a pitiful look, and a heartbreaking little sound escaped her lips.

"Shhh, Daddy's here." Spencer rushed over to her, completely naked. Okay we were all naked.

Jett vacated his place as Spencer started fucking her ass.

"More, I want more," she whined.

"I'm right here, Baby Girl. I'll fill you and knot you, so that you don't feel empty," Spencer soothed.

Why didn't I know that she called him *Daddy,* and he called her *Baby Girl?* It worked.

She rested her warm face on my chest as I made love to her slick, sweet pussy. It still wasn't quite slick, but it was more slick-like than I'd ever seen.

"I want my good boy," she whined as Spencer and I fucked her. Jett was kissing her breasts.

"I'm coming, Little Butterfly," Brennan called from the chaise. "Just a moment."

The fact that she called Brennan her good boy? And he let her? That got me. I was so here for that.

"Okay." Grace looked at me. "Hi." She leaned in and kissed me.

"Hi." I kissed her back.

"I'm here." Brennan grabbed the lube, got right next to Spencer, and casually slid his dick into her pussy with mine. "Oh, look at you. You're so wet for me."

"Um, hi, Bren." I looked at him as he started moving inside her. We were doing this? "Are you okay, Peaches?" I brushed her hair out of her face.

"Feels so nice." Bliss gleamed in her eyes.

This was so different from Evan's heat. But she wasn't Evan, she hadn't gotten sick, and she seemed pretty happy.

"Peaches, do you really want three dicks in your pussy?" Evan grabbed the lube.

"Yes. Dicks, dicks, I have all the dicks," she sang.

Oh, I loved all her cute little songs.

Getting on the other side of Spencer, Evan sort of slid himself in there with me and Brennan.

Fuck, she was full, and I could feel them. It felt good, especially as Brennan's pierced cock moved.

Spencer continuing to fuck her ass. "Feeling better, Darling?"

"So much," she groaned, making a cute little face.

"Are you okay?" I asked again, wanting to make sure we didn't hurt her as the four of us got into a rhythm. All I got was happiness through the bond and a contented hum as she kissed my nose.

She looked around. "Jett?"

"You want my cock, Babydoll?" Jett climbed onto the bed next to me and whipped it out.

"Please." Opening her mouth, he lowered it in, and she greedily sucked on him.

"Peaches, I'm going to cum soon, do you want my knot?" I inquired, as the urge to knot her overwhelmed me.

Grace nodded and mumbled something.

"Brennan, we should knot her together? Evan, you can probably slip out like last time?" I suggested. Evan's dick wouldn't get super squished if it did, would it?

"Oh, this feels so fucking good, yes, please," Evan gasped. He hadn't gone into heat, but he was certainly enjoying himself.

"Yes. Almost there." His expression went pensive, and for a moment there was only the sound of fucking. "On three—one, two, three."

I pushed my knot into her, feeling Brennan's knot rub against me. Fucking shit, I liked how that felt. My cum shot into her.

"Alphas," she cried, coming.

"I'm going to knot you, Baby Girl," Spencer moaned.

I felt his knot through her as he slipped into her ass. Grace came again, flooding the room with her scent.

"You look so beautiful with five dicks in you." Jett stroked her face. "Three knots. So good, now swallow me down."

Grace swallowed his load and slumped onto me. Brennan and Spencer laid on us, too, all three of our knots stuck inside her.

"That was amazing. I'd like to do that again." Evan must have slipped his cock out, because he crawled onto the bed snuggled up next to me. Jett did the same.

"Mmmm, I like dicks." Grace yawned sleepily and nuzzled me like she was a little kitten.

I stroked her hair. "We aim to please."

"Come on, Peaches." I picked her up off the bed and threw her over my shoulder. She'd just finished being the filling in a Jett and Brennan sandwich on the bed, while I fucked Evan on the couch.

Evan and Jett slept snuggled together. Spencer and Brennan seemed asleep, too.

I carried her into the anteroom and grabbed a bottle of water. "Drink."

"Okay." She drank half of it as I brought her into the bathroom. After setting her down, I started the shower.

I wasn't sure how much time had passed. At least she hadn't gotten sick. I tried to stay present in case we needed to rush her to the hospital.

Taking Grace, I plopped her into the giant shower, which had lots of shower heads, a couple of benches, steam, and many things. The bathroom was also dark, lit only by a small nightlight by the sink.

"Are you doing okay, Peaches?" Taking the body wash, I soaped her down.

"I like us all being together." She sighed and rested her face on my chest.

"It is nice," I agreed. Okay, Spencer being with us took a moment to get used to. Especially because he just did everything she wanted with no hesitation, like he'd been doing this for years.

Rinsing off her body, I started on her hair. Someone had stocked the shower with a bunch of products, not the three-in-one stuff we had in the nest shower at the cabin.

"I bonded with Bren. I have the entire set now." She rubbed her chest and then frowned. "No, wait, I didn't get Jett yet."

"Not yet. But I'm sure you can." I tried to get the cum out of her hair. I hadn't actually expected Brennan to go into rut and bond her right away, but given he let her kidnap him, I figured it would come soon.

"I love you, Wes." She gazed up at me as I rinsed the shampoo out.

"I love you, too, Peaches." I kissed her forehead and then conditioned her hair. Well, I hoped it was conditioner.

Letting it sit in her hair for a moment, I washed myself, Grace helping. Mmmm, it was more like she tried to tickle me under the guise of soaping me up.

"Is that how it's going to be," I laughed, tickling her back. I got us all rinsed off. "Ready to get out?"

She shook her head. "Hold me?"

Sitting on the bench that was under the spray, I held her. If she wanted to nap on me in the shower, well, she could nap on me in the shower.

Evan opened the glass door and ducked his head in. "Can I join the shower party?"

"It's more of a shower nap." Exhaustion coated me.

"Sounds good to me," he replied, coming all the way in.

Picking her up, I moved us to the floor of the shower, so that Evan could be with us. Holding the two people I loved most, we sat there under the spray, content to just be together.

Chapter Sixty-Six

Jett

"There you go, take us all, you're so fucking good," I told Grace as I thrust in and out of her ass. She was riding Brennan, with Evan and Wes on either side of me, all three of them in her pussy. Spencer was next to me on the bed, his cock in her mouth.

"So good, Baby Girl." Spencer's hands wrapped in her hair.

While it got a little crowded, she seemed too like all five of us in her at once.

"We're going to knot you now," Brennan murmured as the three of them continued to thrust inside her.

"If they do that, I'm going to cum," I warned.

Mouth full of Spencer, she nodded.

"Good girl, you don't even feel as warm anymore," Spencer praised, stroking her face.

Evan came inside her, slipping out, right as Brennan and Wes knotted her.

I gasped, feeling their knots through her, which made me cum.

"Swallow me down, Darling," Spencer murmured.

Evan handed me the tub of wipes, and I cleaned up him and me.

"Once again, you took us so well." Brennan reached out and cupped her face.

Spencer withdrew his cock from her mouth. She looked Brennan right in the eye. "Night night."

With that, she slumped on his chest and let out a tiny snore.

"Don't have to ask me twice." With a yawn, I curled up with Evan next to Brennan.

Everyone followed suit, since the best thing to do during someone's heat was to sleep when they slept–or were occupied by someone else.

When my eyes opened, the room was completely dark, like someone had turned down the lights on their way back from the bathroom.

Grace was partially draped over me, her foot tangled around Brennan's. Her scent wasn't nearly as strong now, and she wasn't warm anymore.

There hadn't been that many rounds, but even so, this might just be close to being over. Granted, my experience was all Evan's heats, but I had a pretty good feel for this.

My bladder screamed at me. Carefully, I extracted myself from the tangled limbs in our big puppy pile.

Grabbing my phone, I checked the day. Oh, it was late Saturday night. Had we only been going at it for a day and a half? You know, I'd take it.

I went through the anteroom and used the bathroom. Were there any snacks left? I could probably go up to the kitchen and make something. Maybe then have a nap in my own bed.

As I returned to the anteroom from the bathroom, someone jumped on my back.

"I caught you." Grace laughed.

"You did." I leaned back and stole a kiss.

"Can I really?" she asked.

"Of course." Was I not caught? I was already part of her husband collection.

Her teeth dug into my shoulder, hard. Oh, okay. Got it. Omegas couldn't really bond betas the way they could alphas or other omegas. But I could feel Evan just fine through Brennan, just like I now felt her through him much more strongly than I had with just Evan. However, my bond with Evan had gotten a little boost when he'd bitten me, maybe she'd do the same.

"There." She smiled at me. "I've got you all now."

"You do. Do you want a snack?" I asked her, carrying her over to the kitchenette. Yeah, I felt her a little more.

"I'd like you to bite me back while fucking me against the wall." She batted her eyelashes at me. "Is it okay that I bonded with Bren?"

"I'm glad you did. He needs you." I liked how she unabashedly loved him the way she wanted to love him. Brennan needed someone to call him a good boy and take him for rides in the sidecar.

I brought her over to the wall. "Now, someone needs to be fucked?"

"Yes, please."

Moving her to my front, I wrapped her legs around my waist, then pressed her to the wall. "Like this?"

Her eyes blew out with desire. "Please."

I guided my cock into her wet pussy. As I fucked her against the wall, one hand wrapped around her throat. "This is what my babydoll wants?"

"Yes, please." Her eyes closed as I thrust in and out of her, her ass thumping against the wall.

An orgasm ripped through her, squeezing my cock. "I'm going to cum."

"Make me yours," she sighed contentedly.

As I came inside her, I clamped my teeth down on her shoulder. Why not? It wasn't like she wasn't absolutely covered in bites, hickeys, and marks, both from this heat, and being with Brennan on Tuesday.

"Oh, that's hot." Evan stood there as I held Grace tight.

"I love you, Jett." She kissed my nose.

"I love you, too." I kissed her back hoping she could feel it in my kiss.

After a moment, I carried her over to the couch and set her down.

"Snack?" I started looking through the almost empty basket.

"My turn." Evan picked her up and took her back into the bedroom.

Well, then. He'd done an excellent job of letting her be the center of things. I worried about that a little. But it wasn't like he hadn't gotten a ton of fucking, too.

"What do we have left?" Brennan slipped into the anteroom and wrapped his arms around my waist.

"Gummy bears and protein bars." I handed him a protein bar and opened a package of gummy bears.

His fingers traced her bite on my shoulder.

"I have officially been collected," I announced. Honestly, I love how she thought just as much of me as everyone else.

"Me, too. That's okay?" Brennan shot me an anxious look as he took a bite.

"Of course it is." I smoothed his hair. "Wanna take a shower with me before one of them shouts for us?"

I'd like a shower—and a little time with just Brennan. Spencer and Wes could take care of those two.

Brennan kissed me and picked me up. "Perfect."

Chapter Sixty–Seven

Grace

"Oh, Alpha, yes," I cried. Another orgasm shuddered through me as Spencer fucked me from behind over the arm of the chaise lounge.

"You feel so good, Baby Girl," he growled. He pumped in and out of me as I held onto the chaise.

My head lolled back to steal a kiss.

"I'm going to cum, are you ready for my knot?" he asked as his balls slapped my ass.

"Oh, yes, Daddy." I sighed. Mmmm, yes. *Knot me, Daddy.*

His hand stroked my clit as he seated himself inside me. Once his knot sealed inside me I came again, sucking in a breath as he came.

For a moment we just stood there, me over the arm of the chaise as he kissed me on the neck and held me.

"Like always, you take me so well. Mmmm, I love you so much." He picked me up, us still joined, and curled onto the chaise with me, throwing a blanket onto us.

I looked over as Wes fucked Evan on the bed. So pretty. I wasn't sure where Brennan and Jett were, probably in the anteroom. It felt like they were sleeping. I'd been sleeping too but needed a knot after my nap.

The foggy haze that I'd been caught up in since the Bureau of Investigation was leaving. Exhaustion replaced it. My pussy ached. I vaguely remember fitting three dicks in there on more than one occasion.

That was a whole lot of dicks.

My belly also complained. But the rest of me was pretty satisfied.

"I love you, too. I think I've gotten all my dicks and knots. You know, I might be ready for those crepes soon." After that, a nice hot bath with the green fizzies with Evan.

"You think so?" He kissed my forehead. "You're not warm and you don't smell like you're in heat anymore."

"I just feel tired and hungry."

"Okay. Would you like me to make crepes for you, or should we order them and have them delivered? I'm pretty sure it's late morning on a Sunday. We should be able to order from a creperie without a problem. Otherwise, we can order what we need from the store to make them along with any toppings people would like." He kissed my head again.

Toppings? "Like strawberries and chocolate with whipped cream?"

My mouth watered at the thought.

"Are we ordering food?" Jett walked into the bedroom, looking deliciously rumpled, my teeth marks on his shoulder. "If not, should I make something to tide us over until crepe-fest?"

"If we order crepes, could we still get ones with toppings?" I asked. Spencer looked tired, and crepes could be fiddly. Ordering out could be the way to go.

"Yes. Everyone could order what they wish—sweet or savory," he said as Jett went to look for something.

"Later, will you make me soup and feed it to me in the bath? If you're not too tired?" I gazed up at him. Yes, after my bath I wanted a nap, then another bath with soup.

He stroked my hair. "That sounds like a lovely idea. I should make a big batch and freeze some."

"Perfect." I dozed lazily on Spencer.

"We're ordering food? I could eat food," Wes said from the bed.

"If someone brings me my phone, we can see about ordering from a creperie." Spencer held out his hand.

Jett came back over and handed him his phone. "You're ready for crepes now?"

"Yes." I nodded.

"Great. Can we grill later? It doesn't have to be lamb—ribs, steak, or chicken all work," Jett gave me a kiss.

"That sounds doable." Spencer nodded.

He pulled up the restaurant on his phone, and we ordered crepes and coffee for delivery. Even though his knot had softened enough to slip out, I laid there with him on the chaise while he placed a grocery order.

Brennan came over and gave me a kiss. "I'm going upstairs to shower."

He left, leaving the door open, but not before turning up the air filter.

"Evan, off the bed. We never changed sheets. I'm going to toss these in the washer and then go shower." Jett tugged on the sheets.

"Sex party is over?" Evan looked over at me.

"Sex party is hungry. If we need to come back down here, we'll just put clean sheets on the bed." Jett kissed him.

Wes popped up off the bed and tugged on Evan's hand. "Yes, let's take a quick shower before the food gets here."

Evan and Wes helped Jett take the sheets off the bed, and they left.

"A shower before the food comes sounds divine, don't you think, Darling?" Spencer stroked my hair.

I was feeling pretty content, but I could probably use a shower. "With you? I'd love that."

"This is perfect," I sighed, splayed across Spencer's lap on the love seat in the living room as I ate my crepes with chocolate, strawberries, and whipped cream.

Everyone's faces were a little scruffy, except for Brennan who must have shaved in the shower. I would be okay if everyone wanted those grizzly beads.

Brennan nodded from his spot on the floor with Jett. "Your crepes are great, Spence, but I love all the savory options."

Spencer gave me a fond look. "I do aim to please."

"They're delicious," Evan said from the couch where he was with Wes. "When do we want Riley back? Tomorrow after work? Tonight? Are we even going to work? I'm not sure I'm going to work."

"Maybe see if she wants to return tonight since we're going to grill?" Jett asked.

"I think I'll get everything ready for the soup, then take a nap. When you're ready, I'll put it in the pressure cooker," Spencer said.

"Perfect." I gave him a kiss. "Mmmm, I want a bath with Evan, a nap, and then a bath with my soup, then maybe some cuddles, and later we can grill and watch a movie."

"I get a bath with you?" Evan beamed, whipped cream on his nose.

Wes licked it off.

"Yes. I want all the baths." I took another bite of crepe.

Brennan fed Jett a bite of crepe. "When did we get a pressure cooker?"

"We've had a pressure cooker. I keep it in the garage," Spencer replied.

"Can we get a deep fryer?" Jett asked.

Brennan's eyebrows rose. "Where are we going to put it?"

"Okay, Riley will be back in time for dinner." Evan looked up from his phone. "Who's taking her to work tomorrow? She really wants to go because of something they're doing."

"Whoever feels up to it?" Wes offered. "I think Grace should stay home, and someone should stay with her. Just in case she spikes."

"I want to stay home." I snuggled into Spencer. "Can everyone stay home?" I wasn't ready to be apart from them yet.

"We've all called out, so we can all stay home, if we want," Brennan replied. "Grace, maybe we can try out the smoker tomorrow?"

"I'd like that." Oooh, what did I want to make in it?

We finished our crepes, and I snuggled with Evan while the alphas cleaned up. Jett went to throw in more laundry.

"Should we sneak away for that bath now?" Evan whispered.

"Grace?" Brennan came into the living room.

Before I could say anything, he swept me off my feet and kissed me. "Just wanted to say that." Brennan gave Evan a kiss, too. "That, too."

He went back into the kitchen, whistling.

Evan chuckled. "Well then. Bath?"

"Yes, please. I think it's going to be a two fizzy bath." Taking his hand, we went up the stairs to our bathroom, and he started the taps.

When the tub filled, I sank into the hot water. Evan tossed in the fizzies, turned on the jets, and got in behind me.

"Oh, that feels good," he muttered.

I leaned into him. "You're my favorite tub pillow."

"Good. Do you remember anything from the past couple of days?" His finger traced the bite Brennan left.

"I remember a lot. So much more than yours. It was really short. Is that bad?" I looked up at him.

"It was healthy. We'll call that a win. The length and what people remember varies, and that is fine. You should have a post-heat checkup, though," he added.

"Okay. I'll see what they have for after work this week. I was absolutely full of dicks." I didn't even know one could have so many dicks in them at once.

Evan chuckled. "So full of dicks."

"You got enough, right?"

He kissed me. "Absolutely."

"Oh," I gasped. "I don't know where all my presents are. Or my purse or phone."

"I think Jett put your purse, phone, and Wes' sketch in your room. You were wearing all your other presents when your heat started. Someone took them off you at some point, and they're probably in the nest's anteroom." Evan gave me a lazy kiss.

"Thank you. I think I want to get the new sketch made into my wedding dress, or maybe some combination of the two." It was so thoughtful of Wes.

Evan gave me a squeeze. "Perfect. We should probably start planning since your party with Spencer is finished, and I'd like to get a bunch of it done before I start Blanket Brigade training."

"That sounds good, especially if we want to add a pack confirmation. Thank you for saving me." I kissed him. I was frozen, but

I'd seen him leap into the car, roll out of it with me, and then shoot out the tires. He'd come after me. Saved me.

"We save each other, right?" Evan kissed me long and deep.

"You know, I totally had an inter-dimensional advocate the other night."

"Yeah, I had one, too. She was really interesting to talk to. How are you doing with the whole *Rosalind isn't dead* thing?" he asked.

"She and Solomon are the authority's problem now. I hope they rot in prison. I also hope they just kicked Abei back home with fewer memories." Turning, I leaned my face on his chest. "They sold Rydor Corp the equipment, and probably the contacts, without knowing I worked there. Rosalind could have sent me to Wes." The tears leaked out.

It was a lot.

"I have you. The good thing is that you have most of your answers. She's in custody. You can now forget about her and have a revenge-worthy life." He smoothed my hair.

"The best revenge is a good life. I have so many good things to look forward to." Like my siblings. Our vacation. The wedding. Making a virtual super collider.

"We do," Evan agreed.

"Can I come in?" Wes called from the doorway of my room.

"Sure," Evan called back.

Wes came in, looking concerned. "Are you okay, Peaches?"

"I'm okay," I replied, looking up at him. "Because I have all of you."

Chapter Sixty-Eight

Grace

"Are you ready?" Wes stood in the doorway of my office, looking boyishly handsome, as he flashed me a smile with dimples.

"Yes. Let's go." I grabbed my bag. Riley had already gone upstairs to get a ride home with Spencer, Hiro had left, and Blaise hadn't come in today.

Wes's arm wrapped around my waist as we walked down the hall. "How was your day? Did anyone get in trouble?"

"Well, I let the interns do a project with ice cream since my new flavor arrived in the cafeteria. Maybe *I'll* get in trouble." I loved coming up with fun things for the Special Projects interns to do.

He chuckled. "Love that. I have yet to get scolded today."

Margie rounded the corner and scowled when she saw Wes. "We didn't do it."

Wes sighed. "Margie, I'm literally here to get my mate."

"Hummmf." Rolling her eyes, she stalked past us.

"Hey." Creed joined us as we walked to the elevators.

"Hey. The professor still hasn't answered me. It's fine that he's mad at me, but if Tru isn't coming this weekend, I need to know." My belly turned. It had been a week since my brothers had held Nate at gunpoint to get my whereabouts. He could blame me all he wanted, but I'd like him to leave my siblings out of it.

Creed's look softened as we went down to the lobby. "He's not angry with you. I think he's upset at himself for telling them where you were. They got your number from his phone, too."

"He had to protect himself." I leaned into Wes. Solomon probably would have shot him—or one of his students. It must have been a terrifying experience for them all.

"It's all Mum, I'm sure. Having one less adult in the house is stressing her out." Creed pinched the bridge of his nose with his thumb and forefinger.

"Yep, I put her mate in danger. I'm now *persona non grata.*" I sighed. Tru thought that she was still coming, and if she didn't get to visit me, she'd be very disappointed. We'd made plans, including having tea at the Everydoll Boutique with Terrance's kids.

Creed shook his head. "According to Verity, it's still on."

Given Verity was on escort duty, since Tru was too young to fly alone, hopefully she'd be the one to know.

"Also, they're a little upset with me that I won't quit my job and move home to help out," he added with a heavy sigh.

And blamed me for that, I was sure. It would probably all fall to Verity.

"If I hear anything else, I'll let you know," he promised.

"Thanks." We exited the elevator into the lobby.

Creed waved as he left to go catch the bus. Wes and I took the parking garage elevator down to his truck.

"I'll be right there, so if anything goes sideways, we can just leave," Wes assured as we drove to the restaurant.

"Thanks, Wes." I squeezed his thigh. Mrs. K had come through with trying to find me a therapist. It would be online, but better than nothing. However, before he agreed to anything, he wanted to meet me in person first and took the ultra-bullet down from Canada to do so.

Understandable. He probably wanted to make sure I was trust-worthy—and to see if it would even work. Just because he was a therapist who knew other worlds existed didn't mean he'd be right for me.

"If Tru isn't able to visit, we'll figure it out," Wes said. "Is Mercy still coming?"

"She is." And was really excited about it. Mercy was hoping that the skate smash camp could eventually lead to the opportunity to try out for the Rockland Raiders discovery league. Apparently, the league's discovery programs helped promising skate smashers to prepare to go pro.

I glanced at my phone and all my unanswered texts to the pro-fessor. With a sigh, I texted Verity, who was busy with summer research and child-wrangling.

Me

Is Tru still coming?

Also, I hadn't heard from the Authority. No news was good news, but I was curious about what happened to everyone. Hope-fully, I wouldn't have to testify.

It was still hard to believe that Rosalind hated me that much.

This was why I needed a therapist.

"Oh, Mrs. Beekman checked and our documentation for adding me to the pack has been formally accepted." I glanced at a text she'd sent me earlier today.

Yesterday, I met with her at the Center after my post-heat check-up. Apparently, everything looked good. I was still a gamma and would probably stay one. Which was also fine. I had an appointment with a specialist coming up to take a closer look at my seizures. It would be nice to know if they were temporary because of my world-traveling or if they were a permanent effect of everything that I'd endured.

My phone buzzed. But it wasn't the professor or Verity.

Brennan

I keep thinking of how I had you for lunch today.

Ducking my head, my cheeks burned. Brennan had been stealing me most nights. Which I didn't mind. Sometimes Jett or Evan—or both of them—joined in.

And today... today Brennan came to my work at lunch and fucked me on my desk in my office and then fed me onion rings.

Amazing.

Wes glanced over at me. "Evan?"

"Bren." I smiled. I texted him back.

Me

I'd like to make that a regular lunch date.

We pulled into the restaurant. Spencer had arranged everything—a place with a small, private dining room where the two of us could talk but had glass windows so our alphas could see us.

"He's already here," the hostess said. "I'll take you back."

Wes and I followed. I saw him waiting anxiously at the table, on his phone. He was probably about the professor's age, and had dark hair, a dadbod, and a pleasant face.

"There you are. Someone will be with you soon." The hostess returned to her station.

As we approached the door, a man and a woman, both alphas, came over to us.

"You're Grace?" The woman looked me up and down.

"Yes, I am. This is my mate, Wes." Nerves shot through me.

"Milo means everything to us. You understand why we're wary," the man stated.

"I do, and I appreciate it so much," I replied. "Let me talk to him, and if he decides *no,* I won't bother you again."

They stepped aside. I kissed Wes. "It will be fine."

I went into the private dining room and took a small box out of my purse, using it to look for listening devices. Satisfied there were none, I put it back. "Sorry, my mate is in cybersecurity; can't be too safe. I'm Grace."

"Milo." He smiled and looked over the menu. "Apparently we're someplace trendy, and my teenager is jealous."

"Did they come with you to Rockland? Order them something to go. This is all my treat." I looked to see what I wanted.

He shook his head. "The kids stayed with my other mates, they all have summer activities that keep them busy."

"I understand. My pack has a teenager, too." The server came in, and we ordered.

Milo and I made small talk about his trip down from Canada and my day at work.

Finally, the server brought our food and closed the door.

"I don't work for the Authority. I'm not here to put you in danger. As far as I know, there are no plans to make anyone return to their worlds of origin. Omegas are protected by the Authority, and someone once told me there were very few reasons to send anyone back, but I also understand your wariness." I poked at my colorful salad with my fork.

"Well, they sent you back, didn't they? I was told it wasn't the same, but still..." Milo took a sip of his drink, looking a bit nervous.

"They did, but I was taken from this world as a baby and grew up on one without designations. You can see how that might be problematic. I dreamt of my soulmate but couldn't get to him. The only reason I was returned was because I was a witness in a smuggling ring. Someone there realized that I was in the wrong world and returned me out of kindness so that I could be with my alpha." I ate a berry.

Milo nodded, swallowing his bite of sandwich. "It's a lot to go to another world. One with no designations? It's hard to imagine."

"As hard as it is to imagine omegas being illegal. Not that we don't have illegal designations here." I frowned. Spencer and I would find people who could carry out Elaris' work. He was already setting up meetings.

"We weren't illegal in my world, we're just commodities, property, with little choices or rights. I was lucky. I was seventeen when I was smuggled here, so I'd faced nothing truly horrific. Every day I think about those who didn't get out. How fortunate that I have a choice. I can have a job. I can choose who I'm with. I can love." He looked out the window at his mates.

"They know?" I took another bite.

"They didn't at first. I told them after I got pregnant. They took it pretty well, all things considered." He chuckled.

"Wes knew, we talked about it when we dreamt of each other. But not everyone in the pack did when I arrived."

We continued talking. I really wanted to know more about his world, but that's not what this meeting was for. My curiosity could wait. Instead, I told him more about me, since that was why we were here–so he could see if I was a trustworthy person.

"You have a family here? Nine siblings?" He finished his drink.

"I love them, but they're a lot." I showed him the photo of all ten of us from the mating party.

"That's a lot of siblings. My pack has three children." He showed me photos of his kids.

We talked more. Finally, Milo looked at his phone. "My mates are wondering if we're about done."

"That's up to you. Do you have the information you need? You can ask me anything." I used the pad on the table to pay our bill.

"Why don't we try a few online sessions and see where it goes from there. I absolutely want to help you if I can." He stood.

"Thank you, Milo, for taking a chance on me." I grabbed my things.

"I'll be in touch," he promised as we walked to the door of our private dining room.

"Thanks again." I looked at Wes, who was right there.

"Ready to go home? I know you ate, but Brennan's cooking you dinner." Wes grinned.

Awww. We got in his truck and drove off.

"How did it go? I talked to his alphas a bunch. They're really nice," Wes said.

"We're going to give it a try. I really hope it works out." I noticed I'd missed a call from the professor. Oh. I called him back.

"Grace, hi," he said softly.

"Hi, Nate. Sorry, I was in a meeting." Was this where he told me that Tru wasn't coming? If he tried to keep Mercy from camp, Riley would riot.

"It's okay. I apologize for not calling you sooner. It's been a lot," he admitted.

"I'm sorry someone did that to you because they were looking for me." I stared out the window as we drove back to the house. Guilt ate at me.

"It's not your fault. There's just a lot going on with it being summer, and the trials, and everything. And well, Adriana has officially lost her position with the university. Mine is okay, thank goodness. We were a little worried. Still, everything is hectic," he explained.

"Okay, I... I'd understand if you didn't want to talk to me—or if your alphas didn't want your family to have contact with me." I squeezed my eyes shut. I still had so many complex feelings about the professor.

"What, no. Grace, none of this is you. It's mostly just me being overwhelmed and disorganized. Tru's trip is absolutely happening. Between you and me, I'm a little afraid of what might happen if we cancel." He chuckled.

Yes, she would find some way to just come here anyway.

"I'll take good care of her. We have such fun things planned." Relief that it was still on coated me. I knew how much it meant to Tru and didn't want to disappoint her.

"They all had such fun at your party," he added. "Though the boys seem convinced that Compass BioTek works with secret government agencies."

"Would that surprise you if we did?" I shook my head.

"No. Hey, I have to go, but I just wanted to assure you that it's still on. Good night, Grace," he said.

"Thank you. And good night, Professor." I ended the call.

Wes smiled. "Still on?"

"Yep." I did a little dance in my seat. "Now, I wonder what Brennan is making for dinner?"

Chapter Sixty-Nine

Brennan

Carefully, I piped the mashed potatoes into the empty potato skins like the video showed me. The star tip made beautiful swirls. Afterward, I brushed the tops with butter and sprinkled them with cheese and chives.

"Perfect." I put them in the oven. The steaks, having been seared, were now cooking in cast iron skillets and almost done.

Taking the softened butter, I blended it with herbs. Jett sauteed the asparagus and mushrooms.

Riley came into the kitchen. "That smells delicious. Feed me, fuckers."

"Can you set the table with silverware, drinks, and napkins? I'll be plating tonight's dinner." I'd already gotten out the good dishware.

The paperwork had gone through. Grace was officially part of the pack, and it had already populated into her file. She was ours now.

Riley started setting the table.

Spencer came down the backstairs. "Should I select the wine?"

"Please." I took the steaks out so they could rest.

I wanted to do something nice for my mate. I wanted to show her that I could provide for her, feed her, and take care of her in a way that meant something to her—like special potatoes.

Jett finished the vegetables and started plating.

The garage door opened. A moment later, Grace and Wes came into the kitchen and took off their shoes.

"Brennan." Grace's entire face lit up as she rushed over and gave me a kiss. Her pack ring gleamed on her right pinky. She wore the bracelet I gave her, which made me very happy.

"Hi, Grace." I kissed her back. "Wash up, it's almost time to eat."

"Okay. It smells delicious. Hi, Jett." She kissed Jett, said hello to the chicks, then went upstairs.

"She's ours," Wes said softly. "It went through."

"That it did." I checked on the potatoes and took them out of the oven. Perfect.

I finished plating the dinner, drizzling the herb butter onto the steak, and adding some garnish.

"Those look incredible," Riley said as she helped me put them on the table. "I know you can cook, but how did you learn this fancy shit?"

"Mostly it was from all the cooking shows I watched when recovering from my car accident," I admitted. They'd been my comfort shows. Sometimes Jett and I would try things together, other times I'd surprise him.

Spencer started pouring the wine.

Grace came into the dining room and beamed. "This looks amazing."

"I just wanted to make you a nice dinner." I kissed her.

"Thank you. Oh, those potatoes. Did you pipe the filling in with a star tip?" Grace sat down at the table.

"I did." The fact that she noticed made me a little giddy. We didn't have any star tips, so I'd gone to the cooking store and gotten it special.

All seven of us sat down to eat.

"Brennan, this looks spectacular." Spencer raised his glass. "It's official. Grace is part of the pack."

"No take backs, you're stuck with us." Evan laughed.

That she was.

"You are all my husbands." Grace raised her glass. "I have five husbands and a Riley. My life is perfect."

"Yes, your life is perfect, because I'm in it." Riley flashed a charming smile.

"Did anyone get in trouble today?" Jett asked as he cut into his steak. "Cam wants more cookies."

"Next time I make some, I'll send some with you for her." Grace took a bite of potato. Her face was everything. "Oh, these potatoes."

"I'm glad you like them. The sister pack wants us to come over and grill on Sunday afternoon. My dad's coming. But no one else. Did you want to go? After Tru's playdate with Terrance's kids, of course." My father was living in Katie's backhouse right now. The Queen Mum had kicked him out. The Morris company was still dealing with the aftermath of Riley's virus. And a contentious divorce was probably in my mother's future.

"Oh, I finally heard from the Professor. Tru is still coming, so the playdate is still on. If the sister pack doesn't mind us bringing Tre, the cookout sounds fun. I don't remember what time Verity is heading back, but Creed can always take her to the airport. I was hoping to get some time with just her, though." Grace ate more potato, making another blissful face that made me want to fuck her right there on the table.

"Sister time is important. I can do something with Tru. So excited for her to visit." Riley popped a piece of steak in her mouth.

"Tomorrow after work, I need to go buy an enormous toy truck for Pax, will you come with me?" she asked Riley.

"Yeah, if you can drop me off at Kilroy's after. We're gaming at his place." Riley took a bite of potato. "Oh, these are good."

We continued talking about our day and the weekend plans.

"We're going to the gym Saturday morning, right?" Jett asked Grace and Riley.

"Yep. Then Wes, Evan, and I are meeting with the wedding planner. Time to get this party started," Grace laughed.

"Um, we can make it one big, giant wedding," Wes offered. "One where everyone can marry everyone they want, if you'd like to. We can do a pack confirmation or something, too."

"That is very generous, Wes. Grace and I had our moment, I'm fine with you three having yours," Spencer said.

Evan, Jett, and I had actually already talked about this. Evan said he didn't need to marry us. But...

"If you want to marry Peaches, please do." Evan grinned at Jett and me. "Unless you'd rather run off with her and do something private."

That was exactly what Jett and I had come up with. Yes, Jett and I had a spectacle of a wedding, and weddings seemed important to her, but we'd rather just have Grace to ourselves.

"Wait, you have plans." Evan's grin widened.

"Yes, if Grace wants." I looked at her. "Um, Volkov's former residence in France has a beautiful garden. If you'd like to run off with Jett and me for a day when we're on vacation in Greece, and marry us there, I'd like it very much."

"After that, there's a restaurant we want to take you to, too," Jett added.

Grace beamed. Vaulting out of her seat, she gave us each a kiss. "I love it."

"Can we attend or are you eloping?" Evan laughed.

"Up to Grace," I replied. Either way was fine with me.

Riley snorted. "Such saps."

"I would like to do a pack confirmation though, I mean, if everyone would be okay with that," I added. It would be nice, given everything, to publicly celebrate us, our new pack name, our new last name, and everything else.

"I like it," Riley replied.

"That sounds wonderful," Spencer added.

"Perfect. What do you all want so we can tell the wedding planner?" Evan asked.

We spent the rest of dinner talking about the wedding, and I gave them an update of how everything was progressing with the estate.

"Should we clean up and play a board game?" I asked.

"That sounds great. Before dinner, I started the bourbon slushies in the slushie machine." Grace stood. "I'll help clean up. Thank you for the amazing dinner, Bren." She gave me a kiss and started clearing the table.

I blinked. "We have a slushie machine?"

"Yes. It was one of the gifts that we received. I think that one was from the president. She has it in the basement, so that it won't clutter the kitchen," Spencer explained.

I wasn't sure what surprised me more, that the president sent Spencer a present, or that it was a slushie machine. Though if Grace had made them a registry, I could absolutely see her adding a slushie machine–and a meat smoker.

"President of what country?" Jett whispered.

Oh. With Spencer, who knew?

"I get to pick the game." Riley grabbed some empty dishes.

We cleaned up and then settled down on the back porch with bourbon slushies and a board game.

The weather was beautiful, and this was the perfect summer evening with my family.

"I won," Riley said as she moved her game piece. "Again?"

The doorbell rang. Ugh.

"I'll get it." I stood and went into the house.

Opening the door, I saw Agent Weigmier standing there with a woman I might have seen during our time at the Bureau.

"No." I gave him a hard look.

"We're just here for an update," the woman with the pixie cut said. "I wanted to check in with everyone."

"Fine." I sighed. "We're outside."

I led them out to the porch.

"Please don't make me testify." Grace looked terrified. Wes bundled her into his arms.

Her fear coursing through our bond made me want to punch someone.

"There's no need for that. You are not a witness for the trials. Unless you wish to speak on their behalf?" Agent Weigmier said.

"Nope. Not interested in serving as a character witness." Grace rolled her eyes. "Hi, Jira."

"Hello." Jira waved. "Is everyone well? Pimm wanted me to check on the others."

"I'm fine. But if you have any of those candies, I'd be better." Riley gave her a sly look.

Jira patted her tote. "I do."

She and Riley started talking, my attention went back to Agent Asshole, who was looking around as if searching for something.

"See something interesting?" I asked him, wondering what he was looking for.

"I do enjoy seeing how people live on other worlds," Agent Weigmier replied.

"You have so much space here," Jira added. "What are the two tiny houses for? Do children live apart from their parents in this world?"

"No. One is the guest house, for people to stay when visiting. The other is for my chickens, when they get bigger." Grace still clung to Wes.

Yes, her fancy chicken coop had been delivered, and I had to admit, it blended well. I think she and Spencer were going to get his hedgehog next weekend after Tru left.

Jira looked a little baffled by that. Maybe they didn't have chickens in her world?

"I did not steal the cat." Grace looked at Agent Weigmier and made a face.

Agent Weigmier simply nodded.

"Please tell me Rosalind's going to inter-dimensional jail forever?" Wes asked, planting a kiss on the top of Grace's head.

"Rosalind and Solomon will stand trial. He is cooperating, she is not. Though we have found everyone and shut this down," he informed.

"They won't get the possibility to be released on dotage, will they?" Spencer asked. "I'm not sure I want to deal with her coming after Grace in twenty years."

"Me neither," I replied.

Agent Weigmier thought for a moment. "Probably not."

"But they will be found guilty, right? If anyone could talk her way out of this, it would be her." Grace's voice went small.

Point taken. Especially since while we suspected Rosalind was a sigma, we'd never actually got any confirmation. We'd probably never know.

I was okay with that as long as I never had to deal with her.

"There is enough evidence." Agent Weigmier nodded. "The other brother, having been found not particularly involved, had his memory of the past couple of days wiped and was returned to his world of residence, per your request."

Oh, she'd asked that? Huh.

"Thank you. Abel will do whatever they tell him to." Grace nodded. "What about Mrs. Silvers?"

"We wiped her memory, then remanded her to local authorities. But considering they have no memory of Rosalind's re-appearance, I do believe she was returned home," he replied.

Okay, well considering Mrs. Silvers could still get in trouble for her role in Grace's trafficking, and was supposed to be on house arrest until the trial, she probably still wouldn't get off completely.

"I appreciate you helping us clean up this mess," he said.

Grace gave him a look. "I didn't exactly mean to do this. I didn't know I'd somehow put busting Rosalind in motion. Truly, I thought she was dead."

"I know."

Spencer gave him a measured look. "Are you going to erase our memories?"

"Not at this time. You seem trustworthy, and we may need some follow-up. Though I hope very much, respectfully, to never see you again unless by some chance I am returning someone to this world who requires your assistance," he replied.

Well, that was some relief.

"Is there anything else?" I asked him, looking over at Jira, who was handing Riley things from her bag while talking to Evan.

Agent Weigmier shook his head. "That is all. Jira, we should go."

Jira stood. "It has been lovely seeing you again. Have a wonderful evening."

"Thank you," Grace said softly.

"Yeah, thanks for the candy." Riley waved.

I walked them to the door. "I appreciate that you didn't just haul our asses to the station and wipe our memories."

"Most of it was for her. Take care of her," Agent Weigmier said.

"We will." I watched from the doorway as he and Jira got into his weird car and drove off.

Going back to the kitchen, I poured myself some bourbon and joined everyone. Riley was passing around a box of candy.

"That is gross." Jett made a face.

"I know, right? Try these. They're fruity." She handed him something else.

"It's over. All of that is finally over." Grace looked relieved.

"Yes. And with the trials—both of Adriana's and the people who hurt Elaris–coming up, we'll be able to put so much behind us," Spencer agreed.

Evan looked thoughtful. "Spencer, did you tell Elaris' family about the trial?"

"They were contacted, and I believe they are as relieved as I am," he replied.

The chaos had been nonstop, and I was looking forward to everything settling down.

"I got the money from the hospital settlement. How do I transfer it to the foundation for our scholars?" Grace asked.

"I'll help you with that this week." I sat back down. "Should we play another round?"

"Can we go out for ice cream? My treat. After all, I should spend some of it on ice cream," Grace said.

"I like that idea," Evan said.

"Yes, and then go swimming," Riley added.

"That sounds great." As long as I got to spend time with my pack. The past few months had shown me not just how much they meant to me, but how strong they were, we were.

After all, we were the Thanukos pack. And I expected no less.

Chapter Seventy

Evan

Nine months later

"You look fantastic," my sister Sonja said. She straightened my gold bowtie as I got ready in a room the estate had for this purpose.

"Thanks. I'm a little nervous," I admitted as I examined myself in the mirror.

Sonja was one of my attendants, wore emerald green, and looked fantastic, her braids even matching. My sister was tall for a beta, and curvy like Riley. She and her wife had come down from Portland for the weekend.

Today was the day I married Grace. After her being in our lives for well over a year, we were finally having our enormous fantastic wedding.

Actually, the *Enormous Fantastic Wedding* people had reached out to us about filming it for their show. Even if Brennan hadn't been absolutely against it, I didn't want to share this with the world.

Just the people we cared about.

Riley's phone beeped, and she looked at it. "Grace looks amazing in her dress."

"Grace is just amazing," I laughed. While I hadn't been permitted at her fittings, I'm sure she looked incredible.

Riley was dressed in a long, dark rose dress, and looked so grown up.

"Is Sasha coming?" I glanced at my phone, where she'd never answered my texts.

She was supposed to be one of my attendants, too. We'd gotten her a plane ticket, a hotel, and a dress. Sasha was here in Rockland, though she'd missed the rehearsal yesterday, because she'd had an exam and needed a late flight.

"She's coming," Sonja promised.

"Yeah, I mean she hasn't tried to guilt trip you about getting married in weeks," Riley replied, texting someone as she sat on a chair. Probably her boyfriend.

"True."

"It's probably because she's actually seeing someones," Riley added.

Sonja turned to her and frowned. "What? She's not seeing any-one. How do you know that?"

Riley rolled her eyes. "She has secret social media accounts where she posts about her actual life. Though dumbass didn't make it private. Like I can't find her just because she uses another name. Amateur."

"You are absolutely terrifying sometimes." Sonja chuckled.

"This is nothing." Riley made a face.

Riley was now gainfully employed at Compass BioTek and en-rolled in a program where she was taking university classes while still at Hadley Hall. Of course, given she originally learned her computer skills from Grandpa, who'd basically done the same thing Wes had done in the military, then done cybersecurity for banks, we shouldn't be that surprised.

"But yeah, Sasha has some people in her life, and it might be getting serious. So, you know, if she wants to have a wedding, she might need to change her opinions on a few things." Riley shrugged.

Huh. Sasha had been a little nicer in the past few months.

"Hey, Evan, is this the right room?" Sasha knocked on the door.

"You're here. Come in." I let her in.

Sasha came in, dressed in her emerald gown, looking a little frazzled, hair up.

"Sorry. I forgot my shoes, and we had to find me a new pair. Wow, you look good." Sasha gave me a hug.

"We?" Riley smirked.

"Um, I might be seeing some people. Yes, they're here in Rockland but not coming to the wedding. No, you can't meet them yet, because you'll scare them." She sighed and grabbed a soda from the table.

Riley rolled her eyes. "I'm not scary."

"I'm just glad you came," I assured her. "Your test went okay?"

"Yeah. It went great," she replied. "This place is fantastic."

"Bren literally bought it so Evan could marry Grace." Riley gave her a hug. "I'm happy you came too. I suppose you can meet Hiro."

"Hey, I'm excited to meet your boyfriend. Are Marcos, Kilroy, Mercy, and Rose here? I hear so much about them." Sasha gave Sonja a hug.

"Yep." Riley nodded.

Riley had invited some of her friends, but it wasn't like they didn't all know Grace. I was pretty proud of Rose, who'd be graduating high school with honors next month. Mercy was an attendant, along with Verity. Marcos, Hiro, and Kilroy's families were here, too.

Sasha's eyes lingered on Riley's pack tattoo on her shoulder, which she'd gotten last November when she turned sixteen. The entire pack had gotten them together.

I tensed, waiting for her to say something, given she'd been against it.

But she didn't. All she did was sigh.

Sasha took a box out of the bag and handed it to Riley. "I found one of the old videos you used to make of your dolls having adventures, and I feel terrible about what I did. I know it won't replace them. I'm sorry. It wasn't you. I was mad at Evan, but it was easier to punish you."

"Yeah, that's something to talk to your therapist about. But I accept your apology." Riley took the box and opened it. "Awww, is this me and you?"

It was an Everydoll doll holding the hand of a *little sister* Everydoll. They were custom. Grace and Tru had one made of the two of them.

"Yeah. I do love you, and I'm sorry I'm a bitch sometimes. You didn't ask to be born and usurp me as the youngest. You didn't cause Mom and Dad's death. And you didn't become a theta to taunt me." Sasha hugged her tight.

Wow, that was a lot coming from her.

"I'm proud of you for saying that," I told her. While I could handle her being mad at me, her taking out past grievances on Riley really hurt her.

Sonja sucked in a breath. "Are you actually going to therapy?"

"Um, yeah." She looked away for a moment. Sasha would see a therapist once or twice then quit, saying she didn't need to talk to a stranger about her problems.

"Thank you for realizing this. The doll is cute," Riley replied.

"Also, I'm proud of you for getting into that dual enrollment program at Rock Tech. You're doing really well here with Evan," Sasha admitted.

Riley grinned at me. "It's eighty percent Grace."

Very true. Grace took a very active role in raising Riley, and her love for my littlest sister showed. As did Riley's love for her. Okay, so we had chickens, bunnies, and a hedgehog, but it was all worth it.

"Evan, I'm sorry." Sasha gave me a tentative look. "I… I always blame everything on you. But it wasn't you. You're an adult and allowed to leave home and live your life. You and Sonja both offered me that opportunity, and I chose to not take it and play the victim."

I hugged my little sister. "I get it. You were in high school. Understanding things like that I couldn't just leave the Army because Mom and Dad died is hard. We crunched the numbers, and it was better for me to stay and send all my money home."

Sasha didn't have to stay home after high school. Spencer had even said that he'd pay for her to go away to any university she wanted.

"I'm sorry for not moving Wes' ass to Rock Springs with me after we got out of the Army. I could have finished my degree there, and he could have gotten a job locally, instead of here with Spencer." I kept hugging her. While I'd said it before, maybe this time she'd listen.

"You're an adult. I could have left. Grandma told me that enough." She sighed, still holding onto me.

"Hey, it's all good. You're finishing up your degree, and it looks like you're thriving, and I'm happy for you." I squeezed her tight. I could smell two scents on her, and I was happy she'd found some people she cared about.

"Also, I forgive you for being an omega even though I wanted to be one." Her look went a little more solemn.

Oh. Wow.

"Thank you. Believe me, I didn't ask the omega fairy for it, promise. As much as being an omega helped me find my career path, I did like what I was doing for the military," I said.

Sasha nodded. "Yes, I didn't understand what shit omega nurses got until I started this program. I always thought they chose cushy jobs at the Center or specializing in omega medicine or pediatrics. I never realized most were pushed into it."

"Not sure I'd call working at the Center cushy," I laughed. But the working conditions might make up for the salary differences.

"I'll let you know. I'm doing a rotation at the Center this summer," she replied.

"You do that." I grinned.

She let go of me and looked in the mirror, fixing her hair. "Did you pass?"

"I did. I am officially part of the Omega Center Crisis Response team." And I was joining the emergency roster while keeping most of my caseload.

"Hey, Grandma wants to take pictures of us before you go have your moment with Grace. If we're done being saps here, that is." Riley stood.

Grace wanted to do something she called *First Look*. Excitement shot through me.

I gathered my three sisters up in a hug. "Let's do it."

Then I could marry my Grace.

Chapter Seventy-One

Wes

"He's so freaking cute." I held my nephew as Lexi messed with my hair.

She was one of my attendants. Lexi looked amazing in her green dress, considering she hadn't given birth all that long ago.

Katie was also here with her little girl.

"Careful he doesn't barf on your suit." Lexi laughed.

"Wait, I want a picture." My father snapped a photo of the three of us.

There was a knock on the door. "Wes, it's time."

"See you soon." I handed my nephew back to my sister and hugged them and my dad.

I followed the wedding coordinator outside. Brennan had done an incredible job renovating the estate to look like it was straight out of the Tea-Time Britain Era. Every time I came here, more had been done.

It was doing well, too. The ballet having its gala here in the gardens before it was even ready to officially open had gotten him a bunch of bookings. So had us having our foundation Christmas party here and the gala for his dad's foundation.

Brennan's dad was here, and the new foundation was going well. The Queen Mum had stepped back from her business and was letting Liam and Troy try to save it, which so far wasn't going as well as she'd hoped. Especially since Brennan's dad would get a big chunk of it when the divorce was finalized.

Caroline hadn't been heard from since she'd spoken up for Brennan's mom. Riley found her socials, and it looked like she was busy with her pack and kids. Maybe she'd continue to mind her own business and be grateful for what she had.

The wedding coordinator led me to a night-blooming garden with a fountain and benches. No one was there. While family and attendants were here, guests hadn't started arriving... yet.

But I saw the photographer. She was dressed like one of the attendants, so she'd blend in better, which made sense to me.

I heard footsteps and smelled Evan, who was as nervous as I was.

Turning around, I sucked in a breath. "You look as handsome as the day I met you." Rushing to him, I kissed him deeply.

"You look amazing. Guess what? Sasha came." He beamed.

"Good." I know he'd worried about that.

"Keep facing that direction," the wedding coordinator instructed, as I heard more footsteps.

"You can turn around now," Grace said softly.

Evan and I turned around. Grace stood there. Her hair was fluffed, and she had a necklace of little gold roses, with matching earrings.

She wore a fluffy gold dress decorated with gold fabric roses. The dress I'd designed for her as a grown-up version of the one I'd drawn her in long ago. The dress that some big fashion house made custom for her.

But all I saw was her. The little girl in the pink dress told me that one day she was going to marry me.

Evan exhaled sharply. "Grace. You look beautiful."

Going up to her, I cupped her face and kissed her long and deep, ignoring the photographer.

"I do," I whispered.

"Me, too." Her eyes met mine.

Now I realized what this moment was for. To just be with them and no one else. Someone had even left a bottle of champagne and a plate of tiny treats for us.

"My turn." Evan picked her up and spun her around, then kissed her.

"You're both mine." I wrapped my arms around them.

Grace looked up at me. "Yes, we are."

I took my place under the flower arch in the rose garden. Given it had been chilly recently, Brennan had gone to great lengths to make sure it was in full bloom. However, today the weather was cooperating, and we had a lovely, warm, early May day.

The arch itself was done in these incredible roses that were pale peach on the inside of the petals, and dark pink on the outside. The *Princess Grace.* Because Verity, the plant geneticist, had made Grace a *rose* for her mating gift. Something I didn't know was possible.

Besides the roses Verity made, and the flowers in the garden, there were omega lilies *everywhere,* making the air smell sweet and happy.

"You okay?" Evan's grandpa, dressed in a suit, asked me. He was going to be marrying us.

"A little nervous," I admitted.

After Evan, Grace, and I got our private moment, the rest of the pack had joined us for photos. Now, here we were.

Chairs were set up in the garden and filled with our family and friends. Pippa wore a giant hat and looked like she didn't want to be there. Creed was there with a very pretty friend. Surprisingly, *all* of Grace's siblings and their parents had shown up, well except for Adriana.

Trials finished, Adriana was now in prison. Giving the police names of the people who hurt Elaris had lessened her sentences, but considering she'd been found guilty both of trafficking Grace and stabbing Spencer, she'd still been there awhile. Those who murdered Elaris were now in jail and the organization they belonged to had gotten such bad press when the truth came out that it was pretty much dismantled.

Mrs. Silvers had been found violating her house arrest, though she couldn't remember why. Her for that and helping Adriana was that long. She hadn't seemed to be interested in getting to know Grace and that was fine with us.

Spencer's parents were seated next to Evan's grandma. Jett's family had come as well. So had Brennan's dad. And of course, the sister pack.

Many of our co-workers and friends were also in attendance, including Grace's friends from book club and the Daedalus society.

Mrs. Beekman, who was still Grace's advocate, gave me a look that said *I'm watching you.* Carly, from the Center, sat nearby, quite pregnant, her mates with her.

A white runner ran down the center of the chairs, leading right to the flower arch.

Piano music filled the air, as Brennan's friend, Kari, played a piano that had been brought out for the occasion.

Evan came over and joined me. "Here we are."

"Today we marry Grace." So much emotion overwhelmed me.

"I know." Evan hugged me tightly.

"You boys did well. I like her," Evan's grandpa said.

"Ready?" the wedding coordinator asked us.

"Let's do this." I nodded.

"So ready," Evan agreed.

We took our places, one of us on each side, with Grandpa in the middle.

She went off, and a moment later, the piano music changed. Dare, with his cello, joined Kari. He was going to Boston Technical Institute, a well-known science university. We were helping cover the costs so he wouldn't have to take any money from his parents. They didn't know that he was majoring in music–Verity had helped him through the application and audition process.

The attendants started walking down the aisle, which consisted of sisters–Katie, Lexi, Sasha, Sonja, Verity, and Mercy. They all wore emerald green and carried bouquets of flowers. My nephew was asleep in my dad's arms. My niece was awake and being held by Rami, looking around at all the people.

The sisters took their places, three on each side of the arch.

The music shifted again, and now the rest of the pack came, in their suits, with pink accents, omega lilies pinned to their suits. Well, Riley carried omega lilies and wore a pink dress. Jett and Brennan walked in together, followed by Spencer and Riley. They took their places behind us, since the pack confirmation would happen right after the vows.

Seamlessly, the song changed into one that Grace had painstakingly written down for Kari and Dare, one from her world that she'd wanted played.

Pax, in a white suit, came down the aisle, pulling a flower-covered wagon with little Hope in it. She wore a rose-colored dress and tossed flower petals.

When he got to the end of the aisle, Pax pulled the wagon over to the side. Harry helped them take their seats.

Everyone stood as Grace took her place at the end of the aisle. She looked at us with sheer adoration, and I got so much love through the bond. Tru, in a little gold dress, walked behind Grace, carrying her train, beaming.

Giddiness shot through me. After so many years of lying on my bed, or the roof, or sitting in the park, talking about our wedding, of finally being reunited with her and going through everything that happened after she arrived, of patiently waiting so she and Evan could plan their dream wedding, we were finally getting married.

Just like we'd wanted in our dreams.

Evan had a silly look on his face, and I'm sure the other guys in the pack did, too. We were a family. We were complete.

And now we were fulfilling that childhood wish of ours. After all these years, I got to marry my Grace in the wedding of her dreams. My love. My soulmate. My peaches.

The one I loved until the end of the universe.

Chapter Seventy-Two

Grace

Music played and people danced in the main garden under the lights to the band Wes had wanted. We'd finished dinner in the ballroom, but there was still a candy bar, a grazing table, a whiskey fountain, a chocolate fountain, and a full bar, complete with custom cocktails out in the garden.

Hope was running around in circles as if chasing sunbeams. Someone had let her eat way too much candy.

"What are you doing, Hope?" I asked.

She giggled. "Just playing with the cat."

"Have fun." I didn't see a cat, but she was at the right age for imaginary friends.

"You look so beautiful. Thank you for inviting us," Marcos' dad, Antonio, stood there with his mate, the police sergeant.

"Thank you so much for coming." I noticed a lot of people watching Antonio throughout the night, probably wondering how we knew such a famous actor.

"Thank you for making sure my son does his homework," Antonio added with a laugh. I'd been doing a lot of math tutoring this year.

Marcos, Hiro, Kilroy, Riley, Rose, and Mercy had an entire tray of cupcakes and were sitting in a garden alcove.

"I'm glad everything ended well," Sergeant Hawthorne told me.

"Me, too." If he hadn't called Lexi, I may never have found Wes.

We talked a little longer, then I went to find Evan and Wes. They were on the dance floor. But Verity stood in the corner with a glass of champagne, looking wistful.

"How's my sister?" I put my arm around her waist. "I think Hope has an imaginary friend."

"Oh, she's at that age. Hale's imaginary friend was a pink vampire giraffe named Bobo." Verity laughed. "I'm so happy to be here. Just tired, with finals coming up."

It was more than that. With Adriana in jail, Verity had taken on far too much responsibility. Pippa had also become insufferable, micromanaging Verity's time and being generally unpleasant. Not only had Verity pretty much stopped modeling, but Pippa had made her reschedule her much-needed visit to see Creed and me *twice* because they needed her to take care of the little ones. Verity had even dropped a class at Pippa's demand so she could do school pickup.

The only reason she'd even made it to my bachelorette party was because I'd involved all my girl siblings so that Pippa couldn't find a reason to keep Verity away. I'd just hired a babysitter for Tru and Hope for parts of it so we could have some 'big girl' fun.

"Hey, as soon as classes end for the semester, you'll get to come out here. If Pippa tries anything, I'll punch her in the tits. Creed and I have this." I grinned at her.

"I'm looking forward to it." She smiled at me, but fatigue shone in her blue-green eyes.

Verity watched Evan and Wes dance by. Evan waved at me, and I waved back.

"You'll find someone, Verity," I said softly. "You are amazing, and you'll meet someone who will sweep you off your feet and treat you how you deserve."

My sister was incredible and absolutely wasted on her parents, who never thought she was good enough. Which was stupid. One day, Verity was going to tell them to *fuck off,* but even then, I'm not sure anyone other than Nate and Harry would truly realize what they lost.

"You think?" Her look went wistful. "I'm not the traditional alpha."

I don't know why she thought that. Sure, she liked pastels, manicures, and romance novels. But why was that even an issue?

"There's someone waiting for you, Verity," I assured. Of course, it would help if she could date. But her parents were against that, too.

Even Creed, who was flourishing at Compass BioTek, and had made some great friends he'd moved in with, hadn't dated. His 'date' tonight was his friend Inara.

"Sister, this wedding is amazing." Hale came over, in his suit, cowboy boots, and cowboy hat, and rested his arm on my head. "I mean, that other party was great, but this one is better."

"It's like you were looking at my pin boards," Verity laughed. "I'll just hire your wedding planner because this is pretty much my dream wedding. I'd like to get married in a garden. Though I might like a champagne fountain instead of whiskey."

"That was Wes' idea," I told her. It had been quite popular.

Hale shook his head. "I love it."

"When you meet your giant omega and get married, I'll help you have the wedding of your dreams, Verity," I promised.

"What about me?" Hale laughed.

"You too," I agreed. Hale getting a mate? Well, one day he'd mature and find a pack, I'm sure. Some day.

"Hi." Tru came over to me, Hope in tow. "Hopey is tired."

"Oh, I'm sure you are." Verity picked Hope up.

Tru hugged me. "This is so fun. I can't wait to come back for math camp this year."

"Me, too. I'm looking forward to it." I hugged her back. It was all set.

"There you all are." Nate joined us. His vest and tie had chemical equations on them.

"Hi, Professor. Are you having a good time?" I'd seen him and Harry on the dance floor. Zain, the alpha I didn't know well, had been grumpy and in the corner with Pippa most of the night, but Verity's bio-mom Esme had gotten him dancing a couple of times.

"Oh, we are. We'll probably be leaving soon. Are you sure Mercy's okay with you?" Nate frowned.

"She's fine. We love having her over. We'll see you tomorrow afternoon for lunch," I promised.

Okay, so Wes, Evan, and I had a hotel for the night. But Mercy was staying at the house with everyone else. In the morning, Spencer was taking Mercy to the ice rink because she was trying out for the Rockland Raiders discovery team. If she made it, she'd have to move to Rockland, but I had absolutely no issue with her living with us, or Creed, and spending her last year of high school here.

Would they object? Probably. Though this could be her way into the pro leagues.

Honestly, getting Mercy away from the parents was the best way to help her become a professional skate smash player. Because she was good. So good that the Rockland Raiders had invited her to try out for a program that was mostly university students and fed right into the pro leagues.

If only we could get Verity away from them. That would probably have to wait until she finished her PhD, and we could get her a really great job, far away from them. Hale seemed okay. Dare was going to study music in the fall. We'd take care of the others as needed.

If Tru didn't just move herself into our house at some point.

The professor and I would most likely always have a bit of a weird relationship. However, having a therapist that I could tell everything to without fear was helpful. Pippa, Zain, and Esme would probably never like me, because they saw me as the person who destroyed their pack. Not to mention, Pippa still held Solomon and Abel putting the professor in danger against me. Harry and I got along well enough, though.

While I loved all my siblings fiercely, Verity and I had become close. She was the best sister I could have wanted. Not only had she brought so many of her special omega lilies, but she'd created my very own rose for me as a gift. Something she started working on the moment she met me.

I also hadn't had a seizure in six months.

"Grace." Spencer joined us. "Hi, everyone." He offered me his arm. "My good doctor, they're playing our song."

"Excuse us." I waved and let Spencer bring me onto the floor, where we glided across it.

"You look like you're having a great time."

"I am." Everything had gone perfectly. The ceremony. The pack confirmation. The dinner. Our dances.

While it was just Wes, Evan, and me tonight, the day after tomorrow the six of us were leaving for a pack honeymoon, which included using our pack plane for a visit to my beach house, as well as some time at a fancy resort of Brennan's. I couldn't wait.

Riley would stay with the sister pack, since she had school. She absolutely adored the babies. Then, Verity would come visit, and we'd have an amazing time.

"My turn." Jett tugged me away from Spencer as the music changed.

"Hi." I danced steps with him that had once been strange but were now so familiar they were second nature.

Brennan had meant it when he said that Spencer and I were now the face of the pack. Spencer and I went to *a lot* of parties, galas, and science dinners. Also, the virtual super collider project was fully staffed and in progress.

"I love you so much, Babydoll, you know that?" Jett's head got close to mine as we danced.

"I love you, too." Last summer, I'd married him and Brennan in a very private ceremony in the gardens of Volkov's home. It was perfect for the three of us.

Just like tonight had been perfect for Wes, Evan, and me.

"Brennan and I will probably leave right after you three do. Spencer will stay as long as Riley and Mercy want, then bring them home," he said. "I think Brennan's social battery is about done."

He was sitting in the corner holding his niece and talking to Katie, Rami, and his dad.

"We'll be leaving pretty soon. Hale and Dare have our exit planned. They say it's not fireworks and I am afraid," I laughed.

We finished our dance and went off to see Brennan.

I slid onto his lap, careful of the baby. "Hi."

"Hey, Little Butterfly." He gave me a little squeeze.

"Hello, my sweet baby," I told my niece. "Hi, my sweet baby's parents and my sweet baby's grandpa." I grinned at Katie and Rami, who looked exhausted but happy, and Brennan's dad.

"Everything was so beautiful," Rami said.

"It really was. I was sniffling during the pack confirmation," Katie agreed.

"There you are, come on." Evan hauled me off Brennan's lap.

I kissed Brennan and Jett. "Love you."

Where were we going? He, Wes, and I had already made the rounds, talking to everyone, thanking them for coming.

Wes waited for us on the dance floor and the song changed.

"What?" I looked up at him, the tune familiar but unexpected.

"I gave them the song, and they learned it," Wes said, as he and Evan danced with me.

It was the song from my world I'd once played for him and joked that we should dance to it at our wedding. Given we had a live band, we chose something else. I could write out sheet music for Kari and Dare, but doing so for a band was beyond me. It never occurred to me to see if they could learn it by ear.

"You do realize that Mercy and Riley have uploaded a lot of your music to the internet, right?" Evan laughed.

"That's fine with me." While I'd never told Mercy I was from another world, I wouldn't be surprised if she knew. Verity didn't know, but Creed did.

Under the moon and twinkling lights, the three of us danced. "This is the best wedding present ever."

"Yeah?" Evan's eyes sparkled.

"Yeah. I'll show you both how much at the hotel." I gave them each a kiss.

"This is exactly what you wanted, right?" Wes asked, a little anxious.

"It's everything I could want." I kissed him again. We even had a photo booth. I looked at both of them. "You are everything I could want."

I never knew that I needed five husbands until I came here.

We danced together to a couple of songs, then finally left the dance floor for a drink.

Dare, dressed in his usual Victorian rake glory, came over to us. "We're ready when you are. We've got the exit distraction all ready."

"Thank you." I gave him a hug.

"No, thank you, Grace." Dare hugged me tight. "Thank you for being the sister we didn't know we needed."

We went and got some lemonade. Then I found Verity and gave her one last hug. "See you, soon."

"I can't wait," she replied.

Creed joined us and hugged me. "See you tomorrow."

Suddenly, the sky lit up. Not with fireworks, but little lights. What?

"Who ordered the drone show?" Wes looked up in awe.

"That's Hale's distraction," Creed replied.

"Incredible." I tugged on Wes and Evan's hands. "Let's go."

The three of us went back to the main building, but stood there in the doorway, watching the elaborate show, where the drones made hearts and our names.

Evan and Wes quickly helped me change. Brennan and Jett would bring our stuff and the gifts back to the house.

We went out to the parking lot. Spencer, Jett, Brennan, Riley, and Mercy waited for us by our motorcycles.

I hugged Mercy. "Good luck tomorrow. Also, thank Hale for me. How did he even do it?"

"He probably traded drugs for it." Mercy shrugged.

"What?" Brennan's eyebrows rose.

"He invented a party drug that gets past the university athletic drug test," Mercy replied. "The parents were so proud of him that they look the other way as long as he doesn't get caught."

"Wow," Jett muttered.

Yeah, that summed up their parents–proud of the one making party drugs, and hard on the one creating happy flowers.

"See you tomorrow." I hugged Riley. "Thanks for helping to make our party fun."

"Always. Mom." Riley grinned.

I hugged her tighter. "You're the best kid I could ever want."

"Hey, don't ruin it by being a sap," she sniffled.

"It's my wedding, I'm allowed to be a sap," I replied.

"See you tomorrow, my good doctor." Spencer kissed me.

Yeah, I was really looking forward to this trip so I could spend some quality time with all of them individually–and together.

Jett pulled me to him. "Have fun, Babydoll."

"I will." I gave him a kiss.

Brennan wrapped his arms around me and sent me so much love. Until we bonded, I hadn't realized how hard he loved. I loved my good boy with all my might in return.

Pulling him down, I kissed him, too.

"I love all of you so much," I told them, as Evan kissed Brennan and then Jett.

"Wait, is Wes riding in the sidecar?" Brennan frowned.

I caught the tiniest bit of hurt in the bond. Usually, I took him for rides in the sidecar, often with a chicken.

"Yes. But I'll give you a ride tomorrow. Promise." I kissed him again, sending him lots of love.

Wes stuffed himself into the sidecar and put on his helmet. I put mine on and got on my motorcycle. Evan had his helmet on and got on his bike. We were staying at the same hotel that Spencer and I had stayed at. Originally, we'd planned on staying here at the estate. But there had been some setbacks, and it wasn't ready for overnight guests.

I waved as we drove off into the night. My pack. My mates. My loves. My everything.

They were everything I'd ever wanted and needed.

Who said dreams didn't come true? After all, mine did.

The End

Thank you so much for reading Dream Pack and joining me on Grace's journey. I hope you enjoyed the Into the Parallel Omegaverse trilogy. Thanks again for falling into the omegaverse with me.

Glossary of Select Terms

Designations

Alpha: Larger, faster, and with better senses, they make up about a quarter of the population. Their barks and pheromones can influence people. Male alphas have knots, female alphas have locks. Their scent holds a distinctive note that marks them as alpha. Female alphas can carry children.

Beta: They make up over half of the population and are your average ordinary people. Like the other designations, they can have kids, join or form packs, and an alpha can bond with them.

Gamma: Medical designation for a specific type of 'failed' omegas. While sometimes a genetic switch is thrown, halting development, most of the time it's environmental. Something is so dangerous in their environment that the body declares it unsafe to become an omega and halts a genetic process. Gammas can have many omega traits, but it varies from person to person and is often proportional to how close they were to becoming an omega. Gammas rarely respond to barks, pheromones, or danger the way omegas do. Common causes of gammas are war, famine, extreme poverty, and asshole parents, and not as common as they used to be.

Delta: They have a lot of alpha characteristics–especially in regard to size, speed, and senses. They make excellent soldiers and security. They're rarer than the 'big three' designations (alpha/beta/omega) but much more common than any of the rarer designations.

Digamma: Essentially, digammas are 'failed' alphas. Something is so dangerous in their environment that the body declares it unsafe to become an alpha and halts a genetic process. Exceedingly rare to the point where not much is known about them.

Zeta: Sometimes a genetic anomaly creates a designation that is a cross between an alpha and omega, some of them can even switch between the two. Like gammas, each zeta is a little different. Incredibly rare and coveted.

Kappa: The life of the party, they're usually adrenaline junkies with poor decision-making skills. They're an extremely rare designation because they've almost chaosed themselves out of existence.

Theta: Thetas tend to be misanthropic loners who like to amass wealth. While they do mate and form packs, they often aren't with alphas as they don't like to be told what to do. They wanted to be needed, but don't like to be smothered. They're closer to alphas than betas. A rare designation.

Iota: A rare designation, Iotas don't have scents, they also can't smell other scents and don't respond to barks or pheromones. This can be dangerous because they can't catch the scent-cues other designations can. Because they can't be barked or influenced, some iotas think they're better than other designations. They're closer to betas genetically.

Omicron: Omicrons are charming and charismatic but are conceited and don't think the rules apply to them. They want to take over the world and fix it, and aren't afraid to use violence, which has caused this designation, which is an alpha mutation, to be declared illegal. While they often can pass as alphas, because of their size, strength, and speed, and they smell enough like an alpha, they lack knots/locks. Often, they test as alphas when young.

Rho: Medical designation for a feral alpha.

Sigma: Often loners with anger issues, they tend to commit crimes to punish people. They don't want to be part of the system and generally think it's bullshit. Even though it's an extremely rare designation, and an alpha mutation, they're illegal. While they often can pass as alphas, because of their size, strength, and speed, and that they smell enough like an alpha, they lack knots/locks. Often, they test as alphas when young.

Tau: Medical designation referring to someone who lost their bonded scent match, also known as *soulbroke* and *shadow*.

Phi: A rare super-mutation of alpha and illegal. While they can be a loner like sigmas, they can also be fun like kappas, and even charismatic like an omicron. They can become violent and aggressive. Unlike the others, they can more easily hide among alphas, because males have a bulb that can pass as a slightly-deformed knot and their smell is often undistinguishable. Commonly, they test as alphas when young and have the size/strength/speed of an alpha. It is thought that Phis were created for battle long ago and something went horribly, terribly wrong.

Omega: One of the three main designations, omegas are usually smaller than the other designations and tend to be nurturers and caregivers. They're the most physically compatible with alphas, so they're often sought after as mates, even though they make up less than ten percent of the population. They can and do partner with other designations. Omegas have the same rights as everyone else. They have an extra element to their scent that marks them as such. Omega males are very good at making children, though most omega males can't carry them.

Other Terms

Alpha-Blockers: A type of medication that dulls alpha senses and instincts. It's most commonly prescribed to violent alphas, young alphas who aren't in full control, and criminals. There's a huge stigma around them, so many who should take them, don't.

Awakened/Blossomed: When someone fully comes into their designation after puberty.

Bond Test: A government test used to detect an alpha-omega bond.

Designation: The term used to indicate someone's specific genetic dynamic. The three main designations are alpha, beta, and omega. Other designations exist, including ones that are considered illegal.

Equalist: Someone who believes that designations should not be used/recognized so that everyone can be on equal terms.

Fundie/Fundamental: Someone who believed that packs are about population control and the stripping of rights by the government. They think that every alpha has the right to their own omega, even though it's statistically impossible. They often keep to themselves and usually don't take part in government services or programs or go to hospitals.

Heat: An omegas fertile cycle, which results in wanting sexual attention and satisfaction from their alphas and partners. Female omegas often have four to five heats a year; male omegas have two or three. Heats can last from a couple of days to a week.

Heat Spike: A quick rise in hormones, often right before a heat, which result in temporary heat-like symptoms.

Heat Suppressants: A type of medication some omegas take so that they don't go into heat. Heat suppressants are completely legal, though prolonged use can have side effects.

Mate Bond: The connection that forms when certain designations bite another in a certain way where proteins are released into their bloodstream creating a chemical reaction. Some bonds, like alpha-omega, have legal implications. Not all designations can make or accept bonds.

Mega-push: A street drug that can 'push' betas with certain genetic markers over to being an omega and often used in human trafficking. A legal version is available but highly regulated.

Omega Center: Omega Centers offer services ranging from healthcare and pack matching, to education and housing. Omegas don't have to register with the Center, but once registered can use their free services, including having an advocate–an assigned social worker that guides them through the process and helps them understand all their options.

Oxotipoline/Eazy-E: A sedative commonly used in human trafficking. The designer version, Eazy-E, is sometimes used by sexual predators.

Prick-Test: A simple blood test used to test for the three main designations–alpha, beta, and omega. All children are tested in middle school. The test is mostly accurate, but not always. It doesn't test for rare or illegal designations.

Scent-Blockers: A type of medication omegas take to blend in/function in society. These range from light scent-blockers that simply dull an omega's distinctive scent to heavy duty ones that lock down both omega scent and instincts, enabling them to hide as a beta. All are completely legal but can be hard for hidden omegas to get. Prolonged use, especially of the heavy-duty blockers, can make them lose their effectiveness and/or cause health issues.

Scent-Match/Soulmate: That perfect match between two people–usually an alpha and omega. They usually know it by smell. Scent-matches are rare and plenty of people have happy and long relationships without being scent-matches. Sometimes scent-matches dream of each other, but that's mostly in books and movies. A scent match can be 'lopsided' when it is not alpha/omega, usually where one becomes an alpha/omega and the other stays a beta. A 'dead match' occurs when a couple would have been a scent match if they had been an alpha and an omega but instead both stayed betas.

Shadow: A term for someone who has lost their bonded scent match, also called *soulbroke*. The medical term is *Tau*.

Spiral: Dangerous drop in omega hormones which can result in unconsciousness, irrational behavior, and/or hospitalization. Often a trauma response.

Textbook Gamma: A gamma that became a gamma due to external conditions such as famine, poverty, war, or asshole parents.

Trevadol: A commonly prescribed anti-depressant. One side effect is that it can mess with the basic prick-test. This isn't considered much of an issue because this drug is for adults, and once the prick-test is given in middle school it isn't usually given again without reason. Some hidden omegas take the drug solely as a precaution because of that specific side effect,

Ultra-Bullet: Super-fast train that can turn an hours-long drive into moments.

Un-Bonding: The chemical process of removing a mate bond. It's governed by an extensive legal process to make sure that it is not abused.

Variant: A derogatory name for someone with an illegal designation.

The Thorne Family

The Parents

- Adriana Thorne (Alpha, *Mom)* — Chemistry Professor; mated to Nate, mother of Hale and Mercy.

- Pippa Thorne (Alpha, *Mumsy*) — Research Chemist; Mated to Nate, mother of Creed.

- Zain Thorne (Alpha, *Baba*) — Research Chemist; Married to Esme, father of Verity, Dare, and Chance.

- Esme Thorne (Beta, *Mama*) — Translator; Married to Zain, mother of Verity, Dare, and Chance.

- Harry Thorne (Beta, *Harry/Daddy*)–Restaurateur; Married to Nate, father of Pax, Tru, and Hope.

- Nate Thorne (Omega, *Dad*) — Organic Chemistry Professor; Mated to Pippa and Adriana, married to Harry, father of Grace, Creed, Hale, Mercy, Pax, Tru, and Hope.

<u>The Kids</u>

- Creed (Alpha)--Engineering student at National University of Science and Technology

- Verity (Alpha)--PhD student in plant genetics at Briar University

- Hale (Alpha)--Undergraduate student in organic chemistry at Briar University

- Dare (Alpha)--High Schooler

- Mercy (Alpha)--High Schooler

- Chance (designation still unknown)--Elementary Schooler

- Pax (designation still unknown)--Small Child

- Tru (designation still unknown)--Small Child

- Hope (designation still unknown)--Small Child

About Jane Handler

Jane Handler is the author of why choose omegaverse romance, including the HockeyVerse series. A hopeless romantic, Jane grew up reading romance and often got them taken away by her teachers for reading during class. Now she writes why choose, romance. When not writing, she's camping, eating sushi, doing laundry, or binge watching TV.